A MAJOR NEW VOICE IN SLASH FICTION

RISE OF THE QUEER VAMPIRES

Franco De Rocco

Cathedral City, CA

A note to readers:
This book contains adult content, including graphic sex scenes, coerced sex, and swearing.

This is a work of fiction. Names, characters, places, and incidents either are the product of the author's imagination or are used fictitiously. Any resemblance to actual persons, living or dead, events, or locales is entirely coincidental.

First paperback edition October, 2023

Book design by AquaZebra

Library of Congress Control Number: 2023945823
ISBN 978-1-954604-10-0 (paperback)

US Copyright Registration Number # TXu 2-385-642
Effective Date of Registration: August 02, 2023
Registration Decision Date: August 23, 2023

Published by AquaZebra
35070 Maria Rd
Cathedral City, CA 92234
mark@aquazebra.com

Dedication

This book is dedicated to
my husband and best friend.

Author's Note

Welcome to the enthralling universe of *Rise of the Queer Vampires.* This narrative seamlessly weaves together strands of reality and fantasy, creating an intoxicating tapestry of danger, self-discovery, and a riveting fusion of blood and romance. As the author, I invite you into this unique and captivating realm.

Our protagonist is Antonio De Luca, a young Italian grappling with his sexuality against the backdrop of his Catholic upbringing and guilt from sexual encounters. His life takes an unexpected turn when he transforms into a vampire. His journey takes us from a small town in the Pacific Northwest to the lively French Quarter in New Orleans. Along the way, we meet a diverse cast of characters with secrets and desires that test Antonio's understanding of love, lust, and sacrifice.

At the heart of this tale is David, a mysterious figure who embodies passion and intensity, captivating Antonio. However, Robert, a cunning vampire with hidden agendas, threatens their passionate bond and manipulates situations to endanger Antonio's life. With intricate dynamics and engaging storylines, each character will challenge your perceptions, break stereotypes, and stretch boundaries as the plot thickens.

You'll quickly notice the pure joy I find in crafting sensual scenes. But these moments are more than just physical pleasure. They are deep explorations into relationships, emotions, and personal journeys, revealing our hidden desires and vulnerabilities. This story celebrates diversity, promotes acceptance, and fearlessly explores the depths of human passion in gay erotic literature.

Rise of the Queer Vampires goes beyond the traditional vampire story — it embodies my unique perspective, bringing a fresh breath to the genre. Through its rich tapestry of risk, desire, and revelation, it provides readers with an unmatched experience.

In blood and lust,
Franco De Rocco

Antonio

ON THAT fateful evening, following a tiring day at school and a busy shift at my father's restaurant, I decided to relax with a leisurely walk. As I roamed the streets, lost in thought, I unexpectedly stumbled upon Stilettos — a gay bar tucked away amidst the cityscape. The loud techno music emanating from within intrigued me and made me curious about what was inside. Despite my apprehension of feeling like an outsider and my intuition not to enter, something compelled me to step through the door in front of me. Little did I know that this decision would spark a transformation that would change my essence forever.

Upon entering, I was immediately surrounded by a diverse crowd, reveling in Saturday night's spirited energy. Laughter and merriment filled the air as I approached the bar. As I passed the dance floor, the thumping beat of techno music filled the air while scantily clad men danced rhythmically with one another. Their sweat-drenched bodies were undeniably enticing, but I pressed on because my focus wasn't on them. As a lapsed Catholic weighed down by guilt over my homosexuality, I consciously tried to steer clear of local guys. Instead, I used a popular dating app to set up anonymous meetings with men from out of town. Favoring one-time hookups, I never had to face public judgment. This strategy allowed me to navigate my daily life with my secret hidden.

This approach certainly had its drawbacks. Though exhilarating, engaging in intimate encounters with strangers ultimately left me feeling unfulfilled because I wanted to fall in love. However, until I figured out how to overcome my shame, this was how it had to be.

My gaze roved around the dimly lit room, searching for an empty seat at the bustling bar. Unexpectedly, from the corner of my eye, I spotted an attractive stranger motioning toward an open spot beside him. Flattered by his inviting gesture, I eagerly approached and sat down. His demeanor was composed yet inviting, and his sandalwood cologne filled the air with its cozy, woody aroma. I asked if I could buy him a beer to repay his kindness. He replied with an arched eyebrow and a playful smirk.

"I want something far more intoxicating than alcohol. I want — you!"

I laughed at the corny pickup line. "Aren't pickup lines a thing of the past?" I teased, my interest in him growing.

He chuckled and polished off his Stella Artois.

I ordered two more from the bartender and returned my attention to the stranger. He appeared to be around my age — twenty-two — with piercing blue eyes, sandy-blond hair, and a 1970s porn star mustache. Another cheesy element, but somehow it was still hot. I asked his name.

"I'm Robert."

I held out my hand, introducing myself as Antonio De Luca.

His jovial tone of voice indicated that he was from New Orleans. As soon as I thought of his hometown, a wave of nostalgia washed over me, remembering the diverse neighborhoods, the upbeat music, and the cheerful people — not to mention the tantalizing Creole cuisine that was second to none. The mere thought of revisiting this unique place filled me with excitement and longing.

The bartender interrupted my thoughts by placing our cold beers on the counter. As I turned back to Robert, he offered a playful smirk.

"I'm feeling incredibly aroused and passionate tonight."

His fingers moved over the rough denim of his jeans, and he caressed himself, sighing audibly. Moving his hand, he revealed a pulsating erection that demanded attention.

"I'm in the mood to fuck ass."

I couldn't help but chuckle, finding it hard to grasp the sexual confidence emanating from this stranger. As I raised my beer to take a sip, lost in thought, I contemplated whether his overzealous personality would eventually win me over or push me away.

As I pondered this thought, he suddenly turned everything around, catching me completely off guard. His dominating traits surfaced, revealing a new side of him that I hadn't anticipated. He announced that he had beers in his hotel room and casually tossed a twenty-dollar bill toward the bartender.

"Let's go!"

I hesitated momentarily, unsure how to respond to this unexpected turn of events. The assertive side of him was intimidating. As I glanced around the bar, I could sense the curious eyes of other patrons, wondering what would happen next.

He lifted an eyebrow, a discreet sign expressing curiosity and anticipation, while calmly awaiting my response. His body language indicated his eagerness to take the evening up a notch with adventure.

He leaned in closer, his voice low and smooth.

"I promise you won't regret this."

My heart raced as I considered my options. On the one hand, our meeting had been a mix of laughter, engaging conversation, and undeniable chemistry, creating a magnetic pull that was difficult to resist. On the other hand, my intuition wouldn't be quiet, creating a constant feeling that urged me to exercise caution. Ultimately, I chose to heed this inner voice, allowing it to guide my decision and win me over.

Taking a deep breath, I decided to stay. I looked at him and said, "Thanks, but I'm good."

Robert's expression shifted rapidly to anger.

A deep frown creased his face, and his eyes locked onto mine with an intensity I had never experienced before. I felt frozen, unable to look away. Fear initially coursed through my veins, but a strange calmness quickly replaced it. It was like I had entered a trance-like state and was no longer afraid of him.

"Let's get the fuck out of here."

The man's words echoed in my mind, and I felt compelled to follow his command without question. I rose from the barstool and set my half-empty beer on the counter.

Robert

SITTING IN the back seat of the Uber, I admired Antonio's thick, dark hair. It created a striking contrast against the white linen shirt neatly tucked into his black jeans. He finished the ensemble with a pair of loafers, adding an element of refinement. His olive skin and the stubble on his jawline evoked my memories of Italy and its vibrant culture. Antonio's style was effortless yet utterly captivating. I found myself irresistibly drawn to him.

To deceive him, I altered my demeanor and took on the role of a gentleman. Sustaining this facade proved draining, as it required all my energy to maintain the deception. This behavior was unfamiliar, as my true nature was inherently selfish. I was amazed by Antonio's naïveté and the ease with which I could manipulate him. While his gullibility amused me, it also evoked feelings of pity.

Taking a deep breath, I focused on the order my chief of staff had given me — kill Antonio. One benefit of this assignment was that it took me hundreds of miles away from New Orleans, allowing me to indulge in a secret passion of mine — fucking beautiful men. Within my organization, homosexuality is considered prohibited and morally reprehensible. Anyone discovered participating in such acts would face the harshest consequence — death.

A mischievous smile spread across my face while I continued to admire him. I eagerly looked forward to the delight I would experience in tormenting his body. He remained oblivious to the severe pain that lay ahead of him. Eager to fuck his ass, my cock sprang to life.

"Are you on PrEP?" Antonio asked.

"No," I muttered, annoyed by his question.

His eyes widened, hearing my answer.

I could tell he wondered whether I was trustworthy. I thought fast, cursing myself for not saying I was taking the HIV-preventative medication. "I just had a negative test," I lied while caressing my erection through my jeans.

Antonio's eyes widened, staring at my hardness.

I teased him with it, successfully diverting his attention from the drug. As I looked up, I saw the driver in the front seat glancing at me in the rearview mirror.

"What brings you to town?" he asked.

Not in the mood for casual conversation, I responded curtly with, "Business," successfully ending the small talk. As I turned my attention back to Antonio, it became evident that my arousal wouldn't be subsiding soon, so I unbuttoned my jeans and revealed my hard-on.

Antonio caught his breath, surprised by my boldness.

My aggression surfaced, and I raised my hand, wanting to thrust his head into my groin. But I refrained, not wanting to compromise my gentlemanly persona. Instead, I parted his lips and inserted my finger into his mouth. Teasing him with it, I said I fantasized about being pleasured in the backseat of a car.

I removed my finger.

My grin turned into a smirk as he leaned forward. His phenomenal tongue flicked against my cock, igniting excitement within me. Hearing my moans of ecstasy, he started sucking. The sensual technique he employed drove me to the brink of insanity. "Oh, fuck," I moaned, unprepared for his exceptional skill.

He stopped and whispered, "Don't cum yet."

"I'm multi-orgasmic," I said, pushing his head back down. It was apparent Antonio enjoyed giving head. He swallowed all six inches while moaning in pleasure.

I couldn't wait to get to the hotel room. I hadn't fucked a queer's ass in a while. Sensing my eruption building and noticing the driver's gaze, I pushed him away.

Antonio sat up and wiped his grinning mouth.

"How old are you?" he inquired.

I nearly replied with forty-two but quickly corrected myself and told him I was twenty.

"You act much older."

I shrugged my shoulders, feigning cluelessness.

"What do you do?" he inquired.

I hesitated, mulling it over. "I travel the world picking up handsome men," I quipped, hoping this would silence him.

Antonio chuckled, uncertain whether it was a joke or the truth.

As the Uber approached my imposing hotel, I tucked my erection into my jeans and fastened the buttons. Unbeknownst to Antonio, I had a secret I was unwilling to share. My jizz is highly toxic. If I had ejaculated and he had swallowed my load, it would have killed him. I could have ended his life in the back seat of the Uber, but that would have been too easy. I wanted hardcore sex.

The car entered the hotel's porte-cochere.

Antonio's jaw dropped, and he gripped my leg, evidently impressed.

"The Augustus Hotel?" he exclaimed in awe. "Did you know they almost tore it down? But then, someone restored it. I've never been inside one of the rooms!"

I smiled at his enthusiasm.

The driver bid us a polite farewell, wishing us a good night.

As the bellman opened the door, Antonio looked around in amazement. Unlike my companion, I didn't care about the landmark's architecture. All I wanted was to unload inside his ass. "You'll love the Imperial Suite," I said, guiding him forward.

"This is so much better than I expected the night to go," Antonio murmured enthusiastically, glancing at me.

My heart pounded as I considered the task at hand. "Yes, Antonio, this will be an unforgettable night," I whispered, my gaze fixed on his backside, fully aware that his naked body would soon be mine.

Antonio

UPON ENTERING the opulent hotel room, I couldn't help but marvel at the lavish decor and upscale furnishings. The walls were painted in a gentle cream hue, complementing the tasteful artwork displayed throughout the space. Luxurious draperies hung gracefully from the windows, revealing a breathtaking view of the city lights twinkling below. The meticulous attention to detail left me thoroughly astounded.

Without wasting a moment, Robert directed me to remove my clothing and kneel before him. I followed his guidance, and my knees found comfort in the plush carpet below me. I was anxious to see his sex better than I had in the backseat of the car, so I unbuttoned his jeans until it sprung forward in full display.

"Oh . . ." I mumbled in disappointment. It somehow seemed smaller now. Hoping he didn't notice my dissatisfaction. I glanced up and saw his forehead creasing into a frown. I offered an apologetic smile.

Returning to his manhood, I squeezed his hardness, and a drop of pre-ejaculate oozed from the opening. Being on PrEP, I wasn't afraid to taste it, so I licked the fluid. A burning sensation erupted in my mouth. Confused, I glanced up and wiped the substance away.

"Suck me, you ungrateful bitch!"

"You like to play rough," I said as he pulled my head forward. I hoped it was that. Otherwise, I'd made him angry.

He rammed himself inside my mouth, and thanks to my deep-throating skills, I didn't choke. I thought he had become aggressive, but I was willing to go along with the roleplay to get laid. But then he went too far, even for me.

"I'm going to kill you."

I withdrew my lips from his shaft. Glancing up, I saw his lips part, revealing a pair of sharp fangs. A chilling realization struck me — this man was a vampire! My instincts kicked into high gear, alerting me to the imminent danger. Fight or flight became the only option, and I chose the latter without hesitation.

He moved quickly, blocking my way to the door.

"Scared? Little bitch!" he growled, his voice low and menacing.

I backed away while fear swelled within me. Just as I began to turn and flee, he lunged, and his weight pushed us to the floor. I struggled beneath him, desperately trying to break free, but he pinned me with preternatural strength.

Robert

BECAUSE THE whore preferred a well-hung man, I abandoned any pretense of giving him pleasure. I'd forcefully take what I wanted and give him what he deserved. I pinned him down and penetrated his ass, annoyed by how easily he took me.

"Please don't kill me," he begged.

"This is the last cock you'll have, so you'd better enjoy it regardless of its size," I told him and started thrusting away. The excitement I felt overpowering him stirred my balls. As his hole tightened, I shouted, "Fuck!" I quickly pulled out, managing to halt any premature release.

I turned him over and was surprised to see his hard-on. He was circumcised, and it measured around seven inches. The large pulsating vein running down the shaft was so impressive that I licked my lips, wanting to suck on it. But I didn't. If I did, I'd be submissive just like him.

"Why are you doing this?" Antonio moaned.

I didn't answer. Instead, I bared my fangs and hissed at him. His eyes widened as I plunged my teeth into his neck.

After extracting Antonio's blood, I re-entered him, and

my orgasm took over. As I pulled out of his ass, I glared at him disgustingly. "Damn you for judging me based on penis size."

David

STANDING ON the hotel balcony, I looked through the sliding glass door and saw my father having sex with another man. I inhaled sharply, seeing my dad's body illuminated by the bedside table lamp. I admired his broad shoulders, muscular back, and hairy chest. His well-built frame was impressive, and even from a distance, the firmness of his ass caught my attention. I became physically aroused.

Shifting my focus to the guy getting screwed, I noticed he was around my age and unmistakably Italian. His heritage was evident in his dark hair and complexion. His cheekbones and chiseled jawline adorned with stubble contributed to his striking appearance. I knew immediately that this was someone I wanted to get to know better.

I should explain why I'm standing on a balcony watching my dad have sex. My father and I are enlisted soldiers in the vampire army. He holds the esteemed position of a high-ranking master sergeant, while I'm only an E-1 recruit. However, I've been on the run for months after defecting as a conscientious objector. I oppose the killing of gay vampires.

Reading my father's mind uncovered his mission to eliminate Antonio De Luca. To make a long story short, I trailed him here to intervene. My strong contempt for the Army's chief of staff who provided the order fueled my determination to act.

Returning to the erotic scene, I was drawn to my father's

naked body as he screwed Antonio. I could see the sweat on his forehead and the moisture between his ass cheeks. I imagined his masculine body emitted a musky aroma and wished to experience it.

Unexpectedly, he drew me in like I could have never imagined. I grasped myself, not believing my newfound interest in him. I didn't understand my incestuous feelings. However, instead of shaming myself, I decided to embrace it.

With this new revelation, I pondered our fractured relationship. It had been strained ever since he forced me to join the military. My father believed that its discipline and structure would somehow alter me. However, rather than changing me, it drove a wedge between us.

As my dad's thrusts quickened, I knew it was only a short time before Antonio took his load. My prick continued to pulsate in excitement. I wanted to jack off, but I didn't because the time to enact my revenge was coming soon.

Robert

AS THE WARM, sudsy water cleansed my body of sweat in the shower, a surge of annoyance overcame me upon seeing my reflection in the bathroom mirror. At forty-two years old, I certainly didn't appreciate appearing youthful. Preferring to embrace life as an older version of myself, I relied on the vampire powers that enabled me to change my appearance. I reluctantly transformed into my younger self to capture Antonio's attention at the bar.

I closed my eyes and willed myself into middle age.

Opening my eyelids, I saw my body with a forty-two-year-old cock that carried added girth around it. I stroked it back and forth, feeling the need to ejaculate again. I'd hoped raping Antonio would have sated my desire, but it didn't. I decided to head back to the bar. This time I would find a queer appreciative of my dick.

I took a towel and carefully dried my body, removing tangled hair strands. Standing before the mirror, I gazed at my reflection, aware of my good looks. My once old-fashioned mustache, which I adored, was becoming trendy again. I confidently expanded my chest, giving my physique a final glance. With a self-admiring smile, I left the bathroom.

I dressed in an all-black ensemble, drawing strength from its dark hue. With one last disgusted glance at Antonio's unconscious body on the floor, I left the room and approached the elevator.

Once in the lobby, my eyes immediately fell on a handsome figure. His short-cropped hair and muscular body stirred desires deep inside me. Unfortunately, he had taken up a position behind the front desk, and any attempt to entice him upstairs would be hopeless. A wave of disappointment crashed over me as I entered the night air. The only way to satisfy my primal urge was to find a willing partner — then afterward, I'd return to the hotel and dispose of Antonio's body.

Antonio

A COMFORTING WARMTH enveloped my mouth as I consumed a thick, metallic fluid. Its flavor blended sweet and refreshing notes with a velvety texture. The coppery taste suggested something enigmatic. As I gulped it down, I sensed its nourishing properties rejuvenating my body. The noise of my sipping was suddenly interrupted by an unfamiliar voice.

I opened my eyes, feeling disoriented.

"You've drunk too much."

I abruptly sat up, my mind in disarray. Seated before me was a man my age with sandy-blond hair. He bore a striking resemblance to the man who had assaulted me, and that realization unnerved me almost as much as my next discovery. I was sucking blood from his wrist. My thoughts raced, struggling to comprehend the bizarre situation.

"My name's David."

My eyes widened in awe as the gash on his arm healed on its own.

As he began taking off his jeans, I couldn't help but admire his well-defined jawline and striking blue eyes. His prominent cheekbones contributed to a sophisticated yet rugged appearance, and his full lips formed a mischievous grin. Once he had removed his clothes and stood naked before me, I marveled at his physique. It was indeed a sight to behold. I appreciated every aspect of his natural form.

Logically, fear should have taken over, but it didn't. My instincts reassured me that I was not in harm's way.

"Robert drained you of blood."

As I paid close attention, I subconsciously scratched my ass, where a sudden itch demanded my notice. Looking down at my hand, I saw semen. The memories of the attack and the revelation of Robert sucking my blood consumed my thoughts. "Yes. I remember."

"We have to act quickly."

Sensing his anxiety, I quickly asked if he was also a vampire. Much to my dismay, David confirmed that he was. As the shock set in, he revealed that Robert was his father. Hearing this revelation left me breathless. How could it be possible? "You look like brothers!"

"When you become a vampire, you continue to age, but your physical appearance remains unchanged. We embraced this lifestyle early on — I was twenty-one, and he was twenty," he explained and then took hold of my penis.

"What are you doing?" I asked in surprise.

"Don't be afraid," he said gently.

His smile conveyed genuine sincerity, reassuring me. He opened his mouth as if to speak further, but instead, he leaned in and planted an unexpected kiss on my lips. The kiss ended with him kneeling on the floor and inserting me inside his mouth.

Becoming hard, I closed my eyes in pleasure as he sucked me. In no time, he brought forth my ejaculation. "Oh, my god, I'm coming!" I exclaimed. Catching my breath, I opened my eyes just in time to see him swallowing my load.

"The seed of a vampire is poisonous, so I sucked you off while you were still a mortal," he said, smacking his lips.

David elaborated on the situation, revealing that his blood possessed a unique property that counteracted the poisonous venom inside me. And to survive and escape the clutches of death, I needed to ingest his cum. It would seal my fate if I chose not to comply, leading to an imminent untimely demise.

"Isn't vampire sperm poisonous?" The entire scenario was utterly baffling. Seeing the confusion on my face, David gripped my shoulder.

"It's not if my blood is within you."

David's statement left me searching for more answers.

Seeing my bewilderment, he continued, "I don't have time to explain the process of turning someone into a bloodsucker. Just know that it's possible after giving them your blood first. Antonio, do you want to live?"

I nodded.

He further clarified, "For eternity?"

"As in, a vampire," I said, as understanding sank in. I lowered my head and thought quickly, knowing I had two choices — life or death. "I want life!" I blurted out, raising my head.

David sat on the edge of the bed and spread his legs.

I knelt before him and stared at his erection. It pulsated in anticipation of my mouth. I retracted the foreskin and saw the head wasn't red from being hidden away. The length and girth were awe-inspiring. I licked my lips, craving his pre-cum.

"Go ahead. Taste it," he said.

I squeezed his hardness, tasting the clear fluid oozing from his meatus. Confused again, I asked why it didn't burn.

He smiled. "It's because you have my blood inside you."

I ran my tongue down the length of his shaft and licked the area between his anus and scrotum. By his reaction, I could tell he was a man who liked ass-play. I lifted his legs and inserted my tongue into his hole. He moaned loudly, savoring the delicate touch. As I pressed my tongue deeper, he lowered his legs.

"Suck me."

I serviced him as I had never serviced anyone, working his sex until it expelled its life-saving fluid inside my mouth. I moaned, gathering the substance at the base of my throat. I opened my mouth and showed him. He smiled in appreciation, knowing I treasured his fluid.

"Swallow it," David said.

I consumed his load and smiled triumphantly.

David fell back onto the bed, feeling exhausted and spent.

"Rest before we become brothers."

His words took me aback. "Brothers? Why not lovers?"

Feeling a surge of discomfort, I climbed onto the bed. My mentor loomed over me, eagerly awaiting the forthcoming events.

"You have so much to learn."

My breathing became shallow and uneven, and my heart rate slowed down. Fear appeared to surround me from all directions, and soon, shadows encircled me, luring me into their unknown realm.

I calmed myself by closing my eyes and taking a deep breath. At that moment, I realized that eternal peace lies beyond death. With this realization, I let go of all my anxieties and embraced the darkness as it consumed me.

Robert

STANDING IN the shadows, I pushed the fag against the brick wall. The putrid odor emanating from the bar's dumpster was nauseating and suffocating.

He'd approached me soon after I'd returned to the bar, and after a few minutes of flirty conversation, he'd suggested we head out to the alley.

My boner pulsed with desire as he offered his eager ass. He didn't care about cock size, just a hard piece of meat that enjoyed fucking ass. Before I could enter him, he turned and explained that he wasn't on PrEP. He asked me not to come inside him.

I ignored his wishes and turned him back around. I pushed the queer against the wall and started fucking him. His ass muscles felt good. My cock was massaged so well that it stirred my cum-filled balls. I slowed down, not wanting to pre-ejaculate, but it was too late. I couldn't stop the eruption. I moaned loudly and shot my load inside him.

The faggot pushed me out and whipped around. "I told you not to come inside me."

I leaped onto him and tackled him to the ground.

Within minutes, I'd drained him of blood — but I fed too greedily, leaving me in a daze. I cursed myself, wishing I had better control over my thirst. And my ejaculations.

I got dressed, then used my foot to roll him over. A grin formed on my face seeing my jizz seeping from his ass.

The sound of laughter drew my attention to the mouth of the alley. A group of men rounded the corner, heading in my direction. Fastening the last button on my jeans, I took off running. Seconds later, I heard their shocked voices and knew they'd discovered the corpse.

As I made my way back to the hotel, I thought about where to dispose of Antonio's body. I approached a bridge above a rushing river and looked over the railing. I smiled. This would be his final resting place.

Antonio

SNAPPING BACK to reality, I lifted my hands to my face, relieved to see that my olive skin remained unchanged. As I grappled with this new existence, thoughts of doubt and fear washed over me. Was I destined to dwell in darkness forever? What about sustenance? Would I still be able to enjoy the same foods and drinks as before?

"Yes! I'll explain everything," David said.

"Did you just read my mind?"

"I did." He smiled. "It's one of the many abilities of being a vampire."

Excited to learn new skills, I closed my eyes and concentrated on his thoughts to see if I could read them. Nothing came forward. My mind was blank.

"Everyone develops their powers at different times," David explained, then pointed at the bedpost. "Break off the finial."

I gave him a quizzical look.

He explained that I had new strengths.

I grasped the post with my right hand and slightly twisted it. The finial broke off into my hand. My mouth hung open in surprise at how easily I'd done it. "Did you see that?" I asked in amazement.

My mentor nodded, a slight smile playing on his lips. He clapped me on the back.

"Well done! This is just the beginning. I'll show you everything."

My eyes widened in disbelief as I felt my abdomen. The toned muscles rippled beneath my fingertips. "This is fucking unreal!" I'd spent so many hours trying to achieve this sculpted physique, and now, here it was — a six-pack that could grace the cover of any fitness magazine.

"We need to leave before Robert returns," David said, anxiety crossing his face.

I got dressed with my heart racing as I tried to understand what was happening. Questions flooded my mind, especially about his father's intentions. "Why did your father want to kill me?" I asked him.

Then, much to my astonishment, he posed another question that caught me off guard.

"Do you know what happened to your mother?"

Taken aback by the sudden mention of her, I couldn't help but respond defensively, "What do you know about her?" My voice wavered slightly, betraying my shock at his unexpected inquiry.

He looked pensive but didn't respond immediately. His voice was soft and strained when he finally spoke, admitting that he had sinned by making me a vampire. He warned that his father would be furious that he'd saved me.

"He's close. Can't you feel his presence?"

I was perplexed, unable to comprehend why he had suddenly steered the conversation away from my mother. I let him direct the discussion despite wanting to hear what he knew about her whereabouts. "Why would your father punish us?"

David lowered his head. "Being gay is forbidden in my world."

"Your father's gay. He raped me!"

"Robert fools everyone, including himself. He has sex with men and then kills them to keep his secret." He lifted his head. "Antonio, my father's an evil man. Be afraid of him."

"He gets away with this?"

David nodded and walked toward the sliding glass door. "When he returns and finds you gone, he'll track us down."

The sweet, fragrant breath of the late summer air wafted into the room as David cautiously opened the sliding glass door. I was ready for whatever might come next.

"How would he find us?" I asked, following him out onto the balcony.

"He has powers like me, but stronger," he said, wiping

the sweat from his forehead with the back of his hand. "I have committed the worst possible sin by making you a vampire. My punishment will be death."

"But you saved me from dying."

"Only the elders in our Federation decide who becomes a vampire. It's a sacred act and only performed during a special resurrection ceremony. Hold onto me," David said.

I embraced him, and his strong arms held me firmly around the waist, inducing a wave of elation that surged through my body. I nestled myself close to him and savored the security of his embrace.

We slowly descended the twelve stories to the ground. Just as my feet grazed the grass, he kissed me with a passion I had never felt before. I became completely disconnected from reality and my surroundings. In that instant, I knew I was falling in love with him.

Robert

UPON STEPPING into the hotel suite, I instantly realized Antonio was missing. Driven by urgency, I quickly headed to the bathroom, hoping to locate him. When he wasn't there, I came out of the restroom and meticulously scanned the whole room.

To my surprise, my nostrils detected a peculiar and unmistakable scent — jizz. Alongside this scent, the familiar aroma of my son's presence reached me, making me realize he had managed to track me down and rescue the mortal from my grasp. Overwhelmed with anger and frustration, I let out a mighty roar of rage that echoed throughout the room, its intensity strong enough to also reverberate down the hallway.

My heart rate quickened as I sprinted toward the

balcony. Once there, I desperately searched for even the faintest hint of my son's scent. But as soon as I thought I had a trail to follow, it abruptly vanished. Bewildered and frustrated by this unexpected turn of events, I cursed under my breath. Anger surged as I realized David had outsmarted me.

I clenched my fists, feeling my power slipping away. I was no longer in control. They have now become a formidable force to reckon with. I only hoped to find them before my organization realized what had happened.

Making Antonio into a vampire was unforgivable. I wasn't sure how to protect my son from the infantry that would carry out his sentence, but I'd figure something out.

Closing my eyes, I took a deep breath and finally smelled my son's presence in the air. With newfound determination, I flew off into the night to find him.

Antonio

MY HEART RACED while I gazed intently at the drunk man on the street. I couldn't gather the courage to take his life. The very idea of killing another person filled me with dread.

I was caught off guard by David's sudden, forceful shove.

Whirling around to face him, I saw his earnest eyes and could tell he wanted me to succeed. The reassuring pressure of his hand on my shoulder gave me the fortitude to proceed.

My vampire mind instructed me to offer the man a drink. I picked up an empty wine bottle in the gutter and walked toward him.

The intoxicated man halted as he heard my footsteps behind him.

When he spun around to face me, I held the bottle in my hand and waited with bated breath to see whether he would take the offer. He grinned, grasped the bottle firmly, touched it to his lips, and lowered it.

"What the fuck?"

The drunk heaved the bottle onto the pavement.

As it landed with a dull thud and rolled across the street, a foul stench assaulted my senses — excrement. I stared at David in astonishment, questioning his choice of this individual as my initial objective.

David stood unflinchingly — his expression unreadable. I knew he wouldn't explain, as I had no choice. This was life or death. He gestured for me to continue.

I knew I needed nourishment because I was getting weak. I ran my tongue over my incisors and felt my protruding eye teeth for the first time, their length and sharpness. I smiled in wonderment, displaying my fangs proudly.

"Oh, no," he mumbled, stepping backward.

I gazed into his eyes, feeling myself take control of him. As his body froze, I leaped forward and bit into his neck. In seconds, I felt dizzy from consuming his alcohol-tainted blood. His thoughts entered my mind — I saw the wife and children he'd abandoned. I saw a condemned house. My heart went to his wife, knowing she had to raise children on her own.

"Antonio, stop drinking," David murmured. "He's dead."

He snapped me out of my dream state, and I pulled away from the bleeding throat. David took the body and laid it on the street.

"I killed him," I said, feeling remorse.

"The first is always the worst," David said, glancing toward the horizon. "The morning will come soon. Do you know a place we can sleep?"

"My bedroom's in the basement. We'll be safe there," I mumbled, tasting the metallic tang of the drunkard's blood on my lips. His life force filled me with an energy I hadn't known before, giving me a heightened sense of invincibility. A veil seemed to lift from my eyes, making my vision particularly sharp. I felt renewed.

David nodded and gestured to leave.

We sprinted across the street, our feet carrying us faster with each stride. The fear of the rising sun propelled us forward with ever-increasing speed. I felt unstoppable as we ran for the safety of my home. The cityscape blurred around me.

Upon reaching my house a few minutes later, I was relieved as we crossed the threshold. Feeling breathless, I lifted my index finger to my lips, gesturing for David to remain silent. I didn't feel prepared to confront my father while embracing my new identity as an immortal vampire.

"What does your father look like?" David whispered, reading my mind as he followed me through the dimly lit kitchen and down the basement staircase.

"Nothing like me," I said, wishing I looked more like him. "He looks like he just got off the boat from Italy."

David's eyes widened in surprise.

I told him my dad was, in fact, of Sicilian descent and had relocated to the United States after his parents died. His Italian name was Guglielmo, but he preferred using William, the American version.

"He came to the States by himself?" David asked.

I explained that my aunt and uncle, who'd already moved abroad, adopted him when he was about ten. They were childless and were more than happy to have him.

I held David's hand as we strolled through the family room. His eyes twinkled with joy, and I felt my heart swell with happiness. I gestured for him to walk into my bedroom.

I lifted the heavy, patterned quilt off my bed and carefully draped it over the curtain rod on my small window. When I turned around, David pulled me into a warm embrace. His arms were strong yet gentle; I felt safe as if nothing could harm me.

"You're my Adonis. Your beauty brings out my desire," he said, repositioning the erection inside his jeans.

I laughed at his comment, feeling a stirring in my loins.

He grinned. "Let's screw!"

I was captivated by David's alluring gaze as it washed over me. I met his eyes while undressing and couldn't help but think he was the more attractive one. "You're far more handsome than Adonis could ever hope to be," I teased, fully aware of the Greek art's beauty standards. My playful remark blushed his cheeks, and he chuckled softly.

"Did you know he was androgynous?" David inquired.

I shook my head, unable to recall this detail from my Greek mythology class.

"He acted like a man to his wife, Aphrodite, but took on the feminine role for Apollo, Heracles, and Dionysus," David elaborated, gently drawing me back into his warm embrace.

We held each other briefly, and he gently kissed me. His skin felt soft against mine as we shared an intimate moment. As we pulled apart, I couldn't help but wonder if Adonis had felt this kind of love in his lifetime.

My dick sprang to life as I stepped out of my jeans, fantasizing about the muscular Greek gods penetrating Adonis's ass. It felt different, and I realized my transition had given me extra girth. I smirked, impressed.

David stripped off his jeans and had me lay face down on the bed.

He caressed my lower back, and I caught my breath as his fingers slipped between my buttocks. He touched my anus. It puckered and then relaxed, allowing his father's sperm to ooze out. I didn't expect that and was embarrassed. "Oh!" I said and started to roll over.

"It's all right," he whispered, pushing me down.

I was surprised he didn't care about his father's fluid inside me. It turned me on, and I wanted David's load as well. I didn't understand these newfound desires. "Fuck me!"

David grinned and crawled onto the bed, kneeling behind me.

"I have condoms in my pocket," I said, but I was pretty sure they wouldn't fit him. I knew he needed a magnum to accommodate his manhood.

"My jizz would just melt them. I'm taking you raw."

I spread my ass cheeks with trembling fingers, and he entered me. His father's sperm acted as a lubricant and guided him in quickly. I knew David's proficiency in love-making would lead me to experience total fulfillment — a sensation I had never truly encountered before.

David

AS I knelt there, captivated by Antonio's presence, I couldn't help but feel a profound connection with him. Despite knowing that romance between bloodsuckers was strictly forbidden, he made me question the rules and constraints imposed by my organization. However, as this realization set in, I quickly reminded myself that I was acting like a love-struck fool.

I took a deep breath and regained my composure. I cherished my independence and freedom. The excitement of exploring new connections and the variety it brought was something I'd never give up. Being with just one person seemed monotonous and unappealing compared to the adventurous lifestyle I had grown to love.

"So hot!" I murmured, watching my father's cum seeping from Antonio's ass. It took every ounce of my willpower to resist the urge to lap it up. I wasn't sure if Antonio would freak out or not. It was too early to tell; I didn't know him well enough yet.

"Fuck me!" Antonio moaned, spreading his cheeks.

Focusing on the seeping cum again, my resolve weakened, and I scooped the glob onto my finger. I brought it to my nose and inhaled the scent. The aroma was so delightful that it made my mouth open unconsciously. I inserted my finger and savored it for the first time. My eyes rolled back as the rich flavor and delightful texture instantly brought me to the brink of ecstasy. The modest quantity on my tongue didn't cause harm, so I didn't need to expel it.

"I want your dick!" Antonio cried excitedly.

Snapping back to reality and shaking off my momentary bliss, I redirected my focus toward Antonio. The fluid in his ass meant I didn't need lubrication when I entered him. His hole enfolded my prick, and I knew I was home. The fact that I was inside him after my father excited me. I screwed him with passion, unlike anything before.

Antonio

SMOTHERING MY face in the pillow, I muted my moans of pleasure as I took every inch of David's engorged shaft. Hearing his gustatory groans of delight, I turned glassy-eyed and saw his finger in his mouth. His eyes were closed, tasting his father's sperm.

When David opened his eyes and saw me, he quickly withdrew his finger and offered a smile, creating the illusion that nothing improper was happening. He seemed to register my thoughts, and in response, he increased his pace. This calculated move successfully prompted me to disregard his actions.

"I want to screw you on all fours."

"Oh, yes . . ." I moaned as he pulled out and brought me into the doggie-style position. Once again, I took the entire length of his eight inches. In the following moments, ecstasy surrounded us as he adeptly captivated me in every imaginable way.

"Come for me," he whispered, gasping for breath.

Upon hearing his command, my anus tightened around his sex, and I came violently without touching myself. As soon as my body stopped spasming, I turned and looked at him in a state of pleasure.

He bent down and kissed me while thrusting deeply.

I smelt his perspiration. His natural scent aroused me, acting as an aphrodisiac. Then, suddenly, the head of his penis enlarged, and he quickened his pace. He would shoot his load soon. As his moans increased, my erection excreted more fluid.

"I'm coming," he muttered.

David pulled out and deposited his toxic load on the bedspread, then collapsed on top of me, catching his breath. After a few moments of enjoying the afterglow, he rolled onto his back.

Out of breath, spent from my ejaculation, my mind went to his poisonous seed. "I want to taste you again."

"I've warned you," he said sternly, "my cum is highly toxic, so don't think about playing with it. It would be fatal."

I turned around and faced him.

He looked at me intensely, trying to gauge whether I had comprehended the seriousness of his words. He could see that I understood as my eyes widened in disappointment and realization.

"A vampire can only seed someone to turn them — and only after giving them blood first."

"I get it," I murmured sadly.

David looked into my eyes and told me I was different from all the other guys he's screwed. I shrugged, trying to hide the fact that his words made my stomach flutter with excitement. Deep down, I knew he had feelings for me. "I'm just me. I guess that makes me unique."

David gave me a playful smirk, enjoying my answer.

As he leaned in to kiss me, my father's bedside table lamp came crashing to the floor in the room above us.

"What the hell?" I sat up.

David's gentle yet firm touch on my lips silenced me.

I heard a menacing voice threatening my father. In

a panic, we sprang from the bed and hastily dressed. As we hurried away, I crossed myself fervently, knowing the gravity of the situation.

William

A LOUD BANG jolted me from slumber. I reached to turn on the bedside lamp, only to discover that was the source of the noise. My eyes frantically scanned the room, and soon enough, I spotted Robert, my arch-nemesis, the malevolent vampire who longed for me. He lurked ominously in the corner of the room with a predatory glint in his eyes. He bared his teeth and wore a sinister grin.

I trembled as he began to approach me. His deep voice resonated throughout the room, leaving me shocked at his sudden appearance.

"I forewarned you."

His dark eyes gleamed with anticipation of what was to come. My heart was filled with dread, fearing for my son's safety. I knew he had come to take Antonio's life. Robert positioned himself beside the bed, looming over me menacingly.

"Don't be afraid."

My heart raced as he reached into my boxers.

The moment his hand groped me, a powerful surge of anger and disgust coursed through my veins. I forcefully shoved Robert's hand away and leaped out of bed just in time for the door to burst open.

A man bearing a striking resemblance to Robert rushed in, with Antonio following closely behind.

"Run, Antonio!" I shouted, my voice filling with fear for my son's safety. I wanted him to be as far away from danger as possible. As Robert advanced toward Antonio, I threw myself into the fray, determined to stop him at all costs.

Antonio

A SURGE OF terror engulfed me when David unexpectedly charged the unwelcome visitor. My heart sank upon recognizing him as Robert — the man who viciously assaulted me. Frozen in place by sheer panic, I could hardly comprehend my father's desperate plea to escape.

Without hesitation, my dad sprang off the bed, positioning himself beside Robert. The tension in the room became palpable as they faced each other, ready for confrontation.

In a swift, fluid movement, Robert landed a powerful punch in my father's face, sending him sprawling to the floor. Turning around, he wasted no time in showcasing his superhuman strength. With an effortless motion, he lifted David and hurled him against the wall with incredible force. The impact left David unconscious.

With David no longer a threat, Robert's menacing focus shifted back to my father. Grimacing from the pain of the earlier blow, my dad found the strength to rise to his feet, mentally preparing himself for the impending battle.

"Dad!" I screamed, my voice trembling with fear for his well-being.

Looking vulnerable and overwhelmed by Robert's intense gaze, my father stood still, unable to move. It seemed as if the vampire's captivating eyes had cast a spell on him, leaving him motionless.

"It's so good to see you again, William," Robert murmured, taking a menacing step forward. "You look handsome as ever!"

His voice dripped with sinister mockery, sending chills down my spine as he closed the distance between them.

Robert was so mesmerized by the sight of my father's partially nude body that he momentarily forgot I was even there. I held my breath as he raised his finger and traced the hair strip on my father's abdomen.

"Stop molesting my father!" I shouted.

Robert responded with a menacing chuckle and yanked my father's boxers down to puddle around his ankles. I was horrified and couldn't move as he fondled my dad. I stepped closer, realizing my father was hypnotized, determined to intervene.

Robert stopped me with a question.

"Haven't you noticed that you don't resemble your father?"

I couldn't grasp what was happening but knew I had to protect my dad from this predator. Closing my eyes, I mentally urged him to break free from the hypnotic trance.

Astonishingly, it worked.

My father staggered back, tripping over his shorts. His face twisted with anger, and his fists clenched as he shouted at Robert to get his hands off him. Regaining his balance, my father stood ready to fight.

"Didn't you realize this day would come, William? I think it's time you revealed your little secret. If you come clean, your Catholic priest will recite the three 'Hail Mary's' for you."

My dad's face drained of all color.

"Please . . . don't do this," he begged. Robert chuckled, knowing he had the upper hand.

"I'll do whatever you want." My father pleaded, craning his neck toward Robert. "Take my blood but leave my son alone."

Robert smirked. "Oh, William, I'm a sadist. Your pain is my pleasure. I seek your delicious cock, not your neck."

Then he laughed in a low, horrifying voice.

"Take it if it'll shut you up!" my father snapped, stepping out of his boxer shorts and tossing them to the floor. His frustration was evident, and I could tell he was reaching his breaking point.

My gaze was transfixed on my father's sculpted figure as I compared it to Michelangelo's masterpiece, the legendary David. His neck muscles bulged, and his face twisted with disgust. I couldn't help but marvel at his toned body and take note of the only incongruent detail — the small penis. My father grasped his dick and started stroking it back and forth. Then to my dismay, he pointed it toward Robert.

"Take it."

"Tempting, very tempting," Robert murmured, licking his lips in anticipation of my father's erection. "Sucking is a queer's job!" he spat, unbuttoning his jeans. "If you want my silence, get on your knees!"

My father dropped to the floor.

Robert grabbed my father's head and rammed himself inside his mouth. It was evident my dad had never sucked before because unbearable gagging sounds filled the air. I hurried over to David and shook him vigorously. "Get up!" I exclaimed. "I need your help!"

David moaned, his eyes fluttering open.

Hearing Robert grunting in frustration, I turned and saw him pushing my father away, apparently displeased with his sucking skills.

"I'll taste your blood instead," Robert growled.

Gasping for breath, I watched in horror as Robert yanked my father to his feet and sank his fangs into his neck. My dad's painful gasp turned my stomach. Desperate, I shook David again, successfully rousing him to full consciousness.

Suddenly, David leaped into action, propelling himself with such force that he seemed to defy gravity. His teeth gleamed menacingly as he moved through the air toward his father.

Robert ripped his fangs from my dad's flesh and glared at David, halting him mid-air.

"You've sinned by making another vampire! That's a death sentence."

"I'm an infantry deserter, for Christ's sake," David screamed. "They're going to kill me anyway, so who cares?" He levitated closer.

"My son, the queer!"

"And you're not?"

"How dare you call me a goddamn fag!" Robert roared, still clutching my listless father to his chest.

"You fuck men, so you're a homosexual!" David shouted, lowering himself to the floor.

"Damn, you!" Robert yelled, not wanting to hear the truth.

"When was the last time you fucked a woman?"

Robert turned away — his face twisted with anguish. After a moment of introspection, he finally broke the silence.

"Maybe . . . it's true," he admitted softly.

David's jaw dropped, and his eyes widened in disbelief as he took it all in. Then, almost as if he could no longer contain himself, he slowly clapped his hands.

"It's about fucking time!" he exclaimed.

Robert's eyes welled up with tears.

"I could've saved you from the punishment for desertion. But this . . . there's nothing I can do for you now," Robert snapped with a lisp, returning to my dad's neck.

"Please stop," I cried helplessly.

My father's eyes fluttered one last time before they shut completely, leaving me powerless and unable to help him.

Robert tossed my father to the floor, then lunged at David.

I sprinted to my dad and cradled him in my arms. The cold, lifeless stare on his face sent a shiver down my spine. I couldn't believe this was happening.

David yelled at his father while being tackled to the floor, "I never wanted to be a soldier!"

"I wanted you to be a man," Robert snarled.

"I hate you!" David screamed, his voice cracking with emotion. He struggled against his father's grip, but it was too strong.

Feeling defeated by his son's harsh words, Robert hung his head in despair. "I'll hide you from the infantry," he mumbled, lifting his head. The pain of rejection was evident in his eyes.

"I'm not going anywhere with you," David shouted, his face red with fury. He wriggled free from his father's grasp and stumbled backward, his chest heaving as he tried to catch his breath.

"They're going to kill you," Robert implored.

David's expression hardened, and he took a step back. "I'd rather die than be a part of this organization," he declared, his voice filled with resolve.

"We're going back to New Orleans."

Robert bit his wrist and raised his arm, knowing his son was weak and couldn't resist his blood.

With an animalistic hunger, David lunged onto his father's arm like prey. I couldn't believe my eyes when he started sipping the deadly fluid. As I struggled to comprehend how a father could take his child's life, a thought dawned on me — he'd done it before when he turned David into a vampire. That gave me an idea — I could now save my father.

I knew I needed to take advantage of this opportunity to get away. I grabbed his clothes from the top of the hamper, gathered him in my arms, and ran out the door.

***

I put the Honda Pilot into reverse and backed out of the garage. My eyes widened in disbelief when I saw Robert dashing forward. He jumped onto the hood. Before I could even draw a gasp of surprise, he punched his fist through the windshield, leaving behind a gaping hole amidst the shattered safety glass.

My heart raced as I felt the car shake under his weight, but somehow, I managed to keep my composure and maintain control of the vehicle.

Desperately scouring the rear seat, I discovered an empty soda bottle. Clutching it, I forcefully struck it against the dashboard, sending glass shards everywhere. Equipped with a makeshift weapon, I readied myself to fight back.

My adrenaline surged as I thrust the bottle toward

him. The shock of seeing my weapon made him angry. He grabbed it from my hand and threw it into the darkness.

Robert's fist returned with a vengeance.

I knocked his hand away and snapped the wheel to the right, knocking him off the hood. He fell to the pavement and rolled three times. I slammed my foot on the pedal and sped down the street. As I glanced into the rearview mirror, I saw him bending over, catching his breath. I'm sure he was yelling obscenities, too.

The sun peeked over the horizon. I gasped, shielding my eyes, knowing I needed to find shelter quickly.

I rapidly accelerated the car through the city streets and eventually stumbled across a motel. Without hesitation, I pulled into the parking lot and quickly covered my father with a blanket. I then ran to the motel's entrance to pay for one of their rooms in advance. Quickly returning to the vehicle, I opened the door and pulled my dad out, carrying him inside.

The stale and dank smell of neglect immediately assaulted my nose when I entered the room. I took a few steps forward and saw the furniture had a weathered and ancient look. Dark spots littered the carpet beneath my feet, and I soon realized they were stains from years of use.

I slowly made my way to the bed, my heart heavy with unease as I took in the sights around me. Carefully, I laid my father down on the mattress. As I stepped back from the bed, my gaze fell upon the sunlight streaming into the room, and I felt a sense of foreboding wash over me.

With caution, I approached the window, my heart thudding. Gazing outside, I observed the sun ascending and casting its light through the trees.

My vision blurred as my eyes began to burn from the intensity of the sunlight, forcing me to hastily close the drapes and shield myself from its piercing rays. In that instant, the realization struck me like a lightning bolt; this would be the last sunrise I would ever witness.

As I turned around, my breath caught in my throat, and I inhaled in sheer terror. There, lying on the bed, was my father — his once-strong body now frail and withering. He let out a sound I knew I would never forget, the pain and suffering evident in every note. It was clear to me that he was dying.

Robert

"THAT FUCKING bitch! Damn him!"

I stood and brushed the dirt off my jeans. I turned as Antonio honked the horn and waved goodbye, fucking with me. "You're dead!" I muttered, giving him the finger. As steam started rising from my body, I sprinted toward the house to protect myself from the emerging sun.

Entering the house, I rushed headlong to the bedroom, hoping beyond all hope that what I feared was not true. But as soon as I stepped into the room, my fears were confirmed. On the floor lay my son, David, motionless and unresponsive. I'd poisoned him.

I sank to my knees and begged for forgiveness. I couldn't bear the thought of losing him, my only son. What was I thinking? Why didn't I monitor the amount of blood he drank? I was such a stupid fool.

Antonio

I LOWERED MY wrist to my father's lips. His skin had a waxy hue, and his frame was weak. Yet he still turned away from my offering. With an aching heart, I sighed, frustrated. "You'll die if you don't drink," I said, turning his head in my direction. "Father, please. Do this for me."

The sadness that must have been visible on my face resonated deeply with him, stirring a sense of empathy and understanding. It was as if he could see the turmoil I was experiencing, which moved him to consider my plea. After what felt like an eternity, he slowly nodded in agreement, signaling his willingness to grant my request.

As my father drank, I looked around the seedy motel room that charged an hourly rate. I wrinkled my nose at the musty scent; the room reeked of sex. As I glanced down, I saw my handsome, dark-skinned father returning to life. My blood was saving him. I closed my eyes, grateful that he was alive.

I attempted to reach out to David using telepathy, only to realize that my efforts were futile. As I contemplated the possibility that he had passed away, my vision blurred from the blood I had lost. So, in panic and confusion, I retracted my arm before succumbing to unconsciousness. In this moment of darkness, all I could do was hope and pray that David was safe and sound.

Robert

I HAD TRIED to understand why my son disliked me. Was it because we were so alike? The revelation that he was queer troubled me, but I accepted it and asked that he remain in the closet. I was worried that if the elders from the infantry found out, his life would be in danger. I also wanted to prevent him from being perceived as the despised, limp-wristed homosexual.

"Oh, David," I muttered, placing his unconscious body on the bed. I knew he'd die soon if I didn't find him blood.

My mind raced, knowing I needed to do something. I couldn't live with myself if I killed him. As I looked around the room, I thought of what to do. I knew I couldn't leave the house because of the rising sun.

I scoured the house for any rodents. After a thorough search, I was able to locate three rats lurking in the garage. I snapped their necks and carried them to my son. Hovering over David, I bit their heads off and dripped blood into his mouth. As I observed him, he seemed to respond to the fluid, giving me hope for his recovery.

The doorbell rang.

My heart thumped as I rushed to the front door, swinging it open with such force that it caused a draft of warm air to rush into the house. Taking in my surroundings, I spotted an unfamiliar figure. Standing on the front porch was a mail carrier in uniform.

"I have an overnight delivery from New Orleans that needs a signature," he said, lifting a pen toward me.

"Oh?" I said, interested. The morning sun blazed into my eyes. I backed up, shielding its rays. "Please come in," I said, hoping he'd accept my invitation.

The carrier stepped inside the house.

I took the time to thoroughly inspect his slender build, captivated by his alluring face. His hair was a shade of rich brown, and he had a neatly trimmed goatee framing his features. He was on the shorter side, but I could see the bulge in his shorts, causing my excitement to rise. It was then that I realized he was a fag.

My heart quickened as we continued our conversation, and my eyes feasted on every detail of his. I caressed my hairy chest and then grasped my boner inside my jeans.

"Sir?"

"Do you suck cock?" I posed this question only to entice him. My query meant no physical overtures.

The carrier nodded but stepped back, glancing toward the neighbor's houses. "I do, but I'm in uniform. I can swing by after work." I was ready for him when he turned back around.

I displayed my fangs.

The carrier's eyes widened in shock as he looked at my sharp teeth glistening in the sunlight. Before he could escape, I grabbed onto the fabric of his shirt, stopping him in his tracks. I looked at him menacingly, speaking in a cold voice. "Come back here, you little cock sucker!"

His eyes widened even further, realizing the danger he was in. He opened his mouth to scream, but I had already covered it with my hand, muffling his voice.

Without wasting any more time, I quickly pinned him to the floor. His desperate struggles soon stopped as I sank my teeth into his neck. Once he was motionless, I carried him to my son.

Antonio

MY FATHER uttered, "Vampires are monsters."

His words didn't even register with me. I declared, "My blood is only a temporary solution. If you don't swallow my sperm, you'll die soon. It was then that a passing thought of my mother came to me. I wondered if he was thinking of her and whether I had just read his mind. Regardless, I knew what I had to do. I took a deep breath and asked him what he knew about my mother's disappearance. He looked nervous and turned away. I said, "I can handle the truth. Tell me, Dad."

"Oh, Antonio . . ."

"Please, tell me."

"I've held this information from you because I needed to protect you."

I pondered the implications of his desire to protect me. Could I be in peril? Was there something pursuing me that warranted my attention? As I struggled to interpret his message, the dread and unease I experienced were unmistakable. Though uncertain of the situation, I recognized the importance of heeding his words.

"Your mother's disappearance wasn't an accident."

David

AS NIGHT FELL, I awoke abruptly to discover three headless rats beside me. My father must have made me consume their blood to neutralize the poison coursing through my veins.

I sat up with a jolt, my eyes darting around the dimly lit room. Confusion and fear washed over me as I tried to piece together what had happened. I turned and saw my father sleeping beside me, his chest rising and falling in a slow, steady rhythm. The audacity of his actions and the betrayal of trust were too much to bear. My hands trembled with fury, and my heart pounded in my chest.

As I observed his naked body, my anger again transformed into admiration. His chest was thick with hair, and his tan lines revealed something unexpected — did he wear a Speedo? I couldn't help but shake my head, realizing there was so much I didn't know about him. As I continued to stare, he became hard from having a sex dream.

My tongue licked my lips in desire.

I knew my father was gay before he did. His queer tendencies were easy to read — they were for me, anyway. I saw the side glances he gave other men. He thought he was being secretive, but he wasn't because I witnessed his desires.

I looked down, admiring his groin. He wished for something more prominent, but I thought it was perfectly proportioned. My attention shifted to his nut sack, which stirred my desires. Gently, I touched myself, savoring the sensation it evoked. Feeling my willpower wane, I leaned in and took a deep breath. His musky aroma filled my nostrils, igniting excitement within me.

I licked his dickhead.

Overwhelmed with guilt, I sat up, grasping the consequences of my actions. My gaze shifted to his sleeping face, and I acknowledged how simple it would be to end his life. However, a frown crept across my face as I recognized my lack of courage to follow through.

I jumped out of bed.

Landing on the floor, I stumbled across a naked man lying face down on the carpet. I didn't have to check his pulse to see if he was dead because pallor mortis had already set in. I saw the postal uniform lying beside him. I turned him over, looked for puncture marks, and found them on his neck. I must have drunk from him, which saved my life. My eyes glanced toward his post-mortem erection. I touched it. Due to blood solidifying, it was a solid piece of stone. Its hardness made me want to play with it.

Peering away from the imposing carrier, I frantically searched for any method to contain my father. My gaze fell upon a large envelope on the desk addressed to William De Luca sent from New Orleans. The lettering on the package revealed the sender's name as Achilles Chenevert, and underneath that was an acronym: DTAV. Death to All Vampires. I knew this organization. It became evident that William was utilizing them in his desperate pursuit of his wife.

"David?" my father muttered.

"Fuck!"

Turning around, I saw my father levitating above the bed. I grabbed the letter opener, slashed my wrist, and raised it toward him. Blood started flowing from the laceration, dripping onto the floor.

"Damn you!" he hissed, craving my blood.

It was clear he hadn't fed on the letter carrier. His face

looked gaunt and bluish from lack of blood. Slowly kneeling, he reached for my wrist, his eyes full of desperation for nourishment.

"I'm thirsty," he muttered.

"You should have drunk. You're a fool!" I snarled and raised my arm above him. Blood dripped onto his face.

His tongue darted out with enthusiasm, eagerly savoring the delectable sustenance. Overwhelmed by his intense cravings, he tightly gripped my arm and drank my blood. His eyes glistened with pure joy as he relished his meal, occasionally glancing up in delight.

I removed my wrist.

Gazing into his eyes, I knew it would only be a matter of time before he lost his eyesight. A vampire's blood induces blindness before it deprives one of life. However, monitoring the blood amount ensures that this effect is only temporary.

A heavy sigh escaped my lips as I beheld my powerful father, so vulnerable and helpless beneath me. I instructed him to close his eyes and drift off to sleep, allowing me to escape quickly.

Robert

I SAW MY son's blood dripping from his wrist as he lifted his arm toward me. I licked my lips, hungry. Then, I hissed, realizing what he was doing.

He grimaced and raised his arm higher.

I fell to my knees, my parched mouth open as my hand grasped his wrist. My unquenchable hunger was fierce and refused to be hushed; it demanded satisfaction. My stomach growled, and my mouth watered in anticipation of his blood.

I sank my mouth onto his wrist's pale, tender flesh, not needing my fangs. They rested dormant in my gums. I began to suck, feeling his blood course through me. His eight-inch cock stood before my face. As it pulsated, I moaned in awe, worshipping its size. I wanted to taste it more than anything.

Antonio

MY FISTS clenched tightly as my father explained that the vampire infantry had kidnapped my mother. The hatred I felt toward them was boiling inside me. I mustered the courage to ask what she had done. Though I feared his answer, I had to know the truth.

My dad's face drained of all color as he told me the story. He explained how she found comfort in the arms of an infantry soldier, who, due to his exceptional accomplishments, was now the chief of staff. As he uttered these words, his sorrow was almost unbearable. I didn't have the faintest clue what being a chief of staff meant, but it sounded important.

The mother I remember was loving and kind. She would never do this to my father, who showered her with gifts and affection. He pleased her in every way. He was virile. I knew this because I heard them making love every night. None of this made any sense.

"She realized her mistake and asked for forgiveness. Of course, I forgave her. But when you were around eight or nine, the chief of staff had Robert abduct her, and she's been held captive ever since."

"Why did he kidnap her?"

My father stayed silent, lowering his head as he pondered the question. When he didn't respond, I asked if he had tried to find her. He looked up, and I could see the anguish in his eyes.

"I've never stopped looking. The last time I went to New Orleans, Robert confronted me in the French Quarter with a dire warning — that I needed to move on, or else."

"Or else?"

"He would kill you."

"He succeeded! Look at me! My life is over!" I yelled, raising my voice toward him. "I'm a vampire, goddamnit!"

"Oh, Antonio . . ."

I closed my eyes momentarily, calming myself. Then I said, "If you don't become a vampire, you'll die, and he'll win. I'll have nothing."

"Antonio . . ."

"He'll fucking win!"

After a long pause, my father whispered, "There's one more thing I haven't told you."

I shook my head, knowing he was exhausted. "You need sleep," I said and kissed his forehead.

"Antonio, it's important . . ."

"Rest," I whispered, cradling him in my arms. I shook my head, frustrated, not knowing if my father wanted to live or die. "I need your answer. Do you want to live?"

Confused and afraid, he hesitated, not replying.

"Answer me!" I demanded as he lay quiet, saying nothing in return. Finally, I became angry and shook him with all my might. "I want you to live! If I must hold you down, I will. Please take my gift of eternal life."

William

MY HEART felt like it was breaking as I watched my son sleeping. He looked so pale and weak from blood loss. He had asked me a question I didn't answer because I knew how vampires lived — it was not something I desired.

I had to persuade him to get blood, but before I did this, I removed my necklace and placed the crucifix around his neck. It was a gesture of love. I knew it wouldn't stop him from being a bloodsucker, but at least he could seek solace in its meaning.

Antonio awoke with a start, his heart beating as he felt the unfamiliar weight of the cold metal on his chest. He glanced down to see the intricate design. Rays of light streaming from the bedside lamp illuminated the metal, making it sparkle. In shock, he yanked it off his neck, hurling it away.

"Dad, why did you do this?" he asked in shock. "This cross has a practical purpose, too. It wards off evil. It acts as a protective barrier against vampires!"

I was filled with remorse, wishing I had known better. "It seemed like a good idea at the time. I hoped it would have provided you solace," I said, feeling terrible for my mistake, and apologized profusely for not being more informed.

Antonio took a deep breath, exhaling loudly. "I'm sorry for yelling. You didn't know. I'm sorry for destroying it."

I studied the cross on the tattered carpet before me, my heart heavy with sorrow. It had been a cherished keepsake, but I finally understood its meaning and knew I had to release it. Taking a deep breath, I prayed for forgiveness and stepped forward to pick it up. With one decisive motion, I opened the door and cast the cross into the night. Closing the door behind me, I turned to face my son. His pale complexion was even more noticeable in the room's dim light, and his urgent need for blood was evident.

"You need nourishment," I said, gazing into my son's green eyes. They were so much like his mother's. "You've got your mom's eyes," I said with a smile. He paused in deep thought.

"Do you think she'd be proud of me?"

Seeing all he'd been through, I nodded my head. "Yes,

she would," I said reassuringly. "She loved you more than anything." I hugged him tightly.

"Thank you."

I smiled and kissed his forehead. As our eyes met, I gasped, seeing the image of Salvatore Leone, the infantry's chief of staff, staring back at me. I turned away quickly, ashamed for not telling him about his biological father. They looked so much alike. Keeping this a secret was wrong. I should have interrupted him and told him everything. I turned back around. As our eyes met again, he tried to smile, but blood loss was taking its toll.

"I love you," he said quietly.

"I love you too, son. Now go, feed." As I watched him walk out the door, I smiled, proud of him too. He showed me that sometimes you must take risks to be yourself. Through him, I discovered true strength. I had no fear if I died before he returned because I knew he'd go on to make the world a better place.

Antonio

I JUMPED INTO an old maple tree, hearing footsteps. As I focused my night vision, I saw a woman walking through the park. I took a deep breath and pushed the thought of being a murderer out of my head.

The yearning for nourishment became too strong, so I leaped from the tree and pursued my prey. As I ran, I saw the heavily made-up woman wearing a miniskirt. A streetwalker. How many dicks had she serviced this evening? I felt envious. But then, I realized she wasn't gay and probably didn't crave sperm like I did. I'm sure she thought it was revolting and spit it out. Maybe I was wrong; maybe women liked the taste too.

My mind said to turn around, but my body continued to advance. I tackled her. I snapped her neck and silenced her screams. Without hesitation, I ripped into her neck. This person wasn't a murderer or a drunkard. Reading her mind, she was a single parent trapped in a dreadful profession. What had I done?

I stopped sucking, hearing footsteps coming in my direction. Did someone hear her scream? I released the woman and ran through the park at lightning speed. I listened to the advancing footsteps. As I spun around, my assailant tackled me.

The attacker giggled and grasped my groin.

I realized it was David and threw my arms around him. He kissed me and shoved his tongue deep inside my mouth. I returned his kiss with affection. Then I broke the embrace and stared at him, not believing he had found me. "I thought you were dead!"

I had been yearning to hear the words 'I love you' come out of his mouth, but instead, he simply said he missed me. I felt a lump in my throat as tears threatened to break free. Wanting to avoid having to explain why I was so emotional, I lied and told him that I felt bad for killing the streetwalker.

I couldn't help but feel a pang of regret for not being honest with him about how much I wanted to hear those three little words. But instead, I stood up and turned my back on him, not wanting to be vulnerable.

"I don't understand," he said.

"She wasn't homeless."

I cringed, my guilt weighing me down like an anchor. I had been foolish to assume he would feel the same about me.

David grasped the gravity of my situation. He embraced me lovingly and murmured encouraging words to calm my nerves. His arms felt like a secure refuge from the raging tumult surrounding us. In a tender voice, he whispered that we would bury her body.

David

READING HIS mind that he loved me was a surprise, but I quickly realized it was simply his physical desires overpowering him. I didn't want to tell him and hurt his feelings, so I played along with his lie.

I found a hidden place to dig a grave. The task of burying the woman was easy because vampires are great excavators. After burying the woman, we sat in the grass near a tree and discussed vampire life. In our discussion, Antonio cut in suddenly with an anxious inquiry and asked if the woman he killed viewed him as the devil. As much as I wanted to be honest with him, I knew my words would bring pain, so I lied and said no.

I extended my arm, intertwining my fingers with Antonio's as I leaned against the ancient tree. The gentle chirping of crickets filled the night air, and for a moment, all was peaceful. However, that peace was quickly disturbed by Antonio's desperate plea. He asked if I would help him turn his father into a vampire. I agreed to his request.

The offer I accepted was not born out of generosity but rather something more sinister. His father had cast a spell over me. To bask in the warmth of his presence for all eternity seemed to be a dream come true.

Antonio

ENTERING THE motel room, David and I were filled with dread as we encountered my father lying near death's door. His shallow breaths lingered in the air, and a thick silence descended upon us like a heavy blanket. I turned to David for guidance, and without hesitation, he told me to give him more blood. I immediately obliged and produced my vampire fangs to break the skin on my wrist. I dripped blood into his mouth.

I watched his still body with a fear of losing him forever. His eyes opened as if in answer to my silent prayer, and he uttered a feeble whisper that filled me with hope.

"I want . . . to live."

With newfound strength, I embraced him in joy.

"The gift of life needs to come from you, not me. Your blood is already inside him," David murmured, touching my shoulder.

Glancing up, he flashed me a warm smile that sent a wave of confidence through my body. As I glanced down, my father's eyes closed, falling unconscious again. My blood was no longer keeping him alive. I glanced back in shock and saw the urgency in David's eyes. He gestured toward the bathroom and said it was time. I left the room, determined to bring forth the precious elixir to save my father's life.

David

I PULLED BACK the sheet covering William's naked body, and my mind spun. Could it be my issues with my father driving me to him? Was I searching for a father figure without realizing it? Or was something else at work? Uncertainty swirled around me. One thing was sure — I had to find out.

My fingertips delicately explored his chest, tracing the contours of his pecs and chest muscles. I touched his nipple. It stood erect. Feeling a thrill of anticipation, I timidly ventured lower and came to rest beneath the hem of his boxer shorts. My heart raced as I felt an electric excitement tingle through my veins. My fingers skimmed over his smooth, toned abs before stopping at the edge of his pubic hair. Goosebumps rose on my skin. Taking a deep breath, I ventured forward and grasped his softness, feeling its length and girth. Satisfied, I removed my hand and whispered forgiveness.

His beauty entranced me — could he possibly feel something similar? Was he bisexual? If yes, would he even consider me? Wishing my hardness to go away, I looked around the room for a distraction. How many people screwed in here? I frowned, sniffing the air — cigarette smoke. Gross.

I closed my eyes and rested.

Recalling our chat about vampire life, Antonio asked why my father looked so different. I explained that he wasn't content with being a twenty-year-old any longer. When I explained that vampires could take on forms other than themselves, Antonio was astounded and asked for proof. Without a second thought, I changed into a breath-taking man before his eyes. This new form incited carnal desires inside me. Antonio refused when I suggested we fool around because he wanted to return to his dying father.

Turning, I heard Antonio's labored breathing in the bathroom, which snapped me out of my thoughts. As his moans grew louder, I knew it was just a matter of time before he shot his wad. I glanced at William one last time and covered him up, knowing we would become brothers soon.

The door opened, and Antonio stepped out of the bath-room. His face beamed with satisfaction at bringing forth the elixir that would turn his father into a bloodsucker. The sweat that glistened on his forehead was a testament to the hard work and dedication he had put forth to reach this point.

Antonio

I EXTENDED MY arm and passed David the plastic cup filled with precious fluid. His piercing eyes met mine as if he was trying to read my soul in search of any hint of hesitation, but he found none.

I held my breath as David placed the cup on my father's lips. My jaw dropped as his mouth remained closed. "He's refusing it!" I said anxiously.

"Be patient," David murmured.

As David carefully administered the elixir to my father's mouth, I bowed my head in prayer. As soon as I finished and made the sign of the cross, I noticed my dad's eyelids fluttering open — a sure sign that he was alive and fighting. Overcome with joy, I watched him sipping away at the cup, taking in all the nourishment he could. Overwhelmed with relief, I recognized that my prayer was answered and quietly thanked God for His mercy.

The thought of my father not returning made my heart race with fear. He was shaking uncontrollably, and his complexion had taken on the hue of ash. "What if he doesn't come back?" I muttered as my imagination began to run wild with thoughts that could befall him.

"He will," David reassured me.

Moments passed, and his body became motionless. I glanced at David, frightened.

"Look!" David pointed toward my dad's chest.

Looking at his sunken torso, I saw he wasn't breathing. "Look at what?" I yelled, raising my hands in confusion.

"Look inside."

My heart leaped with joy as I noticed the faint beat of my father's heart, visible through his chest. After realizing what David suggested, I used my newfound vampire abilities to look past his skin, delving deeper into his body. His chest rose and fell in a slow but steady rhythm, confirming he was alive.

David and I kissed, celebrating my father's new beginning.

"Antonio . . ." my dad murmured almost inaudibly.

"I'm here, Dad!" I shouted happily. I was ecstatic to be reunited with my father, and I couldn't resist expressing my gratitude to David for making it happen. I wrapped my arms around him tightly and thanked him with another kiss. His face lit up in response. We stood there momentarily, basking in my father's resurrection joy.

***

The motel's parking lot was desolate, with no car in sight. This struck me as particularly strange, given that the motel was open for business. As I surveyed the area, I quickly noticed how run-down and neglected the establishment was. The exterior paint was peeling away. Surprisingly, I noticed a 'For Sale' sign in one of the windows. It all became clear as I remembered seeing something on the news about an organization dedicated to cleaning up the area. The group had long since shut down the porn venues and was working to rid the area of other illicit activities.

Seeing that this community-led initiative had successfully brought about positive changes was heartening. It made me hopeful for the future of the neighborhood. I couldn't help but feel a sense of awe as the area transformed quickly and drastically. It seemed like it was a place of danger just yesterday, and now it was becoming a haven for those looking to start anew.

I whirled around to see my father standing behind me, his expression of utter frustration as he tried and failed to figure out how to lift himself into the air. David then proceeded to show him how to do it. He taught him the basic techniques of focusing his thoughts and using visualization to achieve lift-off. After a few tries, my father finally launched himself into the air.

I could tell David liked my father. His overattentive actions made it obvious he had a crush on him. I thought it was cute. It made me happy that they got along so well. I clapped my hands, excited for my father. As he lowered to the ground, David embraced and congratulated him.

"You did great, Mr. De Luca."

"Call me William."

My father smiled joyously. I knew he felt empowered that he was able to learn something. He thanked David appreciatively by returning the embrace.

"Let's go feed," David uttered.

As my dad's feet lifted off the ground, I recalled David's supportive words not to give up. It was this tenacity that helped my father succeed — it worked.

***

On that balmy summer night, the beauty of my city was on full display as the bright moon's glow illuminated the downtown park. David, my father, and I were on a mission to seek blood. As we moved further into this unfamiliar terrain, my senses heightened with anticipation.

The air smelled of pine needles and fresh-cut grass like nature had expected us. We could hear faint laughter coming from somewhere in the distance, followed by an occasional moan of ecstasy. We continued our stroll until we eventually reached a clearing, where we spotted several men engaging in romantic embraces. We had stumbled across a gay community that blossomed at night. As I stood there watching these men enjoy their moments of tenderness, I couldn't help but feel happy — not only for them but for myself. For the first time, I witnessed what it was to love without judgment or fear of social stigma.

"There!" David whispered, pointing.

My gaze fell upon the burly, heavy-set man leaning casually against a tree, in gay slang terms — a bear. His attire and demeanor suggested he was looking for a sexual encounter.

David gestured for us to stay and then approached the man with ease. I was surprised and began to question his actions. What was he doing?

My father watched the scene, likely hoping to gain knowledge from it. I saw David whisper something into the man's ear. I couldn't determine what was said, but the bear seemed satisfied, forcing David to his knees.

"Is that my victim?" my father asked.

I nodded as anxiety overwhelmed me. "You shouldn't watch." I wanted to run to David and break up the liaison, but I didn't because I didn't want my father to see my jealousy.

I felt my stomach twist as the bear removed an average-sized penis, which David took in his mouth. Watching David perform fellatio killed me. I wanted to cry, but I knew I needed to hold it together in front of my father. Minutes later, my dad stepped forward and joined them. I felt a jolt of confusion. I knew my father wasn't bisexual. Had something shifted after he became a vampire? My worries were needless because he bit the man on the neck and started sucking his blood.

Seeing David suck while my father drank blood was surreal. Then, suddenly, the bear started convulsing, not from blood loss but from ejaculating.

I'm unsure when my father stopped drinking because I was too preoccupied watching David swallowing sperm. I could tell he was ecstatic and guessed it was from tasting the non-poisonous substance again. As I turned to my father, he was staring at me.

"You guys need alone time," he said telepathically, laying the lifeless body on the ground. "I'll meet you at the falls." He turned and disappeared into the night.

Did he see jealousy in my eyes? I wondered.

I went to David, and he agreed with my father. Before I knew it, I was lying on the cool grass with my legs in the air. I jacked off, knowing we were being watched. If another top had shown up to fuck me, I would have allowed him out of jealousy. Fortunately, this didn't happen. I would have felt guilty afterward due to my Catholic upbringing.

I was mad that David had sex with the bear, though I tried to remain stoic and not show my insecurities. I brushed his sweaty hair from his forehead as I lay beside him. We stayed like that for a while, both feeling spent from our ejaculations.

David

EXHAUSTED AND spent, I rested in Antonio's arms. As guilt surfaced, I couldn't help but think of my selfishness. Unbeknownst to Antonio, I took my time sucking the bear. I did this purposely, knowing his dad was watching with interest. I moaned loudly, performing for him. My arduous work paid off because William became aroused. Unfortunately, he turned red from embarrassment and shielded it from me.

I removed my mouth from the bear and locked eyes with William. Telepathically, I thought to him, let me suck you off. His eyes widened, and he glanced at Antonio to gauge his reaction. Thankfully, I realized he was too preoccupied with my prowess to hear me.

Thinking he was granting my wish, he left Antonio's side and stepped toward me. What would I say to Antonio afterward? I wasn't sure, but I was excited to savor William. As I reached forward to caress him, I heard his cautionary voice inside my head.

"Don't hurt my son."

The menacing tone of his voice sent chills down my spine, and I knew he wasn't mincing his words. His warning was clear that he had acknowledged my disrespect toward Antonio. Taking a deep breath, I lowered my gaze to the ground and muttered an apology, filled with regret for what I had done.

My heart raced as I waited for William to address my mistake. As the seconds ticked by, dread began to build up within me. Confident that this transgression would forever stain us, I looked up and saw him nodding in forgiveness. Instead of reprimanding me for my misstep, he provided absolution. I felt such overwhelming relief that I nearly burst into tears.

Robert

UPON WAKING, my vision was obscured by David's blood. I berated myself for being caught in such an obvious trap and desperately sought a solution to restore my sight. I sniffed the air and detected the unmistakable smell of a cat litter box.

Stumbling through the room, I used touch and the strong odor to find my way. My heart raced with anticipation. Soon, I came across a closed door — maybe the laundry room? As I grasped the doorknob, a soft mew came from inside. Carefully, I opened the door and found a small cat, seemingly unafraid of me.

It rubbed against me, purring happily.

I hissed as my fangs grew sharp. I reached for the cat. It tried to fight me off, claws stinging my face. I bit its neck — its death was instantaneous.

I opened my eyes and blinked until I could focus. Once my vision returned, I saw my naked body. My flaccid cock sprung forward, filled with the cat's blood.

Reading my son's mind, I knew he had found the lovestruck queer. The faggot that was trying to entice him into a forbidden relationship. I sighed, thinking about the Federation. What would Salvatore Leone think? I shook my head, embarrassed at my son's actions.

Unbeknownst to David, we teach recruits to be singular. All right — we brainwash them into believing this.

For the Federation to be successful, we must control every aspect of their lives. A love-struck vampire would not be dependable. We need obedience, not emotion.

I hastily stumbled into the bedroom. As I reached for my jeans on the floor, I suddenly felt an overwhelming urge to pee. Instead of heading for the bathroom, I spun around toward the desk and grabbed myself. Actively embracing my momentary rage, I directed a steady stream of piss toward the DTAV envelope to destroy its contents and make a statement against the organization that had been an irritant in my life. At last, having completed this task, I quickly got dressed and went out to find my son.

Antonio

GRIPPING DAVID'S hand nervously, I guided him along the winding path to my hometown's stunning river and majestic falls. I explained that this area, once revered by Native Americans, had become a sought-after tourist attraction, bringing people worldwide to my city.

David seemed intrigued and asked many questions about the history of this area. I told him stories as we continued our walk along the river, listening to its calming rhythm as it cascaded over rocks and boulders. We eventually reached a picturesque viewing point overlooking the falls.

Standing together, admiring the beautiful sight before us, I knew I had found my perfect match. I looked into his eyes and knew it was time to express my feelings. I wanted a monogamous relationship. But before I could get a word out, he explained that enjoying sex is normal, especially if you're a gay vampire. I caught my breath as he muttered that having sex was not a sin. I realized David had read my thoughts during our time together in the park. I shook my head, upset, forgetting that he had the capability. It was clear he didn't understand my reasonings.

"You need to be free of all sexual inhibitions," David said, kissing me with the bear's taste on his lips.

I didn't tell David my jealousy was why I wanted sex with other men. Instead, I explained my religious upbringing and how it shaped my life. He understood the immense weight of religious expectations and how they can burden a person with guilt.

"I enjoy sex. It's fun," David murmured.

His response made me uneasy, so I asked if he would have been annoyed if another individual had joined us. His answer shocked me. He stated that he would have enjoyed seeing me getting screwed by someone else. This reply left me stunned and in a state of contemplation.

"Have you ever been to a bathhouse?" he asked me.

I raised my head and faced him. "Why do you want to know?" My jealousy questioned his motives.

"I belong to one in New Orleans. I'll take you there, and you can have as much sex as you want," he said as if we were best friends, not lovers.

My intense feelings for him were indisputable, yet he continued to parade his sexual conquests before me. Was this a purposeful act of cruelty, or did he fail to understand the ramifications of his words? Either way, it felt like daggers plunging directly into my heart.

Focusing on my thoughts, I said, "I've been to one bathhouse. It was in Seattle." I recalled seeing a hairy daddy getting penetrated by a group of guys in a leather sling and someone getting fisted. I wanted to be like them, but my HIV anxiety held me back. I wondered how many partners David had had and if he was verse.

"I'm a top. I often go because I use it as a hideaway," he said, reading my mind.

I was astonished that he used the bathhouse as refuge, considering it was right under the infantry's nose. When I asked him how long he had been using it, he said he'd been going for years. My curiosity got the better of me, and I wondered if he had ever been in a long-term relationship with someone. He paused for a long moment in deep thought, thinking about how to word his response. In a cautious voice, he said that vampires were noncommittal and that he wasn't looking for a relationship. Just then, a familiar voice shouted behind us.

"David!" Robert shouted.

We both whipped around to see his middle-aged father running toward us. He was back and out for revenge.

David shouted for me to run away, cursing with rage. My heart filled with dread as I fled the scene. David implored Robert not to come any closer. With Robert's return and David's bitter response, I quickly ran in shock.

Suddenly a loud thud echoed behind me, making my heart race in trepidation. Did Robert take David down? Full of distress, I hurriedly ran away in search of my father.

***

I raced to the middle of the footbridge, with my dad following close behind me. I stopped and gazed down at the foaming river below us. "The floodgates must be open," I exclaimed as I shouted over the din of the waterfall. In that instant, Robert emerged from the shadows. He had a mischievous glint in his eye as he clapped my father on the shoulder.

"We meet again!" he chuckled.

I stepped back warily.

My dad clenched his fists and roared, "What do you want from us?"

Robert was unperturbed, his face stretching into a wicked grin.

"I'm here to kill your faggot son."

The words were like a punch in my gut, and before I could react, my father lunged forward and tackled Robert, both stumbling to the cement. However, Robert quickly took control and had my father's neck in a tight grip. They levitated off the bridge and hovered over the river.

Even though my father fought and struggled to release himself, his efforts were fruitless. Robert plunged my father into the water. My heart raced, and I couldn't move because he'd release him downstream if I got any closer. Fear froze me in place, watching helplessly as he surfaced, coughing up water.

"Your wife's been cast aside," Robert shouted.

"Then release her, goddamnit!"

As my father and Robert fought, I listened carefully, trying to decipher what they were saying. Unfortunately, I could no longer hear them because of the cascading falls. The sound was deafening. I hovered, afraid to move any closer.

Robert

I SMILED IN delight as William choked, spitting out the water he had swallowed. Tormenting him was extremely satisfying. "Why doesn't your son look anything like you?" I said mockingly.

William pleaded with me to stop, but I continued. "Is Antonio that gullible?" I asked inquisitively before pushing him underwater once more. His cries of agony echoed through the air as he resurfaced moments later. I grinned, seeing Antonio watching intently from the sidelines. Because I had an audience, I felt compelled to hold him down longer than usual this time around.

I could feel my sense of joy coursing through my veins. It was like some drug-induced sensation that lasted far longer than the few moments it took to push William under again. As he resurfaced, I asked if he had had enough.

Oh, how I had loved William over the years — even

though it was forbidden, I loved him from afar. I thought of him the nights I couldn't relieve myself with a queer's ass. Thoughts of his uncircumcised boner always brought forth my ejaculations.

"Please," he begged.

I smiled at him. "Do you realize how much I desire you? Why don't you accept my friendship?"

"Fuck you!" William uttered.

Even though his words stirred a wave of anger within me, something about his unique Italian accent completely charmed me. It held a certain allure that I found irresistible, captivating my senses inexplicably. This longing filled me with a heavy, unquenchable sadness, so I furiously pushed him back into the water.

Antonio

I LUNGED forward, desperation fueling my muscles as I kicked Robert with all my might. My foot collided with his head, causing him to cry in pain and relinquish his grip on my father. As my dad and I plummeted into the river, Robert's iron-like grip closed around my ankle and refused to let go. Struggling frantically against his hold, I finally succeeded in freeing myself. I levitated and pulled my dad from the roiling waters that had threatened to swallow him alive.

Gasping for air, my father managed to cry out a warning as Robert surged toward us. This time I was ready and braced myself for the impact. Robert collided with us, causing our bodies to separate and sending my father hurtling downriver. I fought to stay afloat against the waves in a desperate battle.

Robert grabbed my arm.

I screamed in anguish as I watched my father vanish into the foaming depths below the waterfall. My heart raced with terror as I felt Robert's grip tighten. Desperation fueled me as I freed myself from his grasp. With a surge of energy, I threw a hard punch at him, sending him spiraling away.

I followed my father over the edge.

The water's icy fingers pulled me in, and exhaustion sapped my strength, knocking me unconscious.

***

I opened my eyes and found myself on the riverbank. The pain had taken over my entire body due to the force of the water rushing over the falls. As I tried to stand, I heard my father's voice and saw him sprawled on the shore. Ignoring my pain, I moved toward him while searching for Robert, who was nowhere to be seen. My vampire body healed with every step, and the pain slowly ebbed away as my ribs reconnected.

Kneeling by my father's side, I softly reassured him, "I'm here." His leg was twisted in an unnatural position, causing apparent agony, which I slowly eased back into place. "The pain will go away," I said and sat down, placing his head on my lap. As I caressed his hair, I stared into his face.

I questioned why I didn't look more like him.

Moving the tattered fabric of his shirt away, I ran my hand across his cold torso, hoping to bring him some warmth. As I did this, I discovered a thick mat of hair covering his well-defined chest. His skin reacted to my touch, and his body suddenly came alive, responding to the heat radiating from my caressing hand.

I brought him to my chest and held him. His breath was warm against my body. I kissed his head repeatedly while waiting for him to heal completely. Raising my head, I searched for Robert again. Not seeing him, I assumed he was dead. The river current had swept him away. "Enjoy hell, you son-of-a-bitch!"

"Antonio . . ." my dad whispered.

I glanced down, seeing my father staring lovingly at me. "Oh, Dad," I murmured, seeing his healed body. I pressed his face against my chest, kissing him once again.

William

AS WE STEPPED through the front door of my home, it was evident that Robert had unleashed his fury. The living room furniture was in ruins. Fragments were scattered all over the floor. The kitchen's condition was even more dire, with broken dish fragments covering every surface. As I took in the pandemonium, I experienced no emotion — only numbness.

We searched the house for Robert and David but couldn't locate them. This confirmed our suspicions that Robert had possibly passed away, leaving us with even more uncertainty about David's whereabouts.

Even though I didn't feel safe in the house, we had to stay due to the approaching morning light. I told Antonio we'd sleep together in his bedroom. I didn't want him alone if Robert returned. Also, my bedroom reeked of urine, and I discovered a postal carrier dead on the floor. As a vampire, I typically feared the daylight hours, but not today. I knew it would give us time and protect us.

I undressed and crawled into bed. As Antonio removed his clothing, I investigated his face, searching for any likeness of me. I knew there would be none, but I still hoped to see something to connect me with him. I feared losing him once he found out about his father.

Salvatore Leone's name echoed in my head. I gazed at my son and saw the familiar features. He looked like a younger version of his birth father. Dismissing the thoughts of Salvatore, I opened my arms as Antonio crawled into bed. His face showed unanswered questions, so I knew he wouldn't be sleeping anytime soon.

Antonio

MY HEAD NESTLED peacefully on my father's chest, and my hand rested comfortably on his abdomen. I was wide awake despite the early morning hour. After hearing tales of Salvatore Leone's mistreatment of my mother, I had many questions. I was determined to find her, no matter the cost.

My father explained that he'd been looking for her for years but had no success. I persisted and convinced him that our newfound vampire abilities would be instrumental in our search. He nodded, understanding my logic, but warned me of the dangers.

As I rested against my dad, I shared my interest in David. He was happy but cautioned me to take things slow and get to know him first. His parental role was clear — protective and supportive.

Suddenly, my father called out my name. I was startled to find myself twirling his pubic hair. I was doing this subconsciously while thinking of David. Embarrassed, I stopped abruptly. My dad showed me understanding as he held my hand. Then he kissed my forehead and said he'd make the plane reservations after we rested.

Lying there, I listened to the steady rhythm of his heartbeat. I felt peace and contentment wash over me as I breathed in his scent. I wanted to savor this moment and never forget it. I wished him goodnight and expressed my love for him.

He said goodnight and fell into a deep sleep. His soft

snores comforted me as I rested, struggling to drift away. My thoughts wandered to the old legend that said if one had difficulty sleeping, it meant you were in someone else's dreams. Instantly, I smiled at the thought of David dreaming about me. Although I wanted to dwell on our intimate moments, reality set in that my father was beside me. So I focused on our plans for the future. We could journey around the world. As I daydreamed about our travels, my body relaxed, and my eyes became heavy. Soon enough, I drifted off into a peaceful sleep.

***

My father and I boarded the red-eye flight to rescue my mother from Salvatore Leone's tyranny.

Hours into the flight and wide awake, I pondered about David. Was he in New Orleans? As I wondered where he was, my hunger kept increasing until I couldn't ignore it anymore. Sitting beside me was a strikingly handsome man whose body exuded strength and power, prompting me to whisper to my father that I wanted his blood.

Knowing all the passengers were asleep, I gently woke him and used my powers to mesmerize him into accepting my request. Taking his hand, I licked his wrist clean before biting down carefully, savoring the sweet taste of his life force. Through his mind, I learned he had a pregnant wife with their fourth child, igniting arousal. Here was another virile man. His masculinity made me excited. Knowing this wasn't the place and time, I willed my hardness to go away to satisfy my thirst. After I finished drinking, my dad leaned in and started feeding.

As my father fed, I closed my eyes and imagined freeing my mother from her captivity. After my father had finished feeding, I checked the man's pulse — it was still strong. We only took what we needed and no more. After tending to his wound, I thanked him and explained that he might feel ill for several days but would recover fully.

Afterward, we shifted our focus to an old card game.

The object of the game was to gain the lowest score possible — an activity that allowed us to share quality time. Dad won in the end, but I was more than content. At this moment, I felt I had already won by being with my father and cherishing our bond.

Disembarking from the plane in New Orleans, my dad and I were excited as we set out to rescue my mother. We both had a fearless spirit and knew nothing would stand in our way.

Robert

DESCENDING THE escalator in the Louis Armstrong New Orleans International Airport, I saw three infantry soldiers loitering around the baggage claim area. My heart sank as David's timid face revealed his fear of them. He had been right — I should have left him alone. With tears welling up, I told him to run away. The first two soldiers began pursuing him, while the third turned his attention toward me.

I stepped forward, and without a hint of respect in his voice, the soldier asked why my son had fled the scene. Not wanting to give him an answer, I used my rank as a form of intimidation and warned him of dire consequences if he didn't show me proper respect. He saluted in response, and I did the same before saying in an authoritative tone, "Your presence scared him." Composing myself, I immediately felt disappointed because I had thought that I could hide my son in New Orleans.

Taking control of the situation, I commanded the soldier to take me to the van because the chief of staff was waiting for my return. He obeyed without question and guided me toward the exit. Before we left, I glanced back and was relieved to find no trace of my son — which gave me hope that he had managed to escape from the chasing soldiers.

At that moment, it dawned on me that he would never forgive me — especially since what I had done was foolish and thoughtless! It became clear that our relationship as father and son was now permanently severed due to this incident. A wave of guilt swept over me, along with intense anger for not considering all the options.

Antonio

MY HEARTBEAT quickened as I walked toward the cab, now dreading what untold horrors lay in wait for us. My father gripped my hand momentarily, his knuckles turning white from the force of his grip. Our eager disposition had now turned negative. I tried to reassure him with a comforting smile, yet that small act seemed inadequate considering our predicament. As we climbed into the back of the cab, I told the driver to take us to the French Quarter.

The airport was much busier than I had anticipated — filled with hundreds of people coming and going, despite being two o'clock in the morning. The temperature was oppressively hot at ninety-six degrees Fahrenheit, with humidity, but thankfully the taxi was air-conditioned and comfortable.

"Welcome to N'awlins," said the driver.

"Thank you," my dad replied.

As I was closing the door, I heard a commotion behind us. Glancing back, I saw two men tackling someone. From where I sat, I couldn't identify whom they'd captured, so I turned around and assumed it was a thief taking someone's purse. I saw my father deep in thought. He had a sad look on his face. "We'll find her," I whispered, understanding he was thinking of my mother.

"I hope so."

He raised his head and embraced me. I waited for him to release me, but he didn't. "Never forget that I love you," he whispered.

"I know, Dad," I said, holding him firmly.

The taxi driver said we'd arrive in thirty minutes. I turned around and saw a man being tackled and thrown into a van. He looked like David to me. No way. What were the odds? I shook the unrealistic thought from my head. As I turned around, I saw a sign that read, '21 miles to Downtown New Orleans.' Memories of David flooded my mind, and I had to cover myself to stop the pleasure it gave me.

"What are you thinking about?" my father asked as a faint smile appeared on his lips.

"David," I replied, blushing slightly and hoping he hadn't noticed what I'd been visualizing. But judging by his expression, it seemed he already knew what had been going through my mind.

He smiled knowingly and said, "I was young once, too. I know what you're going through."

My embarrassment subsided somewhat as my father's unconditional love washed over me like a warm embrace. His mood had changed for the better. It was good to see him happy again. In no time, a road sign that said 'Vieux Carre Orleans Avenue' flew by as the taxi driver pressed the right-turn signal.

"Welcome to the French Quarter, or as we say, the Vieux Carre," the driver said, looking at us through the rear-view mirror. "Business or pleasure?"

I replied, "Business," willing the driver to be silent. I wanted to see the sites of the French Quarter undisturbed. It had been two years since I had vacationed here.

"It's such a relief to have you know the truth about your mother's disappearance," my father whispered so the taxi driver couldn't hear him.

I whipped around and looked at him. "Why didn't you tell me sooner? I could have helped you find her."

"I didn't want your help."

"I don't understand," I said, questioning him. He explained that he wanted me to grow up happy, not hating the world. "Oh, Dad," I murmured, wishing he had confided in me.

***

The French Quarter of New Orleans was alive with energy as we drove through it. The streets swarmed with activity, varying from lavish hotels to buzzing restaurants and packed bars. I saw something new everywhere I looked — the bustling crowds of tourists, the horse-drawn carriages, and the bright lights that illuminated the buildings. It felt like a dream I never wanted to wake up from.

As we drove through the Quarter, my father placed his arm around my shoulder. I was content and didn't care what the taxi driver thought about us. I knew our relationship was changing, so I wanted to hold this memory forever. I felt safe as he held me.

"What are you most excited about?" my father asked.

"Bread pudding with whiskey sauce," I muttered, licking my lips. I smiled, remembering when he'd taught me how to make the dessert in his restaurant's kitchen. My smile broadened, reflecting on him saying I would be the greatest chef worldwide. My thoughts went to the culinary classes I took at the community college. Now that I was a vampire, that was a thing of the past. My whole life had changed — and I wasn't sure it was for the better.

The bright lights of New Orleans welcomed me as I stepped out of the cab. My eyes quickly fell on the wrought-iron railing that lined the balcony of our small boutique hotel. I couldn't help but smile at its beautiful details and the giant potted ferns decorating it. It was exciting to be back in this vibrant city.

***

Our hotel room was in the basement, which I'd requested because of its small windows. I wanted a balcony room overlooking Bourbon Street, but it had a French door leading to an open terrace. It would have been unsafe and too noisy.

"Do you have a plan?" I asked my father as I finished unpacking my suitcase.

"I've made an appointment with the DTAV organization."

"When?" I asked, my heart sinking at the mention of their name — Death to All Vampires.

"Two o'clock tomorrow morning," he replied gravely.

My stomach churned at the thought.

"If they suspect we're vampires, they'll kill us," he said.

"Dad, no . . ."

"Antonio, I've been working with them for years. They know me," he said assuredly.

"You're meeting them at two in the morning? Wouldn't they find that time suspicious?" I responded inquisitively.

"The agents keep the same hours as vampires. I'll be fine," my father said, going about the business of unpacking his suitcase.

"I don't feel good about this," I protested.

My father stopped what he was doing and took me in his arms, reassuring me he'd be fine. As he released me, I held onto him tightly, not wanting to let go.

"Don't worry, Son," he whispered, kissing my forehead.

My head rested against his chest. I listened for his heartbeat, knowing it would calm me. Once I heard it, I took a deep breath and found the determination I felt before coming here.

***

There was enough darkness to eat, find nourishment, and return to the hotel before sunrise. We didn't have time to experience the Quarter properly. We showered and changed clothes. I wore shorts, a garment-dyed cotton polo shirt, and my favorite Italian cologne. I know, not very vampirish, but we needed to look and act like locals.

The tourists on Bourbon Street were drunk at this hour. I laughed at their drunkenness. It was amazing to see the hot men walking around half-naked, egging their girlfriends on to expose their breasts for Mardi Gras beads. If you didn't like breasts and wanted to see dick, you went to the other end of Bourbon Street — the gay district.

My father and I picked a famous twenty-four-hour gumbo restaurant. It was packed, even at this hour of the morning. People ate, wanting to sober up before returning to their hotel. Dad ordered red beans and rice with andouille sausage. I ordered the jambalaya with shrimp.

The waiter served us with apparent eagerness. He winked and tapped his foot against mine, causing a wave of awkwardness to wash over me. I was relieved that my father hadn't seen the interaction.

"Enjoy your dinner," I said to my dad as I adjusted the boner the waiter had given me.

The hardness wouldn't go away. I needed to relieve myself, even in the middle of dinner. The sensation of ejaculation was intense. Usually, I could control it. But not this time. "Dad," I said, feigning normalcy, "I'm going to the restroom."

"Do you want me to wait for you?" he asked.

"No. Eat," I said and stood, covering myself with a napkin. Walking to the bathroom, I wished David was here to relieve my burning desire.

***

As I secured the stall door and twisted the lock, I heard someone else enter the restroom. Unexpectedly, they knocked loudly on my lavatory stall door. "Occupied!" I shouted out of shock.

"Suck me?"

My heart raced as I heard the waiter's voice. Without

any thought, I unlocked the door. Once open, he briskly stepped in and swiftly shut the door behind him. We were now alone in the small space, cut off from the rest of the world. I felt a wave of anticipation and excitement as we stood face-to-face. Without speaking, he pulled me close and kissed me. His hands slowly moved down my body as our lips intertwined.

He then broke away from our embrace and began to undress me slowly. With each piece of clothing that fell to the floor, my desires grew more intense. Then I thought about David, and I stopped him. He pushed my hand away and continued undressing me as his lips traveled down my neck.

"Remove your shorts," he whispered.

As he unbuttoned his black jeans, I inhaled. He pushed down his Levi's, showing me a sidewinder. It was above average in length, circumcised, and curved to the right. As I dropped my shorts, I lowered myself to my knees. Suddenly, the bathroom door opened again, and a customer walked in. I saw him unzip his pants and urinate, thanks to a large hole in the stall's partition. The stall had a glory hole, a hole in the wall of a public bathroom through which fellatio takes place.

"Suck me," the waiter murmured.

As I turned back toward the waiter, I smiled at his excitement in front of me. First, I swallowed him, grabbed his ass, and pushed him back and forth, instructing him to use my mouth.

"I'm coming," he said within seconds.

He shot his hot load down my throat. As quickly as he came, he pulled out, buttoned his jeans, and unlocked the door. I sat on my knees, dumbfounded by his selfishness, as he left the bathroom. I still had the urge to ejaculate, so I looked through the hole and saw the man at the urinal stroking himself.

As I peered into the opening, I could see he was handsome, in his early forties, and his dick was partially uncut. Then, as he turned toward me, he shoved it through the hole.

"Do you want another load?"

I inserted my tongue between the head and foreskin. It was such a turn-on that I started masturbating. As I stroked myself, my testicles bounced up and down. Then, suddenly, the man came. His ejaculation shot to the back of my throat — it was a week's worth of jizz. As I swallowed his heavenly fluid, I masturbated in a frenzy, shooting my toxic load on the bathroom floor.

"Thank you," the man said and zipped up.

As the man exited the room, I wiped my mouth, stunned that I had swallowed two loads. The waiter wasn't appreciative, but the second guy was. I'm sure his wife was waiting at the table and questioning his absence. I thought about the poor guy and realized he probably went without most of the time. After catching my breath, I cleaned up and left the bathroom, feeling satisfied.

Returning to the table, I saw that my father had finished dinner and was waiting for me. I looked at my once-full plate. It was empty. The busboy had put my food into a to-go bag. Sitting down, I asked, "How was your meal?"

Something was different because I could tell his mood had changed. He was depressed. What was I thinking? I should have stayed at the table instead of beating off — what a dumb-ass.

"Mine was fine, and yours?"

"I didn't eat," I said, questioning him.

"I'm talking about the two guys you blew in the bathroom."

I realized he knew about my sexual escapades. Why couldn't I remember he had supernatural powers? "Oh, Jesus," I replied, embarrassed, lowering my head.

"Your illicit activities don't affect me."

"Illicit?" I murmured, raising my head. I sat motionless, unable to speak with guilt. I rarely saw this side of him. I knew he was acting this way out of depression.

My father glanced at his watch. "We need to feed and then get back to the hotel before dawn," he said, throwing his cloth napkin on the table. "I'll wait for you outside."

"I'll pay the tab," I said.

As I watched my father take his leave, I was shocked for some time. Our relationship had changed. We were no longer father and son but equals. It was a frightening development that filled me with apprehension.

When the waiter returned to the table, I requested the check, but instead, he smiled and told me it was on the house. This gesture of generosity made me realize he was appreciative after all.

William

FROWNING WITH sympathy, my son Antonio and I encountered a tall, blond-haired streetwalker while searching for sustenance in the alleyway. She wore a form-fitting blouse, an incredibly short skirt, and high heels. She was struggling with drug addiction.

As if to confirm our suspicions, the woman lowered her blouse and exposed her breasts. Although they were undeniably attractive, I could not take pleasure from them — instead, my heart ached for her plight. This scene only reinforced my understanding that she required assistance from an organization to improve her condition.

"Double penetration costs extra."

"Oh my god!" Antonio muttered.

My heart ached as she propositioned us. Then I remembered the woman's shelter around the corner. Who said we had to drain her entirely of blood and kill her? Was there such a rule? If there was, it was bullshit!

I looked into my son's eyes and told him we would drink but not drain her of blood. He gave me a solemn nod to show his understanding. I reached into my pocket and withdrew a crisp one-hundred-dollar bill. I held the bill up to her. Looking into her eyes with an air of authority,

I explained our intentions. I told her we needed nutrition but had no intention of taking her life. Lastly, I implored her to seek help. I placed the money in her pocket and asked that she never work the streets again.

She responded with a slight nod, seeming to comprehend my words fully. Continuing my actions, I gently raised her blouse over her exposed chest before motioning Antonio to drink first. As he consumed his nourishment from the woman's neck, I cradled her head against my shoulder, using soft strokes to brush away the hair strands that had fallen across her face. Throughout this process, I encouraged her by saying she was beautiful and worthy of comfort — words that caused a smile across her face.

Antonio

I WATCHED AS my father removed his clothing and climbed into bed while I quietly opened the door and slid the 'Do Not Disturb' sign onto the handle. I could see the satisfaction on his face, knowing we had done the right thing by taking the prostitute to the women's shelter. As I undressed, guilt filled my heart for not thinking of saving her. "I'm such a horrible person," I whispered under my breath, lowering my head in shame.

"No, you're certainly not!" my father firmly replied, reading my mind. He raised his arms in an inviting gesture. "With age comes wisdom and knowledge gained from experience."

Meeting his gaze, I saw nothing but unconditional love within his eyes. Without another word said between us, I crawled into bed and snuggled myself into his embrace. We lay together without speaking for what felt like an eternity — each of us deep in thought.

My dad asked if I was alright, breaking the silence. Nodding in response, I lifted my head and asked a question on my mind.

"Did you ever have a girlfriend?"

He shifted slightly to face me better while still holding me in his arms. He explained how much he loved and missed my mother and how no one else could take her place in his heart. His gaze was full of sadness. We stayed entwined as he spoke lovingly of her. I let his words fill me with warmth and comfort as I fell asleep in his arms.

Waking many hours later, I lay in bed, my body still buzzing from a passionate dream I'd just experienced. In my dream, David made love to me with an intense energy that brought pleasure to every inch of my body.

The clock on the nightstand read 12:12 p.m., and I knew I had to release my testicles. I got out of bed and headed for the bathroom.

Once in the bathroom, I shut the door and took a moment to bask in the sensation coursing through me. I closed my eyes, giving myself over to pure instinct. My hands moved down to cup my swollen shaft as images of David flooded back into my mind.

In seconds, a wave of relief flooded me as I shot stream after stream into the waiting palm of my hand. Suddenly overcome with a hunger for what lay before me, I tasted it — only to find its taste nothing but pure poison. Realizing that taking any more would surely end in disaster, I quickly shut my mouth and rose to wash. As I walked back to the bed, I sighed, missing David.

I crawled back into bed but couldn't sleep. My father's snoring gave me a sense of security, and he subconsciously spooned me when I turned to my side. Despite not sleeping, I felt content in his arms.

***

Standing on Bourbon Street, I asked my dad if we could meet for café au lait and beignets after his appointment.

He suggested the coffee shop on Decatur. "I'll see you there," I said, apprehensive that we were separating. What if I don't see him again? I thought to myself as I glanced at his five o'clock shadow and slick-backed hair. His Italian linen suit and crisp, white shirt looked stylish. My father hugged me, turned, and walked in the opposite direction. I felt anxious as I turned and walked away.

I turned back around, needing to see him one last time, and to my surprise, he had stopped and was looking back at me.

"I love you," he said telepathically.

I felt my heart sink as I watched my dad walk away for good this time. I knew he wanted me to be strong and not fear the unknown, so I needed to do that.

***

I walked into the gay district, previously off-limits, and the busy sounds of Bourbon Street surrounded me. People were out and about, enjoying the early morning hours. I couldn't help but feel energized by all of it. As I passed vendors selling hot dogs from every corner, I thought of David. I wondered what he'd think about me having sex with two men. My Catholic guilt came crashing down on me.

Taking a deep breath, I continued fighting away the guilt, focusing on being brave and finding David's whereabouts.

I couldn't help but smile as I watched the unsuspecting tourists explore the gay section of the French Quarter. They seemed to marvel at the extravagance of it all, their eyes wide with wonderment as they beheld the half-naked revelers celebrating in the streets. It was a sight to behold, notably when a plump and raunchy bear with a Prince Albert piercing revealed his most private parts in exchange for plastic beads. I chuckled at the scene and shook my head in amusement. Despite its outrageousness, this moment had a beauty that words cannot describe. It was an incredible display of freedom and joy, reminding me why I loved visiting this city.

I hesitated for a moment, unsure of what to do. Looking up at a group of bare-chested men on a balcony, I heard them laughing and jeering. To my surprise, the most attractive one pointed and shouted for me to show him my dick. His boldness took me aback. I yelled in confusion, "Are you talking to me?"

"Yes, you, handsome!"

Even though I felt the urge to expose myself and join in on their merriment, I needed to find out my boyfriend's whereabouts. If Robert had survived, I knew he'd bring David here. So instead of giving in to temptation, I laughed nervously and waved goodbye, saying I hadn't had enough to drink. As I started to walk away, I glanced back over my shoulder and saw the disappointment on his face, but it was too late now — the moment was over.

William

THE SIGN READ 'Reverend Selene's Voodoo Shop & Spiritual Readings,' located in the historic New Orleans French Quarter. I entered the establishment and walked toward the back of the store. As I entered the back room, the retail clerk, wearing a ritual robe disguised as a Wiccan witch, eyed me closely.

The voodoo shop was only a ruse to hide what happened in the offices beyond a drawn velvet curtain. As I entered the first room, two men in dark suits with DTAV insignias greeted me.

I followed them into the first office. I couldn't help but notice that they looked at me like they knew I had a secret. It wasn't because I looked any different; being a vampire didn't change my appearance, and they knew me from years of visits. I shrugged off the feeling and sat down.

The man I dealt with most sat behind the desk. His name was Achilles Chenevert, and I considered him a friend. I was familiar with the other man but didn't know his name. He stood behind Achilles. "Do you know anything new about my wife?" I asked.

"Mr. De Luca, it has come to our attention that your wife is ill," Achilles said compassionately.

I drew in a sharp breath, taken aback by the news. I pressed further for more information. "Our informant revealed that she has been diagnosed with cancer."

I closed my eyes. Cancer? I couldn't believe it. I needed to find her because I knew she still harbored guilty feelings. She needed to know I had forgiven her. I closed my eyes. My love, I'm so sorry, I thought, feeling a heaviness in my chest.

Achilles explained that even though the chief of staff had discarded her, he had compassion and saved her from immediate death. I opened my eyes and thanked God.

"William, where is your son?"

"My son?" I said wearily. "What does he have to do with this?" I asked in shock as he brought up his name.

He replied that someone had informed him of his new vampire identity. I stood and wiped my forehead with the back of my hand. If he knew about Antonio, he probably knew about me. "I'm sorry, the news about my wife is upsetting," I said and asked if I could use the bathroom.

"Of course."

As I walked toward the men's room, the nameless man followed, likely at Achille's request. Entering the bathroom, I knew he wasn't here for a friendly chat. He knew I was a vampire. Trying to hide my shock, I went to the sink and ran cold water over my face.

Trying to think of an escape plan as quickly as possible, I grabbed a towel and dried my face before moving toward the urinal to buy some time while formulating a strategy.

I continued to urinate, allowing precious moments to pass as I formulated a plan. My eyes shifted to the nameless stranger, and he looked at my body curiously. He quickly averted his gaze when he noticed that I had caught him in the act. Then he asked if what they said was true — that my son was gay. Knowing this question wasn't just idle talk but a reflection of his desires, I answered affirmatively and saw his head nod in realization.

Sensing an opportunity to save myself from whatever fate awaited me in this bathroom, I further engaged the stranger by informing him that I would soon meet up with my son. To make matters even more interesting, I added that my son was single — which immediately produced an interested, yet anxious, look on the nameless man's face. He clarified that he would prefer someone closer to his age, and I nodded understanding as he nervously looked away.

"I see." I turned toward him and presented my erection. I pulled back the foreskin, exposing the head.

His tongue jetted out, licking his lips in desire.

Even though this sickened me, I knew this was the only escape. "I need head," I murmured. "I'm not gay, but I have needs too," I continued, holding my breath for his reaction.

He nodded.

"I'd feel much safer if you could lock the door," I stated while glancing back at the window behind us, which seemed large enough to squeeze through. He obliged and double-checked the lock before returning to me. Although slightly apprehensive about what may come next, I remained composed, knowing that whatever fate awaited me here, I must face it with resilience if there was any hope of surviving this ordeal.

Antonio

I ENTERED A GAY BAR named Ricky's on Bourbon Street. The pulsating techno music played loudly, shaking my body with every beat as it bounced off the walls. My gaze fixed on the middle of the bar, where a muscular dancer moved slowly and sensually on a raised platform. His lack of clothing showcased his toned physique, and his seductive movements captivated everyone in the bar.

One patron became so entranced that he pulled out a five-dollar bill and held it toward the dancer. To everyone's amazement, the go-go boy lowered his G-string just enough to reveal his nine inches. I laughed as the patron fondled the dancer in disbelief. It was unbelievable how progressive the bars were here. This would never happen elsewhere. Showing or touching a stripper was strictly forbidden. As the go-go boy raised his thong, I could see the metal ring he used to ensure his continued hardness, guaranteeing big tips.

I had longed for this experience for years, ever since my father refused to let me out of his sight when we visited the city. Being among those that shared my identity was a feeling unlike any other — a sense of familiarity. It filled my heart with happiness.

I approached the bar and requested a beer to quench my parched throat, either due to the humid weather or sucking two dicks the night before. I welcomed its refreshing taste as it quenched my thirst and cooled my insides.

The cute bartender handed me the bottle with a big smile. I thanked him with a hefty tip. I took a sip and searched the room for a friendly face.

I observed an attractive Black man sitting alone, his gaze lingering on me briefly. Despite the loud music, I was positive he was attempting to communicate something to me. However, my attempts at reading his thoughts proved

futile. It seemed strange that I could not comprehend his intentions when I had been able to read people's minds with such ease before. Nevertheless, I continued observing him as he sat alone in the corner, and I wondered why he had caught my eye in the first place. The man stood and walked toward me.

"Do you have a cigarette?"

"I don't smoke," I said firmly. I noticed he was taller than I expected, with cocoa-brown skin, a goatee, and a shaved head. I guessed him to be around my age.

"Welcome to New Orleans!" he said with a smile.

"Is it that obvious?" I asked, noticing his friendly demeanor and the striking blue of his eyes.

He chuckled softly before replying, "Yes."

I thought I noticed something unusual about him for a moment — fangs peeking from beneath his lips — but when I squinted for another look, I only saw regular teeth.

"My name is Jackson."

He offered a handshake.

I accepted and told him my name.

His eyes studied my face closely.

"You have the most captivating eyes — your skin looks appetizing too. Are you Creole like me?"

I shook my head. "I'm Italian."

"I'm just a shade darker than you," he said, eying me suspiciously.

The strains of an old Chic tune, 'Everybody Dance,' began to drift through the air and fill the room. Jackson's eyes lit up, and a joyful cry escaped his lips.

"Oh, my goodness! I haven't heard this song for ages," he exclaimed, showing his enthusiasm for the music. "It seems like the DJ only plays techno now. Would you like to dance?" He reached for my hand as if I had already agreed to do so.

Though unsure whether I wanted to accept his invitation, something inside me said I should enjoy the moment. Quickly setting my unfinished beer on the bar, I nodded in agreement and smiled at him.

The Creole man, whose tall and handsome figure stood out in the crowd, guided me onto the dance floor. Initially, I was hesitant, but as my thoughts turned to David, I felt a spark of hope that this moment could provide some answers.

Jackson observed me as we danced together, his movements surprisingly graceful.

I was surprised that I wasn't drawn to him romantically — my intuition implied his motives for dancing were beyond just trying to charm me.

I wanted to ask if he knew David. And if yes, did he know his whereabouts? Then I realized that I didn't even know David's last name. This realization brought me to a standstill. How could I be that stupid? What was I thinking? I had a new love and didn't even ask for his last name.

"What's wrong?" Jackson asked as he stopped dancing.

"I need a drink," I yelled.

"Am I not a good time?"

"It's a long story."

"I'm a good listener," Jackson replied, following me off the dance floor.

I felt terrible, but I was sure he would understand once I explained the situation. As we walked toward the bar, I realized my beer was gone. The bartender had disposed of it. "Fuck!" I said, disgruntled.

"What's wrong?" Jackson asked.

"My beer. It's gone!"

As I mentioned my missing drink, Jackson looked slightly nonplussed, but it was soon apparent that he had other ideas. His hand traveled down my body, and I felt a chill as his finger brushed closer to my groin.

"I have a boyfriend," I stammered, taken aback by his inappropriate advance. As he caressed me, it moved, getting hard. "I'd rather you didn't do that." I removed his hand.

"Aren't you looking for a piece of ass like every other damn queer in this bar?" Jackson said, licking his lips.

I stepped back in confusion.

Jackson gave me an apologetic look and sheepishly

cleared his throat. It made me wonder what he was thinking — why did he think it was okay to touch me?

"I could bathe your asshole with my tongue," he purred.

His words shocked me, and I was captivated by the sight before me. He lowered his shorts, revealing an impressive eleven-inch erection that left me in awe. Despite being taken aback by his advance, I knew I had to remain strong and keep my boundaries in place. Gathering my composure and attempting to remain unfazed, I said, "It was nice meeting you," before spinning on my heel and making a hasty exit.

"Hey, wait! Did I offend you? If I did, I'm sorry."

"It's all good. Thanks for the dance." I waved goodbye.

"Let me buy you another drink."

I was suspicious that something wasn't right, and I tried to read his mind, but I couldn't figure out his intentions. His dick pulsating against his shorts confirmed my unease with the situation. Though intrigued by its size and strength, I reminded myself not to be swayed by it and kept my distance, knowing that he posed a potential safety risk.

"Wait here," he said. "I'll be right back."

I nodded yes.

Jackson gestured to stay put, then turned and went to the bar, where he ordered drinks. Moments later, I inhaled sharply in surprise as I watched the mixologist begin making the official drink of New Orleans — a hurricane.

For anyone who doesn't know, a hurricane is a fruit-based rum punch served in a tall glass shaped like a hurricane lamp. The color of the drink is blood red. It's a tasty drink but be forewarned — it'll knock you on your ass if you have more than one. God forbid you have two!

I observed Jackson curling his finger and slowly bringing it to his mouth. His lips twitched around the digit, creating a perplexing puzzle as I tried to figure out if he was biting or sucking on himself. A wave of confusion flooded my brain, and I couldn't help but blurt out, "What in the world is he doing?" As if rehearsed, the bartender handed him two glasses simultaneously. After being presented with the drinks, Jackson removed his finger from his mouth and placed it inside one of the glasses, stirring its contents before turning toward me. The sight of him walking in my direction left me dumbfounded. I couldn't believe what I had seen.

Jackson smiled and handed me a hurricane. Despite feeling flustered and taken aback by his unsanitary behavior, I maintained my composure and accepted the drink without mentioning anything. He then explained that although the hurricane might be more expensive than a beer, it would make up for it in flavor and sweetness. With a bit of skepticism, I took a sip of what seemed like pure sugar mixed with rum — a weird combination that surprisingly tasted good.

Jackson raised his glass.

I politely toasted him and took another sip of my drink, but the intense fruitiness made it hard to discern any unexpected flavors. Soon after, my head spun, and the world blurred.

Jackson's sinister grin revealed his sharp, pointed teeth, sending chills down my spine. It suddenly dawned on me that he had poisoned my drink with his blood. The venom entered my system in no time, and waves of intense pain surged through my abdomen, causing me to retch uncontrollably.

"Antonio? Are you all — right?" Jackson asked.

I watched Jackson's performance of a lifetime. "You bastard," I muttered under my breath.

"I should get you out of here!" He reached for my shoulder and guided me toward the door.

"You son-of-a-bitch!" I shouted as the urge to defecate overwhelmed me. "Get me the fuck out of here!" I cried, having to go, and bad. If I didn't leave immediately, I would shit myself due to the contagion turning my stool into water.

Jackson pushed me through the crowd.

We quickly sprinted away from the bar and down Bourbon Street. We ran past an old house with European charm. Vintage shutters framed its windows, and its white-washed walls were adorned with ivy, giving it a unique, classic atmosphere. The small garden in the back was filled with vibrant flowers, adding to its beauty.

I leaped over the fence to enter this hidden paradise and immediately squatted. Clutching my stomach in distress, I uttered a soft apology to whoever inhabited this place, and without warning or control, I let it all go. By the time I finished, Jackson was standing over me. I knew I couldn't outrun him with the continued pain in my gut. I was his prisoner.

William

I WAS ASTOUNDED by the head I was receiving. This man seemed to have a sixth sense of my desires. He knew exactly how to please me. Losing my wife did horrible things to my sex drive, so I wasn't sure whether I should give him my seed or kill him. It had been so long since I'd been intimate with anyone — but then I realized how selfish that thought was.

The man groaned as he met my gaze, his eyes swirling with delight and expectation as if he knew what reward would come from his actions. I decided it was time to make my move and uttered an apology for deceiving him. "I'm sorry for tricking you. Please forgive me."

I stared into his eyes and tamed him.

As he fell away from me, I immediately grabbed my hardness because I felt my sperm advancing. "No . . ." I moaned loudly, squeezing the shaft until the sensation faded.

I put my penis away and knelt beside him.

Looking into his eyes, I knew this man was kind. He had

done something no one else had ever done. He'd provided me with pleasure beyond anything I could have imagined — it made me feel alive again.

Antonio

"DRINK," JACKSON HISSED.

I positioned my lips over the two small puncture marks, creating a seal. As I began to draw in liquid, an array of flavors enveloped my taste buds. The rich and complex taste of the nourishment caused a sensory overload, making my eyes flutter as though I was euphoric.

Savoring the delectable taste from his wrist, I let my eyes wander around the room, absorbing the exquisite details of the surroundings. Stunning artwork adorned the walls of Jackson's luxurious hotel suite.

"You've had enough," Jackson whispered, pulling his arm away.

He gave me just enough blood to restrain me, making escape impossible. However, my vision stayed clear.

"I'm going to fuck you now," he murmured.

My eyes widened because I didn't think it was humanly possible to take him anally. Looking at his erection, it seemed much bigger than I'd initially thought — twelve inches. It was rock hard, and I wondered about the damage it would cause.

"Why are you doing this?" I asked.

"I was hired to capture you."

As a vampire, he wouldn't be working with the DTAV. Could he be in the infantry? That didn't make sense, either. The military's outdated, prejudiced policies wouldn't accept an openly gay man. His real connection remained mysterious and fascinating.

"Stand up and bend over the bed," Jackson ordered.

Following Jackson's command, I stood up and bent forward, only to be caught off guard by a slap on my ass. The pain rippled through me. This sudden act of aggression sent a shock through my system, making me shudder involuntarily.

I grew nervous upon realizing Jackson's true character. He hid his cruel, violent side well. His face formed a wicked smile. He seemed to enjoy inflicting pain, and I knew it would only worsen if I resisted.

"Show me your hole!"

I spread my buttocks and heard him spit.

The sputum landed on my anus.

"Are you with the infantry?" I inquired, trying to understand his motives as he fingered me, using the spit as a lubricant.

"Correct."

"Why?"

"For a large sum of money."

As if money is everything. You're gay!" I shook my head. "Once they find out, they'll capture you too."

"I'll be long gone before that happens," he muttered and stepped forward, entering me.

I moaned, taking all twelve inches.

The pain and fear melted away, replaced by electrifying sensations. I wanted him to fuck me hard, and he didn't disappoint. He thrust away with increasing intensity, hitting my prostate and sending my body shivers of joy. His steady rhythm drove me wild, pushing me closer and closer to the edge until I finally reached orgasm.

My moans echoed off the walls, marking the end of a passionate session that left me satisfied.

Jackson cried out, getting ready to shoot.

I snapped out of my ecstasy. I had to think fast to stop him from coming inside me — so I pushed him out and knelt on the floor.

"What are you doing?" he asked in surprise.

"Come in my mouth," I said, enacting my plan. Within seconds, his hot, poisonous load shot to the back of my throat.

I gathered it up and spat it back in his face.
He stepped back and screamed.
"Fuck you!" I yelled and tackled him.

William

I COULDN'T BRING myself to kill the nameless man. Instead, I willed him to sleep and dashed toward the bathroom window. Desperately attempting to open it, my efforts were fruitless. Years of dirt and paint had accumulated within the lock's crevices, making it impossible to unlock. In a desperate act, I resorted to shattering the glass with a forceful kick. The sound reverberated through the hallway while glass shards cascaded to the street below.

Achilles Chenevert burst through the bathroom door moments later, his face filled with worry and concern.

Seizing this opportunity, I waved goodbye, expressing heartfelt gratitude for our years of friendship, before leaping onto the cobblestone below.

Looking back one last time, I saw him in the window — seemingly wanting to do something but not knowing what that might be. With that final glimpse, I ran into the night, leaving behind a trail of shattered glass in my wake.

Antonio

I TIGHTENED MY grip around Jackson's neck, the pressure of my hand crushing his windpipe as I screamed,

"Die, motherfucker, die!" But despite squeezing harder and harder, it seemed my feeble attempt at a sleeper hold wasn't doing anything to slow him down. Thinking quickly, I remembered the venomous liquid on the bedspread.

Acting without hesitation, I sat on Jackson's chest, collected the toxic venom, and held it menacingly to intimidate him.

He pleaded for mercy.

He tried to talk his way out, but I refused to consider his pleas. Then he made an unexpected offer. He'd take me to David at the compound if I released him.

As I looked down, the self-assured man who had just raped me turned into a pitiful sight, evoking sympathy within me. I picked up a shirt from the floor and wiped my hands.

"It's a deal!"

"I'm blind now!" Jackson cried out in distress.

"Don't worry, it's only temporary," I reassured him, handing him the shirt to wipe his eyes. "Now, tell me everything you know."

"The council voted to . . ." His words trailed off mid-thought.

I waited for him to continue, but fear held him back. "They voted to do what?" I demanded, raising my voice.

"To enforce the death penalty."

My heart dropped hearing his words, and I immediately grabbed his shoulders, shaking them. "Where's the compound?" I urgently asked.

"It's underground."

I countered that it couldn't be possible due to our sea level position. Jackson maintained it was true, his voice weary.

"If you set me free, I'll take you there."

I warned him against any reckless actions and stood up, extending my hand toward him. Jackson grasped my hand, insisting I escort him to the bathroom to rinse his eyes.

Once in the bathroom, I wasted no time directing his face toward the sink. I turned on the tap and splashed water on his face.

He thanked me.

As he dried himself with the towel, I couldn't help but stare at his groin. Thinking I had just taken him and felt pleasure beyond my wildest dreams was surreal. An overwhelming urge to let it happen again filled me with remorse.

"What's with the guilt?" he asked, reading my thoughts.

I took a deep breath and said, "I was raised Catholic."

Heaving a deep sigh, Jackson shook his head sadly. His pupils shrank at the sudden brightness of the light — he was no longer blind. His stern gaze made me squirm.

"Your religion is fucked up!"

"Despite my religious background, David's going to kick your ass for raping me!" I uttered, quickly leaving the bathroom so he couldn't see my growing erection.

"There's a stack of bills in the top drawer."

I turned and saw him soaping himself, removing all the evidence of my ass. "I'll get it."

Judging by the soiled clothes, room service tray, and dirty dishes beside the bed, it seemed housekeeping wasn't a high priority. I walked to the dresser and opened the top drawer. As I searched for the stack of bills, my hand came across a black, cone-shaped object — a butt plug.

Jackson came out of the bathroom just then.

"Give that to me!"

He grabbed it from my hand, threw it into the drawer, and then fished out the wad of cash.

I stared at the bills, surprised at how much he had.

A loud bang jolted me back to reality.

The hotel door flew open and slammed against the wall.

Two infantry soldiers with batons ran into the room.

"What the fuck?" I shouted and reached for the closest thing I could use as a weapon — the sex toy.

I hurled it, striking the soldier with a misshapen nose. As Jackson tried to back away, Crooked Nose raised his baton and swiftly hit him on the head, making him crumple to the floor. I stood there, staring in shock, instinctively covering my private parts with both hands.

Turning my attention to the other soldier, I couldn't

help but notice his striking blond hair and seductive grin. Even amidst my fear, a desire for him stirred within me. He stood tall, his handsome features accentuated by a strong jawline and piercing eyes that seemed to see right through me. The broadness of his shoulders and the defined muscles beneath his uniform hinted at the power he possessed. His confident stance and demeanor only added to his allure, making it difficult to resist the magnetic pull I felt toward him.

My whorish nature surfaced, even in this deadly situation. At this point, rather than questioning my desires, I hoped I could entice him sexually. If so, maybe I'd survive.

"Looking to fuck ass?" I asked, returning the soldier's seductive grin.

"I am!" Crooked Nose exclaimed as he unzipped his pants.

I turned to the unattractive soldier, wishing it was the good-looking one stepping forward instead. It took everything I had not to look disappointed as I saw his circumcised penis. I had just been fucked with twelve inches, and now this. As he walked toward me, he stroked it, making it hard. It grew to five inches.

"Let me see your fuck hole!" he ordered.

I leaned forward and spread my buttocks. I knew my anus was loose because of Jackson's thick dick. I didn't tighten my sphincter. Instead, I teased them with it. I wanted them to see my used hole. I knew some guys enjoyed sloppy seconds.

I reminded myself that dick size wasn't an issue. His hardness and thickness made up for his shortcomings. I turned, glancing at the handsome soldier. Even though I hadn't seen his sex, I could see from the outline that it was above average. It pulsated as he watched the situation unfold.

I mouthed to him, "Fuck me!"

Blondie's eyes gleamed as he stepped forward, pushed his partner aside, and placed the truncheon inside my ass.

I moaned in pleasure, not in pain.

The soldier grinned, clearly aware of how receptive

I was. As he pulled back the baton, my body quivered in ecstasy. Removing the stick, he played with my erection as it dangled between my legs. I wondered if he was bisexual.

"Let me fuck him first!" Crooked Nose exclaimed excitedly.

My heart raced as I turned, seeing the disfigured-nosed man stepping forward. His pale face betrayed his shock when Blondie grabbed his dick and guided him inside me.

"What are you doing? Get your hands off me!" he yelled, his voice edged with confusion and anger.

Hearing Blondie getting scrutinized by his partner, I shouted, "Fuck me!" By doing this, I shifted the attention toward me. It worked — he grabbed my hips and went to town on my ass. I moaned loudly, even though he wasn't hitting all the right spots. It was too small for me to feel any real pleasure.

"Oh, fuck, you feel great," he moaned.

I tightened my sphincter around his shaft. His moans of ecstasy told me he was coming soon. The blond must have realized it, too, because he dropped his pants.

My eyes widened in anticipation at seeing Blondie's thick, beautiful dick. He took charge, pushing his partner aside, and stepped behind me. I felt myself tremble as he pressed his hardness to my swollen ass lips. I deep-throated his partner at the same time. Finally, after watching scenes like this in porn movies, I was about to experience it for real. My whole body tensed with pleasure as Blondie pushed himself inside me. It was about eight inches, with a mushroom-like head that hit my prostate.

In minutes, Blondie moaned, grabbed my ass, and quickened his pace. Just as he was about to ejaculate, he pulled out and shot his massive load onto the floor.

"It's my turn," said Crooked Nose.

He pulled out of my mouth and entered me anally. He moaned as his eruption built.

"I'm coming!"

"Don't come inside him," Blondie murmured.

Crooked Nose nodded.

He pulled out, shot his load on my ass, and stormed off

to the bathroom.

"I could have seeded and killed the faggot!" he muttered. "We could have said it was an accident."

The hot fluid started to burn.

The sound of running water filled the room as I stared at the blond-haired soldier, hoping for assistance. To my surprise, he grabbed one of Jackson's dirty shirts and wiped the sperm away. He then uttered the words that shocked me.

"I pretend to be homophobic, but I'm not."

His gaze shifted to his partner briefly before turning back to me. His voice was soft and understanding as he whispered that he was letting me go.

A weight lifted from my shoulders.

"I'm gay, and I like you," he confessed.

"What will your partner think?" I asked, turning around.

"Don't worry about him," the soldier whispered. "That was hot. I loved fucking your ass."

I smiled, trying to process the information he had just shared. His gaze was intense and focused — something in it told me he liked me. I felt a thrill knowing that someone else found me attractive.

I woke Jackson and told him we were leaving. As we dressed, I looked into Blondie's eyes and thanked him.

He smiled back.

As I was about to ask his name, he grabbed Jackson and hurried us out of the room. He led us down the hallway with a speed that matched his determination. I had so many questions running through my head, but there was no time. Now, all I could focus on was our escape. We reached the end of the hallway, and Blondie pushed us toward the staircase.

"I'm Angelo," he finally revealed.

I told him mine, attempting to conceal my excitement.

"I know who you are."

He gave me one last look of understanding, protection, and admiration, then disappeared into the shadows around us. A switch inside me seemed to flip — my heart began to race. What was happening? I already had a boyfriend.

Angelo

I COULDN'T HELP but admire the stunning perfection of Antonio's exquisite posterior as he sprinted gracefully down the staircase. My heart raced with anticipation, secretly hoping our paths would cross again. Without hesitation, I quickly returned to the room, just in time to see Philippe, my partner, stepping out of the bathroom. His dick was stiff and eager, clearly ready for round two. However, his expression turned sour when he realized that Antonio and Jackson were no longer present in the room.

"Where did they go?" he demanded with a hint of frustration.

"I let them go," I replied calmly, fully aware of Philippe's strong distaste for homosexuals. "The pursuit isn't over yet," I added enthusiastically, trying to appease his sadistic tendencies. At this, he raised his eyebrows inquisitively, so I quickly explained that I had given them a fifteen-minute head start before we would resume our relentless chase.

"Well, let's get going then," Philippe snarled impatiently, eager for the thrilling game to commence.

I nodded in acknowledgment. Taking my sweet time to get dressed, I could sense his growing agitation. Finally, as I fastened my belt buckle, I lifted my gaze. His arms were crossed tightly over his chest, clearly annoyed.

"It's about fucking time!" he exclaimed exasperatedly.

Picking up my truncheon from the table, I gestured toward the door and said firmly yet courteously, "After you."

***

Taking a deep breath, I inhaled the crisp evening air as we left the hotel. Raising my nose, I could sense the direction Antonio and Jackson had taken moments before. I glanced over to see Philippe sniffing the air as well. Smirking, I knew that his deformed nose was no longer functional. I gestured in the opposite direction.

"They went this way!"

As we strode down the street, Philippe's pace quickened, and I noticed his hand fumbling inside his pocket. Intrigued and suspicious, I couldn't help but inquire about the hidden item. He came to an abrupt halt and revealed a gleaming blade, making it clear that he was intent on seeking revenge, regardless of the consequences.

"They didn't get away," I stated firmly yet calmly, attempting to diffuse his anger. "I told you — I let them go."

Despite my objections, Philippe continued with a resolute stride and unwavering focus, causing my heart to pound in anticipation. I knew his reaction would be disastrous once I admitted we had lost them.

When we had put enough distance between ourselves and the boys, I voiced my frustration. "I lost their scent." My words struck him, and he stared at me, eyebrows furrowed and rage evident.

"What?" he muttered, gazing at me in disbelief.

Feeling the tension radiating from Philippe's demeanor, I suggested we take a break and grab a coffee.

He glared at me angrily and declared that I would pay for it.

I rolled my eyes. "Whatever!"

We headed to the nearest cafe, where I ordered two café au lait and beignets. Sitting at one of the tables, we began discussing our strategy. However, Philippe soon shifted the conversation to a surprising topic.

"I got teased in the gym showers this evening," he said.

"What happened?" I inquired.

"They asked if you were . . . queer," his words trailed off as he gauged my reaction. "They question your sexual orientation," he continued.

"Who?" I asked, taken aback by the entire conversation.

Philippe seemed to choose his words carefully as he spoke again.

"Our comrades. I've been wondering about it too. I see

how you look at me sometimes."

"Just because I fuck ass doesn't mean I'm gay. You do the same! Are you queer?" I asserted defensively.

Philippe lowered his head in deep thought.

"You have a point."

After a long pause, he raised his head.

"Have you told anyone what we do with these fuckers?"

"Hell, no!"

Philippe nodded.

I slowly sipped my coffee, struggling to process my racing thoughts. Feeling exposed, I believed the entire infantry had discovered my homosexuality, and I was sure a court-martial would soon follow.

Desperate to calm myself, I took another sip of coffee.

My partner, Philippe, stared at me intently before reaching into his pocket and pulling out his knife. With a snap, the blade emerged suddenly, shimmering in the light. The sight sent cold shivers cascading down my spine.

He waved it in my direction.

"You grabbed my cock tonight. The infantry is my life."

"I understand," I replied solemnly, my voice soft but audible enough for him to hear. "It's my life too."

Antonio

AS JACKSON and I scaled the fence into Jackson Square, I perched on the railing, utterly captivated by the breathtaking view of the St. Louis Cathedral. Jackson jumped down while I sat, awestruck. My gaze then drifted to the lush gardens within the square. Bursting with vibrant flowers and impeccably groomed shrubs, they created an Eden-like atmosphere that amplified the overall charm. The fusion of architectural grandeur and natural beauty was indeed a sight to behold.

Jumping to the ground, I scanned for Jackson in the poorly lit square. Suddenly, a groan broke the silence.

"Jackson?"

A scary undead creature appeared before me, looking like a grotesque zombie. It was tall and had a thin, pale face with lifeless eyes that seemed to stare into my soul. The skin looked tight over its bony body. The creature's thin lips formed a creepy smile.

As it emerged, my heart raced. I instinctively sought Jackson's support, only to find he was no longer by my side.

Another groan came from the beast.

I stood frozen, not knowing whether to turn, run, stay, or confront whatever lurked before me.

The hideous thing pinned me against the fence.

"I . . . need . . . blood."

As its skeletal finger pointed toward me, I screamed and knocked it away. I bared my teeth, hoping to scare it off, but the creature stood its ground.

"Jackson?" I called out, my voice trembling with fear.

As I panicked, Jackson appeared, brandishing a machete-like knife and forcefully slashing it toward the creature. In seconds, he managed to slice the thing in half.

The creature released an agonizing howl as its two halves fell. I couldn't help but stand, utterly motionless, as I watched in shock while the upper portion of its body squirmed and writhed, attempting to rejoin its lower half. Barely able to speak, I whispered hesitantly, my voice trembling with an overwhelming sense of fear, "What is it?"

"A Reaper," Jackson said, kicking the lower half away.

My jaw dropped as Jackson decapitated the creature, and to my shock, its head continued to wail, even detached from its torso. I blinked, thinking this was unreal.

"This is a vampire depleted of blood. When the sun rises, it'll burn and turn to ashes. However, you need to separate the body parts. Otherwise, they'll reattach themselves," Jackson explained.

I nodded, watching him throw the creature's head

across the square. To my amazement, it landed in a boxwood hedge and continued its loud wailing. I stood silently as Jackson expertly dissected the creature, throwing each piece in a different direction.

"That should do it," he said, tucking the knife inside his jeans. "I'm glad I got to it before it attacked you."

"What would have happened?"

"It would've drained you of blood."

As we exited the gardens, I paused, captivated by the silhouette of Jesus on the side of the building. His outstretched arms conveyed a feeling of welcome and peace, almost like he had just descended from heaven.

Jackson gestured toward a statue on a column amidst the flower bed. It all clicked when I saw the accent light on Jesus, projecting his image onto the wall.

"The resurrection story passed down through generations isn't accurate," said Jackson calmly. "There's more to it than meets the eye . . ." he added in a whisper.

Intrigued, I asked him to elaborate on his statement.

"I'm saying that the Federation resurrected Jesus Christ, not divine intervention bringing him back from the dead."

"Are you suggesting that Jesus is a vampire?" I questioned him, struggling to believe his claim.

Jackson smiled and nodded.

"Is he being held prisoner?"

"Well, yes, but he's not shackled. He's accepted his fate and has blessed the Federation with forgiveness. He's Jesus Christ, after all."

I thought back to Catholic school. After being told the resurrection story, I couldn't believe vampires, not God, raised him. This was surreal. I remembered the drawings of Jesus Christ in class. His masculine frame, long hair, bearded face, and toned body excited me. The Blessed Savior prints depicted him as pleasing to the eyes. Yet even though they illustrated him that way, the church condemned you if you had impure thoughts of homosexuality.

As we passed the sculpture, I smiled, knowing Jesus loved me for me. "Fuck you," I murmured to the Catholic church for teaching me that my gayness was wrong.

***

While crossing the street to meet my father at the coffee shop, a loud car horn startled Jackson and me, causing us to stop. The driver yelled through his open window to watch where we were going. In response, I thrust up my middle finger. We continued until we spotted my dad sitting near the cafe's entrance. Seeing him safe and sound flooded my heart with relief.

As we edged closer to his table, Jackson abruptly seized my shoulder, halting me in my tracks with a shout. Startled by his explosion, I swiftly pivoted to face him, questioning, "What's wrong?" He gestured past my dad's table, where three men clad in ominous dark suits swiftly closed in on him.

"Who are they?" I inquired.

"DTAV agents," he responded tersely.

"They've discovered he's a vampire," I murmured under my breath, watching as the agents encircled him, urging him to depart without a scene. Abruptly, one of the agents reached out and seized a beignet from the plate, demolishing it in just two bites. I couldn't suppress the resentment — what a jerk he was for devouring our dessert.

"Don't get any closer," Jackson cautioned.

I watched as my father stood and left with the agents. "Let's go!" I said, wanting to follow.

"Don't you see the infantry soldiers?" Jackson whispered.

I hadn't noticed them until then, but after watching for a few seconds, I realized several were following my father and the agents out of the dining area.

Jackson

WITH A HEAVY HEART, I hesitantly accepted that I had put myself in a precarious situation. My naive belief that working alongside the infantry would bring me remarkable wealth and success had instead endangered my life. It was clear to me now that leaving New Orleans behind was necessary for my safety, even though it meant departing from a city where I had many fond memories.

Therefore, I would follow through and take Antonio to the vampire compound before I left the area. After that, my future was uncertain and dauntingly wide open. Would I venture off to Florida with its stunning white beaches and pleasant temperature all year round? Or South Carolina, with its delicious Southern cuisine? The decisions were overwhelming and thrilling if I stayed out of harm's way.

"What are we going to do now?" Antonio inquired tiredly.

I fearfully responded, "We will track them down," dreading the worst outcome for his captured father.

Antonio

WE ASCENDED the steps to the Riverwalk, a picturesque trail winding along the mighty Mississippi River, following my father and his captors. Sensing the vampires were trailing them, the DTAV agents glanced back over their shoulders, remaining vigilant in assessing their situation.

The scenic beauty of the Riverwalk was in stark contrast

to the tension that filled the air. With each step we took, the agents grew increasingly uneasy, knowing these supernatural beings could strike at any moment.

My father, ever the stoic figure, appeared unfazed by the looming threat. Despite being held captive, he carried himself with dignity and strength, refusing to let fear take hold. His captors, meanwhile, struggled to maintain their composure, their hands never straying too far from their weapons.

"Where are they taking him?" I asked.

"To the Spanish Plaza. It's almost sunrise."

They were going to burn him in the morning light. "No! We must do something!" I said as more infantry soldiers appeared from out of the darkness.

"We're outnumbered. There's nothing we can do."

My head shook uncontrollably as intense fear and worry rushed over me. With determination, I declared, "I refuse to stand here powerless and simply witness his demise." Immediately after my words left my lips, searing beams of light accompanied by gunfire filled the air. It was obvious the agents were defending themselves against the vampires, blasting them with their rifles that shot flaming balls of energy.

Horrifying screams erupted as the vampires scattered everywhere to escape the onslaught of power. The agents believed they had achieved a triumphant victory, only to be met with the sudden regrouping of vampires. The horrific sight that awaited them was overwhelming. As terror overcame the agents, they dropped their firearms and took off in a desperate attempt to escape. Unfortunately, no amount of running could have saved them as the cruel fangs of the vampires quickly subdued them. Every agent met their demise in seconds, their lifeless bodies strewn about on the pavement.

I inhaled sharply as a vampire hand-cuffed my father. Why didn't he run? Maybe he could have escaped? I thought, not understanding why my dad had surrendered without a fight.

"We need to find cover," Jackson shouted, pointing at

the rising sun.

"But what about my dad?" I cried.

"They're taking him to the compound. We need to find shelter now, or we're dead. Follow me!" he said, running toward the French Quarter.

Moments later, we arrived.

My hands trembled as I descended the staircase in pursuit of Jackson. We had to find shelter fast, and this condemned building on Saint Ann Street seemed like our only hope. My heart raced as he pointed at a wooden door at the bottom of the stairs. Taking a deep breath, I followed him, hoping it would be secure enough to offer us refuge.

Jackson pushed open the dilapidated door.

We stepped inside cautiously, both on high alert for any danger lurking in the shadows. Our eyes gradually adjusted to the darkness, revealing an old, dusty basement filled with broken furniture. With no other options available, we decided this would have to do.

The dark basement smelled musty and reeked of urine. As I scanned the space, Jackson stepped back outside.

"What are you doing?" I asked, alarmed.

"We need our morning meal."

My jaw dropped. "Are you crazy?"

"I'll be right back. Stay here." And he was gone.

I froze, my heart racing as I realized I was the only one in the musty basement. Fearful of what I might uncover, I took a few steps back. The foundation of the building was composed of stone and cement. A filthy mattress lay on the ground, its grimy fabric illuminated by the morning rays from a small window with broken panes.

Surprisedly, I saw a small rodent scurrying across the floor. Staring at the rat as it darted into an opening in the wall, I cursed my bad luck.

While appalled at the thought of lying on that mattress, I decided it was better than nothing. I lifted a corner, intending to drag it away from the sunlight, but an even bigger rat darted out and hurried away. Startled, I dropped the mattress.

As I watched the shy creature scurry away, I felt regretful for the fear it must have been feeling. Lifting my arm, I reached out to catch it before it could escape. However, as soon as I moved forward, the rodent panicked and leaped toward me with a loud squeal. Instinctively, I reacted by catching hold of its tail to prevent it from getting away. The animal wriggled furiously in my grasp, desperately trying to break free. Then, all movement ceased, and it lay still. Its little eyes filled with terror — a feeling that was unfortunately all too familiar.

Jackson

I VENTURED OUT into the daylight, a feat that took immense courage. I knew staying in the sun for too long would make my body feel on fire due to its harmful effects. I remembered seeing a vampire burned alive by the sun's rays. His screams still echoed in my mind as he writhed in agony.

To find sustenance, I had to stay close to civilization without going over the brink and experiencing total immolation. It felt like walking on a tightrope, balancing precariously between two extremes to survive.

"Looking for a release?"

Unable to bear the thought of experiencing the same fate as that vampire I remembered, I lunged forward and sunk my teeth into the neck of a male prostitute. He was barely more than a boy. His blond hair, baby face, and lack of body hair made him look fifteen years old, but he was more likely closer to nineteen. I held his motionless form close and sprinted back to the darkness.

Antonio

MY HEART LURCHED as I spun around to find Jackson staggering into the room with an unconscious figure cradled in his arms. Flames leaped from his body, searing the air with the acrid smell of burning leather. Panic seized me. I quickly dropped the rodent and rushed forward, taking hold of the limp figure in Jackson's arms.

Falling to the dirt floor, Jackson frantically rolled back and forth to extinguish the fire that engulfed him. His agonizing screams filled the air, creating a chilling atmosphere as he desperately tried to escape the flames. I stood there, utterly helpless, unable to block the heart-wrenching sound of his piercing shrieks from reaching my ears.

Gradually, the fire began to subside, and Jackson managed to rise from the ground, his body free from the once-consumptive blaze.

"Give him to me! I need his blood to heal," he demanded urgently.

Overwhelmed with dread, I stared helplessly at his red, swollen face and the blisters that formed on his shoulders where his shirt had burned away. The severity of his injuries was a harrowing sight to behold.

"He's too young!" I snapped.

Jackson's transformation revealed a hideous monstrosity. His screams for the boy's blood resonated throughout the basement, bouncing off the stone walls. Tears ran down my face. I was too weak to defy him, and my heart ached for the boy. I had no idea where David or my father would be if I disobeyed Jackson, so I gingerly laid him on the ground as he woke from his unconscious state.

"Oh . . . to be so young and . . . full of life," Jackson slurred through his swollen lips. His tongue darted out, licking them.

"Jackson, no . . ." I yelled, noticing his fangs protruding menacingly.

He sank his sharp teeth into the boy's neck and began to drink. As he drank, I watched in horror as the blisters on his skin disappeared and his burns healed. Jackson's features then morphed back into their normal state.

The blood dripping from Jackson's mouth awoke my hunger, and the need to survive overwhelmed me. I wanted to push him aside and take the boy for myself, but I knew it was wrong. Jackson lifted his head and scowled at me in disgust.

"He's a street hustler with tainted blood," he spat, wiping his mouth with the back of his hand.

Confused, I asked what he meant.

"He's infected with the virus."

"Oh, Jesus! AIDS?" I couldn't help but feel sympathy for the poor kid. What kind of life could he have had on the streets? My thoughts turned to his parents, wondering where they might be as he opened his eyes. "You're so young," I said, shaking my head in dismay.

"Jesus Christ! He's a nineteen-year-old man!" Jackson suddenly exclaimed, dropping the prostitute onto the dirt floor with a thud.

"What?" I stammered, completely taken aback by this revelation.

"You're so goddamn gullible. He's fooled you too. Are you really that naïve?" Jackson said, shaking his head in disbelief at my apparent gullibility.

I scowled at Jackson.

"That's our meal. So don't get emotionally attached."

"Leave him alone!" I yelled, taking the all-but-unconscious boy in my arms. I saw fear in his eyes. He didn't know where he was or how he got here. I smiled warmly and asked him his name. After a few moments of thoughtful pause, he finally spoke.

"My name . . . is Peter," he said softly.

I introduced myself in response.

"Drink his blood, you fool."

"No," I exclaimed, feeling sorry for him.

I recoiled in shock as Peter dropped to the floor and lunged toward us, his switchblade glinting wickedly in the dim light. His weary, bloodshot eyes were wide with panic and desperation as he brandished the weapon in a feeble attempt to protect himself.

"I'll kill you if you come any closer."

"You little fucker!" Jackson shouted furiously, raising his fists in anger.

"No one's going to hurt you," I tried to reassure the young man, hoping to defuse the situation.

"Get back!" he warned us both. His voice filled with fear.

As Jackson cautiously stepped forward, Peter quickly swerved and swung the knife he had held at him, trying to fend off any potential attack.

"Stay back!" Peter demanded, his voice trembling.

"Drop the knife," Jackson ordered firmly.

"Fuck you!" Peter yelled back, clearly frightened.

The nineteen-year-old was powerless against Jackson's hypnotic gaze. His eyes glazed over into a zombie-like stare, and his knife clattered to the ground as he slumped to his knees.

I quickly scooped up the switchblade and instinctively held it in my hand, ready to use it against Jackson if I had to. But then I thought better of it, slipping the knife into my pocket before I said pleadingly, "Please don't do this."

Jackson smirked and stared deeply into my eyes, making me feel uneasy. I realized too late that he was hypnotizing me as well. He commanded me to throw myself against the rock wall.

I instantly obeyed, hitting the hard stone with intense pain and collapsing. Opening my eyes, I witnessed Peter kneeling in front of Jackson. No! I hate you! I thought, knowing Jackson's intentions.

"Put my cock inside your mouth," Jackson ordered, unbuttoning his jeans. Within seconds his hardness sprang forward.

The words reverberated through my head as a rage

boiled within me. "You're a son-of-a-bitch," I wanted to yell, but I couldn't move a muscle. So instead, I closed my eyes, shielding myself from the horrific scene unfolding before me.

***

I whispered, not wanting to wake Jackson. "Listen carefully. You must drink my blood to stay alive. Do you understand?"

Peter nodded in agreement.

"Trust me," I said, dripping my lifeblood into his mouth.

He snatched my forearm with a powerful grip and began sucking.

I wondered if I had enough blood to give him. A few seconds later, the answer became apparent when I became light-headed and pulled my arm away. Peter at once grabbed my arm, wanting more. I yanked it away, knowing my life was at stake. "I have no more to give you," I said, hoping I had given him enough blood to make him a vampire.

"Blood . . . more . . ." he muttered in desperation.

"I'm sorry," I said softly. "You may not know this, but you have AIDS. You'll die soon if I don't help you."

His expression was puzzled. "Who are you?"

I looked into his eyes and replied warmly, "I'm your archangel. I can give you the gift of life and heal you." My offer took a moment to sink in, and he hesitated before speaking. His voice trembled as he asked, almost in awe.

"Like Raphael?"

I smiled, understanding the enormity of what I had proposed. "Well," I said reassuringly, "that was just a metaphor. But if you're willing, I can make you immortal by turning you into a vampire." He gave me a long look, then slowly drew a deep breath before nodding affirmatively.

Peter

I TOOK A DEEP breath and looked into Antonio's eyes. His gaze was gentle yet powerful — like a warm embrace. He offered me a chance to start over. I knew about vampires, but only that they drank blood and not much more.

Accepting his offer meant I would no longer work the streets. My job as a prostitute wasn't glamorous. Many of my clients were unappealing in both appearance and personality. Unlike those other men, Antonio wanted to help me without any hidden agenda. His kindness filled me with gratitude and hope for a better future. For the first time in quite some time, I felt excited about what lay ahead and eagerly anticipated my new beginning.

When Antonio made me into a vampire, I wanted to suck him off, but he said no. This confirmed my suspicions that he wasn't interested in me sexually. I think he felt protective of me, which was funny because I felt fatherly to him. I had street smarts. He was the naïve one.

Closing my eyes, I realized I was a vampire. That label didn't feel right, though. My mind ran through several possibilities before settling on gaypire.

When I opened my eyes, everything felt sharper and more defined. Looking back, I realized I'd been mud-eyed as a human. Believe it or not, I could see through objects and focus on specific things, such as Antonio's circulatory system. I saw the blood flowing into his prick, making it rigid. It was amazing, awe-inspiring. "I'm a gaypire."

Antonio looked confused for a moment.

The meaning of my new word sank in, and then a smile formed across his face.

"You're brilliant!" he said excitedly.

I could read his mind. It was going a hundred miles an hour. I knew he realized I had coined a vital term, making him realize the importance of a brotherhood.

Antonio

I BIT THE DEAD rat's head off and felt a rush of warmth as the blood filled my mouth. I squeezed its body until it completely drained, and then my stomach growled for more. Peter watched with fascination — his lips still smeared with my drying semen. The atmosphere was intense, with a unique mix of death and lust. It had been necessary to complete his transformation.

Morning light streamed into the basement.

The window was too high to cover with the soiled mattress, so I looked around for another means to cover it. Then, suddenly, I noticed a shovel on the opposite wall. I ran to grab it and raced back to shield us from the streaming light.

Meanwhile, Jackson slept, unaware of the encroaching light.

You motherfucker, I thought. I visualized him waking and screaming in the blinding light. But who was I kidding? I needed him. After only taking a few minutes, I dug a trench with the shovel to protect us from daylight.

I shook Jackson's shoulder, trying to wake him. With a groggy murmur, he opened one eye.

"What?"

My gaze shifted to the morning rays. Pointing in its direction, I urged Jackson to take cover in the trench.

Jackson sat up and mockingly asked if it was a trench or a grave.

Ignoring his jest, I motioned for him to get in.

He did so without further question and immediately fell back asleep.

As I watched him settle into the small pit, relief washed over me that he hadn't noticed that I had made Peter into a vampire. The trench was barely large enough to fit the three of us comfortably, so we'd use the mattress as a makeshift cover instead of sleeping on it.

"What's his story?" Peter asked, stepping into the hole.

"The Federation hired him to capture me because of my father's involvement with their organization," I explained, following him. I sat down against the dirt wall, instructing him to do the same. The deep hole prevented the daylight from reaching us.

"What's the Federation?"

"It's a rigid vampire organization. My boyfriend says homosexuality is considered taboo. They consider it a sin. If you make a vampire without approval, they'll kill you."

Peter glanced at Jackson. "He's a bad guy."

"I know he's not looking out for my best interests, but I need him. He's taking me to the vampire compound to find my father and boyfriend."

"I'm sure we can find it alone."

"I don't expect you to help me. This is too dangerous. If I were you, I'd leave New Orleans and start a new life away from here. If you don't, they'll kill you."

"Would you come with me?

"I can't," I said.

Peter frowned, hearing my response. He glanced down in disappointment and then noticed the size of his dick. He smiled in surprise.

"It's bigger."

"Your body is more muscular too. Look at your abdomen."

"Oh!" He slapped his stomach in surprise.

"How long have you been on the streets?" I asked.

"Since I was fifteen." He ran a hand across his pecs. "One night, my dad caught my friend and me fooling around. He beat me. The next morning when he went to work, I ran away and never returned."

"Your mother let this happen?"

"She's dead."

"I'm sorry," I muttered, glancing at Jackson to ensure he was still asleep. I knew I'd made the right choice but worried about the repercussions.

"I won't let him hurt you," Peter muttered.

"Did you just read my mind?" I asked in surprise.

"Yes."

He was a fast learner. As I slid the mattress over us, the enclosed trench became dark. We'd survive the daylight hours if we were left alone. As I lowered myself to the dirt floor, Peter curled beside me. I knew it wasn't for sexual reasons. Instead, I got the sense that he needed to protect me.

Jackson

WHILE OBSERVING the sleeping figure, Peter's eyes suddenly popped open, filled with fear. I swiftly placed my hand on his shoulder, enforcing my command over him. With an ominous snarl, I stated that I held the power here. In response, Peter bared his sharp fangs, attempting to claim his dominance over me. My mind raced when I recognized that he had become one of us — a vampire.

Even though irritation and fury coursed through him, eventually, he bowed his head in acknowledgment of my authority. A sense of contentment filled me as we finally reached an equilibrium in our power dynamic.

I was thrilled for a sexual reunion, my heart racing and my body responding to the memory of Peter's ability to take me deep without gagging. Pleasurable chills ran through me. But when I caught Peter's gaze, a grimace formed on his lips. I knew not to trust him. Taking him roughly by the arm, I suggested we take a stroll to become better acquainted.

Peter

I ESCAPED JACKSON'S grip and ran from the basement. The fear of what Jackson would do if he caught me spurred me on. But I soon realized it was useless — he was too fast for me, and all I could do was try to prolong the inevitable. As I looked over my shoulder in terror, he lunged at me with all his might and tackled me to the ground. I felt his cold hands around my neck, pinning me down. His mouth opened wide, showcasing his sharp fangs, glinting in the moonlight.

"You're dead!" he said with a lisp.

Hearing his flamboyant stammer, I felt a surge of power course through my veins as I pushed him away. I watched in amazement as Jackson flew across the pavement, unable to believe what had happened. I slowly sat up, eyes wide in confusion, and studied my hands closely. For the first time, I understood I had become something far more than human.

Suddenly, a noise alerted me, and I turned my gaze toward a young couple standing on the trail. I bared my fangs and hissed menacingly at them in warning. They quickly grabbed each other's hand before taking off in the opposite direction.

As I turned back to Jackson, I could see the fear in his eyes as he struggled to comprehend what had just happened. He had become powerless before me, evident by his trembling body and unwillingness to move.

The tension between us was palpable as we locked eyes, neither willing to back down. Finally, I broke the silence and spoke firmly, stating that Antonio needed to feed. My icy glare conveyed my deep distrust and loathing toward him. With contempt, I spat out the words, "I despise you. You piece of shit. I have never met anyone so unpleasant and dishonest as you."

Antonio

OPENING MY EYES, I realized the protective covering was no longer above me. I whipped my head around and realized Jackson and Peter were gone. However, so was the sun. The daylight hours had passed.

I crawled from the pit and noticed an unconscious, naked man on the dirt floor. He had a Southern Decadence festival sticker on his cheek. For anyone unfamiliar with the event, think of Mardi Gras. It's an annual Labor Day event put on by the gay community. The man's fitted faux leather pants and shiny metallic T-shirt lying beside him shouted tweaker boy.

"Hello? Anyone here?" I asked.

No answer.

I knelt and hovered over the man. He was cute, but the beer stench on his breath was overwhelming. I eyed his sex, resting against his thigh, and caressed his chest.

He opened his eyes.

I tamed him.

His eyes fluttered and then became sleepy. His breathing rate dropped. I inspected his neckline, looking for a puncture wound, and found none. Peter must have brought him here. I thought for me to feed. "I'm sorry," I muttered and bit his neck.

As I tasted his blood's metallic flavor, I began to suck too quickly. My stomach tensed up, making me pull away and curse myself for my eagerness. As I looked down, his naked body lay there, relaxed and exposed. His dick measured around five inches and was uncircumcised.

He groaned as he emerged from the trance-like state which had overtaken him.

"You have a beautiful body," I said through slightly lisping lips made visible by my fangs.

"Vampires are real," he gasped in astonishment.

"Of course we are," I replied before leaning forward and slipping his dick inside my mouth. It came alive, and I moaned excitedly.

"I'm on PrEP. Do you swallow?" he asked.

I stopped sucking and raised my head. "It doesn't matter if you're diseased or not. It won't affect me." Then I realized his fear seemed to have evaporated, and he responded with a smile when I offered to make his vacation memorable. "Why aren't you afraid of me?"

"I can tell you're a kind man."

As he laid back, I licked his testicles. His scrotum was firm, not saggy. Then, I lifted his legs and ventured toward his anus. He moaned loudly as my tongue glided over his hole. Here was another man that enjoyed ass play.

"Oh, yes!" he moaned, wanting to get fucked.

Seeing his erection dangling above his face turned me on. I wasn't a top, so I screwed his ass with my tongue. He stroked himself, moans increasing. I went back to his testicles, tonguing them as they bounced back and forth. Suddenly, sperm shot from his dick and landed on his face.

"Oh, yeah, don't stop! I'm still coming!" he moaned, masturbating in a frenzy.

I watched, impressed, as he caught the remaining fluid in his mouth. Lowering his legs, I kissed him deeply, tasting him. My craving was so intense that I licked his face clean.

Dangerously unsatiated, I realized I had to get him out of the basement before my blood craving took over. I thought I owed him that much for permitting me to play with him.

He was still weak, so I dressed him. "Thank you," I said, kissing him one last time. Then I got dressed and lifted him in my arms.

"I had sex with a vampire," he mumbled, grinning in his delirious state as I carried him from the basement.

I smiled at his contentment despite my own rising hunger. Outside, I figured the tourists would assume he was drunk and ignore him if I left him on the sidewalk. I sat him down, then waved goodbye and thanked him again.

As I walked back toward the basement, it was hard to think because I needed blood. I didn't know where the boys were, and the anxiousness surfaced again.

I came upon a drunkard around eighty years old. The yellowing of his skin told me he had jaundice — liver disease. He'd be dying soon. I yanked him up and dragged him into the alley. I smelled piss as it ran down his pant leg — he realized his life was ending.

I bit him before he could shout for help. When his heart stopped beating, that was my cue to stop sucking. He was dead.

I dropped him and ran from the alleyway.

As I returned to the basement, I lowered myself into the pit. I was still determining where Peter and Jackson were. Alright, I'll be honest, I was too afraid to leave and waited for their arrival. It was strange, as I had never been afraid of doing things alone. I didn't understand why this fear had suddenly taken over me.

As I stretched out on the dirt floor, I tried to calm my racing thoughts by listening to the rhythmic sound of my heartbeat. Hoping it would lull me to sleep, I eventually drifted into a deep slumber. But then, suddenly, my eyes shot open, and everything seemed cloudy at first. Gradually, though, as my vision came into focus, I saw Robert pushing my father into a holding cell, causing him to stumble and fall to the floor. Confused and disoriented, I mumbled, "Dad?" realizing this wasn't just a dream. Somehow, I was experiencing some form of telepathy.

I could see them even though I wasn't present in the room. The cement walls told me they were underground in the compound. There was nothing I could do but watch in horror, feeling both helpless and powerless.

"Stand up," Robert demanded.

Bruised and battered, unable to fight back, my father continued to lie on the floor, helpless.

"Do you remember the evening I stole your wife?" Robert asked, unbuttoning my dad's pants.

"Don't do this . . ." my father pleaded.

"It was you I wanted to kidnap, not her."

"Stop . . ."

"This is my last chance to play with you before you die. It's now or never."

Robert took out my dad's dick.

"It's time I sucked my first cock."

"No . . ." I cried out.

"You have no idea how long I've wanted to do this. I'll be honest with you. I feared I'd enjoy sucking too much and turn into some limp-wristed fairy. I know that's not the case now. How naïve of me, don't you think?"

"Robert, please . . ."

"Do you find me attractive?"

"No."

"That's upsetting." Robert frowned. "Many nights, I beat off thinking of you. There, I said it. Oh, William, why couldn't we have been friends? I think we belong together."

My dad shuddered, disgusted and sickened to hear Robert's innermost feelings.

"I deceived myself, believing I wasn't gay. I wasted so many years that could have been filled with joy."

"Just kill me."

"Oh, no . . ." Robert moaned, eyeing my father's uncircumcised dick. "It's beautiful! William, everything about you excites me. I would save you if you promised to spend eternity with me."

My father looked resolute and mumbled he'd rather die.

I watched in disbelief as Robert bent down and took my father inside his mouth. Feeling embarrassed and uncomfortable, I wanted to look away, but something held me there, watching the scene unfold.

Suddenly, Robert pulled away with a sour expression.

He wiped his mouth, trying to remove the pre-cum from his tongue. Giving up on fellatio, he began masturbating my dad. The rhythm started slowly but increased as my father moaned in pleasure.

"No!" my dad wailed in surprise as seminal fluid erupted from his shaft. His body spasmed as load after load squirted onto Robert's hand.

I couldn't believe what I was witnessing. I knew this was something I was never supposed to see. "Oh, Dad. I'm sorry."

"Fuck, that's hot," Robert exclaimed, grinning.

"You bastard," my father said, disgusted and spent.

"I've never seen someone come so much." Robert wiped his hands on my father's boxer shorts. "You're the epitome of a virile man."

"Damn you!"

Completely taken over by his lustful desires, Robert tore off his military fatigues and straddled my father's chest. He proceeded to pleasure himself with such vigor that it only took seconds until his load exploded from deep within.

William

DAMN HIM! I turned away as Robert's load landed on my chest in large amounts. That bastard molested me. I hated him for it. I smelled his semen, and it repulsed me.

I grimaced as he rubbed his dickhead through the warm fluid. He smeared it across my chest, proud of his achievement. The burning sensation became too intense, so I flicked it off my chest.

"Maybe I'll kidnap you and keep you as my slave," Robert murmured as his smile broadened into a sinister grin.

"Kill me," I said, disappointed in myself for ejaculating. Was it because I hadn't beaten off in a long time, or did the DTAV man awaken the fluid inside me? I was confused. This infuriated me, and I blamed myself for getting hard. I let this happen.

I clenched my fists as I stared at Robert, vowing revenge.

My hatred for him was so intense it felt enjoyable to think about killing him. The infantry soldiers beat me up badly. And the shock of what just happened shut down my brain. As my eyes closed, Antonio's face flashed before me in a moment of clarity, and I mentally whispered an apology for failing to shield him from this predator. If only I had seized the opportunity to eliminate Robert, none of this would have transpired.

Antonio

I AWOKE FROM a deep slumber to the sound of my father's apology. Feeling disoriented, I sat up to see my brothers lying next to each other. Peter was spread out on his back, while Jackson lay face down. Not understanding what was happening, I scrambled out of the trench and rushed toward them.

Upon closer inspection, I saw blood seeping from Jackson's ass. In a state of panic, I shook Peter until he woke up. "What did you do?" I cried out, gesturing toward Jackson.

"I raped him. The scoundrel got what he deserved," he replied, sitting up, perplexed by my line of questioning.

"You've killed him!" I accused.

Peter stared at me in shock, unable to grasp the severity of his actions. As I continued to gaze at him, he shook his head and raised his hands in confusion.

"What are you talking about?" he asked.

I sighed and grabbed his shoulders. "Your sperm is poisonous. It's lethal to other vampires," I yelled, regretting not explaining this. "I'll never find my father and David now!"

"My jizz is poisonous?"

"Yes!" I said, shaking him.

Peter sniffed the air, smelling something peculiar. His face contorted with disgust, finding its origin — shit on the head of his dick. He quickly stood and looked for something to wipe it off with.

"Did you come inside him?" I asked urgently.

Peter shook his head, perturbed by my questioning. Spotting a newspaper in the corner of the basement, he walked away, gesturing for me to stop with my line of questioning.

"He's not dead then!" I yelled, elated.

That woke up Jackson, and he opened his eyes.

I watched as the recollection of the assault returned to his face. He stood, raising his fists.

"Where's that fucker?"

"He's cleaning the shit off his dick," I said, pointing toward Peter in the basement corner, holding a dirty newspaper.

"That bastard raped me!" Jackson wailed.

"Hopefully, it was a lesson well learned," I said, inhaling the repulsive scent. "Clean yourself up. You smell like shit!"

Robert

AS I ENTERED the compound's office, my eyes immediately landed on the nameplate on the desk. It was neatly engraved, reading 'Chief of Staff.' As I stepped forward at attention, Salvatore Leone, the man in charge, pushed his chair back and stood up. As he crossed his arms, my eyes couldn't help but wander over his imposing six-foot-two-inch frame. His muscular build was captivating and could easily grace the pages of a vintage beefcake magazine. Despite his intimidating presence, I couldn't help but feel intrigued by the man before me.

Waiting for my reprimand, I hoped it would be non-judicial and not dismissal from service.

"How does reduction in grade sound?"

"Sir, I completed the job. David saved him behind my back," I said as I became mesmerized by his looks. It was apparent he was Antonio's biological father. They could have been identical twins, excluding the age difference.

"Who has the bigger dick?" I wondered. The chief of staff was in the steam room once, naked. I remembered being impressed by its circumference, and I could tell it got massive once hard.

"David, your son, the defector?"

I was jolted out of my thoughts, a wave of shame washing over me. "Yes, sir." Salvatore inhaled deeply, his head bowing in contemplation. After a few moments, he raised his head, his gaze piercing mine as if seeking the truth.

"Does my son know about me?" Salvatore queried.

"He has no clue. His father hasn't . . ."

"Jesus Christ! I'm his father!" he snapped.

Salvatore's anger boiled over uncontrollably. Clearly, he found the thought of his illegitimate son being attracted to the same sex unbearable. Perhaps, he felt a bizarre sense of responsibility. Could his genetic composition be the blame for his son's sexuality?

"William has not told him."

"Once my soldiers find out about my queer son, they'll question my honorable service. Do you get that? I told you to kill him. I gave you a simple order, and you failed. You're incompetent, and I should dishonorably discharge you. I will not have this whoreson ruin my career."

"Sir . . . I'll make this right. I'll find and kill him."

***

As I stared at David through the cold, unforgiving bars of his jail cell, my voice took on a tone of accusation. "Your actions have left me disgraced in front of my superior officer." I deliberately held back the words of Salvatore

Leone, worried that revealing them would only fuel his sense of victory. David's face twisted into a sneer.

"This is your fault!"

In response, I could only shake my head, the disbelief evident in my voice as I retorted, "I don't deserve this." His eyes bore into me like two fiery daggers.

"Are you serious?" he barked, his voice echoing off the walls. "I told you to leave me alone!"

"I'm sorry," I stammered, trying to keep my composure. "I thought I was helping." His answer was swift and brutal.

"Fuck you!"

Despite the hurtful words, I held my ground. "I've apologized," I shot back, my voice stern. "I'm your father. Show some respect." But David was not moved. Instead, he gestured rudely with his middle finger, his defiance as clear as day. "Your mother would be ashamed," I said, trying to appeal to his conscience. But his response was like a punch in the gut.

"My mother, who you killed?"

His words hit me like a freight train, leaving me in shock. I hadn't anticipated such an accusation from him. A flood of thoughts washed over me, each more troubling than the last. My heart pounded like a drum, and I struggled to respond coherently. But no words came. I stood mute, unable to defend myself, overwhelmed by a wave of guilt that threatened to consume me.

"I know you killed her!" David murmured.

Laced with bitterness and hurt, his words hung heavy in the air, their sting refusing to fade away. "She didn't want to be immortal," I finally managed to utter, my voice barely above a whisper. Shame weighed heavy on my words. The gravity of what I had done and its consequences began to sink in, leaving me feeling small and remorseful.

He spat in my face.

I wiped away the sputum.

David knew joining the ranks of the infantry came with stringent directives. The most crucial rule: relationships are forbidden. I offered her immortality. She had the opportunity to flee New Orleans and escape death. At first, her initial reaction led me to believe she was interested. However, her facial expression soon shifted dramatically, leaving no room for doubt about her rejection. She refused my offer, not out of fear of the unknown, but because I repulsed her. Her understanding of my bisexuality and my history of unfaithfulness with men significantly influenced her decision.

"I did everything within my power to save her. I truly did!" The desperation in my voice was palpable. I hung my head, guilt gnawing at me for the lie I'd just told.

"Bullshit!"

I looked up, locking eyes with my son. The truth stood between us, an unavoidable reality. "You're right," I admitted, my voice barely audible. "I took your mother's life, not because I was ordered to. I killed her to protect my secret." The words left a bitter taste in my mouth. "She intended to expose me to the infantry and reveal everything."

Salvatore

AS ROBERT departed the office, I found myself drawn to the top drawer of my desk. There, nestled between old reports and miscellaneous items, lay a photograph, a relic of my past. It was a picture of Antonio's mother, her smile forever captured in the stillness of time.

I lifted the photograph.

Settling back into my chair, I let myself get lost in the memory it invoked. The room around me faded as I sat there, my gaze transfixed on her image. I felt a sense of nostalgia as I traced my fingers over the photograph. I remembered the times we spent together.

Reflecting on the past, I couldn't ignore the extent I had

gone to safeguard my identity. The mere thought of her discovering I was a vampire filled me with an overwhelming dread. Had the infantry caught even the slightest whiff of my relationship, it would have altered my fate, prematurely ending my military career.

While serving brought me personal pride and satisfaction, it unintentionally brought tension to my relationship. The extended hours, regular deployments, and unpredictability of my profession meant I frequently had to place my responsibilities above my personal life. This left Antonio's mother feeling overlooked and marginalized, ultimately leading to the dissolution of our relationship.

Years later, I traveled to the Northwest to see what kind of life she had built for herself. As soon as I laid eyes on her, she was holding the hand of a young boy who reminded me so much of myself when I was his age. It all became clear at that moment — I was staring at my son.

She had become pregnant and didn't tell me.

The anger swelled inside me. Desperate to make things right, I returned to New Orleans and commanded Robert — my Master Sergeant — to kidnap her immediately.

After her capture, curiosity compelled me to take trips back north to watch over my son and observe his growth into adulthood. While tailing him through town one fateful evening, he stumbled into a hotel, unaware of my presence.

Using all my energy, I levitated onto the room's balcony undetected like some vengeful spirit from beyond the grave. I had a deep sense of dread, anticipating the worst possible outcome. And there it was, played out before my eyes in vivid detail. My son was submitting himself willingly to a man with no sign of resistance whatsoever. That was enough to shake me to the core of my being, for my son was nothing more than a filthy queer.

In a fit of anger, I scrutinized the photograph once more. The recollection of our shared history now carried a bitter aftertaste. She had breached my trust, giving birth to a monster. With a swift motion, I discarded the photograph into the trashcan.

Antonio

I GLANCED OVER at Peter and noticed the curiosity etched on his face. He was deliberating whether to join us on our journey or go his own way. Given the increasing danger in New Orleans, it would be understandable for him to leave rather than risk his life by staying here. So, I quietly asked him what his plans were. Peter responded quickly and confidently, declaring that he was going with me. However, I couldn't help but notice the disgruntled look he shot toward Jackson as he spoke those words.

I was amused as I watched Jackson attend to his bodily needs in an inappropriate place. The ravishment had caused the contents of his bowels to stir. When he requested a sanitary item to clean himself, it prompted me to stifle a smile at the situation. Peter paused in his movements and seemed to recognize this as an opportunity to assert his dominance within the group. In a swift motion, Peter grabbed a piece of discarded newspaper from the ground and fiercely warned Jackson not to lay a finger on either of us again. He thrust the paper forward as he spoke, making his point clear.

Jackson's expression shifted from brazenness to quiet submission as he grabbed the newspaper, mumbling that he got it.

With our arms folded, we held our ground, purposefully encroaching on his comfort zone. His embarrassment was more than obvious, mirrored in his reddened face. Having seen enough, I turned to Peter and smirked knowingly. He returned the nod, assured that Jackson had learned his lesson.

Jackson

AS I STOOD THERE, my nakedness exposed for all to see, I felt a deep humiliation and degradation. Evidently, they had deliberately chosen this course of action to humiliate me, and I had no choice but to comply. Yet, with every passing second, my rage was growing stronger.

I shot Peter a fierce glare, communicating through my eyes that his behavior was not going unnoticed, and he would eventually pay for it. But, as if reading my thoughts, he spun around and shook his finger, warning me not to think about retaliating.

I was frustrated by his power over me, and I couldn't help but mutter an expletive under my breath, wishing I could drain him of his blood. After all, he was new to the vampire world and seemed to think he had a certain level of control. The audacity! However, a plan suddenly occurred to me, and I quickly tried to mask my mischievous smile from them, hoping they wouldn't catch onto my secret scheme.

I caught sight of their smirking faces. In response, I flashed a defiant grin as I picked up the shovel leaning against the wall. Standing tall, I shrugged off any lingering embarrassment. With one final act of rebellion, I flipped them off and filled the hole I had just soiled.

Antonio

AS WE APPROACHED Lafayette Cemetery #1, we felt a sense of foreboding creeping up on us. The moon was full in the sky, casting an eerie glow over the entire area. Looking up at the wrought iron gate, I couldn't help but be drawn to its twisted spires and intricate design. Despite the warning signs surrounding the cemetery, I felt a powerful urge to explore further, to uncover the hidden secrets.

With a deep breath, the three of us clambered over the gate, our hands grasping at the cold metal as we hoisted ourselves up. As we landed on the other side, the gate let out an ear-splitting creak as though protesting our intrusion. We looked at each other nervously, wondering if we had made a mistake coming here.

As we made our way through the cemetery, which was thick with the presence of death, my dad's words echoed in my head. He had told me that they buried their dead above ground due to the high water table. Otherwise, the coffins would resurface in storms. This bizarre fact made me shudder, especially as I noticed Jackson had distanced himself from us. I called out loudly for him to wait, sure that his sullenness stemmed from Peter screwing him over.

"Damn him!" Peter said, running to catch up.

When we turned the corner, he wasn't there. "Goddamnit!" I said, knowing I was fucked without him. "You made him angry! Now, what are we going to do?"

Peter levitated into the air.

I watched as he rose and scanned the cemetery. Then, he smiled and pointed in Jackson's direction.

"He's up ahead, playing games."

"More like punishing us!" I said, following Peter as he returned to the ground and headed toward Jackson.

I ran into Peter seconds later.

"Fuck!" I yelled.

He'd stopped abruptly, seeing a Reaper walking in our direction with outstretched arms. I couldn't help but question why the creature was hunting in the cemetery. And then I realized the locked gates imprisoned him. He didn't have the strength to climb the fence. I imagined his only meals were rodents.

"Give . . . me . . . blood . . ."

"I'll take care of him," I said as the creature stepped forward, hissing at us. I felt sorry for him because he was old and missing a fang. I decided to give him blood instead of slicing him in half. I slashed my wrist with my sharp fingernail.

The Reaper grabbed my arm and started sucking.

As he drank, I read his mind. He'd been an infantry soldier but was now retired. I realized he was drinking too fast. I tried to pull away, but he wouldn't release my arm. I remembered Jackson's warning.

"Help me!" I yelled.

As Peter moved in to pull the thing off me, the Reaper pulled away and grasped at his throat. My blood had poisoned him.

The Reaper fell to the ground and took his last breath.

The next moment, he turned ash-white and started deteriorating. First, his face caved in. Then his chest, and lastly, his extremities. Finally, all that was left was a pile of clothes.

Peter's eyes went wide with disbelief.

"We should have cut his head off," I said, realizing my foolish mistake.

We hurried on. As we turned a corner, there stood Jackson with his arms crossed.

"It's about time," Jackson said.

"Why didn't you wait?" I asked, irritated.

Jackson didn't answer. He just pointed. "The entrance to the compound is straight ahead."

He'd explained earlier that we'd use the emergency exit to enter the facility. I chuckled, visualizing the vampires lined up in an orderly fashion while exiting the compound.

I asked him about the water table because it seemed like an underground compound would flood. He said the complex was safe because of an elaborate pumping system.

We continued, passing an old mausoleum with a missing front panel. I looked inside, expecting to see scattered bones. But instead, a startled rat scampered away into the darkness.

"Pay attention!" Peter said, pushing me forward.

"All right!" I whispered.

I tried to focus, but I couldn't. The dates on the crypts interested me. And then, I noticed a mausoleum defaced with graffiti. 'Death to All Vampires' was spray-painted across the front plate. I caught my breath. That was the organization's name. Did the DTAV do this, or was it kids playing tricks on the ghoulish creatures of the night?

Peter sighed in frustration, pushing me forward again. "Keep walking," he whispered.

My mind continued to wander. I thought about David. I couldn't wait to hold him in my arms. But then, I thought about the anonymous sex I'd had. My anxiety surfaced again. Would he care about my sexual affairs?

Jackson halted at a crypt and raised his index finger toward a concrete statue above it.

Upon closer inspection, I discovered that the sculpture atop the structure was a cherub — an infant with a rosy complexion and a pair of wings. To my amazement, its head moved, and it made eye contact. I immediately shut my eyes, thinking my vision had been playing tricks on me. When I reopened them, the first detail I noticed was its tiny, uncircumcised penis. It gave me a mischievous smirk as I focused on its face while two sharp fangs peeped beneath its lips.

The cherub bit Jackson's finger.

"What the fuck!" I yelled, not believing my eyes.

The statue tasted his blood and smacked his lips.

"You have the blood of a vampire," he said in a child-like voice.

"Thank you," Jackson replied with a bow.

"You may enter."

A loud rumble erupted, and the heavy marble door slid open. Jackson entered the tomb. As Peter and I stepped forward, the door abruptly shut in our faces. We stepped back, surprised and bewildered.

"What the hell?" I shouted.

The statue turned and pointed at me.

"I have never seen you before. Who are you?" he asked.

Afraid of the living statue, I froze.

"Give him your finger and tell him your name," Peter murmured, pushing my arm forward.

"I'm Antonio," I said.

The statue eyed me cautiously.

It was apparent he didn't like me. I wasn't sure why, and then I realized it had read my mind. The statue questioned my authenticity. Did he figure out I was an imposter? I blocked my mind, stopping him from gathering any more information.

"Can we enter?" I asked.

"Let me taste your blood!"

I raised my finger toward his mouth. As the cherub started to bite down, it scowled at me. I pulled my finger away, frightened. The longer our eyes remained locked, the more I hated him. I raised my clenched fist toward his scrotum without realizing it.

Peter swiftly grabbed my elbow, stopping me in my tracks.

"Do you want to break your hand? It's a concrete statue."

"My hand would heal," I muttered, defiantly lifting my middle finger toward the statue's mouth, silently mouthing, "Screw you." I had reached the end of my patience with its delaying tactics.

The statue eyed me suspiciously once again and then grabbed my finger. As it bit down, I winced in pain. I held my breath as it smacked its lips, waiting for permission to enter. Finally, the concrete figure made his pronouncement. This time his infantile voice had an edge to it.

"You have the blood of a vampire. You may enter."

The door opened.
I entered.
The crypt door slammed shut behind me.
I stood still in the darkness until my eyes adjusted. As I stepped forward, I saw the staircase descending into the belly of the vampire compound. I put a hand on the glistening cement wall. It was wet. Adding to my anxiety, a drainage gutter ran alongside the staircase. Behind me, the mausoleum door opened, and Peter stepped through.

"I should have kicked that angel's ass for you!" he said, appraising the entrance to the compound.

"I don't like this place," I muttered.

"I don't either!"

I closely followed Peter, carefully matching his steps as he descended the steep staircase. The lack of a railing made the descent somewhat precarious, so I instinctively reached out to grasp the wall for support, steadying myself as I continued downward. Approximately every twenty feet, low-wattage bulbs lit the way.

We descended the winding staircase until we arrived at the entrance of an expansive room. Peering into the darkness, multiple pathways meandered away in different directions. Suddenly, hurried footsteps echoed off the walls, prompting us to take defensive stances.

"Jackson?" I whispered.

"I hope so!" Peter replied.

Peter crouched down with his fists clenched, ready for battle.

Jackson burst out from one of the hallways, sprinting toward us.

"What the hell are you doing?" Peter yelled, his voice filled with confusion and anger.

"Peter!" I interjected, trying to calm the escalating tension.

"The holding cells are in that direction," Jackson informed us, pointing down the hallway. He then turned to Peter — his face twisted into a displeased expression.

"Stop!" I yelled, seeing Peter's fist rising, poised for an attack.

Jackson smirked, taking a step back. He then turned around and motioned for us to follow. As we carefully proceeded through the dimly lit hallway, with Jackson leading the way, I could hear faint voices echoing from somewhere up ahead. This sudden realization made me stop in my tracks, straining my ears to listen more closely.

"I hear voices!" I whispered urgently.

"The guards are up ahead," Jackson confirmed in a hushed tone.

"What are we going to do?" I asked, my voice wavering with uncertainty.

"Jump them?" Peter suggested, barely above a whisper.

"We'll poison the fuckers," Jackson said.

Before Peter or I could utter a single word, Jackson swiftly slashed his wrist, causing blood to start dripping onto the cold cement floor. I caught my breath as I saw the oozing red fluid. Instinctively, my tongue darted out, moistening my lips. Recognizing my excitement, I mentally reminded myself to stay calm.

Taking a deep, calming breath, I watched as Jackson continued down the hallway toward the source of the muffled voices, leaving a trail of blood in his wake. As he vanished from sight, I became lost in my thoughts, contemplating the gravity of our situation. At that moment, Peter suddenly jolted me back to reality, breaking me free from my intense reverie.

"What's he doing?" Peter asked.

"He's leaving a trail. The guards won't be able to resist following the blood. They'll become poisoned by the time they reach us." I noticed Peter's eyebrows furrowing as he regarded our comrade with concern and suspicion.

"He's up to something."

I could sense Peter's suspicion toward Jackson. I attempted to decipher his thoughts, but he turned and shook his head.

"Keep out of my mind."

"What are you planning to do?" I whispered, knowing he was up to something too.

"The less you know, the better."

The sound of Jackson's hurried footsteps echoed through the hallway. I peered over my shoulder and saw him sprinting toward us. A mischievous expression was etched on his face as he glanced back to see the guards in pursuit. I watched his grin widen, almost as if he were taunting them.

Jackson stopped before Peter — his cold stare as icy as his words. He grinned as he declared, "You're dead!" His remark sent a chill down my spine. It was then that I knew we were in trouble. Jackson had his agenda, and I knew it wouldn't end well.

Jackson

OBSERVING THE guard's reactions was amusing as I shouted an expletive and rudely gestured in their direction. They seemed taken aback and exchanged expressions of astonishment before jumping out of their seats and pursuing me from the desk.

My pulse raced with adrenaline. As I approached Peter, I taunted him with the words, "You're dead!" Then, I ran toward the staircase, chuckling with amusement as I glanced over my shoulder at the guards. I repeated my obscene gesture again to rub salt in their wounds.

My plan to kill Peter was going to work. Unfortunately, Antonio would succumb to death too, but oh, well. This was payback. That little queer had it coming to him. How dare he take advantage of me? I'm a top, not a bottom.

"Jackson!" Antonio shrieked.

As I ran up the stairs, I heard Antonio's voice screaming

my name in a terrified tone. The urgency in his voice made me stop and turn around to check on him. I saw the security guards advancing toward them, and he looked helpless and defenseless. Despite my initial excitement about the plan to stop Peter, my conscience immediately kicked in, and I realized the gravity of my actions. Damn it! I cursed inwardly, feeling a wave of shame and regret. As I watched the guards closing in on them, I couldn't help but wonder what it was about Antonio I liked so much. Raising my hands in defeat, I descended the staircase.

Antonio

AS I RETREATED from the guards advancing toward me, my heart filled with an overwhelming sense of disbelief. The sting of betrayal sliced through me like a sharp blade, leaving a gaping wound that threatened to engulf me. I couldn't shake off the disappointment and sadness that consumed me. Everything seemed to unravel, and I had no control over it.

The guards continued to crawl toward me on all fours, their faces contorted with a feverish hunger that seemed otherworldly. They resembled ravenous beasts, their tongues eagerly lapping the blood from the cold, cement floor. Their movements were slow and calculated, and I could feel their eyes boring into me from every direction. It was a terrifying sight, and I wondered if this was how it would end. Suddenly, one of them crumpled to the cement, overwhelmed by the toxic effects of the blood.

Peter pushed me out of harm's way and declared he'd take care of the other advancing soldier. I offered him his knife, which I had been carrying in my pocket, ready for any situation. He accepted it gratefully and stood his ground, prepared to fight for our lives, no matter the cost.

"Step back!" Jackson shouted, surprising us.

As I turned to see Jackson's sudden and unexpected return, I felt a glimmer of hope wash over me. He charged toward the now-standing vampire, swinging his machete with all his might, aiming for the creature's throat. The blade sliced through the air with a sharp whooshing sound before contacting the vampire's neck. The machete sliced through the guard's flesh like a hot knife through butter in one swift motion. Blood gushed from the opened jugular as the vampire's head fell to the floor, signaling an end to his reign of terror. The sight of the vampire's lifeless body twitching on the cement as it gasped for its last breath was gruesome and satisfying.

Peter turned toward Jackson and threatened him with the knife. "You son-of-a-bitch! You left us to die!"

"I returned, didn't I?"

"I don't trust you," Peter stated firmly.

The intoxicated guard managed to stand up and began staggering toward us, his eyes glazed over and his movements unsteady.

"Guys?" I said nervously, pointing in his direction, urging Peter to shift his focus to the imminent threat.

"I'm going to fuck you up!" Peter forewarned Jackson, then ran to the advancing guard and slit his throat.

***

As we stepped carefully over the guard's bodies, I couldn't help but shiver at the cold, lifeless look in their eyes that seemed to follow us even as we moved farther away. However, we had no time to lose, so we pressed on, our footsteps echoing ominously in the dimly lit corridor. Finally, we reached a door that led us into a room bathed in bright fluorescent light. My eyes struggled to adjust to the harsh glow as row after row of inmates stared back at us from behind metal bars, a sea of hopeless faces that sent a chill down my spine.

My heart raced with anticipation as I scanned their faces, searching for any sign of my father and David. But as I reached the end of the cell, my heart sank like a stone in my chest — they were nowhere to be found. I took a deep breath, still weighed down by the shock of Jackson's actions. My heart was heavy with sadness, and my mind reeled with confusion, unsure how to proceed.

"We'll find them," Peter said, consoling me.

"I need nourishment," Jackson shouted, getting our attention. I turned, seeing him eyeing the prisoners.

"We all need to feed," I said, hating his selfishness. "What are you doing?" I shouted moments later, seeing him lift a set of keys off the guard's desk. I held my breath as the prisoners backed up, startled to see him unlocking the door. I shouted for him to stop, but he ignored me and entered the cell, grabbing the closest prisoner — a middle-aged man.

The inmate screamed, seeing his fanged mouth.

"I should kill him now," Peter grumbled.

Peter ran inside and pushed Jackson away. He silenced the prisoner with his fangs. Then he feasted, leaving Jackson to find his own meal.

As I entered the cell to calm the frightened inmates, Jackson captured one of them and started to feed. I restored calmness by hissing and threatening the remaining prisoners with my incisors.

As my comrades fed, I saw a handsome, curly brown-haired man with sparkling green eyes stepping from the group of inmates. He appeared to be a little older than me, and the weird thing was he wasn't frightened. He was average height, clean-shaven, and masculine but had a feminine flair. I knew he was gay, and I was willing to bet he was verse and liked it both ways. "What's your name, and why are you here?"

"My name is Harry. I accosted a Federation soldier on Bourbon Street. I was drunk."

"I see."

"Can you help me?

"Escape?"

"Make me into a vampire?"

I knew we didn't have time for this, but I was mad. Mad as hell. The infantry changed everything in my life. I was bent on revenge now. "Yes," I said as Jackson lifted his head from his blood source, questioning my response. I raised the palm of my hand to quiet him.

I didn't know if Harry would be our ally, but, at this point, it didn't matter. I wanted to make as many gay vampires as possible. This would piss off the organization.

The handsome man stepped forward and craned his neck toward me. My fangs poked out, and I bit his neck. In no time, I drained him of his blood, almost to the point of unconsciousness. Afterward, I slashed my wrist with my fingernail.

"I'm so thirsty," he said, staring me in the eyes.

I could tell he trusted me. I momentarily got lost in his beauty. He had a European look that I liked. I didn't know if he was uncircumcised, but I thought he could be. I was pretty good at guessing. I wanted to suck him off, surprising myself. I realized my sexual desires were getting stronger.

Harry moaned, snapping me out of my dream state.

"I'm sorry," I said, raising my wrist to his mouth.

He grabbed my arm and started sucking.

I closed my eyes, and then, after a few minutes, I pulled my arm away because I was getting weak.

"I want more," he moaned.

I lowered Harry to the floor and straddled his chest.

Unbuttoning my jeans, I masturbated, thinking about David fucking my ass. "You must swallow my sperm if you want to be immortal," I said breathlessly.

Harry opened his mouth wide.

His tongue shot out, wanting to catch every drop of my life-saving fluid. He moaned in anticipation.

I groaned in pleasure as I shot a big load in his direction. He caught my milky substance and immediately consumed it.

His body began to shake uncontrollably, and I looked down in disbelief at how quickly the transformation was happening.

Then a familiar voice grabbed my attention, and I whipped around to see Robert pushing David into the cell. My heart raced as I tried to make sense of the situation.

"What do we have here?" Robert asked.

"David!" I cried, almost forgetting that I was sitting on Harry's chest. I took my hand off my spent dick and leaped up. The expression of disgust on David's face froze me in place.

"You're a fucking whore!" he spat.

"I told you he was a tramp and worthless!" Robert said while unbinding David's wrists. "You shouldn't have saved him. He's a scum-sucking-whore, and he doesn't deserve your big cock!"

My guilt came flooding back. I lowered my head and thought about the business travelers I had sex with at home. The two guys I blew in the bathroom stall, Crooked Nose, Angelo, Robert, and Jackson. Even though Jackson raped me, I enjoyed it.

"Antonio!" Peter shouted, frightened.

I turned to see two soldiers tackling him and Jackson to the floor. I should never have taken the time to make Harry into a vampire.

"Peter, I'm so sorry," I shouted.

"You're trash!" Robert smirked, pointing at me.

"I concur," David uttered in agreement.

My mouth dropped, dumbfounded at hearing them. Why is my lover saying this? The hatred he felt toward me was eye-opening and shocking.

"I blame you for everything!" Robert hissed and back-handed me.

I hit the cement hard, my head spinning from the impact and the betrayal. As I struggled to regain my bearings, I knew I had to find a way to save Peter and myself while also discovering the truth behind David's sudden change of heart. Opening my eyes, I heard Harry returning to life. I knew Robert would kill him if he knew I'd made him into a vampire. "Keep quiet if you want to stay alive," I whispered, seeing Robert and David's heads bent, conversing with each other.

"This man is evil and will kill you."

Harry blinked, acknowledging my warning.

"When it's safe, feed on one of the prisoners. You'll die if you don't get nourishment. And never, never drink from a vampire. Their blood will kill you. Make as many gay vampires as possible. I hope we meet again."

"Thank you," Harry whispered.

Turning, I recognized one of the guards restraining Peter and Jackson with a rope — Crooked-Nose. As he escorted them out, I stood and placed my wrists together for Robert, resigned. "Do what you want with me. I don't care anymore."

Robert

AS I FORCEFULLY pushed Antonio out of the cell, I could feel the atmosphere becoming tense when David suddenly grabbed my arm, bringing me to a halt. I spun around in surprise, taken aback by his unexpected concern. His facial expression revealed that he no longer harbored the same intensity of hatred. Instead, he inquired about my intentions for Antonio — a question that left me perplexed and curious about why he would even care.

Dismissing the thought, I shook my head and concentrated on the task. Once I had successfully locked David inside the cell, I grasped Antonio's arm firmly and encouraged him to move forward.

As we returned to the hallway, I forcefully pressed him against the wall, my grip tight on his arm. And as I fixed him with a piercing gaze that left no doubt about the impending consequences he would face if he dared to defy me, a shiver of fear ran through him.

"Listen to me," I stated coldly, my voice low and menacing. "If you want to avoid a fate worse than death, you will do as I command from now on. Do you understand?"

Antonio nodded in agreement, his eyes wide with terror.

He promised to comply without further resistance, knowing full well the consequences would be severe if he failed me. Feeling satisfied with his response, I released my grip on his arm and began to lead him down the hallway toward the fate that awaited him. No amount of pleading would be able to sway my resolve now.

Antonio

NAKED AND VULNERABLE, I nervously glanced around the small, confined cell, my heart pounding as I stood in my new environment. I couldn't help but nervously glance around, taking in the sight of the other inmates who were also stripped down and standing in line. Some of them fidgeted nervously, their movements mirroring my apprehensive behavior, while others fixed their cold, steely gazes directly at me, making me feel incredibly uneasy and unprotected.

I felt violated when Robert pushed me against the cold metal bars, his strong hands firmly grasping my shoulders. His breath smelt of cigarettes as he leaned in close, whispering threats that made my skin crawl.

Nevertheless, I remained composed, reminding myself to stay brave to get out alive. I kept repeating this thought as I looked around the cell, praying for the moment I would be set free.

"I want you to fuck him," Robert shouted to the prisoners.

The inmates stared in disbelief as I stood there, my heart pounding, trying to process what was happening. No one dared to challenge Robert or utter a word of dissent.

"You!" Robert gestured at the youngest inmate, who was shielding his genitals. "Remove your hand from your cock!"

The inmate promptly uncovered his groin.

The prisoner stepped forward, and I saw with relief that he was uncircumcised. His life was in Robert's hands now. No matter how much I feared the situation, I knew that if he followed Robert's orders, there'd be a chance he'd make it out alive. As the inmate walked toward me, I whispered, "Follow his orders, or he'll kill you."

"Shut the fuck up!" Robert yelled, slapping me on the ass.

Bowing down, I parted my buttocks, hoping the young man would perform, escaping Robert's demise. As his fingers ran through my hair, I sensed his warm body pressed against mine.

Suddenly, he thrust his seven-inch erection inside me, causing me to moan and shudder with pleasure. With each movement, my body trembled with exhilaration, taking me closer to ecstasy.

I used to fear what others would think if they knew the truth. I was scared to try something new and experience the pleasure and freedom it could bring me. But something shifted — I suddenly found the courage to let go and indulge in temptation. This situation became my opportunity to embrace my body and celebrate the journey of self-discovery.

This young stud had fucked ass before. I could tell he liked it. Even though it was pleasurable, I had to play the role of someone getting tortured. I groaned and grunted each time he thrust inside me. I didn't need lubrication because my hole was moist in anticipation of getting screwed by all these men. This was a dream — a fantasy coming true.

I squeezed my anus as he climaxed inside me. As he

pulled out, Robert pointed toward the floor.

"Get on all fours."

I got in position with the young man's sperm leaking from my ass. Robert smirked, scooped it up, and fed me.

A new prisoner stepped forward with an enormous dick, and I trembled, anticipating what was to come.

My used hole excited him.

As he fucked me, I moaned as his hardness hit my prostate. To my surprise, it quickly brought me to the brink of orgasm. "I'm coming!" I shouted and stroked myself. I shot my load on the concrete floor as the man pounded me. Looking over my shoulder in ecstasy, I could see Robert's concern that I was enjoying this. Shit! I thought.

"Please make them stop!" I cried out, play-acting. It must have been believable because the sadistic bastard pointed to the next prisoner.

"You!" Robert said. "Fuck his throat."

My mouth serviced his six inches as the other man continued to screw me. I thought about David. I hoped he was watching via telepathic powers. How could he be disgusted with me when he said vampires were noncommittal all along? He was such a liar! The more I thought about it, the more it upset me.

The prisoner pulled out of my mouth.

Most of his sperm landed on my face, but the last squirt shot to the back of my throat. I swallowed, licking my lips. I moaned as if a demon had owned me.

"Fuck me! Fuck me!" I shouted, the desperation feeling more overwhelming every second. The prisoner quickened his thrusts, making me scream even louder in pleasure. I felt his hot breath on my neck as he climaxed and shot his load inside me. As he pulled out, two more prisoners stepped forward, eager to receive my service. I moaned as they entered me, once again filling my ass with their seed and shooting their load down my throat. Then the next two stepped forward, and I serviced them too. My body became a vessel for their pleasure, and the more I serviced them, the more out-of-body my experience felt.

Robert motioned the last three over, pushing the guy with the biggest dick toward my ass, gesturing for the other two to fuck my mouth.

I choked and almost suffocated as the two cocks took turns thrusting deep into my throat. The more I gagged, the harder they got. It turned me on that they loved torturing me.

I was ready for the finale. I had performed so well that Robert couldn't help but unbutton his trousers and start masturbating. As I took another load up my ass, the other two dicks simultaneously emptied onto my face. I pushed the guy out and knelt, licking my lips.

"Fuck me!" I yelled at Robert, feeling alive and empowered in a way I never had before. I wanted to be fucked again, to feel more of that overwhelming pleasure. I fingered my dripping hole, urging him to take me. It seemed my newfound whorishness had turned him on because he moaned excitedly and stepped forward. He pushed me back and lifted my legs into the air, and I inhaled sharply, expecting him to fuck me hard. But instead, he rammed his tongue inside my ass.

What the hell was this? He ate cum for the first time, moaning in delight. I pushed it out, giving him everything I thought I had. I'd lost count of how many loads I received.

I gave it to him, and he ate it.

Then, in his excited state, he screwed me.

"Fuck me! Fuck me hard, goddamnit!" I yelled. Even though I hated him, he knew how to screw ass. "Damn, you're good," I murmured, delirious. His testicles slapped my cheeks as he pounded me. It was a turn-on. And then suddenly, I felt another orgasm building.

"You're going to make me come again. Harder! Oh, here it comes!" I shouted as my eyes rolled back.

As seminal fluid shot from the head of my dick, I realized I was now multi-orgasmic. Then suddenly, I heard David's telepathic voice shouting a warning inside my head. It was a jolt of energy, an urgent message that seemed to echo through every corner of my mind.

"Don't let him cum inside you," he screamed, his voice

filled with panic and fear.

My eyes widened in shock at hearing him.

"Don't let him cum inside you!" David shouted again.

As Robert's movements quickened, my body responded with greater fervor, and I lost myself in the waves of ecstasy that washed over me. But as the rush of pleasure subsided, a nagging sense of wrongdoing crept up, filling me with shame.

My mind raced with thoughts of the Catholic church's teachings, and the guilt deepened with each passing moment. The pleasure may have been intense, but it was fleeting, and what remained was a feeling of despair and worthlessness.

***

As the jail cell door closed, I felt relieved that I wouldn't have to endure more of Robert's torment. But that feeling quickly dissipated as I began to feel a burning sensation. It was the poisonous fluid that he had injected into me during our encounter. I knew I had to act fast to expel it from my body before it caused any harm.

With my heart pounding, I mustered the strength to run for the commode. All around me, my fellow prisoners watched in silence, their fear of me seemingly replaced by a sense of pity or disgust. But I didn't care about that now. The only thing that mattered was getting rid of the poison, knowing my life depended on it. As I sat down on the cold, hard seat, I gasped in pain as I pushed with all my might. Every muscle in my body ached, but I refused to give up. I had to get as much out as possible. As I finally managed to cleanse myself of seminal fluid, it dawned on me with a newfound clarity that the fluid of the other prisoners had neutralized Robert's seed. I experienced an overwhelming sense of relief and gratitude, realizing it had genuinely been a miracle. It saved my life.

Thinking back, I struggled with a profound sense of insignificance. The teachings of the Catholic Church made me feel powerless and inadequate, preventing me from resisting Robert's advances and permitting him to seed me. Even though I could have pushed him away, my ongoing emotional turmoil left me unable to fight him. However, sitting on the toilet, I soon realized these thoughts were foolish.

I investigated the milky substance in the toilet. I couldn't believe my rectum held that much. Then, as I looked closer, I could see Robert's sperm. It had an orange tint to it. It looked different from the rest.

Anger flared within me like a raging inferno as I thought about Robert. "You're dead!" I vowed under my breath. That son-of-a-bitch would get what was coming to him. I felt violated, humiliated, and disgusted at what had just happened.

Feeling sore and physically exhausted from servicing everyone, I slowly wiped my ass, wincing in pain. Every movement was a struggle, but I knew I had to press on. I summoned all my strength to grit my teeth and brave through the torment. Despite the discomfort of my exhausted body, I needed to catch my breath and unwind for just a few moments. Thus, I stumbled and settled down on the cot, letting my muscles relax. Finally, I surrendered to the alluring temptation of slumber and drifted away into a deep and peaceful rest, completely unaware of my surroundings.

Peter

AS THE MAN with the deformed nose forcefully dragged Jackson and me down the hallway, I couldn't help but feel a sense of fear and uncertainty. My mind was racing, and I couldn't help but think about Antonio and what they might be doing to him. I closed my eyes and tried to reach him telepathically, but the thick concrete walls blocked the transmission, leaving me even more worried and anxious.

My heart raced as the man stopped before a door and pushed it open, revealing the arena beyond. As I stepped through the threshold, a gasp escaped my lips from the sight before me. I was completely taken aback, unsure of what would happen next, but completely enamored by my surroundings. The arena was magnificent in its design, with every detail carefully thought out and executed to perfection. It was clear that the designers had transformed an outdoor garden into a stunning theater set against the backdrop of a sprawling landscape. The most notable feature was the clear glass ceiling, which replaced the once-open sky and provided an unobstructed scenery view.

"This place will be filled with spectators in a matter of hours," the deformed nose man said, interrupting my thoughts.

I saw the staggered terraces. The tinted glass ensured the vampire's safety from the sunlight while allowing them to watch and enjoy the festivities. Despite the beauty of the arena, the thought of being a part of this entertainment filled me with dread.

He then spoke in a harsh tone, telling us to undress. My heart raced with fear as I looked at Jackson, silently questioning what was happening. I couldn't help but wonder if the guard was interested in our bodies or if something even more sinister was at play. As the soldier's gaze lingered on us, I tried to take comfort that we were in this together. It was clear that Jackson also felt the weight of the situation. His face contorted with fear as if he knew the guard personally.

As I began to undress, I couldn't help but wonder what would become of us. The situation seemed unreal, and I couldn't imagine the horrors ahead.

"This is the soldier who assaulted Antonio. We call him Crooked Nose," Jackson whispered so the soldier couldn't hear him.

"Is he gay?"

"Sadistic."

The soldier greeted Jackson in a manner that suggested they knew each other. His words were contemptuous as he accused Jackson of being a fool for coming to the vampire compound. With a firm grip, he turned Jackson around and delivered a sharp slap to his ass.

"You missed the party at the hotel. Now it's your turn."

"I'm not interested," Jackson spat.

"I am!" I said and walked toward him, wanting to do anything to keep us alive. Crooked Nose stepped back at first, surprised that I was advancing. "I find you attractive. I'll give you a blowjob," I said, smiling eagerly, grabbing his groin.

The soldier nodded in agreement, enjoying my flirtatiousness.

I found his looks repulsive.

I unbuttoned his military uniform, but he stopped me and removed a small bottle of amyl nitrate from his pocket. I found it unusual for a straight man to know about poppers.

"Unbutton my pants," he commanded.

As I lowered his trousers, his erection sprang out before my face. I opened my mouth and began to suck him.

He inhaled the amyl nitrate and exclaimed, "Oh, fuck . . ." under his breath. His cheeks turned a rosy shade of pink as he closed his eyes, feeling a rush of blood to his head.

As I quickly serviced him, I couldn't help but feel surprised and curious about this soldier's unexpected behavior. Nonetheless, I was pleased to have saved us from a potentially dangerous situation. Once he reached orgasm, I spat the harmful substance out and wiped my mouth.

He looked at me with both annoyance and appreciation, saying that I was a cock whore, while he buttoned up his trousers. I shrugged, not particularly bothered by his comment.

Antonio

I RUBBED MY eyes, trying to shake off the hazy fog of sleep and make sense of the situation. Slowly, my senses began to focus, and I saw Robert motioning for me to stand up. Though groggy, I managed to rise from the cot, my limbs feeling heavy and sluggish. As I stood there, trying to make sense of what was happening, I couldn't help but notice the smirk on his face. It made my stomach churn with disgust, and I realized he enjoyed watching me get gangbanged. The thought was sickening, and embarrassment and shame washed over me.

"We're going back to David's cell."

I felt a sense of unease wash over me. I couldn't bear to face David after what had happened. His behavior left me feeling disgusted and betrayed. I knew this wouldn't be an easy reunion, especially after what transpired between us.

"David despises you now, so there's no reason to keep you apart," Robert sneered, his voice dripping with hatred.

I couldn't help but think about how much my life had changed in such a short amount of time. Everything felt like a nightmare, and I couldn't wake up, no matter how hard I tried.

As I glanced down, I noticed the dried semen on my thigh, and I felt a wave of disgust wash over me. It must have trickled out while I slept, and the realization made my skin crawl. I quickly tried to wipe it off, but it seemed stuck, an unwanted reminder of the horrors I had experienced.

"Let's go!" Robert barked, his tone harsh and unforgiving.

He pushed me into the hallway, and I stumbled forward, still feeling disoriented from my deep sleep. I tried to keep up with him as he led me back to the original cell, my heart racing with fear and uncertainty.

As we arrived, Robert unlocked the door and shoved me inside, his actions rough and unforgiving. I stumbled forward, unable to regain my balance, and collided with the hard, unforgiving floor. It was a painful reminder of the brutality of my situation.

David stood up from his sitting position, and instead of offering a helping hand, he closely observed the situation. As I looked down, I realized I had an abrasion on my knee.

David hissed when he saw the blood.

I stood up and surveyed the cell. My heart sank when I realized the other prisoners, who had been held captive with us, were nowhere in sight. David and I were the only remaining prisoners. The reality of my situation hit me like a ton of bricks, and I recognized that the elders had likely killed them for their blood. Was Harry dead too? Trapped in this grim cell, I wondered if I would meet the same fate as the other captives.

Taking advantage of the situation, Robert inflicted even more pain on us. With a cruel glint in his eye, he turned his attention toward David and began to taunt him about me, using vicious words to degrade me and undermine our relationship. His words cut through the air like a knife, and I could feel the tears prickling at the corner of my eyes. Then, Robert dealt us the final blow, locking the cell door behind me. I stared at him in horror, realizing I was trapped and defenseless. The lock echoing through the cell was like a death sentence. Robert left the room, leaving us alone.

I couldn't contain my hatred toward David and spat out, "Damn you!" The words hung heavy between us, dripping with emotion. I could see the hurt and confusion reflected on his face, but my anger and resentment overpowered me, and I didn't care. I couldn't believe someone I loved had betrayed me so quickly. The feeling was like a knife to my heart, cutting deep into my soul.

"Antonio!" David pleaded.

I turned away from him.

"Please listen . . ."

I detected a distinct shift in his tone of voice, and I couldn't quite comprehend what was happening. His expressions of anger and bitterness were suddenly replaced with ones of empathy and understanding, which left me quite bewildered. Although I was still grappling with the impact of his previous outburst, I was caught off guard by this sudden change in demeanor. "You called me a fucking whore!" I shouted, determined to speak up, assert myself, and call him out on his shameful behavior.

"It was all for a show," he murmured, his voice barely audible.

I narrowed my eyes, questioning him.

"It doesn't bother me that you had sex with all those men," he said. "It turned me on because you enjoyed yourself. I wanted to be the last guy to fuck you."

"You're not disgusted?" I asked incredulously.

"Far from it," he said. "I masturbated excitedly."

Before I could say anything else, he took me into his arms and kissed me deeply, filling our momentary silence with a passionate embrace full of emotion and understanding. This healed my broken heart and rekindled hope for things to come.

Breaking apart from our hug, I said softly, "You upset me."

His voice was filled with an apology as he replied, "I'm sorry. I didn't mean to hurt you. I didn't want Robert to know the truth."

"I understand."

"Still horny?" he murmured, pressing his hardness against me.

My heart raced erratically. I moaned in response — wanting him. He kissed me again before undoing the buttons on his jeans.

As he slowly revealed himself to me, I couldn't help but feel overwhelmed with need. Watching him undress was like watching a scene from a steamy movie. My senses heightened as I could feel every inch of my body yearning for him. He pushed me down to my knees without hesitation and gripped my head firmly, urging me toward him. I could feel the excitement building inside me as I took him into my mouth. His taste on my lips was intoxicating, and I found myself moaning in pleasure as the sounds of our lustful encounter filled the air. Our bodies were in perfect sync, driving each other wild with pleasure. I felt him quiver and shake as he reached his climax, his hands gripping me tightly as he came. It was an unforgettable moment of pure ecstasy.

I savored every drop before spitting it out. Breathless, he pulled me back up, kissing me hard. We were lost in passion, forgetting everything but the sweet intensity of each other. At that moment, nothing else mattered, and we were blissfully lost in our mutual desire.

David

AS I GAZED at Antonio's ravaged body, I couldn't help but feel envious of all the men who had been with him, including my own father. This realization left me with an acute sense of longing. Despite the gravity of the situation, I was still horny, even after just coming. I maneuvered him onto his back, and before penetrating him, I lifted his legs and buried my face into his ass. The sensation of the fluids, still lingering from his encounters, burned my tongue. Despite this discomfort, my desire to taste every man who had sullied his body became overpowering.

I felt a thrill rush through me as Antonio moaned in pleasure. The cum was like an aphrodisiac, driving me wild with desire. I wanted more and more of it, and Antonio had no problem supplying me with the material. My tongue dragged over his fuck hole, eagerly savoring the salty flavors that filled my mouth. With each taste, a feeling of ecstasy flooded my mind.

I quickly entered him, giving him what he wanted

— my big prick. "I'll cum inside you if you push it out immediately," I said, hoping he'd agree.

Antonio let out a moan of pleasure while nodding his head.

His used hole begged for more as I plunged inside him. The feeling was incredible. The sensation of filling him with every thrust sent a wave of electricity through me.

I felt the intense pleasure building up inside me, making my body tremble with anticipation. I claimed my territory with one final thrust and was the last to seed him. The sensation overwhelmed me, leaving me gasping for breath and completely satisfied.

Jackson

AS THE DEFORMED-NOSED soldier exited the chamber, I realized that Peter's quick thinking had spared us from the unspeakable horrors of torture.

My gaze drifted to the empty seats beyond the tinted glass, and my thoughts wandered to the ancient Roman assemblies, where citizens gathered to watch gladiators fight each other to death. It dawned on me this arena was no different. Vampires gathered to watch the same brutal spectacle. Enslaved humans being forced into the role of gladiators filled me with dread, and I shuddered at the thought.

As the possibility of us becoming the next victims in this blood sport dawned on me, an overwhelming sense of fear coursed through my veins. The thought of fighting for our lives before a bloodthirsty crowd of vampires was bone-chilling. With every passing moment, my apprehension grew, but I refrained from voicing my concerns, not wanting to add to Peter's already obvious stress and anxiety.

I didn't blame him for wishing me dead. He had valid reasons for his hatred toward me. I was acutely aware of my flaws and had brought this horrific situation upon myself. Clearing my throat, I managed to catch Peter's attention.

"Thank you," I whispered.

"For what?"

"Taking care of Crooked Nose."

"It was nothing."

Apologies can open many doors, and I wanted to show him this was the case. I gazed at Peter and spoke earnestly, conveying my sincere regret. Despite my previous focus on the money I earned from the infantry, I yearned to demonstrate my commitment to choosing the right path. We were engaged in a heated battle together, so it was clear that we needed to trust each other if we were going to win. After moments of our eyes locking together, I could tell his skepticism had started to melt away, and he now believed me.

Peter's sudden exclamation caught me off guard.

"There's an emergency exit in the ceiling!" he exclaimed, gesturing toward the hatch with a tilt of his head.

I saw the small opening sixteen feet above us as I looked up. It was our only way out of the arena, but how would we get up there? Our wrists were bound tightly with rope, making it impossible for us to levitate or climb.

Peter shook his head as he surveyed the situation in frustration. I noticed the push rail embedded in the hatch. That was our escape. If only we could find a way to get up there.

Antonio

AS DAVID worked his magic on me, I couldn't help feeling like I was in heaven, experiencing waves of euphoria that made me forget about everything else. David used his powerful tool to strike all the right spots, bringing me closer and closer to climax. The sensation was beyond words; each time I vocalized my pleasure, he became more determined to elevate my ecstasy to new levels.

However, as we simultaneously came together, the heavy cell door burst open without warning, interrupting our moment of bliss. With the sudden intrusion, my body jerked, and I was pulled back to reality. I recognized the figure being forcefully shoved inside by Robert — it was my father, looking frail and disoriented.

"What the hell is going on here?" Robert shouted.

Infuriated by the steamy scene before him, Robert's voice boomed, demanding an explanation. He was at the peak of his anger, and the questions he hurled at David were overflowing with emotion.

Ignoring his father, David looked at me with concern and suggested that I should push the fluid from my ass. I nodded in agreement, and he tenderly took my hand, assisting me to stand.

"David, answer me!" Robert yelled.

I immediately recognized the urgency of my situation and knew that I had to act fast. Without wasting any time, I promptly squatted and applied pressure on my pelvic muscles. I instinctively slid my hand beneath me to catch the expelled fluid.

As I felt the spent cum splash into my palm, I knew I had successfully managed to control the situation. Standing up, I was amazed by the sheer amount of substance. At that moment, a devious idea crept into my mind. Grinning mischievously, I began plotting a plan for sweet revenge.

With newfound confidence, I raised my hand to my mouth and took a tiny sip of the viscous fluid, teasing Robert with it. The taste was vile and bitter, but I savored the moment.

As I lowered my hand from my mouth, a sudden jolt of surprise overcame me when David reached out and firmly grasped my wrist. His bold move caused me to pause momentarily, uncertain how to respond. However, my initial hesitation was quickly replaced by a feeling of intense arousal as I watched him eagerly lick the substance. My heart raced as I observed him raise his head, seeing a thin strand connecting us.

Robert observed the scene with intense longing, yearning for the same experience. He moved closer and bit into the string, his eyes closing in ecstasy as he savored it. At that moment, I realized what was necessary and promptly tackled Robert to the floor.

David exclaimed in shock, "What are you doing?"

The man before me had committed two heinous crimes — rape and molestation of my father. Determined to commit an unforgivable act myself, I pinched his nose shut with one hand. And with the other, I placed the poison in his mouth, threatening him with lasting consequences if he didn't swallow it.

With beads of sweat flowing freely down my forehead, I could feel a raging fury within me that threatened to consume everything in its path. I knew without a doubt that I had to complete this task at all costs, no matter what it took or how much I had to endure. Fueled by my anger, I seized the opportunity to shout at Robert, calling him out for all the injustices he had inflicted upon me.

David tried to pull my arm away, but I refused to budge an inch.

My voice rose to a fever pitch as I demanded Robert to swallow the fluid. Despite his reluctance, he obeyed my command.

Silent anticipation filled the room as Robert began to choke on the fluid he had just consumed. I watched his face contort in agony, struggling to keep his breath. I leaned forward, excited and scared, as my revenge peaked. Suddenly, his body shook violently with every muscle writhing, capturing my attention. However, just as suddenly as it had come, the convulsions stopped, leaving his body devoid of activity.

David

MY HEART ACHED as I gazed at Robert's lifeless body lying motionless on the floor. Every fiber of my being longed for him to get up, even though I knew it was futile. Despite Antonio being by my side, I felt utterly alone. His attention was only focused on his rage toward my father, leaving me to grapple with my sorrow.

I reminisced about all the times Robert had tried to protect and love me throughout my childhood, even though we didn't always see eye-to-eye. My mind raced with questions about how I would manage without him. If only he had come to terms with his sexuality, perhaps we could have been allies and best friends instead of being locked in a lifetime of conflict.

Tears streamed down my cheeks uncontrollably as I watched his chest slowly deflate and turn to ashes. The sadness that engulfed me soon transformed into overwhelming fury — I knew what to do. Rising from my bowed position, I snarled viciously at Antonio, vowing revenge.

Antonio

As DAVID WEPT, I couldn't help but feel empathy for him. With every sob, his shoulders trembled, and his face was etched with the weight of his sorrow. Despite my desire to reach out to him and offer comfort, I knew the situation was too complicated.

My dad's weak voice interrupted my thoughts, calling my name. I shifted my gaze away from David and looked down at him in my arms. His words struck me like lightning, jolting me out of my reverie.

"I'm not your biological father."

A striking silence filled the air after my father's shocking revelation. It felt like an eternity before I could take another breath. The words seemed almost surreal.

"Salvatore Leone . . . is your father," he continued.

As I gazed into his eyes, my thoughts raced. I couldn't believe what I was hearing. It was as if everything had been a dream until now. "Dad?" I gasped out in confusion upon hearing the news.

"I tried to tell you earlier, but you interrupted," he spoke softly, barely above a whisper. "I'm dying . . . and you need to know the truth."

As reality set in, a whirlwind of emotions overtook me, and a flood of thoughts overwhelmed me. My world had shattered instantly, and everything I thought I knew suddenly became uncertain. It was a lot to process, but the truth was evident as I looked at him. William wasn't my biological father, which explained why I didn't resemble him. Despite my best efforts to remain composed, tears streamed down my cheeks as he continued to speak. I couldn't find my voice and sat silently, trying to understand what had just been revealed. It was a moment I would never forget that changed everything.

"I loved you as if you were my own son," he said softly.

Bursting with questions that demanded clarity, I asked about the length of my mother's relationship with Salvatore. He paused momentarily before revealing their paths had crossed during her college years. She kept their relationship hidden from her parents due to his military status. Their relationship ended because his job took precedence over her. However, they rekindled their relationship after we were married, which resulted in her becoming pregnant.

"Does he know about me?" I whispered, still in disbelief.

"He's aware of you now, but he wasn't back then. She also kept her infidelity a secret from me," he stated, shaking his head in sorrow. "He has disowned you."

"Why?"

"Your homosexuality."

"Seriously?"

William's eyes were filled with a profound sadness that he couldn't hide, and I could sense his pain so acutely that he didn't even need to speak the words aloud. As much as I wanted to cling to the hope that my biological father might take me in, I knew that the truth was much harsher than that. William's eyes revealed I was nothing more than an illegitimate child with no status or honor — a bastard in every sense of the word.

The weight of that realization hit me like a ton of bricks, and I was overcome with a pain that felt physical. Just as I was trying to process the news, William spoke up.

"He wants you dead," he said bluntly.

Those words hit me. I could feel my heart stutter.

For a moment, I was frozen, unable to process the gravity of what he had just said. I struck my chest, trying to force my heart to start beating again as I turned to David. He had been listening to our conversation, and I had hoped he might show me some compassion. But as I looked at him, all I could see was hatred burning in his eyes, and I knew that my troubles were far from over.

Angelo

UPON HEARING from Philippe that Antonio was being held captive in one of the compound's cells, I knew I had to act fast before his execution. However, the task ahead of me was daunting, as the compound had three separate jail cells, making it difficult to locate him. Time was of the essence, and I needed to find Antonio before it was too late. My mind was distracted by the imminent ritual about to unfold in the arena where five men were to become vampires through the seed of Jesus Christ, followed by a brutal battle between two gay vampires. It was a rare spectacle that occurred only twice a year, and it had captivated the attention of everyone within the compound.

Fueled by determination, I hurriedly searched all three cells until, at last, I discovered Antonio in the third cell. He was in a pitiful state that broke my heart, and I knew that time was running out to save him.

Although I had not known Antonio for very long, there was a connection between us beyond mere acquaintance. I would consider leaving military service and running away with him, especially now that my fellow soldiers were becoming aware of my sexuality. Reflecting on our past encounter, I remembered Antonio's expertise, which enabled me to experience pleasure unlike before. Thinking about him warmed my heart and brought a smile to my face, and I knew that I had to save him no matter what.

Antonio

AS SOON AS I saw Angelo standing before me, memories of our previous encounter in Jackson's hotel room came flooding back. My heart raced as I took in his handsome features, and my eyes were drawn to his groin, where I could see the outline of his hardness pressing against his uniform. The intensity of my attraction to him shocked me, and I felt a wave of heat and excitement spread through my body, settling deep between my legs. The idea of him fucking me again made my ass wet.

"Hello," he whispered, smiling gently.

My desire for him was so strong that it felt like an ache deep down, but I had to put it aside for now — my father needed help. I pointed to his unconscious body lying on the floor and looked into Angelo's eyes pleadingly.

"He needs blood," I said.

Angelo's understanding was immediate, and I felt comforted as he pulled me close. Our lips met in a passionate embrace, and I felt my heart swell with emotion. The kiss was slow and gentle before blossoming into something more intense. As we continued embracing, I felt his hands slip around my waist, pulling me closer. His lips were warm and soft against mine, and I got lost in the sensation. At that moment, I realized no other kiss had ever made me feel this way. Not even David's kisses could compare to this one. It was as if the entire universe had aligned to bring us together.

As our lips slowly parted, our eyes met, and I could see the depth of his affection reflected back at me. It was a moment that I would always cherish, a moment that filled my heart with contentment.

"You're beautiful," he whispered.

I felt my cheeks flush at the compliment and glanced down at my own hardness — a physical manifestation of the desire that had been building since we met. It was as if, with his presence, Angelo had sparked something in me that had been dormant for far too long. My body ached with a desire that I could no longer ignore.

As I looked up at him, I knew in my heart that he was the one who could satisfy the cravings that had been gnawing at me for so long. I was grateful for the opportunity to explore this newfound desire with him. This man did something to me — something good.

David

TRAPPED IN THE CELL with Antonio and William, my emotions spiraled out of control. A powerful surge of jealousy overwhelmed me as I witnessed Antonio embracing a mysterious stranger. Their passionate kiss appeared endless, and it seemed as though my heart was tearing apart. Betrayed and furious, I couldn't believe Antonio would brazenly display such intimate affection in my presence. It was one thing for him to engage in promiscuous activities, but sharing his love with someone while I stood there was an entirely different matter.

My mind raced, trying to comprehend what had just happened before my very eyes. Who was this person? How were they connected? As these questions filled my head, with each one came a new wave of anger and resentment toward them. No matter how much I tried to control it, my jealousy kept seeping.

I looked down and took a few deep breaths to calm myself and regain my composure. But no matter how hard I tried, the negative emotions came flooding back each time my gaze returned to them. I was consumed with rage and could not bring myself to look away.

It seemed as though my world had turned upside down. Antonio had killed my father, and now this. The feelings of betrayal were too much for me to handle, and all I wanted at that moment was for them to be gone. But I knew that wasn't possible. I had to come face-to-face with the reality of the situation. This night would forever change how I saw Antonio and, more importantly, how he saw me.

Antonio

ANGELO'S GAZE darted from one hallway to another, every twist and turn a potential hazard. Guided by his instincts, we maneuvered through the maze-like corridors of the compound with the precision of a seasoned captain guiding a ship.

In my arms, I cradled my father. His body felt heavy, but at the same time, it was fragile. Every step I took was calculated and deliberate, with the utmost care not to jostle him more than necessary. I understood the seriousness of the situation. My father's life depended on me, and I was fully committed to ensuring his safety no matter what it took.

Behind us, David sulked, his emotions a mix of self-pity and bitterness. His gaze, fixed on my back, was intense and penetrating.

Hit by a wave of realization, I drowned in a sea of remorse and self-blame. I had acted impulsively, giving in to my desires by kissing Angelo in front of him. Consumed by a deep sense of shame, I couldn't help but question my actions. What had I done?

We stepped into a large room where Angelo unlocked a cell door. This was no ordinary jail; it housed prisoners chosen to nourish Jesus. Their selection was based primarily on their health and vitality. A surge of hysteria swept over me as soon as we crossed the threshold. The inmates scurried around in panic, desperately seeking places to hide.

I motioned to David, signaling him to grab one of the captives. However, instead of following my instructions, he whirled around and stormed out. His sudden exit left me baffled and worried. I called out to him, my voice bouncing off the concrete walls.

"Where are you going?"

David shot me a glare in response.

I looked down, my father's frail voice breaking the silence.

"I'm thirsty."

My father's eyes fluttered open, meeting mine with a glimmer of recognition. "We're going to feed," I announced, a wave of relief washing over me, thankful he'd regained consciousness.

I lifted my head, seeing David from my peripheral vision. I noticed him making a hasty exit. Prioritizing my father's health over a lover's spat, I gently laid my dad on the floor and pounced on one of the prisoners.

***

I sank my teeth into the captive's wrist, allowing the blood to flow freely. Holding the bleeding limb above my father's mouth, I dripped blood into his mouth. He had once again lapsed unconscious, his face pale and lifeless against the cold floor.

As the blood dripped into his mouth, I waited for signs of life. Time seemed to elongate, and hope began to wane as he remained motionless. Just when despair was about to engulf me, his eyes snapped open, and he started to drink. However, the prisoner stirred, pulling his arm away, leaving me filled with desperation. In a split-second decision, driven by the urgency to save my dad's life, I pounced on him and sank my teeth into his neck, forcefully silencing him again. The act was gruesome and violent, leaving me shaken, yet I knew I had to do whatever it took to save my father's life.

"Antonio . . . I need . . . blood."

Lifting my head from the lifeless prisoner, I noticed my dad's outstretched arms. His need for blood was evident. Without thinking, I returned to the prisoner's neck and drew nourishment into my mouth. With a sense of urgency, I rushed to my father's side and gave him what I had collected.

He drew from my mouth, his body quivering as energy coursed through him. His tongue darted inside me when the blood ran out, seeking every drop.

A wave of pleasure surged through me, so powerful that it was impossible to resist. My self-control wavered, and I surrendered to my most primal desires. I knew in my heart that what I was doing was wrong, but I couldn't stop myself — my tongue invaded his mouth, intertwining with his in a dance as old as time. The shockwaves of the horrifying act reverberated through me, yet I found myself unable to stop myself, entranced by the illicit thrill of the moment.

My father's pained groan jolted me back to reality.

Horror-stricken, I realized the magnitude of the line I had just crossed. What had I done? My actions were beyond redemption.

As I glanced at Angelo, I saw my horror mirrored in his eyes.

My father's plea for more blood pierced the heavy silence.

I had to act swiftly. Despite trembling hands, I drew the prisoner closer, allowing my father to sink his teeth into his wrist. Blood spurted forth, and my father began to drink greedily. Sitting beside him, I found myself apologizing continually, the weight of my transgression pressing heavily upon me. At that moment, I knew I had committed an unforgivable act. Would he ever forgive me?

David

EMOTIONS SWEPT over me like a tsunami as I knelt next to my father's ashes. Tears welled in my eyes cascading down my cheeks as I whispered, "I'm so sorry." Amid this torrent of sorrow, a memory bobbed to the surface — a conversation I'd had with a comrade about bringing back the dead. He claimed all it required was to plant one's seed onto the ashes. The idea seemed so unbelievable that I brushed it off as pure fantasy.

As I pushed the thought from my head, the anger that surfaced inside me was overwhelming — a seething rage that threatened to consume me entirely. My love for Antonio was melting away, leaving behind only a bitter sense of betrayal and hurt.

Memories flashed before my eyes with dizzying speed. I couldn't help but wonder where things had gone wrong. We had been so good together, compatible in every way. Our sex had been passionate, a heady mix of desire and raw emotion. And yet, despite all of this, Antonio had betrayed me. The hurt and pain of his actions cut deep, leaving behind wounds that would never heal.

A profound sadness weighed down my heart as I thought about my father. His presence was more vital to me now than ever before. His understanding of the vampire realm was essential in our dangerous, shadowy world. In his absence, I felt unmoored, adrift in a vast ocean of darkness that seemed ready to engulf me.

"Oh, Dad . . ." I sighed.

To prove my comrade's words true, I knew what I had to do. With my fingers, I traced over the sensitive skin on my thighs and stomach. My prick grew hard almost instantly. I undid the buttons on my jeans and began to masturbate, lost in the moment. Shuddering and gasping, I directed my release onto my father's ashes.

Angelo

IMMERSED IN THE moment's passion within the cell's confines, the distant sound of Antonio's father's snoring gave us the freedom to relish in each other's presence, oblivious to the prisoners around us. William had just finished a delicious feast, and although he had regained his color, his exhaustion was still evident and demanded rest.

My body couldn't help but respond to Antonio's touch as he skillfully worked toward bringing me to the brink of satisfaction. His head bobbed up and down, and his grip on my hips became firmer, guiding me effortlessly deeper into his mouth. I ran my fingers through his soft, silky hair, reveling in the sensations that his movements were creating within me. Despite the intensity of our passion, Antonio remained focused and unwavering in his efforts to fulfill my desires completely. My breathing became ragged and uneven as I felt ecstasy rising within me. Suddenly, I withdrew and began to stroke, wanting to take extra precautions to ensure his safety.

"I'll spit it out," he moaned softly, trying to ease my fears.

Despite the risks, I understood and accepted his desire, allowing him to continue pleasing me with renewed vigor. Minutes later, I warned him again with a sharp gasp of air, which prompted him to increase his speed, pushing me over the edge and into the abyss of pleasure. Finally, unable to hold back any longer, I released into his waiting mouth with a cry of pure bliss.

Antonio

I OPENED MY MOUTH and showed Angelo the seed I had collected at the base of my throat, feeling exposed and vulnerable in a way I had never experienced before. Despite this, I cherished this moment with him. As the burning sensation grew intense, I had to spit it out. Angelo didn't flinch or judge but instead kissed me, sharing the remnants of the fluid like it was a sacred symbol of our blossoming love.

In his embrace, I found myself questioning my earlier actions. I was still stunned that I had kissed my father. Processing this thought, Angelo lifted my chin. He looked at me and asked what was on my mind. Knowing there was no point in lying, I told him what I felt. Angelo was understanding, reassuring me that I had done nothing wrong.

Despite his reassurances, my Catholic guilt returned, and I lowered my gaze in embarrassment. Angelo lifted my chin again and smiled. He said he was taken aback initially but understood how these things happened.

My father unexpectedly cut short our intimate moment by waking from his slumber. We hastily pulled apart, both of us visibly startled to see him slowly rising from his resting place. He cleared his throat apologetically.

"I'm sorry to have interrupted your tender moment."

My cheeks burned with embarrassment, but before I could respond, my father continued speaking, saying he believed we made a suitable pair. A warm smile spread as I realized that my father liked Angelo. In the past, whenever our conversations turned to David, I couldn't help but notice a certain guardedness in my father's demeanor, as if he didn't fully trust him or thought he wasn't the right one for me.

With newfound confidence, Angelo stepped forward and lovingly embraced me once more. Sensing our need for privacy, my father turned around, allowing us to share this special moment without further interruptions. As I looked into Angelo's eyes, I could tell he loved me.

David

WITH MY EYES fixed intently on the pile of ashes before me, an incredible sense of awe and anticipation surged through me. I watched in amazement as my father's form slowly took shape, emerging from the ashes as if reborn. As his form grew more distinct, my initial fear and apprehension melted away, replaced by a growing sense of excitement and joy at the sight of his returning figure. As I looked at him, a smile crept across my face, a sense of wonder and amazement washing over me. I knew there had been secrets for far too long between us, but now, seeing him return to life, I could sense that things would be different.

"We'll work together," I said out loud, imagining all the possibilities now open to us.

My heart started racing as the success of my experiment dawned on me. I realized it had been possible because of my DNA. Using my genetic material, I created the ultimate resurrection. My father would return with a perfect blend of his previous memories and a new, stronger mind. With this enhanced foundation, we'd achieve anything, overcome any hurdle, and surmount any challenge. I knew our bond would be unbreakable, forged in love and innovation.

William

MY WIFE'S CONDITION was critical, and her life hung in the balance. I could feel time slipping through my fingers like grains of sand, and the thought of losing her was unbearable. With a heavy heart, I turned to Antonio and told him that we needed to split up. He hesitated, and I could see the reluctance in his eyes, but I knew it was the only way to cover more ground and find everyone in time.

As we stood there, I considered giving him a farewell hug, but my emotions were too overwhelming. I longed for him to hug me first and reassure me that he still loved me, but when it didn't come, I wished him safety and walked away.

As I walked down the corridor alone, I felt desolation and sorrow.

My only companion was Antonio, and feeling the truth shattered our bond. Deep in thought, I contemplated whether I had made a grave mistake by sharing the truth with him. Not able to answer my question, my mind wandered toward the kiss. My heart rate quickened, and a knot began forming in my stomach. I should have broken away and clarified that it was wrong. I should have told him how much I loved and cared for him and that his actions had no impact on our relationship. However, in the heat of the moment, I was too absorbed in the shock of the kiss to make the right choice.

I couldn't help but worry about Antonio's mental state and the guilt he must be carrying. I knew my son well enough to understand his emotional turmoil as he tried reconciling his actions with his moral compass. As for me, I was emotionally detached from the entire situation. Despite the impropriety of what had transpired, I didn't feel attached to the kiss. It was as if it had happened to someone else, some distant figure I could only observe from afar.

Finally, I came across a sign that read 'Sick Bay.' Seeing it filled me with dread as my heart sank at the thought of my wife's dire condition. I didn't know what lay ahead or if she would recognize me. But I knew that I had to face it with courage and strength. I took a deep breath, put my fears aside, and entered the room.

Peter

AS I SURVEYED the vast arena, I saw the terraced area teeming with vampires eagerly awaiting the event. Their eyes sparkled with anticipation, and an uneasy knot formed in my stomach as I noticed the four ominous crosses. The elders had already chosen the sacrificial victims — Antonio, David, William, and the victor of the gladiator battle, which would come down to either Jackson or me.

Jackson and I were seated before the dreadful crosses, our wrists tightly bound together by ropes. As the vampires bustled about, preparing for the impending ceremonies, I could feel Jackson trembling at my side. It was evident that the odds were not in our favor.

Despite the seemingly inescapable situation, I refused to resign myself to doing nothing. Instead, I decided to attempt something daring, at least. Leaning toward Jackson, I suggested that we sit back-to-back, hoping this position might allow us to free ourselves from restraints.

He nodded his agreement, understanding the plan, and shuffled closer to me.

The entire arena was illuminated by dozens of flickering lanterns, casting an eerie, orange glow over the scene.

The vampire's movements seemed joyful and excited as they eagerly looked forward to the forthcoming events.

As they busied themselves around us, we had become invisible to them. Seizing the opportunity, I slowly loosened the knots that held us captive, determined not to surrender without fighting.

Angelo

I HELD ANTONIO'S hand firmly, my heart pounding with urgency as the foreboding echo of the guard's boots grew louder in the corridor. We should have exited sooner, but our emotions had held us captive. "Have you ever attempted shapeshifting?" I asked. My voice tinged with desperation.

Antonio seemed startled by my question and responded with a head shake, stating that while David had mentioned the concept, he had never personally tried it. I tugged at his arm, urging him to focus on visualizing someone else. I further explained that if he managed to shapeshift successfully, the guards would be unable to identify him.

He closed his eyes, and within seconds, his body began to morph into a series of energy patterns. However, the transformation process abruptly ended due to his overwhelming fear. I encouraged him to release the anxiety obstructing his progress. Moments later, he had fully transformed into Heracles — the mighty son of Zeus. He stood before me, wearing nothing but a beard and wavy hair, which was surprisingly captivating. I awkwardly adjusted my now bulging member and remarked that Heracles might not be the most suitable disguise for the situation.

Antonio

THE MUSCLES in my body tensed and flexed as I successfully assumed the form of Heracles. However, Angelo pointed out it was too conspicuous, and I needed to adopt a different disguise. After weighing my options, I concluded that the best course of action would be to blend in with the other prisoners. Angelo urgently reminded me that time was running out as the guards were fast approaching. Closing my eyes, I concentrated on altering my appearance once more, and within seconds, I had transformed into a robust and muscular young man. My new physique was striking, boasting broad shoulders and impressive biceps.

"Undress!" Angelo commanded just as the guards entered the room.

Since I was already unclothed, I stood there boldly, my powerful form on full display for everyone to see. As the other inmates removed their clothing and arranged themselves in a line, two armed soldiers stepped through the doorway of our cell.

"Eyes front!" Angelo shouted, ordering us to stand at attention.

My heart rate quickened as the men methodically paced back and forth, examining each of us with keen precision. After an eternity, they stopped before me and nodded approvingly. I could sense their admiration for my physical prowess.

As the command to step forward rang out, my heart pounded even faster. I obediently moved toward them and stood still, fixing my gaze straight ahead. The taller of the two men spoke loudly, directing me to turn around. I complied without hesitation, now facing away from them. I could feel the weight of their gazes on me from behind, likely taking in the sight of my muscular backside as I awaited further instructions. Then came the command to face front, prompting me to turn around and look up at him. Our eyes locked briefly before his gaze shifted to my exposed jugular vein. A satisfied grin spread across his face as he declared me a 'prime specimen' for Jesus's sacrifice.

I stood frozen with fear, my mind racing a million miles a minute, trying to process what had just happened. It was then that I felt Angelo's thoughts penetrate my mind, calming me down enough to understand that my fate was not a foregone conclusion. He reassured me that all would be okay if I kept calm and controlled. His words were like balm to my frayed nerves, and I felt a sense of relief wash over me.

The soldiers selected two additional prisoners.

Angelo directed me to extend my arms so he could link the three of us together with shackles. I did as he asked, allowing him to bind the other two prisoners first. When he turned his attention to me, I offered my wrists to him. Our eyes locked, and the concern etched in his features for my safety brought comfort. As soon as the cold metal cuffs clamped around my wrists, a wave of fear washed over me. However, the steadying influence of his gaze quickly quelled it, replacing the fear with a calm resolve.

As the soldiers began to lead us away, I glanced at Angelo, my eyes reflecting my apprehension. He read the silent plea in my gaze and told the soldiers he would accompany us. A wave of relief washed over me. I took a deep, stabilizing breath. Knowing I wouldn't face the looming uncertainty alone brought a comforting sense of reassurance.

David

THE FIGURE before me was a grotesque caricature of the man who had once been my father. His familiar features were now warped and distorted, rendering him unrecognizable. He started moving toward me, slithering in a way that was far from human. The sight of his unnatural movement sent a bone-chilling shiver down my spine.

I stood rooted to the floor, frozen by pure, undiluted fear. I could not move, scream, or do anything other than watch the horror unfold before my eyes. The scene before me was like something straight out of a horror film — my father had transformed into an abomination, a monstrous creature.

I couldn't help but feel a pang of guilt, knowing that his transformation into this hideous creature directly resulted from my actions. I had failed to produce sufficient sperm, leading to an incomplete process that resulted in this nightmare.

The room was filled with his anguished cries, each ricocheting off the walls and reverberating in my ears. The bright, unrelenting fluorescent lights exposed his terrifying figure in vivid detail. His back and legs, twisted and warped, blatantly defied the laws of human anatomy. Grotesque angles bent his body, churning my stomach with disgust.

"I need cum!" he screamed, his voice filled with desperation and pain.

His demand was clear — he required more to complete the transformation and reverse the horrifying effects he was undergoing.

A sudden realization washed over me — standing idle was no longer an option. I needed to save my father and reverse his monstrous transformation.

Antonio

ANGELO DEFTLY undid the cuffs restraining me, then leaned in close and quietly suggested that I should transform back into my body after he and the other officers departed the chamber.

"You're a vampire. He cannot drink your blood," Angelo said telepathically.

I felt relief wash over me as I understood his original words — I wouldn't die. Taking a deep breath, I nodded my agreement and uttered, "I understand." Turning around, Angelo followed the officers out of the room and closed the door behind him.

I quickly returned to my original form. The other two prisoners saw this and started whispering anxiously, terrified at what they had just witnessed. I couldn't blame them. I would have been just as scared if I were in their shoes.

"Come forward!"

I turned, hearing the Savior's voice.

I lowered my head immediately, seeing a golden light illuminating the entire chamber, filling it with tranquility. His compassionate voice filled the room as he beckoned us forward again, drawing the two inmates from hiding behind me.

As we moved forward, I fell to my knees, honoring him.

Lifting my gaze from the floor, awe caught my breath when I saw him sitting atop his throne, wearing nothing but a loin cloth. The light revealed the glow of his olive-hued skin. His long brown hair and beard were stunning. Despite the cruel crown of thorns on his head, he radiated an indomitable strength and courage that filled me with admiration.

Every inch of his body was sculpted gracefully, and his toned physique made it clear how powerful he was.

I looked upon him with respect.

He acknowledged me with a smile and set a chalice filled with a glowing substance on the table.

"My brother."

Is that the Holy Grail? Is that his semen? I wondered as I looked into his blue eyes. He was everything I thought he would be and more. I started to cry because he was the most beautiful man I had ever seen.

"Be not afraid to surrender your blood to me. For I will bless you for your lifesaving offering."

"I'm honored to be in your presence, the Son of Man," I said and kissed the soft skin of his foot, no longer calloused and sun-scorched from wearing sandals.

"Thank you."

He placed the palm of his hand on my head and blessed me.

My heart thudded heavily, and my eyes filled with tears that ran down my cheeks as I realized the extent of my sins. According to the teachings of the Catholic Church, it was clear that my lifestyle, deemed immoral, was a direct path to an eternity in Hell. Desperately yearning for divine forgiveness, I uttered between sobs, "I'm a homosexual. I've lived a life of sexual immorality." As soon as he heard my confession, he sighed with empathy.

"The teachings of the church are wrong."

These seven words offered me a glimmer of hope as I lifted my head to regain composure while struggling through my ocean of emotions.

"My father loves you as you are. My dear brother, you are not a sinner if you lie with another man in consent. Shine in my light," he said, gesturing for me to stand before him.

I did so, sniveling, covering my nakedness.

"Be not ashamed," he said softly, his voice carrying an air of reassurance that made me feel somewhat comfortable despite the situation.

I slowly lowered my hands and stood before him, completely exposed. His gaze trailed down my body, his smile widening as he reached my groin.

"My father has made you in his likeness."

Suddenly, his eyes glowed a deep red, and his long fangs emerged from his mouth — it was time for him to feed. I should have been frightened with fear at this moment. Instead, I felt strangely calm and collected. "I cannot give you my blood," I informed him while showing him my sharp teeth to prove my statement was true. "You see, I am a vampire too."

Jesus nodded.

I wasn't sure if he was disappointed, but a heavenly light, much brighter than his, erupted from the ceiling. I could feel the air around me vibrate as a trumpet blast echoed through the chamber, and wings fluttered above us. The supernatural display took me aback.

Jesus seemed just as surprised, and we both stared in amazement as we beheld an angel descending from heaven. The divine messenger was nude and held a golden trumpet in his hand. In astonishment, Jesus placed his left hand over his heart at the sight of this heavenly being in front of us.

"I'm Gabriel," he proclaimed, "God's messenger sent to announce your return."

He gestured for Jesus to stand.

The prisoners behind me started weeping. I turned to them as they bowed their heads in prayer.

"You are Christ's Savior."

As I witnessed them praying, my mind raced with confusion. Were the words just spoken directed toward me? I turned around at the sound of Gabriel's voice. His finger pointed at me in confirmation.

"You are the chosen one."

I fell to my knees, knowing not to say anything more.

Overwhelmed with emotion, I watched as Jesus stood in front of me. His loincloth fell to the floor, and I saw his nakedness. His arms now outstretched — he looked toward heaven. A bright light filled the room, and a reverent silence fell over us — as if Jesus and God were having a conversation that none of us could hear. With a smile, he bent down and retrieved the cup from the table. He slowly rose again, holding the chalice in both hands, illuminated by the heavenly glow.

The sight was majestic — so much so that I sat still and felt my breath catch in my chest. My gaze never left him as he continued to commune with God. He seemed to be discussing something vital — what it might have been. I can only imagine. Then with one last glance upward, he lowered his head and turned back toward me — as if he'd just received an answer from high above. He stepped forward, looking into my eyes with a knowingness I still can't quite understand.

"Stand, my brother."

I caught my breath as I stood before him, staring at his nude body. It was perfect in every way.

"This is my gift to you," he said, handing me the chalice.

He kissed me tenderly on the lips and then held me close. I felt his groin resting against me. It was long and slender. My breath caught in my throat as it moved against me, filling with blood.

He gestured for me to drink.

Putting his hardness from my mind, I swallowed his seminal fluid. Immediately, a profound shift began to occur within me. Each cell in my body seemed to undergo a magical yet terrifying metamorphosis. The fluid had an inexplicable taste, unlike anything I had ever experienced. I felt compelled to consume more of it, unable to resist its charm. Once the cup was empty, he gently took it away from my lips, his face adorned with a satisfied and knowing smile.

He leaned in to kiss me, his lips gently brushing mine as the sweet taste of his nectar lingered. I felt my heart swell with love and appreciation. When he finally pulled away, I asked what I could give him in return for such a precious gift. His answer was simple yet profound — all he wanted was my poisonous blood.

David

THE SIGHT before me was horrifying. My father's body convulsed violently after consuming more of my seed.

"The pain!" he cried out.

I stood frozen, my feet rooted to the floor by fear and uncertainty. Was there anything I could do to help him? Or would my attempts only exacerbate his condition?

As I struggled with my indecision, my father's screams reached a crescendo, then abruptly cut off, becoming still. Then, to my shock and horror, I heard the sickening sound of bones snapping. His once prominent hump flattened out, disappearing back into his body, and his bent legs stretched straight.

The transformation was gruesome and terrifying.

I held my breath, waiting anxiously for any sign of movement. Then, after what felt like an eternity, his eyes fluttered open.

"David . . ."

He looked at me, confused, not believing the pain that had consumed him just moments ago was gone.

My father's eyes were full of love and understanding. He was no longer in pain, and his body was free from the ailments that had plagued him. As he reached forward, his hands cupped my face. His caressing touch felt right. We stared at each other with a newfound love, then, suddenly, without warning, he leaned forward and kissed me. It was a gentle kiss that conveyed so much emotion and tenderness. Initially, I didn't know how to react, but his touch was comforting, and I soon relaxed feeling his touch. Pulling away, he kept his hands on my face and looked deeply into my eyes.

"I love you," he said softly, his voice breaking with emotion. "I've always loved you and always will."

Tears welled up in my eyes as I felt the weight of those words. All these years, I had struggled with my feelings toward him, unsure how to deal with the complex emotions swirling beneath the surface. But now, at this moment, everything felt clear. I loved him too, and his kiss was all the proof I needed.

We stood together for an eternity, neither saying anything, but the silence was enough. It was a moment of healing and release, of letting go of all the anger and confusion plaguing me for so long.

Antonio

I CLOSED MY eyes with anticipation and fear coursing through my veins. I could feel the soft yet unyielding pressure of Jesus's lips against the surface of my skin. This intimate connection sent shivers up my spine and made my heart flutter uncontrollably.

With each upward and downward motion of his throat, I could feel him sipping the venomous fluid within me. It was a poison, a toxin that could bring about unimaginable pain and suffering. But to Jesus, it seemed more like a drink of life.

After he had consumed his fill of the venom, a sense of calm enveloped us. With strength waning from the exchange, I slowly, almost ceremoniously, lowered myself to the cold concrete. I embraced him, our bodies entwined in a moment of shared vulnerability.

This tableau of ours was reminiscent of the iconic statue La Pieta. Just like Mary cradling the lifeless body of her son Jesus, I held him close. Our roles reversed in this intimate echo of art and history.

The moment's tenderness was almost too much to

bear, and I could feel every emotion coursing through me as his body lay limp in my arms.

His breath was light and steady, yet so powerful that it seemed to reverberate through me and into the world beyond. As I held him close, the air around us was alive with divine energy that weaved between us, creating a bond that would never be broken.

"You're my savior," Jesus spoke with a hoarse voice.

Jesus, with his dazzling blue eyes, looked directly at me, and I felt held captive by his gaze. It was as if he could see into my soul. Tears streamed down my face, and I couldn't help but feel overwhelmed with emotion. I looked to Gabriel, who had been guiding me through this moment, for reassurance, and he nodded, indicating that everything that was happening was as it should be.

As Jesus said, "I am the light of the world," my heart swelled with love and admiration. I knew those words were true, and he had dedicated his life to guiding all who would follow him.

His head lolled listlessly to the side, and at that moment, I knew the Son of God had perished.

I let out an anguished wail and brought him to my chest, holding him tightly as the presence around us grew even more intense. A brilliant expanse of white clouds filled the room, and I wondered if God had come to take him home.

I felt movement as Jesus began to rise.

I wanted to hold on to him but knew I had to release him. Lowering my arms, the lifeless body of Jesus suddenly started to rise toward the heavens.

The whole room seemed to shimmer and glow brighter than ever, and a heavenly chorus of angels filled the air with beautiful music. As he continued his ascent, a white portal suddenly opened above, revealing an expanse of shining clouds.

The voice of God echoed all around us, his words filling me with peace and hope despite my sorrow.

"My son! Rise and come home."

With those words, Jesus rose and continued his journey through the clouds. I turned to Gabriel with tears streaming down my face. He encased me in his wings and comforted me.

***

The prisoners cowered in fear before me, aware of what I needed and that they would provide it — blood. I was exhausted and weak from the lack of nourishment. The light of God had changed my hair from black to white, making me look years older than my actual age. What else had changed since ingesting Jesus's gift? I thought before jumping forward, grasping the larger of the two inmates.

The inmate screeched.

My fangs protruded and bit into his neck, silencing him. I drank his blood too fast, which made my stomach churn with pain. But I didn't stop. As I drank, my mind played back to the miracle that just happened. No one would believe Jesus Christ had given me his seed. That's when I realized the other prisoner had to live. He would be Jesus's prophet and my seer.

Still drinking, I tamed the other inmate, explaining telepathically what I needed of him. His mind told me two things — he understood and was gay. This made me happy — he'd fit in with his good looks and be a welcome member of our newly formed brotherhood.

"My name is Lucien," he whispered.

I lifted my head from the prisoner's neck. "I'm Antonio. It's a pleasure to meet you." Lucien's eyes locked on mine. I could see the sexual desire in them. I dropped the dead prisoner and stepped toward him. He wasn't afraid any longer and embraced me. I felt his hardness against me.

I glanced at his dick and wanted to suck on it, but there wasn't any time. Although slender, it was beautiful — I was no longer concerned with size. My attention now turned to expressing love through mutual pleasure and physical closeness. "I must drain you of blood first. Do you trust me?"

Lucien nodded.

My pointed teeth shot forward, and I hissed instinctively as if it was second nature. I apologized for scaring him, though it was out of habit. I sunk my teeth into his neck and quickly drained him of his blood. His legs shook beneath him, so carefully, I guided him to the floor — never releasing my grasp from his throat.

Full of blood, I absorbed myself in a moment of passion — pleasuring myself inside his mouth. I saw his body twitch as he succumbed to death. Seconds later, it was born again into eternity — an immortal creature of the night.

I explained everything about becoming a bloodsucker — the dos and don'ts. He seemed to be a fast learner. He wanted to escape as badly as I did, but I explained I needed to find my father, Peter, and Jackson first. I didn't say David because he was no longer part of my life. Just thinking of him, I could feel his hatred toward me. I would go on without him.

"Let's go find them," Lucien said.

I smiled, knowing I'd made the right decision. We had no clothes to put on, so I led him to the door. Peering into the hallway, I didn't see anyone. I took off running, knowing Lucien was behind me.

Peter

THE AIR WAS tense as we sat there, waiting for the resurrection ceremony to begin. The bloodsuckers had become increasingly impatient, and their agitation was intense. Like us, five humans stood on stage, all naked, waiting to become vampires. They seemed to be in some trance, eyes closed and bodies swaying from side to side. Suddenly, a soldier appeared, carrying a golden cup. Fear rose as we thought this might be the beginning of the ceremony.

The soldier walked up to the stage, holding the cup for the elders to see. Their faces registered varying degrees of disappointment and confusion.

As I watched, confused whispers began circulating among them on stage. They talked about Jesus having disappeared, and there was no semen in the chalice. None of it made sense, and I wished for some explanation.

I glanced over at Jackson, relieved that I had finally managed to loosen the rope from his wrists. "What's going on?" I asked him in a calm voice, hoping he had some idea. He shook his head and shrugged, indicating he was just as clueless as I was.

A high-ranking military officer made his presence known, ascending the stage, distinguished by his collection of ribbons and medals. His arms flailed about frantically as he sought to understand what had gone wrong. With a booming voice, he commanded that the Son of God be tracked down. In response, I glanced at Jackson, seeing the potential advantage this could bring us.

An unexpected announcement was made that sent shockwaves through the arena. The officer declared that the resurrection would take place the next day. Loud boos filled the arena. He lifted his hands, quieted everyone, and elaborated on his statement. He said that while the resurrection would be delayed, the execution would go as planned.

The crowd erupted in cheers.

Jackson stared at me, his eyes wide with fear. I couldn't console him because I didn't have a plan to escape. There was nothing we could do to save ourselves.

William

I PUSHED OPEN the door, expecting it to be locked shut. Surprisingly, the knob turned quickly, and the door creaked open. I cautiously stepped into Sick Bay, feeling apprehension washing over me. Various vampires could be seen throughout the room, some lying in beds while others were seated in chairs. I.V. bags were attached to poles, providing them with much-needed blood. It was clear that these were vampires requiring transfusions to live. It was silent except for an occasional muffled sob or moan from a patient in pain.

My heart skipped a beat when I saw my wife seated on one of the beds in the corner of the room. Her head bowed, her lengthy hair cascading down her back. Despite my urge to run toward her, I waited until she noticed me. When she finally looked up, tears streamed down her cheeks as she stared with an expression that seemed to contain hope and despair.

I took a few steps forward before finally stopping right beside her bed. We looked at each other for what felt like an eternity. Our emotions were too overwhelming for either of us to speak — until she finally managed to whisper my name between sobs.

"I'm so sorry," she whispered, wanting forgiveness.

Clutching each other for dear life, I embraced my wife and breathed reassuring words into her ear. She looked much older than before — her hair had been transformed from a deep black to a dull grey. Her body felt fragile in my arms, making me hug tighter. I kissed her forehead and whispered, "I'm so sorry I didn't save you." The rage toward Salvatore and Robert flared within me. They deserved to die for what they did to her.

Without even a moment's hesitation, my fangs extended from my gums and protruded outwards, overcome with the urge to make her a vampire. Carefully, I turned her head away and exposed her neck. But before I could do anything, she spoke up and pushed away from me.

"No . . ."

Her voice was soft but firm, making me stop in my tracks. I looked at her with pleading eyes, begging for understanding. After what seemed like an eternity of silence, she spoke again.

"Let me go . . ."

And I did. With my fangs slowly retracting, I let go of her and stepped away, allowing her to choose. She didn't have to be like me, and that was something I had to accept.

"Drain me of blood."

Tears streaming down my face, I kissed her forehead before my fangs protruded again. She knew her life would be hell, even as a vampire.

"Do it now . . ."

I couldn't take it slow, or else I would never be able to fulfill her wish. As I drank from her neck, I explained telepathically that I loved her.

Salvatore

MY HEART RACED with adrenaline, pounding in my chest as I surveyed the chaotic scene unfolding before me. Everything in the vicinity had been thrown into complete disarray, leaving a sense of confusion and disorientation.

Soldiers were running around frantically, their faces etched with panic, as they desperately searched for any clues or traces of information about the whereabouts of Jesus and the fate of my Master Sergeant. It was evident that they were struggling to make sense of the situation and were grasping at straws to find answers.

Suddenly, I was ushered onto the stage, thrust into the spotlight to confront the bewildering situation head-on. As I stood there, a wave of anxiety washed over me, and I felt utterly overwhelmed by the magnitude of the task. It appeared as if everyone's gaze was fixed on me, relying on my ability to restore order amidst the turmoil and offer essential direction during this critical moment.

My mind swirled with questions and doubts — why would Jesus leave now? He had accepted his fate at our base and blessed us with forgiveness, never attempting to break free in the past. I felt a wave of worry coursing through me at the unexpected turn of events, tarnishing my reputation.

I peered down at the gold chalice in my soldier's hand standing beside me, noticing it was empty. The cup glimmered with a thin layer of residual moisture. The sperm had been there once, but now it was missing.

I checked my wristwatch and realized there were still a few hours until sunrise. At this point, the vampires had already begun to clap impatiently, eager for the execution to begin. Realizing that I had to entertain the troops, an idea popped into my head — I would subject the queer vampires to torture as an alternative form of entertainment. So, with swift resolve, I organized an excruciatingly painful activity for them all to witness. The crowd erupted in excitement when they heard my plans, quickly shifting from boredom and restlessness into gleeful anticipation.

Robert

TAKING A DEEP breath, I pushed away from David and felt a pang of regret at his groan of protest as I ended the embrace. As I looked into his eyes, I couldn't help but notice the blissful joy filling them. I couldn't ignore my erection. My cock was pressing up against him, and as I looked down, I could see that it had grown from its previous six inches to a full eight. It was now the same size as his, and I wondered if this was a testament to his DNA. Although my looks and body remained the same, this sudden difference in my manhood was hard to ignore. David's gaze shifted downward, and I could see the desire flickering in his eyes as he noticed me. He reached out and caressed it, sending pleasurable sensations coursing through my body. It was almost too much to handle, and I had to pull away before pre-ejaculating.

Panic surged through me as I contemplated what had just occurred. I had kissed my son, and it wasn't just a simple kiss — it was a profoundly passionate embrace that two lovers would experience. My mind screamed at me that it was wrong, that I needed to run away and act as if it never happened. But my heart betrayed me, telling me that what I felt for David was real and that nothing could change that. David grabbed my arm before I could do anything, forcing me to focus on him. He looked directly into my eyes and spoke softly yet firmly, his words cutting through my confusion like a knife.

"Don't feel ashamed."

We looked at each other, our eyes conveying the forbidden truth we both wanted. We had found solace in something society deemed wrong. Still, it felt right, and the moment lasted longer than it should have, giving way to the undeniable desire and chemistry between us — something that only a father and son could feel.

David broke the silence. "I raised you through my seed. If anyone finds out about this, they'll kill us."

I nodded and stepped away, both of us unsure of what to do now that our reunion was over. I knew I needed to get dressed before someone noticed us, but part of me wanted to keep holding him in my arms. We had been apart for far too long, and this moment was the first time in years we could be together without any judgment or prejudice. We gave each other one last lingering look before I gestured toward the gymnasium, explaining I had a spare uniform in my locker. David kissed me once again and nodded his head in understanding.

David

AS I STOOD in the infantry's locker room, my dad handed me a military uniform and said that I should morph into a soldier but not exaggerate my appearance. Little did he know, after hearing his wish, I planned to make one tiny alteration. I wanted to be different for once, so I shrank my eight-inch prick down to a more modest size. My dad noticed immediately and exclaimed loudly.

"What the hell?"

I replied simply, "I'm tired of fucking size queens." His face lit up with shock.

"You're crazy!" he said incredulously.

I wasn't about to give up that easily. I was determined to make my point — having a big dick isn't everything.

A naked, aroused soldier walked out of the showers, surprising us both. We paused, unsure of his intentions. He looked at my father and gave him a nod toward the showers. I watched as he re-entered, hoping my dad would follow. This person shared my struggle yet was stronger than me — he couldn't care less about society's expectations and followed his desires.

The soldier's gesture gave me a slight sense of happiness for my dad, who had never seemed to find pleasure in anything until that moment. As much as I wanted him to follow through with the invitation, he knew we had no time for something like this, so he stood there proud and tall before turning away regretfully.

Changing into the uniform, my dad told me that Salvatore Leone was Antonio's biological father. "Yes!" I said. "I know all about it."

Watching my father button his shirt, I couldn't take my eyes off his sculpted physique. His firm ass was perfectly rounded. But my eyes were soon drawn to his groin. The thought of his raging erection stirred an overwhelming longing within me. As he continued dressing, I brushed my hand over his backside, marveling at the feel of his firm muscles rippling under my touch. Unable to resist any longer, I allowed my fingers to trail down the crack of his ass, reveling in the sensation of his thick, curly hair against my skin.

"You've got a great ass," I mumbled in awe.

My touch lingered over his anus, and as it pulsed and relaxed under my fingertips, I felt a surge of heat between my thighs. I let out a low moan, aching to taste him, to feel his hot seed spilling into my mouth. But our moment of passion was abruptly interrupted as my father reminded me of our time constraints.

"We don't have time for this."

"I know."

My father grinned.

I lifted my fingers to my nose. I took a deep breath, smelling his musky scent. My prick pulsated in excitement. Robert saw this and caressed me gently while smirking seductively.

"We better go."

I nodded. Reluctantly, I lowered my hand from my nose and finished getting dressed, unable to shake the image of my father's backside from my mind.

Following my dad dutifully as we left the locker room, I smiled and waved goodbye to the cruising soldier as he peered out from the showers.

As we stepped into the hallway, I could hear murmurs of anger and disappointment coming from the arena. Inside my head, I felt their thoughts like a hurricane of confusion.

Jesus disappeared.

. . . empty chalice . . .

. . . no resurrection . . .

At last, the execution.

Kill the queer vampires!

I hadn't met the two gay vampires they discussed but knew they were Antonio's friends. They deserve to die. I thought as a sinister grin crossed my face.

"This way," my dad said, gesturing to hurry.

As my dad sprinted down the long hallway toward the Chief of Staff's office, I followed, my gaze fixed on his toned butt. I couldn't believe that this strong man whom I desired was my father. I was eager to feel his hardness again.

Antonio

AS WE SEARCHED for Peter and Jackson, the unending labyrinth of the compound quickly became overwhelming. My heart sank with each wrong turn, and I began to worry that we would never find the arena. Despite the signs posted along the hallways, there was no mention of where the stadium might be. I glanced at Lucien and saw the same frustration on his face. But even in the face of our mounting disappointment, he remained calm and focused. His unwavering dedication gave me a glimmer of hope that we would eventually find my friends.

"We need to keep moving," Lucien said, his voice steady.

I turned to him, my trust deepening as we continued to work together. The bond we had forged since I had turned him into a vampire had only grown stronger, and I knew that he would do anything to help me. I nodded in agreement, knowing we couldn't give up yet.

As we made our way through the complex maze, our determination to find Peter and Jackson had never been more vital. Every twist and turn seemed to bring us further from our goal, but we kept soldiering. Then, suddenly, my mind flooded with a weak telepathic message. Despite the interference caused by the dense concrete walls, I somehow managed to pick up Peter's statement.

He informed me the execution chamber was filled with vampires. We were outnumbered and outmatched. Our only hope was to find my father and devise a new plan. As we continued to navigate through the compound, the weight of the situation weighed heavily on us.

I called my father telepathically and asked where he was. He responded by saying in Sick Bay. However, he didn't want me to come. I stopped abruptly in my tracks, bewildered by my father's response.

I gasped as he revealed that my mother had passed away. The shock of his words was so overwhelming that I felt like a bolt of lightning had struck me. Lucien noticed my distress and was quick to offer his condolences. As tears streamed down my face, I announced the need to see her, despite knowing the futility of it. But my father's response was stark and unyielding.

"No, son. You need to remember her the way she was."

The weight of the situation was unbearable, and I couldn't imagine how my father must have felt at that moment. As our telepathic connection faltered and we lost contact, I knew we had to find each other. The situation's urgency was greater than ever, and we had to band together to face the looming threat that awaited us.

Lucien and I continued onward. We soon turned a

corner, and I heard the loud sound of machinery. Curious about what it could be, I slowly opened the door and peered inside. What greeted me was a large and complex pumping system that worked tirelessly to ensure the compound remained dry. As I wiped the tears from my eyes, my mind started racing with thoughts until Lucien tapped my shoulder and gestured that someone was outside in the hallway. I quietly closed the door and told him we'd wait until it was safe to leave.

David

AS SALVATORE and my father's conversation ebbed and flowed in hushed tones, I perched at Salvatore's desk, my mind drifting to Antonio's thoughts. Although his father had denied him access to the infirmary to see his deceased mother, Antonio still had an overwhelming desire to go there. I couldn't help but smirk in response to his selfish intent. Serves you right, asshole, I thought without an ounce of sympathy. As the smirk on my face grew into a wide grin, an idea dawned on me — my morphed identity would make it easy to surprise him. With a sense of daring, I contemplated the possibility of following through. However, Salvatore soon interrupted his conversation with my dad and approached me. Despite my disguise, he knew who I was. At that moment, all that mattered was that I was on board and fully committed to his cause — he no longer cared that I was a defector.

I felt excited as I shook Salvatore's hand, captivated by his firm, tall frame and commanding presence. His military uniform turned me on in a way I had never experienced before. As our eyes met, I couldn't help but think how attractive he was despite our differences — which were quickly forgotten, given his offer for freedom if I helped kill his son.

Wishing to subdue my arousal, I left the office to find Antonio.

Salvatore acknowledged my exit while my father gave me a perplexed expression. I told him I had something important to care for and the details would come later. I departed as he questioned my actions.

***

Entering Sick Bay, I was surprised to find William without Antonio. I approached him cautiously, my heart heavy from the sight before me. He was paying his last respects to his dearly departed wife. His glance was weary and fear-filled, yet he looked upon me with surprise as I entered in disguise. I lifted my hand in friendliness. "I'm not here to hurt you," I said softly.

The fool believed me.

William's naiveté was evident. I knew Antonio had inherited this foolishness from his father. Taking advantage of the opportunity to get back at Antonio, I willed William to stand and remove his clothing. He fell into my trance and followed my orders without hesitation.

He stood naked before me.

Without wasting time, I closed the curtain around the bed and dropped to my knees. Grasping William's groin, my tongue excitedly explored the head as I pushed back the foreskin. I savored the taste, feeling my arousal growing. I unbuttoned my uniform and began to stroke. My balls were full in anticipation of having sex with my father, so I needed to release my built-up sexual energy.

William stiffened in pleasure. I licked his prick from the base to the tip. His moan soon changed in intensity as I ran my tongue over his nut sack, eliciting a reaction of delight. His body was hot, and I could feel his desire emanating forth. His manly scent only added to the experience. Had he ever been rimmed before? I turned him around and bent him over so that I could spread his ass cheeks. I drove my tongue right into his hole. His moans grew louder as he enjoyed the sensation. A thought crept in — would it be revenge if I fucked him? But then another idea presented itself, what if he screwed me instead?

I rose to my feet and turned him around. In his trance-like state, his eyes were captivated entirely by me. Bending forward ever so slightly, I pressed my lips against his. My tongue glided through the opening and into his mouth when he parted his lips. Although he didn't reciprocate with a tongue of his own, it was still wonderfully sensuous.

With a slight grin spreading across my face and a glint in my eye, I spat into my palm and coated his boner with my saliva, rubbing it around the head and down the shaft. Anticipation coursed through me as I presented my eager hole, pushing back eagerly against him. As he slid into me, I felt an initial burst of pain that quickly converted to pleasure that had me arching my back and moaning with satisfaction. The sensation of his six inches filling me was intense, and I relished the feeling of being so completely filled. And despite the allure of a monster cock, I knew that nothing could compare to the satisfaction of this perfect fit.

He grasped my waist firmly and started thrusting in and out with the motion of a passionate lover. As I felt his presence, I couldn't help but smile and think of Antonio. I sent him a mental message, exuding confidence and power: "Look at me, bitch. Your father's fucking my ass!"

Telepathically, I felt Antonio's shock echoing through me. With a sly smirk, I declared, "Yes, it's me, David. I'm in disguise." I turned around, seeing William's eyes widening with lustful anticipation. Knowing he hadn't screwed in years, I realized he would come quickly.

"Come inside me," I moaned, my body ushering him toward his climax. His eyes rolled back, and his orgasm built until, finally, the eruption came forth like a tidal wave of pleasure.

"Oh . . ." William moaned.

I reached down and grasped myself tightly and stroked. "Yes! Oh, yes. Pound me, goddamnit! Fuck me!" I shouted. I orgasmed simultaneously as he pumped his cum inside me. Once finished, I eagerly turned around and licked him clean. The salty spunk burnt my tongue, so I spat it out, but the pleasure was unmistakable.

I ordered him onto the bed next to his wife.

I felt the jizz burning inside me.

With a sense of urgency, I quickly took a deep breath and tried to calm my racing heart. I knew I needed to depress my pelvic muscles to expel the unwanted fluids, so I braced myself against the wall. Despite my best efforts, nothing came out, and the realization worsened my panic. I pushed harder, gritting my teeth as beads of sweat broke out on my forehead. My face turned red with the effort, and I could feel my breathing become more labored. "Oh shit!" I muttered to myself in frustration as the pain became overwhelming. "This will be the death of me!" I felt utterly defeated momentarily, the weight of the situation bearing down on me.

I heard Antonio's obnoxious laughter echoing inside my head. The bastard thought this was funny. My revenge had backfired. But then, taking a deep breath, I gathered my composure and tried again. This time, I focused on relaxing my muscles before contracting them with more force, bearing down with everything I had. And finally, with a sudden gush, the jizz flowed out of me. I let out a relieved breath, knowing I wouldn't die. I admired the large amount on the floor and then returned to William. "My father was right," I said. "You're the epitome of a man."

Antonio's voice entered my head again.

"You fucker! I'm on my way, you son-of-a-bitch!"

I couldn't help but smile as I heard his reprimand. I quickly morphed back into myself, dressed, and made my way to the door. As I closed it behind me, I locked it from the outside for good measure.

Robert

DAVID EXCUSED himself from the office, leaving Salvatore and me alone. Relief flooded through me as I realized my son's execution wouldn't take place after all. My appreciation was evident as I shook Salvatore's hand in gratitude. His expression suggested he had a few unanswered questions, so I peered deep into his mind using my powers to ascertain what was troubling him — he knew I was a homosexual.

"My sexuality doesn't affect how I serve you," I forced out, my voice wavering slightly. The anxiety on Salvatore's face dissipated as he took a long breath to compose himself. "I've been an incredibly committed comrade. Please don't let this come between us," I finished, looking him in the eye with determination.

He slowly nodded, realization dawning on his face.

"I get it," he said.

By this point, I had preserved our bond and ensured that my son was safe from harm, and I felt confident in my actions.

Salvatore and I exchanged a few more words before leaving to meet David at Sick Bay, as he had telepathically instructed me to do so. As I reflected on what had just happened with Salvatore, I felt we both had grown stronger because of it — now understanding each other a little better than before. Hope filled my heart for the first time in what felt like forever, and I let out a contented sigh.

Antonio

LUCIEN AND I sprinted down the hallway, determined to confront David and ensure he didn't get away with what he had done to my father. It was personal now. As we ran, I glanced at Lucien, who was keeping pace with me. "Listen closely," I said breathlessly. "If something happens, I need you to run back and destroy the pumping station. We need to flood this fucking compound!" Lucien nodded in agreement, his expression serious.

"I won't let you down."

I felt a surge of pride at his words. Lucien was a good soldier. I knew he had my back. We pushed ourselves harder, sprinting down the corridors toward Sick Bay. The twisting labyrinth felt never-ending. We'd be lost if it weren't for the signs pointing us in the right direction. Despite my shaking hands and deep dread, I was determined to confront David and ensure that he would face the consequences of his actions. As we made our way toward the infirmary, I paused momentarily and turned to thank Lucien for being with me. His presence provided comfort and security as I faced what could be one of the most challenging moments of my life.

"You're welcome," he said, smiling at me warmly.

I warned him to be ready for anything if David put up a fight. "He's evil, like his father," I muttered darkly. "So, don't fall victim to his deceitfulness." Lucien nodded once again.

"I'll be fine. Don't worry," he said.

My palms were slick with sweat as my mental faculties scrambled to process the magnitude of the situation. As we cautiously advanced, a sign that identified Sick Bay loomed ahead of us. I inhaled deeply and mentally steeled myself for what was to come.

Salvatore

AS I WAITED in the corridor, accompanied by Robert and David, my thoughts wandered to what life could have been like had I convinced Antonio's mother to divorce William and live with me. I could have raised him as my son and developed him into a masculine individual, not one with delicate features that gave off effeminate vibes.

I remembered my mother's brother, Alessandro, the only other person in our family I knew to be queer. The last time I'd seen my uncle was at a family dinner in 1485. I was too young to understand the situation fully, but while we ate, he talked about a man he'd fallen in love with. My grandmother became so emotionally overwhelmed she left the room in tears while my grandfather and Alessandro exchanged harsh words.

My grandfather rose to his feet, thrusting a finger toward the door in a bold gesture, and roared for him to get out. His voice reverberated throughout the room, vibrating the walls and causing a chill to run down my spine.

My uncle dropped his gaze in shock at being dismissed from the residence. As he shuffled out the door and into the darkness, I knew I would never see him again.

My grandfather settled back into his chair, a silence filling the air. I admired him for his courage and the wisdom he imparted to me. That night he taught me a valuable lesson — sometimes reality must be accepted, and moving on is best.

I sighed wistfully, my mind drifting back to when I was thirty-four years old and living in Florence, Italy. The Middle Ages were prosperous for many Florentines, thanks to the generous patrons who encouraged and funded the writers and artists who hailed from the region.

On one fateful night, as I made my way home after an evening spent drinking and carousing with loose women, I crossed the Ponte Vecchio arch bridge and was confronted by a stranger dressed in black. Instantly my life changed forever as he revealed himself to be a vampire.

For hundreds of years since then, I have borne witness to numerous events in history while at the same time accumulating countless memories throughout my five-hundred-and-forty-five-year lifespan. It's been an extraordinary journey, but I can still recall when it all began on that eerie bridge in Florence many years ago.

The man moved quickly. Before I knew it, he had bitten me on the neck. As he began drinking my blood, I heard his voice inside my head, explaining what he was doing — transforming me into a vampire and what I needed to do once I woke up. Though I could not see his face, something about him seemed strangely familiar, almost as though I had known him before.

After he drank my blood, his eyes glinted with an insatiable hunger as he urged me to pleasure him. With my heart pounding in my chest, I reluctantly complied, feeling the weight of his dominant and powerful presence upon me. This was the first time I had ever felt a man's cock in my mouth, and as the taste of his salty essence flooded my senses, I knew without a doubt that it would be my last. The vampire's voice echoed through my head as he declared that his seed was the gift of eternity, so he made me swallow every drop. Despite the intimacy we had just shared, he left without even a word of explanation, leaving me to wonder why he had selected me.

I awoke in the street to the warm morning sun on my face, feeling an unnatural heat coursing through my veins. Quickly, I ran until I found shelter, remembering the vampire's words. When it was safe for me to venture out again, I left Florence behind and traveled to Rome — leaving my family without explanation. In 1895 I moved to America and started a new life, never looking back on what had transpired in Italy.

I've lived a long life of loneliness.

I exhaled slowly, a wave of apprehension washing over

me as I heard thundering footsteps coming ever closer. I knew my son was just moments away from turning the corner, and it seemed like an eternity before he made his appearance. Anxiety bubbled inside me — what would he do when faced with the three of us?

The footsteps suddenly stopped, and I held my breath, waiting for the inevitable moment. My son slowly stepped around the corner, his face a combination of shock and fear. He looked from me to David and Robert standing beside me. Standing tall out of nervousness, I took a deep breath and brushed the creases from my shirt.

Antonio

I WAS SURPRISED to see my biological father, Salvatore, standing in the hallway with Robert and David. It felt like I was looking into a mirror since he looked so much like me, with his Italian ancestry on full display. Questions ran through my mind. Where did he come from? What was his story? Why did he hate me?

Despite being outnumbered by the three of them, I stood firm and held Salvatore's gaze. David stepped back in surprise at the sight of my white hair. Lucien must have sensed something terrible because he turned and ran back toward the pumping station.

I never stopped to think how I'd react once I saw my birth father. I stared in shock, oblivious to Robert and David moving to surround me. So many questions continued to run through my head. Why did he mistreat my mother? The questions wouldn't stop surfacing.

"Antonio?"

He said my name. I backed up, afraid, as he raised his hand to shake. Was I supposed to forgive everything he did to my mother? Within seconds I realized it was only a gesture to distract me because Robert and David grabbed my arms, holding me captive.

I turned, reading David's mind. He hated me. "You're a bastard," I said under my breath. I'd never forgive him for molesting my father.

He smirked and gloated that my father had seeded his ass well.

Salvatore stepped boldly forward and fixed his gaze upon my groin with an intensity that made me uncomfortable. He seemed to be looking for something, though I could not be sure if it was a resemblance to him or simply a desire to examine this strange new body part more closely. After what felt like an eternity, he finally exhaled, a sound of disappointment emanating from his lips.

"She circumcised you," he said softly, almost as if he was speaking more to himself than to me. "How disappointing."

I opened my mouth to express my displeasure at the comment, but he quickly shot me a warning that made it clear that I should remain silent. His gaze shifted up and away from my groin, and he pointed at the hair on my head.

"What's with the white hair?" he said scornfully. "It's so gay!"

An intense feeling of inner turmoil surged within me, stemming from the awareness of the truth about my hair color. Its unique hue was a manifestation of divine light. However, the prospect of disclosing this revelation to him filled me with an unbearable sense of dread and apprehension.

After being severely tested, my patience had finally reached its limit. Holding back my disapproval of his actions was no longer an option. My mother's unfair treatment weighed heavily on my mind, and I knew it was a matter I could not let pass without addressing it directly. All around me, the air in the room was thick with tension and unease as I steeled myself for what was to come. Despite the fear coursing through me, I mustered all the courage I could and decided that now was the time to confront him. My voice shook with rage as I looked directly into his eyes and demanded that he answer for his actions. "Why did you mistreat my mother?" I said, my voice rising in anger.

"How dare you speak to me without permission?" he snarled.

"She loved you at one time!" I shouted.

He roared with rage, slapping me across the face.

At that moment, I noticed David's satisfied grin and saw his erection poking through his uniform. The situation turned him on. In response, I spat in Salvatore's face and declared defiantly, "Fuck you!"

Wiping away my sputum with revulsion, Salvatore sneered down at my groin — recognizing the similarities between our members. With pure contempt dripping off every syllable, he snarled at me.

"You repulse me."

He turned and walked away, leaving me feeling hatred for him. His callousness was infuriating as he turned to Robert.

"Do what you want with him — I couldn't care less."

His cold indifference seethed within me, bubbling up into a shout of rage. "I hate you!" I yelled after his retreating figure, but he didn't look back. The realization that my queer identity sickened him filled me with disgust. Suddenly, the grip of David's hand on my arm startled me out of my reverie — and the seductive grin on his face indicated what kind of punishment he had in mind.

Lucien

MY HEART raced as I ran, desperate to reach the pump station, before it was too late and the vampires caught Antonio. I fumbled with the doorknob with shaky fingers and hastily shut myself in. I had no idea what I was up against, but my sharp mind told me that if I succeeded in destroying the pumps, Antonio might have a fighting chance.

My heart pounded in my chest as I frantically searched for something, anything that could help me.

Finally, I spotted a small control panel near the corner of the room. It seemed to be the key to shutting down the pumps — all I had to do was figure out how to use it. I took a deep breath and began tinkering with the various buttons and switches until, finally, with a triumphant roar, the pumps stopped running.

Antonio

AS I DESPERATELY tried to free myself from their grip, David and Robert effortlessly dragged me down the hallway toward the locker room. Even though I stubbornly fought against them, their superior vampire strength made it impossible for me to resist. I mumbled in a confused stupor, "I killed you. I saw you turn into ashes." This comment caused Robert to hiss while David chuckled with amusement.

Finally arriving at the men's locker room, they pushed me into the shower enclosure, trapping me in hopes of preventing any escape. They began removing their uniforms when I fell to the tile floor. My assumption was correct — the father-son duo planned on breeding me.

Fear and terror flooded my mind as I watched Robert lower his military-style pants, revealing an eight-inch erection that had previously been just six inches. Nothing made sense to me at that moment — all I could do was huddle against the wall, paralyzed with fear. Horror spread across my face as I pleaded desperately. "Please don't hurt me." This wasn't a game anymore, and I knew it.

My dick shriveled, mirroring my fear.

With swiftness, Robert lifted me and turned me to face the wall. His hand slowly explored my muscular ass before unexpectedly delivering a sharp slap. He then spread my ass cheeks wide, a menacing gesture that filled me with dread and caused my breath to catch in my throat.

"Look at that fuck hole!" he moaned in excitement, displaying my puckering anus.

"Finger him," David whispered, stroking himself.

I gasped in pain as Robert's unlubricated finger entered me.

He growled, "Dry bitch!"

Robert quickly removed his finger, squatted down, and began to rim me. His long tongue expertly slipped into my hole, again and again, making me wet. I couldn't believe how far Robert had come. In the past, he would never think of sucking, swallowing sperm, or rimming ass!

Robert stepped back and gestured for David to come forward. As David stepped closer, I turned and saw Robert standing, kissing him passionately.

Their tongues intertwined, and their moans filled the room with pleasure. It felt like a scene from a horror movie — two people engaged in an act of incestuous pleasure. I couldn't believe what I saw and shouted, "You're sick!"

David pulled away from his father, smiling mischievously. He then squatted down, and I watched in disbelief as he deep-throated his dad. I moaned in disgust, unable to utter a single word. With my eyes closed in repulsion, I prayed that this nightmare would end soon.

I opened my eyes in pain and disbelief as David entered me. He thrust deep, his scrotum hitting me with every thrust. I tried to push my ass out to lessen the pain, but he seemed hell-bent on hurting me. My face pounded against the tile wall as he thrust back and forth.

"Take his big cock!" Robert shouted.

David pulled out each time, only to quickly ram his

erection back inside me. My moans seemed to turn him on, and I knew it wouldn't be long before he came. He increased his thrusts, pushing me further and further into the wall.

As his cum spilled into me, my head shot back in pain. I knew what was coming next. His toxic seed would kill me instantaneously.

"Die, you fucking whore!" he spat and pulled out, gesturing for Robert to finish the job.

But instead of Robert entering me as expected, he knelt and spread my ass cheeks wide, rimming me again with his tongue.

"Oh, fuck!" he moaned, lapping up David's sperm.

I didn't understand why these two had such a sexual fascination for each other. It scared me greatly, and I felt violated in the most horrid way. Then an unexpected idea came over me — maybe if I pushed David's seed into Robert's mouth, he'd stop this hateful act — so that's exactly what I did. "Fuck you!" I whispered, pushing it out of my ass.

The sound of David's seed exiting was loud and obnoxious. However, it didn't bother Robert. I heard him moaning loudly in sexual bliss, relishing the taste. My plan backfired. He wanted to savor every drop. He held it inside his mouth for as long as possible, then spit it out.

I braced myself for his hardness.

"Spread your ass cheeks!" Robert demanded.

I did as he told me. He wasted no time. He stood up, grabbed my waist, and started thrusting inside me. The pain was intense, and all eight inches felt like it enveloped my whole rectum. Seconds later, he let out a loud moan signaling the end of his penetration as he filled my insides with his sperm. The force of his ejaculation took me by surprise, and he shot it so deeply that I knew it wouldn't be coming out anytime soon.

"Can I have a piece of that ass?"

A soldier stepped into the shower, and I couldn't help but notice how his eyes flicked over me with a knowing gaze. It was clear that he had been cruising the bathroom, and his hard-on stood at attention as he moved toward us. It became evident that Robert was already familiar with this stranger as their eyes met in a silent understanding. With a sudden exertion of force, Robert pushed me to my knees, his lust filling his mind as he looked down at me. I felt a mix of fear race through me as I took in the soldier's dick, standing proud and ready for action.

"Shoot inside his mouth!" Robert demanded, gripping tightly onto my hair, keeping my head firmly in place.

I opened my mouth, and that was where the third load went. The soldier continued stroking until he emptied himself inside me, gathering at the base of my throat. I then looked at David for assistance, only to find him mouthing, "Screw you." At that moment, I knew this was it — this would be my end.

"Swallow it!" Robert commanded as the spent soldier stepped away from me.

I swallowed the sperm, and as Robert released my hair, I wiped away the residual fluid on my face and waited for the poison to take effect. I prayed it would be swift, not wanting to satisfy them with a prolonged death. David crossed his arms, expecting me to collapse, but nothing happened.

"What the fuck?" David shouted in surprise, "Why isn't he dead?"

His words echoed my thoughts. I lowered my head in contemplation, surprised that neither my rectum nor throat was burning. Had Jesus's seed changed all that?

Lucien

I SHUT THE pump down, but someone could quickly turn it back on, so I needed to damage it to ensure it would never work again permanently. I hurriedly rushed to the tool closet at the far end of the room and grabbed a mallet off one of the pegs along its walls. Without wasting time, I dashed back to the pumping device and raised my weapon above my head, striking it against metal with each blow. The sound reverberated throughout the chamber, causing a man resembling Antonio to burst through the door.

I frantically sprinted toward the alarm on the side of the wall. I knew I needed to forewarn everyone that the pumps had stopped working. The elder Antonio was hot on my heels, his anger evident in every step he took.

With great urgency, I reached out and pulled the lever. Suddenly, a loud ringing filled the room, and the walls began to vibrate as the emergency evacuation alarm became activated.

Antonio

THE SUDDEN blaring of the alarm jolted us out of our moment, and Robert screamed in frustration. As Robert and David dressed, the cruising vampire made a swift exit. Just as I stepped out of the shower, David tackled me, his hands gripping tightly onto my neck. I stared back in shock, feeling nothing despite his fingers squeezing harder around my throat. His body pressed against mine, but I no longer felt any attraction toward him. In fact, being so close to him made me feel somewhat sickened.

"Why aren't you dying?" David shouted as sweat poured from his forehead.

His grip tightened around my neck.

I launched myself forward, my body radiating with powerful energy. David recoiled in fear, his eyes widening in disbelief as he took in my newly acquired strength. As he backed away, I raced toward freedom, leaving him behind me.

"What . . . the fuck?" David stammered in confusion, struggling to comprehend what he had just witnessed.

It was as if I had vanished instantly — another strange occurrence courtesy of the Son of God.

I rushed down the corridor, my feet splashing through the torrent of water that had flooded the compound. Sending out a telepathic distress call to Peter, Jackson, and Angelo, I told them to flee the compound and meet me at the bathhouse in the French Quarter. I received multiple acknowledgments in response, but soon their voices started to stutter, and everything went silent.

Panicking, I frantically scanned my surroundings for an escape route as the water level rapidly rose. With every passing minute, the floodwaters submerged more of the compound. My heart felt like it would jump out of my chest as I pushed deeper into the hallway, desperately seeking a way out before it was too late.

I swiveled in circles, feeling disoriented and confused as the water reached my waist. Desperately I called out for my dad, but there was only silence.

Taking a deep breath, I tried to steady myself and stay calm to survive this ordeal. I spotted a reddish glow radiating from an exit sign further down the hallway. I ran toward it with renewed vigor while shouting for my dad again — but still no reply. A sense of dread crept over me at the thought of living eternity without him by my side.

Salvatore

I RACED AFTER the perpetrator, desperately trying to catch him before he could cause more damage. With every step, my anger at him for endangering us all grew. When I finally managed to corner him, we both tumbled into a pool of murky water. Instinctively I pushed his head beneath the surface and cursed him fiercely. He gripped my neck in a futile attempt to break free, but his scrawny body was no match for me. Tears of rage filled my eyes as I held him underwater, screaming profanities.

Just then, the door suddenly opened, and a surprised Angelo stepped through with a vengeance on his face. Before I had time to react, he punched me square in the jaw with enough force that I lost my grip on the perpetrator and fell back into the water with a splash.

Angelo yanked the exhausted man from the water, leaving me stunned and submerged up to my chest. Angelo abandoned the prisoner and came at me again. I stood and instinctively raised my arms to protect my face from his strike. However, instead of hitting me with his fist, he lifted my body and tossed me like a rag doll toward the broken pump. I felt powerless as I crashed into it, and then everything went dark because I lost consciousness.

Peter

AS THE EXECUTION chamber rapidly filled with water, I struggled to maintain composure amidst the chaos. Peering through the glass, I caught sight of the lifeless bodies of the vampires, submerged and floating in the seating area. Turning my attention to the elders, I noticed their motionless forms carried away by the forceful currents. Aware that our demise was imminent, I quickly assessed the situation. Spotting the escape hatch, I urgently gestured to the five men who were to become vampires and Jackson, making it clear that seizing this opportunity was crucial for our survival.

Gripped by terror, Jackson thrashed his arms wildly in the water, yelling that he couldn't swim. Doing my best to suppress my rising panic, I offered him calm guidance on how to tread water to stay afloat. Suddenly, a loud boom reverberated throughout the chamber as the door succumbed to the immense pressure of the surging water. In a matter of seconds, the entrance to the seating area blew open, causing a torrent of water to flood the execution chamber with even greater force.

Jackson shrieked for help.

One of the humans grabbed and held him. Jackson clung to the handsome man, frightened for his life as the water rose.

Terrified of impending death, I positioned myself under the hatch, just six inches between us and the glass ceiling. I took a deep breath and hit the bar on the emergency door. The hatch flew open with force, slamming back against the glass.

"Let's go!" I shouted, reaching for Jackson.

The human beside him pushed him to safety. He gestured for me to exit next. I did and pulled each of the humans through the doorway.

Sitting on the glass, I looked at Jackson and smiled. Despite the odds against us, we managed to survive. I took his hand in mine and embraced him tenderly. As I pulled away, I saw kindness in him that I had never seen before.

William

THE SITUATION was critical as water seeped under the Sick Bay door and quickly rose to waist level. I panicked when I realized my cries for help were drowned out by the alarm, leaving me stranded with no escape. I had to think fast and plan before it was too late. The vampires in the room could not swim and drowned immediately, their bodies sinking below the water.

Despite my frantic attempts to contact Antonio, he was my last hope, and I couldn't reach him. A sense of hopelessness washed over me as I looked around at the rapidly filling room. Suddenly, I felt something in my arms — my wife's lifeless body. In desperation, I cradled her and kissed her forehead one last time. To my shock and disbelief, she gasped for air and opened her eyes.

"William?"

As I looked down, my heart sank. I screamed in pain and frustration, hoping she could find peace in death.

She passed away after her eyes closed once more, fulfilling my prayers. I was left alone to face the rising floodwaters. I held her tight as the water rose above my chest and sobbed uncontrollably. The darkness surrounded me, and I knew my time was running out.

Harry

THE SITUATION seemed almost hopeless, yet a faint glimmer of hope remained. Antonio's telepathic warning had come just in time, allowing me to evade the rapidly rising floodwaters. The fact that I was still alive was nothing short of a miracle.

Earlier, when the guards had led us out of the cell to have our blood drained, I had taken advantage of a brief distraction and managed to slip away without being noticed. Even now, I could scarcely believe my audacity and that my bold move had worked.

My heart pounded with fear and adrenaline as I followed the exit signs through the compound. Had Antonio made it out in time? I couldn't be sure. The water rose higher and higher, eventually reaching my chest. It was a struggle to keep moving forward, but I knew that giving up meant certain death.

As I stumbled through the darkened water, I encountered dead vampires. It was a strange sight — could they not swim? Why were they all dead? Suddenly, my heart skipped a beat as the sensation of something grabbing my ankle sent shivers down my spine. Panic set in as I struggled to free myself from the unknown entity lurking beneath the murky water. The darkness made it impossible to identify what had taken hold of me, and my mind raced with terrifying possibilities.

A forceful tug yanked me underwater.

I fought with all my might to break free from its grasp. With each passing moment, my lungs burned for air, and I knew that time was running out. It was a fight for survival, and I could only hope to emerge victorious against the unknown force pulling me deeper. With all my strength, I shook off the hand and resurfaced for air, gasping for breath.

But it wasn't over yet. The hand pulled me back down. I felt a surge of fear and anger rise within me. I started kicking with all my might, hoping to push my attacker away.

Finally, my foot connected with something solid. With a burst of adrenaline-fueled power, I pushed my attacker away and surfaced. As I looked around in confusion and horror, my attacker emerged with me — dead. I realized that the being pulling me down was a young boy in uniform.

The realization of the situation hit me like a ton of bricks. This boy was too young to be a soldier. How had he ended up here? My mind raced with questions as I contemplated what to do next. Should I try to revive him? I answered my question and reached for the boy, starting CPR. But unfortunately, it was too late. With a heavy heart, I let him float away and continued wading through the rising floodwaters.

Antonio

MY HEART plummeted with the crushing realization that my seemingly perfect escape had been a fleeting illusion. As I trudged through the water, I couldn't help but glance back, only to witness Robert and David closing in on me with unnerving speed, their eyes locked onto me with deadly resolve.

Without any warning, David initiated his assault, propelling himself from the water's depths like a missile aimed directly at me. His powerful strike caught me off guard, causing me to lose footing and tumble headfirst into the water.

As we clashed, I could feel the adrenaline surging through my body, fueling every punch and kick with an intensity that matched my opponent's. Our battle was fierce and calculated as we traded a series of forceful blows, each of us determined to emerge victorious.

In a swift motion, I managed to kick David away, creating much-needed distance between us.

However, it wasn't long before Robert sprang into action, launching his relentless attacks. He started pounding me relentlessly, forcing me to cover my face and brace for the impact.

Summoning all the strength I had left, I kicked him.

To my surprise, my newfound strength was enough to overcome the resistance of the water and send him flying like a rag doll. I watched triumphantly as he slammed against the unforgiving cement wall before falling into the water. A surge of adrenaline coursed through my veins as I shouted in defiance. "Fuck you!" With a final show of contempt, I raised my middle finger in scorn toward Robert's fallen form.

As I continued, I saw David pulling his motionless father from the water. Quickly refocusing, I headed toward the exit sign. As I reached the staircase, the rising water propelled me upwards with great force.

***

Stumbling toward the stone door, I couldn't find a way to open it. Frustrated and scared, I shouted at the concrete cherub on the other side of the boulder to let me out. After fighting off David and Robert successfully, I didn't want to die this way.

I instinctively cried out desperately, imploring Jesus to aid me in this seemingly hopeless situation.

Feeling overwhelmed by the intensity of my emotions, tears streamed down my face as I sobbed uncontrollably. My heart was heavy with despair. I pounded on the door, desperately seeking an escape from my predicament. Then, without warning, the room was bathed in a brilliant, almost blinding light that left me squinting and struggling to comprehend what was happening.

As the dazzling brightness gradually subsided, I was astonished to find the figure of the archangel Gabriel materializing before me again, his divine presence filling the room with serenity.

I observed Gabriel, devoid of a loin cloth, without his iconic golden trumpet. I couldn't help but notice his chiseled body, free of hair, except for a small patch above his groin. His shoulder-length tresses displayed a blend of rich brown hues intermingled with subtle blonde highlights, framing his ethereal visage. I couldn't help but notice his uncircumcised penis, which appeared long and slender, completing the striking image of this celestial being.

"I've been appointed your watcher."

"My guardian angel?"

Gabriel nodded.

I couldn't remove my eyes from his body. He was beautiful, as if he stepped out of a Rembrandt painting.

Despite the rising water, Gabriel remained calm, comforting me as the water reached the landing and rose above my ankles.

"I don't know how to open the door."

He became aroused.

I caught my breath, surprised to see this from him.

"I appreciate beauty, too," Gabriel whispered. His mischievous smile gave him away as he stared at my groin.

His comment stunned me, and I couldn't help but wonder if angels had sex. Before I could further ponder the question, Gabriel gestured at the stone door and floated toward it. I watched as he pointed to a concealed lever at the base of the wall.

I depressed the lever, causing the stone door to open. But when I turned around to thank him, he was nowhere in sight — he had returned to heaven. Despite his mysterious departure, I felt grateful for his guidance during our brief encounter.

I left the compound, feeling a mix of relief and rage. The concrete statue, which seemed to despise me, confronted me with flailing arms. I couldn't resist taunting him about the compound's destruction and everyone's demise. As I reached for him, he hissed in fear. In anger, I grasped his head and pulled down, causing the concrete to crack before his bulbous head fell from his body. I shouted my final insult at the statue as it screamed its last breath and collided with the granite base.

Angelo

AS I PAINSTAKINGLY navigated my way toward the exit, the burden of Lucien's frail body weighed heavily in my arms. The severe beating inflicted by Salvatore had left its mark, and I was acutely aware that every passing second was crucial if we were to escape with our lives. "Stay with me," I murmured, hoping that my words would bring some solace to Lucien as we trudged through the ever-rising water. Then, unexpectedly, he spoke up, his voice barely more than a hushed breath.

"Antonio swallowed Christ's seed. It was a gift."

His enigmatic words lingered between us like a thick haze, filling me with confusion and uncertainty about their meaning. Before I could inquire further, Lucien's body sagged against me again, slipping back unconscious. I couldn't help but dwell on his cryptic remark as we pressed on. Had Antonio undergone some transformation?

My train of thought was abruptly interrupted by the sight of a staircase emerging from the shadows up ahead. The path to our escape seemed tantalizingly close, but I knew we couldn't afford to let our guard down.

Upon reaching the stairs, I felt a surge of renewed determination course through me. With careful haste, I ascended the steps, avoiding any missteps that could result in us falling into the treacherous waters below.

As I arrived at the landing, I pushed the lever downward. A wave of relief swept over me while I waited for the massive stone door to open — we were finally out of harm's way. However, as we stepped out of that perilous environment, I couldn't help but notice Lucien's delicate figure resting on my shoulder.

"Stay with me," I murmured once again.

Lucien came to, lifting his head toward me.

"You saved me. Thank you."

After Lucien expressed his gratitude, I felt a sense of unease. "We're not out of harm's way yet," I warned him, bracing myself for obstacles that might come our way. Holding Lucien close, I ran into the darkness without looking back, determined to keep us both safe from whatever lay ahead.

Robert

A WAVE OF relief washed over me, enveloping my entire being as I regained consciousness in the secure embrace of my son's arms. There he was, my guardian angel, keeping me afloat in the water and ensuring my safety. With a gentle voice filled with concern, he asked how I was feeling, wanting to ensure I was alright. I could only nod in response, unable to express my gratitude through words. Instead, I leaned in and tenderly planted a heartfelt kiss on his cheek.

"We'll survive this nightmare and take that bastard down!"

David's words instilled hope and fortitude within me. United as father and son, we were determined to triumph over the situation — whatever it took.

By now, the water level had risen alarmingly, leaving us with two feet of breathing space. Evidently, we would meet a watery end if we didn't exit swiftly.

"I'll follow your lead," David instructed.

I began swimming toward the exit, feeling my body heal and my strength return. With each passing moment, I swam more rapidly, my eagerness to escape intensifying. Upon reaching the staircase, I spun around to check on David — but he was nowhere in sight.

"David!" I yelled desperately, plunging back into the

murky water without hesitation. Frantically, I searched for him, extending my arms and kicking my legs to cover as much ground as possible. The darkness and swirling debris made the search even more challenging, but I refused to give up.

Despite my relentless efforts, there was no trace of him. With a heavy heart, I resurfaced, gasping for air. That's when I spotted David's lifeless body floating beside me. A cold dread gripped me — what had happened? He was an adept swimmer. Such a fate seemed impossible.

I quickly grabbed him, pulling his head above the water's surface. Desperately, I attempted to revive my son, administering rescue breaths and chest compressions with tears streaming down my face. I couldn't bear the thought of losing him after everything we had been through.

My tears flowed as the realization that I might lose him began to set in. A thunderous boom reverberated through the water, causing the walls around us to tremble. The explosion within the compound propelled us upwards, forcing us onto the staircase and toward safety.

With unwavering determination, I hoisted David's unresponsive body and approached the open stone door. As we emerged into the open, I gently laid him down. Refusing to give up, I continued my efforts to revive him, administering CPR with desperation and hope.

Antonio

THE SOUND of Robert's frenzied voice pierced the stillness of the cemetery, snapping me out of my daze. I turned quickly to see him kneeling over David's lifeless body outside the mausoleum, his hands shaking as he attempted to revive him. A sharp gasp escaped my lips as I realized that David had drowned, and the gravity of the situation hit me like a ton of bricks. Without thinking, I muttered through gritted teeth, "Burn in hell." Deep down, I knew it wasn't the right thing to say, but I couldn't control my emotions.

Not wanting to draw attention to myself, I lowered my head and walked away from the scene. I navigated the cemetery maze quickly, passing two Reapers with outstretched arms. Ignoring them, I ran toward the cemetery gate, feeling a sense of relief wash over me as I jumped over it and landed on the other side.

As I surveyed my surroundings, I couldn't help but notice the eerie emptiness that enveloped both the cemetery and the adjacent street just beyond the entrance gate. It was a haunting silence devoid of any signs of life or activity. I couldn't help but wonder, where had everyone gone? The unnerving possibility that I may have been the sole survivor began to take root in my mind, and a wave of grief washed over me.

Memories of my father, who had gone missing amidst the chaos, flooded my thoughts, and I could not hold back the tears. Uncontrollable sobs erupted from deep within, and I hastily covered my mouth to muffle the heart-wrenching cries. Desperately, I tried to regain control of my emotions and compose myself, but it proved arduous.

To find some semblance of hope, I clung to the idea that perhaps everyone had managed to escape unharmed and were now gathered together at the bathhouse, waiting for my arrival. Deep down, I knew this was likely a fabrication, a desperate attempt to ward off the crushing despair. Yet, believing in this version of events gave me the courage and determination to keep moving forward.

Peter

"WE'RE ONLY making queer vampires," I declared with unwavering conviction, perched confidently on the transparent barrier that formed the ceiling of the execution chamber. I was fully conscious of the weight my words carried. The five men chosen for transformation stood before me — their fates now intertwined with mine.

A heavy, silent tension filled the air as each man stood in anticipation of what was to come. The stillness was shattered when one of the humans bravely decided to step forward. As he moved, every eye followed him, eager to know what thoughts he wished to share.

Exuding confidence, the man started to speak, his voice unwavering and resolute. He motioned toward two of his companions, drawing everyone's attention to them as he addressed me.

"We're bisexual. Our wish is to become vampires," he declared, asserting their desire to join the ranks of the undead.

I couldn't help but feel a sense of satisfaction at his revelation. It was a glimmer of hope, a sign that our mission to create a new generation of vampires might be possible. But at the same time, I knew this revelation also put these humans in great danger. By coming out, they had become outcasts, distinguishable in ways that made them vulnerable to the hostility of our adversaries.

His buddies nodded in agreement.

The three humans, as though on a mission to prove their sexuality, closed ranks and locked themselves into an embrace. Their bodies interlocked in a jumbled mass of limbs, muscles, and flesh as they held on tightly to each other. The raw passion that they shared was evident in their kisses. The physical signs of their arousal became more pronounced. Their crotches bulged and hardened as their erections stood up straight and proud. But soon, a sudden noise pierced through the air, jolting me out of my reverie and back into reality.

I looked down to see a vampire submerged underwater, pounding on the glass of the execution chamber. Panic filled his eyes, and then they went blank. It was a gruesome sight, but I couldn't help feeling a sudden pang of sympathy for the dead vampire, even though he had probably killed many humans in his lifetime. I realized that I should have jumped in to save him. Even though he was my enemy, it would have been the right thing to do. My mind raced with conflicting thoughts, and I knew this moment would stay with me for a long time. It was a reminder that sometimes, even our enemies deserved compassion and mercy.

As I sat there, lost in thought, the good-looking human touched my shoulder and pulled me away from the gruesome scene below. I took his hand, and he helped me stand.

Suddenly, the handsome man pulled me in for a deep kiss. I felt electricity course through my body. I pulled away, aware that the two straight humans were recoiling in disgust. They were shocked by the sexual activity unfolding before them. In response to their disapproval, I hissed and bared my sharp teeth, causing them to run away. But the handsome man stayed by my side, and I grasped him tightly, stroking him back and forth, unable to believe the size and girth of his erection.

"Suck it," he whispered.

I could feel my heart beating faster. I lowered myself to my knees and engulfed him in my mouth, his manly scent driving me wild with desire. I wanted nothing more than to bring him to ejaculation, but I knew we needed to keep moving to survive. I stopped sucking and smiled at him, introducing myself as Peter and pointing to Jackson, who was perched on the glass ceiling and smiling at us. I informed them of our plan to visit the bathhouse and invited them to join us.

The handsome man spoke up. "I'm Doug," he said,

gesturing toward his friends. "This is Bennet and Parker. We want to be vampires."

"Come with us," I said, my eyes drinking in his sturdy frame. "We'll have sex there, and then afterward, I'll make everyone into a vampire."

David

AS MY EYELIDS gradually lifted, revealing the world around me, my vision was filled with the familiar sight of my father's face. I could feel his protective presence hovering above me. The dampness of my clothes pressed against my skin created an uncomfortable sensation that weighed heavily upon me. At that moment, I became aware of my surroundings, realizing that I was sprawled on the cold ground just outside the foreboding walls of the vampire compound.

My eyes locked onto my father's, seeking answers to the questions racing through my mind. His expression, laden with worry and etched with fear and concern, communicated more than words ever could. In that instant, the truth dawned on me — I had been swallowed by the watery abyss, drowning in its dark embrace.

"Dad," I mumbled, my throat sore.

"You're alive!"

I nestled into the warmth of his arms, never wanting to let go. His embrace provided me with a comforting sense of security. I breathed in his familiar scent and relaxed as he wrapped his arms tightly around me.

"I thought I lost you," he said and smiled, removing the matted hair from my forehead.

As I gazed at him, his eyes became teary. I waited for him to say something more, but he remained silent and appeared deep in thought. I knew the thought of losing me scared him. I stayed quiet, feeling content in his arms.

The ground beneath us shook violently as another explosion rocked the compound. In the chaos and confusion, Salvatore Leone suddenly emerged from the depths of the water, struggling to stay afloat as he gasped for breath. My father didn't hesitate, immediately springing into action and pulled him to safety. I watched anxiously from a distance, my chest heavy with dread and uncertainty. As they emerged from the water, I approached them, my steps measured and cautious.

Salvatore couldn't catch his breath. "A prisoner . . . destroyed . . . the pumps."

"What?" my father exclaimed in shock.

Salvatore nodded, sitting down. "I tried to kill him . . . but a soldier entered . . . and saved him."

"A soldier?"

"Angelo Bianchi."

"Oh, my god!" my dad said.

"The bastard tried to kill me. I lost consciousness . . . when he threw me against the pump. The only thing that saved me . . . was coughing. I woke up swallowing water."

I sneered, knowing to whom he was referring. This was the soldier that kissed Antonio. It was rude and disrespectful of him to do that in front of me. I knew he liked Antonio because I saw his erection in his uniform.

"Did Antonio make it out safely?" Salvatore asked.

"He made it out," my dad replied.

Salvatore caught his breath before speaking up, "We need to lose these uniforms. We look too obvious."

As he unbuttoned his shirt, he paused to catch his breath again.

My father reached for Salvatore's top button to help him, and Salvatore nodded, letting him. However, I noticed Salvatore closely watching my dad and seemed to question his intentions.

I stripped myself naked.

As Salvatore stood and stepped from his pants, I saw

his uncircumcised prick. It was a replica of Antonio's — except he had foreskin.

"What are you looking at?" Salvatore murmured.

"I'm sorry," I said, covering my hard-on. "You may not know this, but your son and I were . . ."

"What? Friends?"

"Lovers. Even though we had just met."

Salvatore grimaced. "I'm sure he was your submissive bitch!"

I nodded.

"It figures," Salvatore sneered.

Antonio

I WATCHED a homeless man pushing a shopping cart that contained his belongings. It was clear that the cart was his only means of storage. I felt sad knowing that he had a mental disability. As I scanned the contents, I wondered if he had extra clothes. If he did, they were most likely to be dirty. "Excuse me?" I shouted, stepping out from behind a flowering hibiscus shrub.

The homeless man looked at me strangely as I stood there naked. I realized I must have looked crazy, so I asked him kindly if he could spare some clothes.

"In trade for liquor?"

"I have nothing to give you," I said, as the corners of my mouth turned downward, knowing I had nothing in exchange. Suddenly, I heard snickering behind me. I turned and saw two men in their late twenties pointing toward me. I wasn't sure if they were pointing at me in general or specifically at my muscular ass. Regardless of their actions, I pounced on the man closest to me.

The man inhaled sharply at the turn of events while the

homeless man ran away, pushing his cart into the darkness. Within seconds, I tackled the man and undressed him. As he stood in his underwear, his shocked friend backed up. I hissed at him, and he ran away.

"Please . . . don't hurt me," the unclothed man cried.

I glanced down, ignoring his plea, and saw the outline of his dick. I caught my breath, impressed with its size. I stepped forward and lowered his briefs to view it more closely.

His penis tumbled out.

"What are you doing?" he wailed.

As I reached for his groin, I stopped suddenly, hearing Jesus's voice inside my head. He wasn't addressing me directly, but I remembered him stating that sex needed to be consensual. I quickly removed my hand from the elastic band of his underwear and turned away in shame. "Please forgive me," I muttered, quickly gathering his clothing and dressing.

Feeling confused and terrified, the man grabbed the shirt I was buttoning up, causing it to rip. In response, I hissed and bared my sharp teeth. The man let out a shriek of terror before running away.

As I heard a clackety sound in the distance, I turned to see the St. Charles Streetcar approaching. I smiled as I realized it was the quickest way to the French Quarter.

I finished dressing and bolted toward the trolley, which was moving around fifteen miles per hour. Within seconds, I managed to jump into the car. The operator looked up, surprised to see me and my hastily put-together outfit. My shirt was untucked and torn from the earlier event.

I waved at him and walked past him without paying the fare.

"Hey . . . you haven't paid," he exclaimed with a Cajun accent, still shocked that I appeared out of nowhere.

I turned back and stared into his eyes.

Within seconds, he grinned and gestured that everything was fine, and I should sit down. It was unbelievable how easily I was able to charm him.

"I'm grateful," I said, captivated by his beauty. His sleek

black skin and slender frame were simply irresistible. I'm sure he had a long uncircumcised dick as well. I snapped out of my thoughts, seeing him questioning me.

Sitting down on the streetcar, I couldn't help but admire its interior. The wooden bench beneath me was smooth and polished, with a rich, dark stain that resembled ash. The intricate carvings on the wood gave it an antique feel, like I was sitting on a piece of history. The walls were lined with elegant brass fixtures and ornate lighting, glowing warmly. The windows were open, allowing a gentle breeze to enter and cool the space. I couldn't tell if this was the original streetcar or a replica, but one thing was for sure — the interior was simply beautiful.

As I peered through the open window, my breath caught in my throat at the awe-inspiring view that unfolded before me. A magnificent tunnel of majestic oak trees stretched along the length of St. Charles Avenue, their branches reaching out to one another as if in a loving embrace. The sight was so captivating that I couldn't help but inhale sharply, filling my lungs with the fresh, crisp air that carried the scent of these ancient giants.

And behind the oaks stood the old antebellum mansions, each grander and more imposing than the last. They stretched miles with their stately columns, sweeping verandas, and intricately wrought iron balconies. Even from a distance, I could see the meticulous attention to detail that had gone into their construction — from the ornate carvings on the doors to the delicate lacework on the windows. I admired their size and beauty, returning to an era of elegance and refinement.

The streetcar passed a gay couple dressed for a celebration. It reminded me that Southern Decadence was happening in the French Quarter. To avoid risks, I decided to go to the parade instead of the bathhouse and get lost in the crowd. This area was safe, and I could blend in with everyone else.

Robert

A VAMPIRE COULD only follow a trail for a limited time before losing it. Knowing that Antonio was smart, he probably used some form of transportation to escape. We needed to leave soon if we wanted any chance of catching him. As I helped Salvatore up, we noticed the smashed head of the concrete statue on the granite base.

David exclaimed, "What the fuck?"

As I turned around, I saw Philippe, one of my soldiers, escaping the rising water. He stumbled toward us and fell to the ground in exhaustion. His chin hit the concrete floor with a loud thud, and water splashed everywhere as he cried out in pain. I knew that his already deformed nose must have taken an additional beating.

In the distance, I heard a shout and saw a man in his underwear waving his arms frantically. Despite feeling terrible for Philippe, I knew that David, Salvatore, and I couldn't stay behind to help him. Gesturing for them to follow me, we approached the man standing in his underwear, who pointed toward the moving St. Charles Streetcar.

"The guy on the trolley stole my clothes!" he exclaimed.

The three of us ran forward without saying a word. We caught up with the trolley and jumped onto the car's roof. After leaning over the edge and checking a few windows, I saw Antonio inside. He had his head down and was in deep thought.

As I sat up, Salvatore sat down so he wouldn't fall off the trolley. My eyes scanned his muscular naked body. His gorgeous Italian physique made me squirm with excitement. I sighed, wishing to run my fingers through his chest hair and caress his magnificent uncircumcised cock.

As Salvatore looked up, sensing my stare, I looked down

and concealed my blossoming erection. The last thing I wanted was to make him feel uncomfortable. Things were good right now, and I didn't want that to change.

Antonio

AS THE STREETCAR arrived at the Riverwalk, memories of the DTAV agents and vampires fighting over my father flooded back. It felt like ages ago, even though it had just happened. I knew I had a thirty-minute lead on Robert. The streetcar gave me some extra time. Although the bathhouse was my sanctuary, I couldn't run there as it would reveal our meeting place.

"Hey, Antonio!" a familiar voice shouted out.

I turned and saw Robert, David, and my biological father standing on the trolley car. They waved, seeing my shocked expression. I couldn't believe David and my birth father had survived the flood. "Fuck!" I stumbled backward.

"You can't hide from us," Robert shouted.

I realized I could use my new superpower to outrun them, so as they jumped off the roof, I sped off and disappeared in a flash. Running across Decatur and up Toulouse Street, I arrived at the parade moments later. Stopping there, I bent over to catch my breath. I looked up and saw a sea of faces in front of me. All gathered to celebrate the Southern Decadence festival. I saw men dressed in jeans and T-shirts adorned with rainbow flags and glitter. Their energy was infectious as they danced to the music blasting from nearby speakers. But it wasn't just the men who were out in full force. Lesbians and straights joined in on the festivities, flocking to the sidewalks to watch the parade go by. They, too, were dressed in colorful clothing, some sporting rainbow accessories and others waving pride flags high above their heads.

Everyone was eager to be part of the celebration, despite their differences. The atmosphere was full of laughter and excitement, with people chatting and cheering at every passing float. Clearly, this wasn't just an event for the LGBTQ+ community. It was a time for everyone to come together and embrace diversity.

I wandered further into the crowd and bumped into a naked man wearing a locked silicone chastity cage and nothing more. His boyfriend wasn't at the parade, and he didn't want him fooling around.

The police officers looked amused as they watched the parade, leaving the spectators and marchers alone.

Due to the excessive crowd on the sidewalks, I stepped onto the street to maneuver more efficiently. I sped through a group of marching women wearing purple costumes and pointed Madonna-like cone bras. They sipped on alcohol while performing a synchronized dance.

"I'm so sorry," I shouted as I disrupted their performance.

I pushed forward, passing by a band playing jazz music and then a group of men in speedos, pumping and grinding to the beat. Some spectators were so drunk they exposed themselves. Despite feeling exhausted, I viewed each presentation in amazement as I ran toward the gay bars of Bourbon Street.

David

AS WE SPRINTED down the street, completely naked and exposed to the world, the cheers of onlookers filled our ears. They mistakenly believed we were part of the parade, and their enthusiasm only fueled our adrenaline. My dad and I seemed unfazed by our state of undress, but I could sense Salvatore's uneasiness with the situation.

Out of the corner of my eye, I spotted three men in jeans and T-shirts casually smoking cigarettes in a dimly lit alleyway. Seizing the opportunity, I gestured toward them, and we hastily darted into the alley, hoping to avoid any further attention from the crowd.

As the men turned to face us, their eyes widened in surprise at seeing our naked bodies. Without hesitation, I signaled for us to attack. In perfect unison, we pounced on our unsuspecting victims, swiftly draining them of their lifeblood. Once they had been rendered unconscious, we stripped them of their clothing and donned it ourselves, knowing that it would better suit the festive atmosphere of the celebration.

Leaving the lifeless bodies of the three men concealed behind a dumpster, we dashed back into the crowd, making our way toward the vibrant and lively gay section of Bourbon Street.

"There he is!" My dad uttered.

I spotted Antonio in line for Charlie's, the biggest nightclub in the French Quarter. I motioned to the back of the line, where the sea of people hid us from his view.

I was sweating heavily, so I removed my T-shirt, and my dad followed suit. The drag queen in front of us was a sight to behold. She wore towering, platform heels, while her makeup boasted bold colors. A voluminous wig cascaded down her back, and her sparkling costume hugged her curves perfectly. She caught my father's eye as she turned and flirted with him by playfully touching his chest. My dad basked in the attention while I inhaled sharply in surprise at the unexpected encounter.

I hissed at the queen, feeling protective of my father.

The impersonator raised her hands dramatically in response.

"Excuse me! I didn't know he was your private property!"

"Back off, bitch!" I retorted firmly, placing my hand on my dad's chest to claim my territory. However, as the drag queen turned around, I felt embarrassed and dropped my hand upon seeing my dad's shocked expression. I raised my hands in a conciliatory gesture and smiled unapologetically at him.

Robert

AS DAVID'S face flushed with embarrassment, he quickly averted his gaze, unable to meet my eyes. Sensing his discomfort, I didn't hesitate to reach out and enfold him in a comforting embrace. My arms wrapped tightly around him. Leaning in, I whispered tenderly into his ear.

"I am yours."

Feeling him nestled into my embrace, I welcomed the warmth that radiated from our entwined forms. I pressed a loving kiss upon the crown of his head, providing reassurance and solace. I was captivated by the bouncer calling out to Antonio, gesturing for him to enter. As I watched Antonio slip inside, a grimace formed on my face, acknowledging his successful infiltration.

The opportunity before me was clear. If I played my cards right and eliminated Antonio, I could secure a high-ranking position within Salvatore's organization. My mind raced as I pondered the immense responsibility that would follow – rebuilding the decimated infantry with countless new vampires.

Salvatore's voice cut through the whirlwind of thoughts swirling in my head, reminding us to advance in the queue. Reluctantly, I loosened my grip on David and stepped away, catching a glimpse of confusion in Salvatore's eyes as he tried to make sense of our intimate connection. Gripping David's hand tightly, I offered a reassuring smile, a silent affirmation of our love.

Antonio

AS I PUSHED my way through the crowded lower level of Charlie's, I couldn't help but notice the striking decor. The walls were adorned with vibrant Mardi Gras masks, and colorful beads hung from the ceiling. The dim lighting created an intimate ambiance, making it the perfect spot for a night out in the French Quarter. Go-Go boys wandered freely and intermixed with the crowd, adding to the lively atmosphere. As I ascended to the upper level, I knew that whatever awaited me upstairs would be just as visually stunning as I had seen.

The energy on the dance floor was electric as the celebration of Southern Decadence continued. The men in attendance were diverse, each with a unique style and personality. Many had shed their shirts in the heat of the moment, revealing chiseled abs and toned muscles. They moved to the blaring techno music with an impossible intensity to ignore. Some danced alone, lost in their world, while others formed groups and danced together, feeding off each other's energy. It was a sight to behold and perfectly captured the celebration's spirit.

I searched for a dark room area, looking for a moment to catch my breath and take in the sights. That's when I noticed him — a man my age with dyed gray hair and a five o'clock shadow leaning against the wall. Our eyes met, and he gestured me over. As I walked toward him, I couldn't help but undress him with my eyes. "You have a drink? Lucky you," I said with a smirk.

He smiled back. "The waitperson should be back soon."

We introduced ourselves — his name was Mason. As we shook hands, his gaze went to my torn shirt. Without hesitation, I took a deep breath and flexed my muscles, displaying my upper torso for him to see.

The song ended abruptly as an announcer interrupted

our moment by inviting everyone to participate in the go-go-boy contest. The prize money was one-thousand dollars. Though Mason seemed interested in the announcement, I ignored it and focused on his beautiful face.

"The contest?" he asked, pointing up at the speaker.

"I'm sorry . . . I wasn't paying attention," I admitted.

"They're having a dance contest. Are you participating?"

I shook my head.

"I am," he replied confidently.

Mason then reached out and caressed my chest. As I glanced down, I saw what appeared to be an impressive bulge in his jeans — either he was wearing a foam cup or genuinely packing heat.

"It's real," he said, smiling mischievously.

The way he grinned told me that he wasn't lying. "How long have you been dancing?"

"I cut hair for a living. Dancing is just something on the side."

"Can you do something with this?" I inquired, gesturing toward the unruly mass of white hair atop my head. Since God had worked his inexplicable magic, transforming my once youthful locks into a sea of silvery gray, it had become unmanageable and desperately needed proper styling. The strands seemed to have a life of their own, rebelling against any attempt to tame them, leaving me at a loss for how to regain control over my appearance.

"Is that natural?" he asked curiously.

"The color?"

"Yes."

I nodded without wanting to go into specifics.

As if sensing our conversation coming full circle, he pinched my nipples sensually while giving me another seductive smile.

"I'm glad you're not entering the contest. You'd win."

I smiled at his compliment and felt relieved to have company. He explored my body while I sent a telepathic message to everyone but received no response, which worried me. Mason noticed my concern and asked what was wrong, but I reassured him that everything was fine with a smile — even though it wasn't.

Robert

THE BAR'S ATMOSPHERE buzzed with energy as a diverse crowd of attendees filled the space. From twinks and lesbians to transgender individuals and flamboyant drag queens, the variety of people gathered here created a vibrant and welcoming environment.

As I surveyed the scene, I couldn't help but feel a thrilling mixture of excitement and danger, fully aware that this establishment was strictly off-limits to active-duty personnel. The air of forbidden allure surrounding the place heightened the experience. If the Military Police were to catch a vampire entering or exiting the premises, the consequences would be severe.

The atmosphere was electric, with the sound of pulsing music and the chatter of patrons filling the air.

As I searched the room for Antonio, I noticed a cluster of young men chatting excitedly by the bar. They were clad in snug-fitting attire and flaunting vibrant hairstyles. Turning, I saw several hairy daddies, some sitting at tables and others standing at the bar.

I noticed the side glances that my son David was receiving. The conversations would abruptly cease, and all eyes would turn toward him. He was clearly the most handsome, with a striking appearance that drew attention wherever he went.

For his twenty-first birthday, I had decided to turn him into a vampire, knowing that his youthful appearance would be eternal while he would continue to age in years. As a father, I had hoped that enlisting him in the infantry would do him good, but unfortunately, it only served to drive a wedge between us. Our relationship changed for the worse, and David began to despise me.

To make matters worse, his comrades in basic training knew he was homosexual and taunted him relentlessly with derogatory terms like 'Bum Chum.' It broke my heart to see my son mistreated in this way simply because of who he was. Despite our strained relationship, I couldn't help but feel protective of him and wished there was something more I could do to ease his pain.

My pride as a father suffered.

I bribed the drill sergeants to keep quiet. I snuck prostitutes in every night. The senior and junior drill sergeants would party with them for hours. My plan worked until David graduated boot camp and defected from the infantry.

The drill sergeants told all.

Salvatore threatened to demote me once he heard what I had done to keep my son's secret. I apologized profusely and asked for forgiveness. He forgave me under one condition — never screw up again.

"There aren't many guys here my age," I said matter-of-factly.

"Wrong bar!" David yelled in return.

I nodded. It was apparent Antonio wasn't on this floor. "Let's go upstairs," I shouted, gesturing toward the staircase.

David

WEAVING MY WAY through the crowd of revelers, I spotted a familiar face — one of the men I had slept with before. We exchanged glances before someone else grabbed my arm and turned me around to face another acquaintance. After exchanging pleasantries, I went upstairs with my father and Salvatore. The bright lights momentarily disoriented me but then dimmed to reveal a drag queen on stage announcing the start of a go-go boy dance contest.

I scanned the open room. I knew Antonio would be hiding in a dark corner, and to my surprise, I found him immediately. I tapped my dad on the shoulder and pointed toward him. He was talking to Mason, a hairstylist I had fucked a few years back.

Salvatore smiled upon seeing his son. As I watched, Mason began to fondle Antonio's crotch. Meanwhile, the drag queen on stage droned on for too long about a gay organization needing support. Despite the distraction, I remained focused on Antonio, trying to devise a plan to capture him.

"All contestants, please line up in front of the stage. In groups of three," the drag queen announced.

I turned to my father, looking for a plan of action.

"Let's see what he does," my dad whispered.

I nodded and turned back, noticing Mason striding confidently to the front of the line, ready to take his place on the platform. He watched as eleven other hopefuls lined up behind him, eager to join in on the dance contest. The drag queen confidently issued clear instructions, leaving no room for confusion. She stated that the same music would play for every group. Once the song ended, the following three dancers would take over as the current three stepped down. All contestants acknowledged and understood the instructions.

"Could the first three step to the platform, please?"

The techno mix started in the background as Mason and two other contestants stepped forward.

"Okay, boys. Let's dance!"

Mason stood out amongst the clothed go-go boys, his moves mesmerizing the audience. They chanted at him to remove it, and he obliged, revealing a chiseled physique. He wore only a white jockstrap, which blatantly showcased his muscled backside. I couldn't help but gasp in awe at how beautiful it was.

The crowd went wild as he gyrated his hips back and forth, showcasing an impressive bulge that enthralled me. As much as Mason's performance had captivated me, my father's sudden grip on my arm brought me back to reality. He gestured toward the outside balcony and informed me that Antonio had seen us and left the room.

Antonio

UPON STEPPING onto the balcony, a rowdy group of men tossing beads at tourists on Bourbon Street caught my gaze. Their laughter echoed through the night as they cheered each other on, utterly oblivious to anyone else around them. I quickly realized I could not get past them and jump to the ground below. Panic began to set in, and I took a deep breath, focusing on finding another way out. That's when I noticed another entrance into the bar at the end of the balcony. With renewed hope, I decided to wait and see which way my pursuers came out before moving in the opposite direction.

David was the first to emerge, his dad and Salvatore behind him. I ran in the other direction and slipped in the door.

Mason and two other competitors had just disembarked the platform as I entered. At once, I noticed the drag queen waving the next group forward. The first two contestants advanced in response, prompting me to act quickly. I seized the arm of the third contestant and declared that it was my turn in line. He seemed taken aback by my actions, and though he attempted to contest them, I refused to back down. Without hesitation, I hopped onto the platform and shoved him away from me — a reckless move but one necessary to protect myself from my assailants. All the while, I was aware of the curious stares from the crowd and made sure to hold my head high.

I inhaled deeply, feeling the crowd's energy as David, Robert, and Salvatore re-entered the bar. My heart began to race as I heard shouts for me to strip. Knowing what a go-go boy does from my extensive YouTube research, I ripped off my torn shirt and started to caress my chest with both hands rhythmically.

I unbuttoned my jeans, and the crowd cheered as they saw my pubic hair. I realized I wasn't wearing any underwear and panicked. I had forgotten to take them from the man whose clothes I had stolen. The crowd wanted me to get naked, but I didn't know what to do. The two dancers joined in and started stripping too. Suddenly, I saw my biological dad watching me in disgust. Angry, I mouthed, "Fuck you!" and lowered my jeans. The crowd cheered, but the drag queen screeched as I exposed myself to the bar.

"No nudity, boys."

The crowd continued chanting.

The song switched to a popular dance mix by a well-known music producer. When I heard the first beat, I recognized the music from the attractive Israeli-born DJ from Tel Aviv and couldn't help but smile. I followed his techno mixes on YouTube and Facebook, saving each picture of his toned muscular body. His social media posts mainly featured him in underwear that outlined his groin, igniting my fantasies about being intimate with him at night.

I stopped dancing and stepped out of my jeans. I stood for two seconds as my dick filled with blood thinking about the Israeli-born DJ. As I started dancing, the crowd gasped in shock, seeing my hardness bounce back and forth.

The other two dancers ceased their movements and stared at me. I gestured for them to remove their clothing. In an attempt to match the situation, they complied. The chaotic atmosphere made the drag queen feel anxious. She desperately implored the contestants to adhere to the rules. This irritated the two other dancers, who quickly fled the stage, losing the audience's attention.

As David, Robert, and my father approached me, I observed envy evident on David's contorted face. To my astonishment, David stepped onto the platform and commenced dancing. As he swayed his hips, he began to undress. Within moments, his impressive size became exposed, causing the audience to react with astonishment.

As David enjoyed the limelight, he momentarily forgot about me. I observed Robert take his turn on the stage. The crowd looked at him in shock, thinking he was past his prime. However, Robert surprised everyone by being the better dancer.

The crowd responded enthusiastically.

Robert stripped.

It took the crowd about two seconds to realize David and Robert were father and son. The audience lost it, seeing their matching eight-inch dicks moving to the beat of the music.

This was my chance to escape because all eyes were on them. I grabbed my jeans and torn shirt and jumped off the stage.

Mason came up to me as I dressed.

"What the fuck?"

"They're trying to kill me," I yelled, pointing to David and Robert. "I need to get out of here!"

"Follow me!" he shouted.

I finished dressing, and we ran to the staircase. As I descended the stairs, I saw David and Robert still dancing. With all the chaos in the room, it didn't look like Salvatore had seen me leaving.

Mason

ANTONIO AND I fled the bar and emerged onto the bustling street. As the gravity of the situation set in, memories from the past flooded my mind. The person pursuing Antonio was someone I knew — a one-night stand. The realization was stunning, and I felt a mixture of disbelief and apprehension. It was unimaginable to think that this man, who fucked me, was intent on harming him.

Nonetheless, I asked Antonio where he wanted to go, and without hesitation, he indicated my apartment. I told him my residence was further up the street behind my salon. Upon hearing my place of business, Antonio amusingly asked if I could tend to his messy white hair. In return, he offered payment for the service. I accepted his unconventional proposal without hesitation and decided to style his hair like mine with the desired spiky quaff. Since his hair was already white, there was no need for dye. "There's no need for payment," I happily said. "How about we exchange a deal instead?"

"I have nothing to swap."

I smiled and pointed at his crotch.

Antonio assented to our arrangement, but his expression showed unease. I knew proposing an intimate encounter was a bit rash, but I hadn't been with anyone for ages because I devoted most of my time to my business.

Familiarizing ourselves with each other as we walked to the salon, Antonio remained wary and scrutinized our environment in search of any potential pursuers. In no time at all, we had reached our destination. Antonio seemed to relax as we entered, and I led him directly to my hair-cutting station.

I explained the classic yet modern style — short on the sides with some length on top. Antonio looked good when it was all said and done, and he thanked me profusely for taking care of him.

Antonio had worked up a sweat while dancing at the nightclub, leading him to desire a shower. However, I implored him to wait until after we had engaged in sexual activity, as his sweat was an immense turn-on. It was manly. A musky scent that I desired. He readily agreed with my peculiar request, nonchalantly shrugging his shoulders to signify his assent.

Heading to my bedroom, I undressed in front of him. As I lowered my jeans, he gazed at my circumcised cock springing forward, anticipating what was to come. His eyes widened, seeing the length and girth of it.

"You never said why you're on the run," I murmured.

Antonio unbuttoned his jeans, ignoring me.

My curiosity shifted to his groin. We'd deal with the unanswered question later. I held my breath as he stepped out of his jeans and presented his magnificent erection.

Antonio

MASON'S HAIR salon was situated in the residential district of Bourbon Street. As I sat in the chair and caught sight of my white hair, anxiety washed over me. Should I lie and say it prematurely greyed or be honest and tell him that God had done this? I opted for the former, thinking he would think I was mad if I said the latter.

As Mason cut my hair, I felt its coarse texture as it fell onto my lap. When I looked up in the mirror, there was a clean-shaven side of my head. The look was distinct, giving me a military-like appearance.

"This hairstyle looks good on you," Mason said, beaming at me.

He seemed to enjoy being a hairstylist and was happy

to help me. This made me feel grateful, so I knew I had to honor our agreement despite him assuming the submissive role. It meant that I had to be dominant, which made me uncomfortable.

***

I closed my eyes, reveling in the sensations that Mason was igniting within me. His talented mouth worked wonders, and I was lost in the pleasure coursing through my veins. The sound of his moans only served to heighten my desire. As he finally withdrew from my dick, crawling onto the bed, I watched him with longing. My heart pounded in my chest as he reached for the lube. It was clear that he knew what he was doing, and I couldn't help but feel a sense of anticipation building within me.

As I took a step forward, Mason grasped me, expertly lubricating the length of my shaft. My heart continued to race as I watched him get on all fours, lifting his ass toward me. Without hesitation, I knelt behind him and slowly spread his cheeks apart.

"Rim me," he moaned.

Eager to please, I leaned forward and tasted his hole, enjoying the clean and satisfyingly delicious taste. As I licked and probed, I knew it was time to move on to the main course. With him loosened up, I placed the head of my cock against his pulsing anus. Taking a deep breath to steady myself, I slowly began to push forward, gradually entering him until we both gasped in pleasure. Starting to move slowly and gently, I began to screw him deeply, reveling in the feel of his hot body. Our moans and gasps of pleasure filled the room as we surrendered ourselves to the sensations.

Mason

ANTONIO WAS relentless as he flipped me over onto my back and pounded fervently into me. With one hand gripping my leg, he moved his other hand down to stroke my cock. The intense pleasure quickly built up inside me until I couldn't hold back any longer, shooting my load all over my stomach. Judging by how Antonio stared at the thick, white substance, I could tell he wanted to taste it.

Without hesitation, I wiped the jizz off my abdomen and offered it to him. He eagerly savored the flavor, his cock stiffening even further. "I'm on PrEP. Come inside me," I moaned, craving more of him.

"I can't," he murmured, reluctantly pulling out of me.

As I sat up in confusion, I watched Antonio begin to jack off furiously. Within seconds, he shot his load all over the comforter, and I couldn't help but stare at it in disbelief. To my horror, I noticed steam radiating from the fluid as if it was some form of poisonous substance. "What the fuck?" I exclaimed in shock, still trying to process the bizarre and unexpected turn that our encounter had taken.

I quickly grabbed my shirt and wiped away the fluid, saving my bedspread from stains.

As I was tidying up, I heard a sudden hiss. It prompted me to pause and look up, feeling perplexed.

Antonio reared up, snarling fiercely, exposing sharp fangs. Fear overcame me, causing my legs and arms to shake uncontrollably as I scrambled for cover. My panic intensified as he lunged forward with lightning speed and pinned me to the bed. However, I was taken aback when he didn't bite me. Instead, a creepy smile formed on his lips, and he began to giggle in a disturbing manner.

Exhausted, he collapsed onto the bed.

As my mind raced with uncertainty, unsure of whether

to flee or stay, he seemed to sense my unease and apologized for the dramatic way in which he revealed his identity. I remained still, barely able to speak, as my gaze silently asked for an explanation. With a heavy sigh, he explained that he didn't know how else to tell me, so he showed me instead. His words soothed my worries but stirred my curiosity. I reached out and laid my hand on his chest before prompting him to tell me everything.

"Those men following me are vampires too."

His hand caressed mine as he began to spin his tale with a warmth that belied its sorrowful content. I found myself captivated by his story, eager to learn more.

Antonio

MASON WAS drawn to becoming a bloodsucker, as it allowed him to escape a life of loneliness and find companionship. He saw joining a brotherhood as an appealing prospect, where he would never be alone again. Moreover, he stood to benefit from the supernatural qualities that being a vampire entailed, such as enhanced strength and immortality.

I drained him of his life fluid and then made love to him again. Instead of pulling out this time, I shot deep inside his rectum, not believing the sensual feeling it brought me.

As Mason's body trembled and he breathed his last breath, I held my own, anxious and scared once again that the transition wouldn't work. His muscles twitched uncontrollably, and I watched in awe as his conversion began. Staying by his side, I couldn't help but think of the gay bar he had told me about with the hidden backroom. He said we could go there to create an army of gay vampires to fight against the organization we were up against.

Mason was more than a new acquaintance. He was a mentor who taught me to think like a soldier. His intelligence and unique perspective made me see things differently.

Suddenly, Mason's body ceased trembling. His eyes widened as the successful conversion into a vampire took place. I had done it. I screwed him and came inside his ass. I felt overwhelmed with achievement. After all my hard work, the impossible thing I thought could never happen had become a reality. I was now a butt fucker.

Salvatore

AS I STEPPED out of Charlie's, the gay bar, I trailed Antonio and Mason down Bourbon Street. A sense of determination washed over me, knowing they had no idea I was following them. I had to take matters into my own hands because my queer Master Sargent and his son had failed to do the job, and now it was up to me to set things right. I left them dancing in the bar, their erotic movements sickening me.

Standing on the sidewalk, I watched my son and the dancer disappear into the salon. My mind wandered to more profound thoughts. With nobody around to distract me, I had time to reflect on everything that led me to this moment. I stepped to the window and stared at Antonio sitting in the stylist's chair. I couldn't help but marvel at his beauty — a combination of masculine and feminine features that made him irresistible in an almost otherworldly way. Even as I recognized our similarities, it was clear that he was the better-looking one.

As I looked at his face, something shifted within me. Despite my reservations about his sexuality, I found myself seeing things in a different light. It wasn't that I suddenly approved of his choices — far from it. But the rules and beliefs that had once governed my every action had been shattered with the collapse of the vampire compound. In this new world, there was room for change and growth — even if it meant accepting things that were previously unthinkable to me.

As the haircut ended, my son rose from the seat, and they made their way toward the back of the salon — his apartment. Seized by a sudden urge, I slid open the window and entered the salon. Navigating my way through, I turned the corner and entered the bedroom. To my dismay, I discovered my son engaged in oral sex.

I left the room behind and hurried down the hallway, seeking refuge from the sounds of passion. Reaching the wall, I leaned against it and closed my eyes tightly, longing for some respite from the overwhelming sensations assaulting my senses.

I waited restlessly for the impassioned moment to pass. When the sounds finally fizzled away, I listened as Antonio revealed his true nature. To my amazement, the dancer welcomed the invitation to join their brotherhood of queer vampires.

As the dancer exited the room to shower, I suddenly manifested myself in his place, exposing my menacing fangs and startling Antonio with my abrupt and unexpected intrusion.

To my surprise, after noticing me, he didn't seem afraid. Instead, he had a confident aura around him I hadn't seen before. He asked if I had watched him having sex. My answer was honest — no, but I heard everything.

"I feel sorry for you," Antonio murmured.

Confused, I asked him to explain himself.

He revealed the painful truth — that I hated him and wanted him dead despite being his only son. The weight of his words hit me hard as I struggled to come to terms with what he had just said.

"Who cares that I'm queer! This is my life, and I'm the

one living it, not you," he stated with a sense of defiance.

I watched Antonio's fists clench and rise in front of him. It was clear that he was prepared for a physical confrontation. But who was this man that stood before me? He wasn't the effeminate person I had initially thought him to be. Instead, he was courageous and unafraid to face me.

"Come on!" he shouted, baring his teeth like a wild animal. "Let's settle this once and for all before Mason returns."

"Put your fists down," I mumbled, realizing my initial judgment of him had been foolish.

"I'm not scared of you anymore," he declared. "No matter what you do to me, I won't die. I drank the seed of Christ."

Before I could fully process the weight of his revelation, Antonio lunged at me, forcefully knocking me to the ground. Helpless, I lay beneath him, feeling the weight of his naked body on my chest.

Fear coursed through me as his hand rose. I braced myself for an incoming blow. To my surprise, Antonio tapped my chest angrily. The unexpected gesture perplexed me, leaving me uncertain of his intentions. Antonio's voice was cold and menacing as he gave me an ultimatum.

"You have two choices," he said, eyes locking onto mine. "Leave town, or I'll kill you now."

His threat hung heavily, leaving me with dread and uncertainty. The thought of leaving the Federation behind was overwhelming. "I have to rebuild the infantry," I protested weakly. Antonio's response was swift and uncompromising.

"The infantry is no more. Go back to Italy," he said firmly. "Contact me when you're ready to become father and son."

After his response, he bared his teeth, hissing at me. I knew he was serious. I had no choice but to agree with his demands. His words were like a knife twisting in my gut.

"There's now a brotherhood of gay vampires."

I watched my son take charge and assert his strength.

Even though I was frightened, I couldn't help but feel a sense of pride now. He resembled me in so many ways — from his authoritative demeanor to how he confidently carried himself.

"Take the next cruise ship to Europe."

As I nodded in agreement, my mind raced with thoughts of what lay ahead. The idea of being on a boat as a vampire was terrifying, and for good reason. It meant being surrounded by water — an element that posed a significant threat to vampires. For one, it limited our ability to move around freely. We couldn't simply jump into the water and swim if we needed to escape danger. Furthermore, prolonged exposure to water weakened us significantly, making us vulnerable to drowning.

Additionally, being on a boat meant being in close quarters with humans — something that could quickly turn dangerous if they discovered my true nature. But despite the hazards, I had no choice but to comply with Antonio's demand. The alternative was certain death at his hands.

"Leave now before Mason comes out of the shower."

"I'm sorry," I whispered, hoping he could forgive me. "I realize my mistake now." My son stood and pointed toward the door. I knew not to say anything more — it was clear that our conversation had ended.

As I left the room, I felt a sense of sadness and regret wash over me. It wasn't just about the mistake I had made — it was about all the moments we had missed together because of it.

Angelo

LUCIEN NEEDED clothes, so we targeted a lone man strolling the street. Dressed casually in jeans and a T-shirt, his breath smelled of alcohol, suggesting he had spent his night barhopping. We stripped him of his clothes, during which I wrestled him to the ground.

A primal urge stirred within me, and I wanted to drain his life-sustaining fluids. However, Lucien's calming voice reminded me that we could satiate our thirst later.

We watched as the man staggered off into the distance, left in nothing more than his undergarments. His eyes were wide with fear, causing guilt to resonate within me. The terror we had instilled in him was unmistakable. Lucien's voice shattered the silence that followed, laced with a sense of urgency. "We should go now," he insisted. Heeding his words, I steered him toward our next destination — the bathhouse.

As we cautiously entered the building, a wave of darkness washed over us, accompanied by the powerful scent of chlorine, almost suffocating in its intensity. Behind a pane of plexiglass, a man rose from his stool and approached us. His question hung in the air.

"Are you looking for a room or a locker?"

"We'd like to rent the largest room you have available," I said, reaching for the wad of cash inside my pocket.

"Eight hours?"

"Sixteen."

"That'll be sixty dollars."

I placed the exact amount of cash on the counter. As the man took it and opened the register, I turned to look at Lucien. His face was now unblemished, and his body had healed from Salvatore's savage attack. He appeared perfectly normal to anyone else, and no one could have guessed the ordeal he had just endured.

The man behind the plexiglass returned with two bleached towels, keys attached to plastic bungee cords, and four unopened rubbers. He informed us that the 'suite' was available and reminded us to check out on time to avoid being charged again.

I thanked him for his assistance as he handed us our items.

The attendant pushed a button that made an obnoxious sound as the door unlocked. I depressed the lever, and we stepped inside.

Lucien

ANGELO AND I navigated the crowded lounge area with men of all shapes and sizes. Some were naked, but most had towels wrapped around their waists as they conversed and shared drinks. This room served as a space for socializing rather than participating in sexual activities.

As we arrived at our locker, the room bustled with activity. Men were undressing left and right, revealing their naked bodies for an evening of sexual exploration. I couldn't help but stare at them as they stripped to nothing.

Once Angelo and I had undressed, we put our clothes inside the designated locker before wrapping towels around our waists. The atmosphere in the bathhouse was electric, with an intense energy that caused my heart to race.

Entering the main area, I felt excitement and apprehension about what lay ahead. The sound of running water filled my ears as I gazed around at the various rooms and pools surrounding us.

There was an air of relaxation and excitement here, with men everywhere. Some lounged in hot tubs, while others watched excitedly from their lounge chairs. It was a completely different world than anything I had ever experienced.

Angelo gestured me forward. I could tell he was in a hurry to find our room. The hallways were narrow and dark, almost claustrophobic, and the acrid smell of poppers filled the air.

Making our way through the maze-like corridors, I felt disoriented by the twists and turns that seemed to lead in every direction. We came across open doors and witnessed men lying face down with their backsides raised, indicating their readiness for sexual encounters. The moaning and groaning echoing through the corridors confirmed that men were engaged in intimate activities behind closed doors.

Upon reaching our room, I eagerly took notice of the word 'Suite' displayed on the door, generating high expectations in my mind. However, as Angelo unlocked the door and we entered, my dismay became palpable.

Seeing a king-sized bed, two metallic chairs surrounded by dull walls, and an unpainted plywood ceiling shocked me. Unable to hide my disappointment, I muttered, "This is the suite? I can't stay here."

"It's a room for sex and nothing more," Angelo assured me.

"It's dirty."

Angelo could see the disappointment in my eyes and quickly explained that it wasn't about the room itself but rather the experiences we would share within these walls.

However, looking at him, I could tell he was excited about Antonio's arrival and planned to ravage him throughout the night. The anticipation of what was to come filled the air with electric energy.

I pushed aside my reservations and let myself get lost in the moment, eager to see what was in store for us.

As Angelo closed the door, his towel slipped from his waist, revealing his muscular body. Seeing him was an instant turn-on, and I found myself drawn to him in a way

I couldn't explain.

He had an erection. I wondered if his arousal stemmed from thoughts of me or was triggered by the presence of other naked men in the hallway. Contemplating the situation, I questioned whether I could handle him, observing the impressive size of his penis. Perhaps I could accommodate him if he took his time and adequately prepared me.

Angelo smiled affectionately. "I find you attractive," he said, "but my interest lies with Antonio."

I nodded in understanding, realizing he had read my mind. Embarrassment washed over me. He cupped my chin and looked into my eyes.

"You're my brother, and I love you," he continued. "You'll meet that special person when least expecting it."

I nodded.

Angelo picked up his towel and turned to leave. I couldn't help but notice the outline of his groin pressed against the fabric. Before I could say anything more, he asked me to make another vampire.

I nodded in agreement, excited at the thought of creating a new brotherhood member. He smiled tenderly one last time and left the room.

Angelo

I INFORMED ANTONIO telepathically that we were at the bathhouse. He updated me on his meeting with Mason and their plan to create more vampires. When he asked about his father, I sensed his anxiety. I admitted I had no new information but reassured him we'd find him.

"What if he drowned?" Antonio inquired.

"He's still alive," I responded, sounding as confident as possible.

"I hope you're right because I couldn't go on without him," Antonio said, his words heavy with sorrow.

Antonio's comment left me feeling uneasy. I couldn't quite grasp what he meant when he said he couldn't go on without him. The thought that he might be suicidal hadn't crossed my mind, and I worried about his well-being. After our conversation ended, I returned to my task of finding a safe place for us to rest. I discovered the building had three levels, with the first two floors dedicated to the bathhouse. Ascending the staircase, I noticed the 'Do Not Enter' sign when I reached the top floor.

I opened the door.

Struck by its cavernous size and unfinished appearance, the third floor appeared to be undergoing renovation. The walls were adorned with wood moldings and lined with glass doors that led to small Juliet balconies that provided a picturesque view of Bourbon Street. The floors were made of polished hardwood, adding an elegant touch to the space.

As I contemplated, my mind wandered to the endless possibilities for this space. A vivid image materialized in my thoughts — an orderly array of coffins stretched out in rows before me.

Continuing to examine the room, I entered through a closed doorway and stood in a fully furnished studio apartment.

The space was cozy yet spacious enough to allow comfortable living. Looking around, I couldn't help but think that this would be the ideal place for Antonio. The apartment had a luxurious California king-sized bed, a large comfortable sofa, a well-sized dining table, and a fully equipped kitchen area.

I couldn't help but wonder if the proprietor used this as their own living space or simply a fuck pad. The attention to detail in decorating and furnishing the apartment was evident. Every aspect of the room exuded comfort and style, from the tasteful artwork on the walls to the plush throw pillows on the couch.

Lucien

I CASUALLY SLUNG the towel over my shoulder as I left the room. Glancing at myself, I couldn't help but appreciate my slender and hairless physique. While it may not conform to society's narrow standards of masculinity, I knew plenty of men enjoyed a more feminine look.

Making my way through the crowded hallways, I knew that making a vampire would be challenging. With so many guys around, I would have to find someone alone in a room. I passed by countless men, but they barely gave me a second glance. And you know what? That was perfectly fine. I didn't need their approval. I was content to keep searching for my elusive prey, undeterred by the indifference of those around me.

Looking in open doorways, I found a room at the end of the hallway with a middle-aged man sitting on a bed. He stood and motioned me inside. As I entered, I could see his oversized belly and small dick. He smiled, attracted to me immediately. I could tell he was kind and decided he would be my first.

The door shut behind me as I took my partner's hand, allowing him to guide me to the bed. I could feel his excitement as he ran his fingertips across my bare skin. His lips found their way to my chest, eliciting a sigh of pleasure from both of us. I bared my fangs as he looked at me, anticipating what would come. His eyes widened in surprise, and he shrank away. As he attempted to call for help, I pounced on him and bit into his neck, silencing him.

I opened my eyes, knowing he was drained of blood. Reading his mind, I realized he had a wife at home and two grown kids.

I dripped blood down his throat.

Lowering myself to my knees, I masturbated inside his mouth. His body immediately started convulsing and stopped a moment later. The transformation took only minutes.

I helped him sit up and apologized for taking his life without consent. He was saddened not for himself but for his wife, who would be alone. I explained that he could acquire wealth and still provide for her at arm's length if he was smart.

Peter

THE SOUND of shattered glass echoed through the empty street as I broke into the casket supply company. Carefully, I reached in and unlocked the front door, allowing Jackson and me to slip inside.

Once in the lobby, we froze as we heard footsteps approaching. My vampire vision allowed me to see through the darkness, revealing that the night attendant was coming to investigate. We waited silently, ready to defend ourselves if necessary.

Looking at the attendant, I couldn't help but be mesmerized by his Viking-gold hair, defined cheekbones, and beautiful blue eyes. He was captivating. The way he carried himself in his pressed uniform hinted that he might be gay, which made me even more drawn to him. He would make a great addition to our brotherhood. With his confidence, he would fit right in with the rest of us.

Without hesitation, I lunged forward and sank my fangs into his neck before Jackson could react. As I tasted his blood, I communicated telepathically that I was turning him into a vampire.

As I raised my head from my now-dead victim, I saw Jackson standing above me. "Don't just stand there," I muttered impatiently. "We need to find the caskets." With a grimace, Jackson flipped the bird and entered the warehouse. I remained behind to complete the transformation process.

I was about to unbutton my jeans when Antonio's voice suddenly echoed in my head. He informed me that Angelo and a vampire named Lucien were already at the bathhouse, getting things ready for us.

I reassured him that we would fulfill our part of the plan and return as soon as possible. With his words in my mind, I fed the night attendant my blood. Then, I quickly unbuttoned my jeans, eager to make him a vampire.

Turning toward the guard's face, I felt a longing wash over me as I gazed into his eyes. He was undeniably attractive, and the thought of playing with him crossed my mind. However, I quickly pushed those thoughts aside, realizing that time wasn't on our side. With a heavy sigh, I reminded myself to stay focused and resist any temptation that may arise along the way.

Beating off, I shot my load into his mouth. After my body stopped spasming from the eruption, I wiped the residual cum away that landed on his face and fed him. His tongue lashed out and cleansed my finger.

Doug, Bennet, and Parker entered the room, their eyes scanning for any signs of danger. I quickly instructed them to split up and search for caskets.

Fear raced through me as I watched the man on the floor convulsing in agony. I knew that I couldn't abandon him in his moment of need. I placed my hand on his chest and whispered, "This will only take a moment. And a brand-new world will be revealed to you."

Jackson

AS I PEERED inside the semi-truck, I couldn't believe my eyes. The trailer was packed with caskets of all shapes and sizes. Some were ornate and intricately designed, while others were plain and simple. The coffins were made from various materials such as wood, metal, and even glass, each one seemingly more unique than the last.

I ran my fingers over the smooth curves of a polished cherrywood casket, admiring its craftsmanship. As I moved further into the trailer, I noticed some coffins had intricate carvings etched into their surfaces, depicting scenes of angels and demons.

The air inside the trailer was heavy. Despite this eerie atmosphere, I couldn't help but feel excited at the sight before me.

"Can you believe it?" I exclaimed to Doug as he emerged from the warehouse. "This is like something out of a horror movie." We both stared in awe at my discovery, knowing I had hit the jackpot.

Doug's masculine body caught my eye. His physique reminded me of my all-American high school gym coach. Excitement coursed through my body, visualizing his nakedness. His chest swelled, knowing I was enthralled with him as he stepped inside the trailer. I took a chance and reached for his groin.

He stopped, surprised at what I was doing.

"Does this bother you?"

"Have I removed your hand?"

I smiled as he became hard. My fingers caressed the head of his cock. This excited me. I investigated the length and thickness of him. His tool was massive. It pulsated eagerly in my hand, letting me know he was interested. Looking around for the others, I knew this wasn't the place or time, but the urge to ejaculate overwhelmed me. I needed to come. Doug glanced at my erection pressed against my jeans.

"I want to get fucked."

He smiled and turned toward the warehouse, searching for his comrades.

"What if we get caught?"

"Who cares. Afterward, I'll make you into a vampire," I said, hoping he'd take the bait.

"Peter's going to do that."

"Does it matter who seeds you?" I asked, reading his face closely, looking for any signs of favoritism.

"I guess not."

I unbuttoned my fly, wanting to entice him. His eyes widened as my twelve inches sprung forward. "Drop your pants and turn around."

"Fuck, dude!" he moaned, unbuttoning his jeans.

I watched as he turned around and dropped his pants. I stared at his muscular ass excitedly. As he placed his hands against the truck, he pushed his butt outward. I stepped forward and spat in the palm of my hand. I lubricated my shaft and entered him.

All twelve inches slipped right in.

Doug moaned in pleasure.

He was good. There was no hesitancy. I could tell he had serviced large cocks before and enjoyed the deep penetration. It was a turn-on for me, too, seeing my dick thrusting back and forth inside his white ass. Whenever I pulled out, he'd gasp, wanting it back inside.

"Oh, fuck! You're going to make me cum!"

I leaned forward and bit his neck. He inhaled as his blood entered my mouth. I drained him of his nutrient-rich fluid as his moans increased from his rising orgasm.

"Oh . . . I'm coming!"

I placed my hand in front of his dick.

My boner triggered his ejaculation, and my hand filled with his milky substance. I removed my teeth from his neck and lifted the palm of my hand. I ate his juice, savoring every drop. Afterward, I sunk my teeth into my wrist and forcefully placed it into his mouth.

The intense pleasure I felt from the ecstasy resulted in my orgasm. Tilting my head backward, I released my life-giving fluid inside him.

Angelo

I POLITELY KNOCKED on the door of the bathhouse office, and I was surprised when it immediately swung open, revealing the inquisitive expression of the attendant. He pointed at the 'Employees Only' sign and asked why I was there. I apologized quickly for interrupting him.

The attendant's expression softened as he observed my features, causing a shift from a negative to a more positive attitude. He kindly inquired about how he could assist me.

Recognizing the unfortunate situation of this man having to work while others enjoyed themselves, a playful remark slipped from my mouth. "I noticed you as soon as I walked in. I must say you're quite handsome," I said, teasing him lightly, emphasizing the undeniable presence of my aroused state.

His eyes glanced at my groin, licking his lips.

"Can I come in?" I asked.

He glanced into the lounge to check for onlookers and found it mostly devoid of people. Confident no one was around, he signaled me to come in hastily.

"This is against all rules," he warned.

"Give me head, and I'll be on my way."

He gestured to the back office.

Once I entered the backroom, I removed the towel from my waist and assumed a wide-legged stance. I compelled him to kneel and satisfy my desires. His name,

George, was apparent due to his nameplate. George displayed exceptional oral skills, leading to a swift climax. However, to my dismay, I suddenly recognized the missed opportunity to drain him of his blood.

He moaned as he swallowed my cum.

I gently pushed him aside and engaged in a passionate kiss with him. He responded by moaning, and our tongues intertwined. I patiently awaited his demise from consuming my toxic substance, but nothing was happening. Growing impatient, I revealed my sharp teeth.

"What the fuck?" he muttered, pushing away, feeling my incisors jetting forward.

I opened my mouth and let out a menacing hiss. Before he could scream for help, I pounced on him and sunk my fangs into his neck, draining him of blood. With my telepathic powers, I explained he'd guard the bathhouse and its inhabitants against any potential threats who might seek to enter.

Moments later, his motionless body fell into my arms. He was close to death, so I lowered him to the floor. Biting into my wrist, I started dripping blood into his mouth. After giving him my nourishment, I started stroking, and within seconds, my juice erupted again. The force of my ejaculation shot to the back of his mouth, seeping down his throat.

Mason

THE CATACOMBS BAR had an unassuming exterior, with a plain brick facade and a small sign above the door. The doorman checked our identification and gestured to enter. As we stepped inside, I felt excited as I introduced Antonio to the infamous gay bar.

The interior was dimly lit, with low-hanging lights. The walls were covered in corrugated galvanized steel, giving the space an industrial feel that made me smile. The air was thick with the scent of alcohol and cigarette smoke that only added to the gritty atmosphere.

The wooden tables and chairs were well-worn, evidence of countless patrons who had come before us. A jukebox in the corner played classic tunes at just the right volume — loud enough to be heard over the din of conversation but not so loud to be overwhelming.

Behind the bar, shelves lined with various shapes and sizes of bottles stretched toward the ceiling. Bartenders moved quickly and efficiently, mixing drinks and serving them to eager customers. Overall, it was clear that this was a place where people came to let loose and have a good time — no frills or pretensions here.

The patrons of this establishment were a unique bunch, with many of the regulars sporting leather pants and going bare-chested or wearing white T-shirts. Some even wore hats and sported beards and long sideburns, giving off a rugged, masculine vibe that suggested they might ride motorcycles.

However, it quickly became clear that their attire was merely for show — these were ordinary, hard-working men who enjoyed expressing themselves in a different way at night. As they mingled and chatted over drinks, their personalities seemed to shift slightly, as if they were shedding the constraints of their daytime lives and embracing a more carefree side of themselves.

Despite their unconventional appearance, these leather-clad men were friendly and welcoming to newcomers. This bar was a safe space for people to express themselves however they chose — whether through fashion, conversation, or letting loose on the small dance floor.

The bartender that helped us was certainly a memorable character, his striking appearance commanding the attention of patrons throughout the bar. His cop uniform was eye-catching, with a badge and handcuffs dangling from his belt.

Despite the somewhat intimidating nature of his attire, he exuded a friendly and approachable demeanor that quickly put us at ease. He listened to our requests with a warm smile and attentive ear despite the music blaring in the background.

As we sipped our beers, we couldn't help but admire the bartender's unique style and professionalism. He moved about behind the counter easily, serving drinks and engaging in friendly conversation with customers without missing a beat.

I looked around the room for guys who would make good vampires. Two men caught my eye, and I smiled, giving the sign of fellatio. One of them, who was naked except for a jockstrap, smiled back at me in response to my invitation and nodded toward the staircase. His partner had a tattoo and nipple piercings, and I was certain that they were a couple who played together.

I teased my lips with my tongue and whispered, "These guys are suitable candidates," gesturing toward them. Antonio looked over at them and approved, waving in their direction.

Antonio

THE CATACOMBS on the second floor were a complex network of passageways and rooms. The air was damp and musty. The only light came from flickering fluorescent bulbs mounted on low ceilings. The walls were made of plywood and painted black, giving the space an eerie feel.

As we walked through the winding passageways, I felt a sense of unease. The darkness seemed to swallow us whole, and every creaking sound echoed loudly against the plywood walls. It was as if we were walking through some macabre underworld where anything could happen.

Despite its unsettling atmosphere, something was alluring about this place — perhaps it was the thrill of exploring such a mysterious and foreboding space. Whatever it was, I found myself drawn deeper into this underworld, eager to discover what secrets it held.

A sign on the wall directed men to the gloryholes, fuck rooms, showers, and toilets. Smelling spent cum and poppers, I realized the 'backroom' was a miniature bathhouse.

I followed Mason down the dark passageway and into the fuck room. There were platforms, benches, and slings available for use. However, there was no privacy. Anyone could watch you having sex. This was not the place for the shy at heart.

Mason took his clothes off and instructed me to do the same. I looked around the room for a locker but didn't see one. I undressed and folded my clothes. Lifting my head, I saw two men in the darkness. I couldn't see their faces but could tell they were waiting for sex.

One of them stepped forward and pushed Mason to his knees without warning. I stepped back in shock and watched Mason give the man head. The man moaned loudly and shot his load down his throat quickly. Flicking the residual cum off his dick, he zipped up and left the room.

I raised my hand in question. "We're here to make vampires, not have sex," I said telepathically.

"It's been too long for me. I'm horny!"

Mason gestured the next guy over.

I thought I was promiscuous, but he took the cake. The next guy stepped forward, stroking himself.

"Fuck me!" Mason moaned.

I watched Mason bend over and spread his cheeks. I envied him because he had no guilt or limitations. As the guy fucked him in the ass, the two men from the downstairs bar entered the room. They stood and watched as Mason took another load. Once again, after finishing, the man zipped up and left, not saying a word.

"Are you just going to stand there?" Mason whispered, glowering at me. "Now is the time," he said telepathically.

I took a deep breath and crawled onto the platform. It was now or never. I set my clothes to the side while pushing my guilt away. The tattooed man stepped forward, interested in me. I lifted my ass, demanding that he screw me. The man complied with my wishes. He drilled me with his hardness just seconds later, and I knew I couldn't masturbate as I needed to save my seed to turn him into a vampire.

"Kiss each other!" the jockstrap man ordered.

I turned to Mason and saw him getting fucked. I kissed him deeply. As our tongues intertwined, I moaned, tasting the sperm in his mouth. It tasted heavenly.

Both men ejaculated simultaneously.

After they stopped spasming, we pushed them out and tackled them to the floor. We drained them of blood and then gave them nourishment in return. Afterward, we jacked and shot our loads inside their mouths. As their bodies began to convulse, we turned quickly, hearing footsteps coming in our direction.

"Hide the bodies!" Mason shouted.

We dragged our victims into the corner of the room, ran back to our spots, and kneeled, waiting for the next unsuspecting visitor.

The downstairs bartender entered.

"He must be on break," I thought aloud as he looked at me and pointed toward the sign reading 'showers'

***

The bartender gestured toward the shower floor. "Kneel. I'm going to piss on you."

I had never experienced golden showers before, so my mind raced with all the diseases I could encounter. The worst was getting exposed to the hepatitis B virus. The F-bomb erupted from my mouth when I remembered I was a vampire immune to all diseases.

I knelt as two guys entered the bathroom and stood beside the bartender. I figured they wanted to participate due to their eagerness. I glanced at their groins. They were both well-endowed and circumcised.

"Open your mouth!" the bartender ordered, pointing his dick toward me.

My mouth opened in anticipation of piss. Indeed, he wouldn't make me swallow it. I thought as the first stream hit my face. I flinched, not expecting the force.

"Open wider!" the bartender shouted.

I followed his direction. A stream of piss entered my mouth. It tasted salty, so I pushed it out.

From the corner of my eye, I saw Mason entering with our newly made vampires. The two men standing next to the bartender stepped forward and started urinating. Three streams hit my face and chest. As the streams diminished, I sat still and waited for further direction.

The bartender murmured his thanks and turned around to leave. Drenched in piss, I telepathically messaged Mason to stop him from going.

I jumped into action, attacking one of the other men as Mason attacked the bartender. When my victim fell, he also caused the third guy to fall to the floor. I grabbed his leg to prevent him from getting away and shouted at our newly made vampires to attack and drain them of blood.

The vampires immediately obeyed and began feeding on the helpless victims. I watched as they replenished their bodies with nourishment and then jacked off into their mouths. As their victims convulsed, I turned to Mason and smiled as I saw the realization in his eyes that our newly made vampires were fast learners.

Peter

I DROVE THE semi-truck filled with caskets since Jackson claimed he didn't know how to operate a manual transmission. "What a pansy!" I thought to myself as I was left to do the job.

The streets of the French Quarter were narrow and lined with old brick buildings and balconies adorned with wrought-iron railings. Some buildings were painted in pastel shades of pink, blue, and yellow, giving the area a quaint and charming feel. Despite their beauty, however, the streets themselves were treacherous to navigate. Cars parked on either side made them even narrower than they already were, and sharp turns forced drivers to slow down considerably.

Despite these challenges, I managed to drive the truck through them successfully. It was nerve-racking at times — I had to be careful not to hit any drunk pedestrians or other vehicles — but eventually, I caught sight of the lights of the bathhouse in the distance.

I turned to look at Jackson in the passenger seat, my disbelief evident. I couldn't believe he had turned Doug into a vampire without my consent — the audacity was mind-blowing. As I slowed down, the truck lurched forward, and I could feel Jackson's eyes on me. He was questioning my driving abilities. "Fuck you!" I thought, feeling a surge of hatred toward him once again.

Suddenly, there was a loud bang from the back of the cargo area. One of the caskets must have come loose and hit the wall when I changed speeds. I panicked about the four men back there — two were vampires, and two were not. Pressed for time, I hoped to convert them before sunrise.

Glancing at my watch, I saw that it was already 2:30 a.m. My anxiety grew as I realized just how little time we had left. With over thirty caskets in the trailer, unloading and carrying them to the third floor would take us a while.

I turned to face Jackson again, glaring as he looked relaxed and sexually fulfilled. My hatred for him only grew stronger.

We finally arrived at the bathhouse, and I depressed the blinker before turning into the alleyway where Antonio had instructed us to unload.

Harry

I WAITED FOR Antonio's father to wake up while sitting under the massive oak tree that sheltered us. He was exhausted from almost drowning.

Closing my eyes, I thought back to the flooded compound. The pounding on the Sick Bay door told me someone was inside, so I stopped to investigate the situation.

I unlocked and opened the door.

The water rushed in with a deafening roar, filling the room and pushing against the door with incredible force. As I opened it, the total weight of the deluge hit me like a punch. The surging current buffeted the naked man's body, his arms flailing as he struggled to stay afloat. The water was murky and dark, swirling around us in an angry dance. Despite its chaos, I could feel its power tugging at my legs and threatening to drag me under. With all my strength, I pulled the man toward me and held him close, shielding him from the relentless onslaught of water. It was a battle — we were lucky to survive.

As the masculine, naked man reached out, I grabbed him and pulled him into the hallway. He was so exhausted that I cradled him in my arms.

"I've got you!" I said, gazing into his eyes.

"My son . . . Antonio . . . Where is he?" the man muttered.

"I know him!" I exclaimed. "He made me into a vampire." As I continued staring at him, I couldn't see any resemblance to his son. Perhaps it was the difference in their eyes or how they carried themselves.

I saw the staircase leading us to safety. "I'm Harry. Don't you worry. I'll get you out of here."

"Is Antonio safe?" he asked again.

"I don't know," I replied honestly.

I continued to hold him in my arms because he didn't have the strength to stand alone. "I'm sure he made it out safely," I said reassuringly. Despite not having a concrete answer, I tried to comfort him.

I ascended the staircase slowly because the first five steps were underwater. I moved carefully, making sure not to slip or lose my footing.

As we ascended higher, I glanced down and saw the man's naked body. My eyes widened, and I inhaled sharply, momentarily mesmerized by his masculine physique. His uncircumcised penis draped on his thigh, adding an unexpected element to the situation.

"My name is William."

"We're almost out of here."

Despite the unexpected distraction, I quickly refocused on our task and continued up the stairs. The safety of William and I depended on reaching the top as quickly and safely as possible.

I pushed aside any distractions that threatened to slow us down, focusing solely on each step. Every movement was deliberate and calculated, ensuring we made progress without risking injury or danger.

As we finally emerged from the water onto the cement landing, I sighed in relief. We made it to safety.

Approaching the stone door, I couldn't see any obvious way to open it. Frustration mounting, I let out a groan of exasperation. William's voice broke through my thoughts, and he pointed toward the base of the wall.

"Depress the handle," he mumbled.

Without hesitation, I ran forward and used my foot to depress the lever. To my surprise, the door opened with ease.

With adrenaline pumping, I sprinted away from the mausoleum and into the darkness. My heart was pounding, and I could barely catch my breath. Suddenly, I stumbled from exhaustion. Fortunately, I managed to keep William from crashing to the ground by falling on my knees. I took a moment to catch my breath before continuing the run.

I ran for what felt like ages, my only focus being to escape the horrifying nightmare of the mausoleum. Finally, after what must have been a mile of running, I came across a large oak tree. Breathless and exhausted, I collapsed against its trunk and caught my breath.

Now in the present, I opened my eyes and glanced at William. He was now asleep in my arms. Surprising myself, I raised my hand and fingered his hairy chest. He moaned unknowingly, feeling my touch. My jaw dropped, taking in his beautiful body. He became aroused. Yes, most men had bigger dicks, but his was the prettiest I had ever seen.

My tongue shot out, licking my lips, wanting to taste it, but the exhaustion I felt stopped me. It was overwhelming, a combination of physical exertion and emotional intensity that drained me. Only then did I realize how much energy I had expended during our escape.

A wave of drowsiness washed over me. Even though we were in the open, exposed to anyone who might happen by, I was slipping into a deep sleep. How long I slept is unclear — it could have been minutes or even hours.

***

My eyes snapped open at the sound of footsteps behind me. I quickly turned to see who was approaching. My heart began racing as I saw a man with a bleeding, crooked nose, his features twisted into a dangerous and menacing expression.

Despite his apparent injury, an air of strength and confidence about him made me uneasy.

For a moment, I struggled to the place where I had seen him, but before I could figure it out, he hissed and bared his sharp teeth. My heart raced with fear as I sat William down.

I frantically searched for anything that I could use as a weapon. But it was no use — I was utterly defenseless against this creature of the night. As he lunged toward me with lightning speed, I closed my eyes and braced myself for the impact.

Philippe

THE TAKEDOWN was swift and decisive, as my years of experience as a hunter kicked in. Harry, the newly made vampire, posed no real threat to me, so I didn't waste any time. I tackled him with all my might in one fluid motion.

He struggled beneath me, his movements wild and erratic. But even as he thrashed about, I could feel the adrenaline coursing through my veins, heightening my senses and sharpening my focus.

With one hand firmly around his throat to keep him pinned down, I reached for my knife with the other. The blade glinted menacingly in the dim light under the tree. I had feasted earlier on a guy in the park standing in his underwear, but now I needed to nut. My balls were full of cum.

"Get off me!"

Harry continued to struggle until I raised the knife to his throat. The glint of the blade seemed to snap him out of his frenzy, and he became motionless. "You're going to surrender your ass."

I could feel his eyes on me as I made my demand — he

nodded in agreement, seemingly resigned to his fate.

He screamed as my cock penetrated his non-lubricated asshole.

I covered his mouth as I started thrusting back and forth. I knew I'd come quickly, but that was fine because I needed to find Salvatore Leone, my superior officer.

I felt the intensity of my building orgasm, and my body was wracked with pleasure as my head shot back. But then, suddenly, a sharp pain exploded at the back of my head, and I fell to the ground in a daze. The sensation was jarring and disorienting, causing me to lose all focus on what had just happened.

Frustrated that my eruption was abruptly interrupted, I swiftly turned to investigate the cause — only to discover Antonio's father towering above me, his foot poised mid-air. Anger and disgust twisted his face while his intense gaze sent shivers down my spine. All I could do for a moment was stare at him in shock.

William

AS I HELPED my rescuer, Harry, stand, I asked if he was hurt. He replied that he was fine and turned toward the unconscious vampire with the crooked nose on the ground.

"You son-of-a-bitch!" he yelled, delivering a swift kick to his chest.

"What should we do with him?"

"Leave him be," he replied tersely. "It'll be sunrise shortly."

I looked up at Harry, my eyes traveling to his face. He was gazing at my groin. I wasn't surprised — this wasn't the first time a gay man had ogled me in such a way. But instead of responding with outrage or embarrassment, I ignored it. "I don't know where the meeting spot is. I tried to reach Antonio, but the transmission didn't go through."

"My apartment is in the French Quarter."

"Is it safe?" I asked.

He nodded confidently.

Harry flinched from pain, touching his asshole.

I turned him around, feeling a sense of dread as I saw the look of pain etched on his face. Carefully, I spread his cheeks to get a better look, and my heart sank at the sight that greeted me. Blood was seeping from his anus, staining his skin. "You're bleeding," I said softly, my voice barely above a whisper.

As the reality of the situation hit me like a ton of bricks, my mind raced with anger and disgust toward the crooked-nosed vampire who had brutally sodomized him. Frustration consumed me as I acknowledged the urgent need to cleanse the wound promptly. "Let's get going," I said firmly, taking charge of the situation. "I'll clean you up." The urgency in my voice left no room for argument or delay. Harry turned toward me with tears and gratitude etched across his features.

"You'd do that for me?" he asked incredulously.

"You saved my life," I replied without hesitation. "Of course, I would." Despite the gruesome nature of what we were dealing with, there was no question about helping him through this ordeal.

Harry

I WAS STUNNED when William generously offered his assistance. Before I could respond, the bloodsucker emerged from unconsciousness and swung a jagged stone into William's temple. The force of the impact sent him reeling and left me struck dumb with shock.

I could feel my anger boiling up, and without hesitation, I lunged forward and began throwing punches in the vampire's face. Each punch connected with a sickening thud against his skull as I continued to rain down blows until he eventually fell unconscious again.

As I picked up William, my heart sank at the sight of his bleeding wound. The side of his head was gashed open, with blood trickling down his temple. The wound looked raw and painful, with bits of dirt and debris sticking to the edges. My mouth opened uncontrollably in shock at the sight of his injury. But I quickly gathered my wits and breathed deeply to calm myself. While assessing the wound, a pang of sorrow washed over me for the brutal attack he had endured. Realizing the gravity of the situation, I knew I had to act fast and administer medical attention. I picked him up without wasting time and raced toward the French Quarter.

Breathless, I sprinted through the alleyways, my heart pounding. The darkness seemed to press in on me from all sides, making it difficult to see where I was going. The tall buildings flanking either side of the alley loomed over me like menacing giants, casting deep shadows stretching out and swallowing me whole.

Despite the fear that gripped me, I kept running. My feet pounded against the cracked pavement beneath me, ringing echoes through the narrow passageways. The only sound that accompanied me was my ragged breathing and the occasional flicker of light from a distant streetlamp.

Darting from alleyway to alleyway, I avoided the patrolling police officers. Adrenaline coursed through my veins as I made our way to safety, each breath feeling shallow and ragged as I pushed myself harder and faster toward our destination.

Franco De Rocco

William

EMERGING FROM the fog of unconsciousness, I felt a firm, steady grip enveloping me. The arms that held me belonged to a young man who appeared to be in his late twenties. Though slightly blurred by my dazed state, his face struck a chord of familiarity. However, despite my best efforts, I couldn't pinpoint where I had seen him before.

As he sprinted with me in his arms, his curly brown hair bounced around his face in unruly waves. He was clean-shaven. Something about him suggested a European origin — perhaps his style or a particular accent that drifted into my ears, hinting at a far-off homeland.

The name "William" slipped from his lips during our frantic escape. The utterance, brief as it was, left me puzzled. Who was this William he mentioned? Was it his name, or perhaps someone else we were running from or towards?

The furrowed brow and tightened jawline on his face hinted at a deep worry. It was clear that the situation was more complex than I initially perceived. After what seemed like an eternity, his pace gradually slowed until we came to a halt. His gaze fell upon me, filled with concern, adding another layer of mystery to the already baffling situation.

"Are you alright?"

Bewilderment washed over me. My mind felt like an empty canvas, devoid of memories or knowledge about myself or my past. The sense of self, the familiarity of my identity, seemed to have vanished into thin air.

As I continued to gaze at the young man in front of me, my puzzled expression must have been clear as day. He seemed to pick up on my disarray, his eyes softening with a hint of understanding.

"William?" he muttered.

I managed a shrug, my muscles feeling heavy and

uncooperative. A sense of loss and disorientation engulfed me, making it difficult to comprehend the situation. "I . . . don't . . ." I stammered, my voice barely more than a whisper, grappling to form a coherent sentence. "Understand," I finally managed to articulate, though it did little to convey the whirlwind of confusion within me.

One of his eyebrows arched upwards, creating a slight asymmetry on his otherwise symmetrical face. His next words, however, sent a chill down my spine.

"You've been struck on the head." His voice was steady yet laced with concern, filling me with dread and curiosity.

I tried to act cool. In truth, I was far from fine — my head was spinning, and my thoughts were jumbled. But for some reason, I felt the need to hide my confusion out of embarrassment. Perhaps because I didn't want this stranger to see me as vulnerable, or maybe it was simply a reflexive response to the traumatic situation.

As my fingers grazed the side of my skull, they met the raw, wet sensation of an open wound. A sharp sting of agony shot through me, but I managed to suppress a grimace. Striving to maintain an air of nonchalance, I looked at the man before me, my expression filled with bewilderment.

"Let me stand," I declared firmly, my voice unwavering. Despite the throbbing pain, I was determined not to exhibit any signs of vulnerability.

Harry

AS WE AMBLED side by side toward the French Quarter, a nagging suspicion gnawed at the back of my mind. Something about William seemed amiss. Acting on this intuition, I halted abruptly and seized his shoulder.

He turned, surprised at my sudden and unexpected action.

In a voice that resonated with firmness, I asked, "What's your name?"

For a moment, he remained silent — as if struggling to remember something important. His eyes furrowed in concentration as he searched his memory for the answer. And then he stammered out a response.

"William . . . My name's William."

I felt relief wash over me as I realized that the man's memory had returned and that his earlier confusion was no longer an issue.

This realization made our journey together less fraught with worry and concern. We were able to continue toward our destination without any further interruptions.

As we walked through the city streets, I felt a sense of comfort and reassurance in the presence of this stranger. Our shared experience brought us closer together, and it was clear that there was a newfound connection between us. It's funny how life sometimes works — how an unexpected event can bring two people together in ways they never imagined.

William

THE STAIRCASE to the man's apartment was narrow and twisted deep into the building. The steps were steep and challenging. The walls around us were a dull gray. A dim, yellow light bathed the stairway, emanating from a lone, flickering bulb. Its erratic glow added an unsettling undertone to the climb, enhancing the eerie ambiance of the scene.

We reached the third floor, a welcome respite from

the seemingly endless climb. The man stretched his hand toward the door frame, retrieving a hidden key. As he unlocked and pushed the door open, a wave of anticipation washed over me, filling the air with an almost tangible expectation.

Upon entering, I was immediately captivated by the room's warm and intimate atmosphere, which enveloped me in a sense of coziness and comfort. It housed only a few essential pieces — a bed that had seen better days, a small couch that bore the marks of frequent use, a humble kitchen table, and two chairs that matched its simplicity. Despite the modesty of the furniture and their obvious signs of wear, everything was arranged with meticulous care, creating an atmosphere of order and cleanliness.

I ventured further into the room, drawn toward the window draped in faded curtains. Pushing them aside, I found myself peering into the darkness. Bourbon Street, usually teeming with tourists and locals alike, now lay deserted, its usual hustle and bustle silenced as the visitors retreated to the safety of their hotel rooms.

Glancing upwards, I felt a twinge of pity as I saw two men laboriously boarding up the third-floor doorway of an adjacent building. Without thinking, I waved to one of them, and he waved back. I wondered what led these men to work such odd hours. Were they trying to finish a job before a looming deadline? Whatever the reason, it was clear they were putting in long hours. The neon sign above the building's entrance caught my eye, flashing a bright light in an entrancing rhythmic sequence. I couldn't resist taking a closer look. As the sign came into focus, it read 'N. O. B.'

I stood there contemplating the letters and whispered, "New Orleans . . ." But before I could ponder further, the man who brought me here suddenly touched my shoulder. Startled, I quickly turned to him. He looked at me curiously.

"What are you looking at?"

I gestured toward the building across the street and replied, "The one with the neon sign."

With a knowing smirk on his face, he informed me matter-of-factly. "That's the Bathhouse."

Confused by his response, I released the curtain and stared at him with a puzzled expression. He explained that it was a place where men went to have sex.

As I stood there, trying to understand his words, my mind began to race. I struggled to recall where I had heard the word 'bathhouse' before, but then my thoughts were interrupted as I glanced down and noticed his naked body.

My eyes widened as I took in his uncircumcised penis and bushy pubic hair. I quickly glanced away, hoping he hadn't noticed me looking. Suddenly, he touched my chest without warning, causing me to inhale sharply.

I waited for him to remove his hand, but he didn't. Instead, he let his finger trail down my abdomen until it reached my groin. Despite my racing thoughts and questions, his touch didn't threaten me. In fact, I wasn't appalled by it at all.

"Let's get cleaned up."

The man led me toward the bathroom.

As we passed the small kitchen table, I saw an open correspondence with a name written on it. Forgetting his name, I leaned closer and read the lettering, muttering "Harry" out loud. I glanced at my companion to see if he recognized the name, but my attention was drawn to the blood on the back of his legs.

Suddenly, my mind flooded with questions and concerns. My confusion overwhelmed me again. I pressed my fingers to my forehead, thinking I should know what happened, but I couldn't remember anything.

The man turned, answering my call.

"Yes?"

I pointed to the blood on the back of his legs.

His eyes followed the direction of my finger and frowned. "Don't you remember what happened?"

I nodded, pretending to remember.

I followed him into the bathroom, relieved to have learned his name. As I looked around the room, I noticed that instead of a shower, there was a bear-claw bathtub. It was massive, big enough to fit two men.

Harry turned on the bath water and pulled two towels from a rack above the toilet. I was grateful for his hospitality as he gestured toward the sink. He soaked a washcloth in hot water as I stepped forward and began cleansing my face. Out of the corner of my eye, I saw the washcloth and noticed it was stained with blood. My heart raced with fear as I looked at myself in the mirror. That's when I saw an open wound filled with dirt and small stones. It was clear that something had caused a deep laceration on my face, leaving me wondering what had happened.

"Turn back around."

Feeling confused, I looked back at the man tending to my wound. He smiled at me sincerely. Despite my curiosity, I never asked him what had happened. Once he was finished washing my wound, he gestured toward the tub as if to indicate that it was time to take a bath.

I stepped into the tub and sat down on the edge.

As I relaxed, I glanced at the man helping me. His naked body caught my eye again, and I felt intrigued by him. When he grasped me earlier, I got aroused. Knowing his hand felt good on my erection, I questioned if I was gay or bisexual.

Harry stepped forward and caressed my upper back, interrupting my deep thoughts. I didn't flinch because it felt good. His touch was sensual, and I became hard once again.

I was lost in thought when he spoke up. "Your wound has healed," he said matter-of-factly.

Without thinking, I raised my hand to feel for myself. To my amazement, he was right — it was as if the laceration had never happened.

"It healed instantly after I cleaned it," he explained.

As I lowered my hand, Harry stepped into the bathtub with me. Our eyes met, and he smiled with a look of desire that sent a thrill of excitement through my body.

Harry

AS I GENTLY lowered myself into the tub, the warm water enveloped my body, providing a comforting embrace. Meanwhile, William sat perched on the tub's edge. His gaze fixed on me. I couldn't help but notice the firmness in his posture and the way his muscles tensed and relaxed every time he breathed. As my eyes locked onto him, I felt a stirring within me, a surge of arousal hidden beneath the water's surface.

I studied him more intently, trying to decipher his sexual orientation. Was he straight, bisexual, or gay? His actions were subtle, leaving room for interpretation. The way he met my gaze, however, was comforting. There was an element of appreciation in his eyes, a silent affirmation that put me at ease.

My attraction toward him surfaced. Surprising myself, I leaned forward and kissed him tenderly. He didn't grimace or pull back. Instead, he kissed me in return. His tongue entered my mouth. I moaned and surrendered to his masculinity.

William pulled back and stared at me. The look on his face told me everything. He enjoyed the sensual kiss.

I smiled and sat back in the water.

As he stood, his erection pulsated before me. I reached forward and caressed him. A moan of ecstasy escaped his mouth. This man was beautiful. He wasn't well-muscled like a bodybuilder, but he was toned. His body reeked of masculinity.

I leaned forward and placed my lips around his throbbing shaft. With a teasing flick of my tongue, I delicately traced the contours of the head, savoring every breathtaking moment. The symphony of his moans reverberated through the air, a testament to the overwhelming pleasure he was experiencing. As I pulled back the foreskin, revealing him thoroughly, the heightened sensitivity he felt from my skilled tongue only deepened his moans of ecstasy. It was almost surreal to think that here was a man, a figure twice my age, allowing me to pleasure him. Driven by an insatiable hunger, I eagerly and confidently took him deep into my throat, thoroughly enjoying the sensation of his shaft filling me, momentarily losing myself in the moment's passion.

"It feels so good," he moaned.

I think he was surprised someone could deep-throat him. He wasn't big, so it wasn't a problem. This made me realize he was inexperienced when it came to sex. I didn't know his back history and wouldn't ask him. This wasn't the place and time.

He pushed my head backward.

As I glanced upward, my heart raced with anticipation. His hands cupped my face and pulled me in. I could feel his warm breath on my lips as he kissed me.

Lost in the moment, I surrendered myself entirely to him, letting him take control of our passionate embrace. His touch was gentle yet firm as he explored every inch of my mouth. It was a feeling unlike any other — pure bliss and ecstasy all rolled into one unforgettable experience.

I was verse and enjoyed both roles, so I'd play the submissive if he played the aggressor.

He pulled away from me slowly, breaking our intimate moment. Once again, I tried to read his mind but found myself unable to do so. He seemed confused and lost in thought as if trying to come to terms with something new and unfamiliar. Perhaps this was his first time kissing a man, and he struggled with his emotions.

"Stand up," he whispered, helping me to my feet.

His touch was gentle yet firm as he guided me up, his eyes still locked onto mine. I could feel the tension between us building once again. I didn't know what would happen next, but it didn't matter. He turned me around. Is he going to screw me? I wondered. As he leaned in, I felt his warm breath on my neck before he kissed my upper back softly.

"Can I make love to you?" he asked.

His words echoed in my mind, their profound impact sending a shiver coursing through my body. I found myself turning to look at him, my gaze meeting his. In his eyes, I saw a fervor that was impossible to ignore. It was evident that he was not a man to rush things. He savored every moment and experience like a connoisseur savoring a fine wine.

He was a stark contrast to the other men I had encountered who were only interested in fleeting encounters. But not William. He yearned for something deeper, a connection that transcended the physical. His desire to connect on an emotional and intellectual level was unmistakable, and this depth of character set him apart. At that moment, I knew that I wanted him more than anything.

With longing, I whispered my response, "Yes," and watched as he leaned in to kiss me softly. It was the beginning of an early morning filled with intimacy and connection, where nothing else mattered but the two of us.

I spread my cheeks with trembling fingers, and I held my breath. My head shot back as he entered me. He was gentle, and his size didn't disappoint. My ass had completely healed, so I was no longer in pain. Turning in ecstasy, I glanced at him. His eyes were closed, feeling the sensation of my ass lips around his shaft.

I moaned, knowing this man administered pleasure, not pain. He grabbed my waist and started making love to me.

As his moans elevated, I knew he was getting ready to orgasm. He didn't seem to know his cum was poisonous.

"You can't come inside me," I forewarned.

He was a gentleman and pulled out.

I turned around, knelt in the water, and then proceeded to suck him off. The first stream of cum shot to the back of my throat. Then four more jets shot into my mouth. The texture of his jizz was joyous, and I wanted to savor it forever.

As he pulled back, I sat with his load gathered at the base of my throat. I held it in my mouth as long as possible until the burning sensation caused me to lean forward and spit it out.

"You don't like the taste?"

"Your seed would have killed me."

I saw his look of confusion. "You're a vampire. Your jizz is poisonous," I explained, seeing him thinking deeply. Did he not know this? I thought, questioning him once again.

He lowered himself into the water and held his forehead. I could tell he was in deep thought.

"I'm a vampire?" he muttered softly.

"Yes."

"And my sperm is lethal?"

I leaned forward and grasped William's shoulder, hoping to snap him out of his confusion. "William, do you remember what happened earlier?" I asked him urgently.

He shook his head slowly, looking bewildered and lost. It was clear that something was seriously wrong. "Does your head hurt?" I asked him gently, trying to gauge the severity of his condition.

I gazed at him. My heart filled with a profound sense of pity as his lips moved to form words. His voice echoed in the room — each syllable heavy with a bewildering mix of confusion.

Earlier on, he had introduced himself as William. But it wasn't a spontaneous introduction. Instead, it was a parroted response, a mere echo of my words when I informed him of his name. His identity was a borrowed one, given to him by me because he couldn't remember his own.

As I studied him closely, his eyes met mine. They held a depth of sincerity that hadn't been there before. It was as if, for the first time, he was truly present in the conversation, genuinely responding instead of just repeating what he was told. I could see a flicker of comprehension and a realization that made me believe his response was authentic this time.

My heart sank as I realized he had amnesia. This was a

serious medical condition. Taking a deep breath to steady myself, I tried to remain calm as I assessed the situation.

As we sat together silently, my mind raced with questions and concerns. How severe was his condition? Would he be able to recover? And most importantly — how could I help him through this challenging time?

William

CONFUSION WASHED over me like a tidal wave as I struggled to make sense of the dizzying sensations inside my head. The room seemed to spin around me, and my head was pounding intensely, making it difficult to focus. I could hear his voice through the haze of my muddled thoughts, asking if my head hurt. It took me a while to even begin to process his words. The knowledge that I had shared an intimate and passionate experience with him just moments ago left me with questions. The unknown terrified me, and I struggled to reconcile my inner turmoil. Feeling him touch me gently on the arm sent shivers of both fear and pleasure down my spine. I instinctively pulled away from him, my mind racing as I tried to process my conflicting emotions.

"I climaxed inside your mouth," I mumbled.

"Everything's fine. Sit down," Harry whispered.

I sat down and stared at him. Moments later, his smile assured me that everything was all right. He grabbed the bar of soap and started bathing me.

Closing my eyes, I felt his gentle touch. It soothed and relaxed me, easing my tension.

Focusing on what little memories I could grasp onto, I remembered that I had a son — but for the life of me, I couldn't recall his name or what he looked like. And then there was my wife — gone now but still present in my thoughts and dreams.

"You're safe here," he said softly, sensing my unease. "I'll take care of you."

His words were like a lifeline during all this confusion. They gave me hope that things would eventually get better.

Nodding slowly, I took comfort in his calming presence. At that moment, it didn't matter who or what we were to each other — all that mattered was that we were together, and he was looking after me. For now, that was enough.

Robert

THE BOUNCER stationed at the entrance of the Catacomb Bar scrutinized my son's ID before motioning us inside. I could tell he questioned our age difference from how he looked at us. However, his opinion or what he thought of us didn't bother me. At this point, all that mattered was our mission to locate Antonio.

As David and I stepped into the bar's foyer, I urged him to undergo a metamorphosis and assume the appearance of a leather man. Once we had both completed our transformation, I turned and saw his conversion. David's attire was quite eye-catching and distinctive. His chaps were made of high-quality black leather and hugged his legs tightly, accentuating the muscular definition of his thighs. The front panel of the garment was embellished with a captivating arrangement of silver studs, forming an elegant geometric pattern that enhanced its visual appeal. David's bare chest was oiled and glistened in the bar's dim light, drawing attention to his impressive physique. He also wore a leather harness around his torso that crisscrossed over his sculpted pecs, further emphasizing his masculine features. His long sideburns and full mustache added to his overall air of masculinity and confidence. Overall, David looked like a rugged and alluring figure who commanded attention.

I reached forward and caressed his buttocks. He smiled, and, in return, he grasped my cock. I had morphed into a leather man too. I wore chaps, but instead of exposing my ass, I chose to expose my groin. I was proud of its new length and thickness and wanted everyone to see it in all its glory.

David led me through the bar while holding my dick. I surveyed the scene — it was clear that chaos reigned supreme. With only one bartender serving a room full of leather-clad men, it was no wonder that he looked stressed and overwhelmed. His eyes darted toward the staircase, hoping for backup to arrive at any moment. Antonio was nowhere in sight, so David led me upstairs.

"He's up here."

I nodded as he released his grip on me.

As David turned and ascended the staircase, he shared his knowledge of the catacombs. It was clear that he had been here before and knew all about what lay ahead. The excitement in my veins began rising as I realized the adventure awaiting me. I was eager to see and experience everything this mysterious place offered. After hiding my gayness from the world, I was ready to make up for lost time and embrace every opportunity that came my way.

David opened the door, and we entered a dimly lit room with a map on one wall listing each room's directions. He pointed to 'showers,' and I knew that's where Antonio was. With a nod, I followed my son as he led me into the maze.

Antonio

AS MASON and all the newly made vampires gathered in the shower, I explained that it was crucial that we act fast and efficiently to succeed in our mission. With that in mind, I explained the plan — our goal was to split up and make as many bloodsuckers as possible within a half-hour timeframe. Once that was done, they were to take their recruits and meet us at the bathhouse. Everyone nodded in agreement and went their separate ways. Mason stayed with me as I finished showering. Suddenly, two men dressed in leather entered the room, catching me off guard.

As the two men undressed and stepped into the shower, I realized they were our next target. Mason joined me under the same showerhead, sharing my thoughts. As I observed them more closely, I couldn't help but notice how comfortable they were with each other. It was unclear whether they were in a romantic relationship or just close friends, but their bond was undeniable.

I watched as the scene unfolded before me. The men embraced each other. Their lips met passionately, and their hands explored each other's bodies. After a few minutes, the submissive one broke away and fell to his knees to perform oral sex.

Mason walked over to the kneeling man and ran his hand through his hair. He then leaned in and kissed the man receiving head, their tongues passionately intertwining. I, too, joined in on the liaison, and we all surrendered ourselves to our primal urges and indulged in the moment.

Robert

I GLANCED DOWN as David deep-throated me. I was surprised he didn't gag when my balls touched his chin. I couldn't help but acknowledge my son's skill and professionalism. I watched him work, the expression on his face one of utter bliss. It was clear that he took great pleasure in dedicating himself to the task at hand. I was overwhelmed with a feeling of excitement as Mason leaned in and kissed me. I closed my eyes and softly moaned as the kiss deepened.

I opened my eyes to see Mason's mischievous gaze. Without a word, he reached forward and teased the sensitive skin around my nipples, adding to my pleasure.

David pushed Mason's hand away.

I couldn't help but feel a sense of confusion and frustration. Our mission was to kill Antonio, not to engage in petty displays of dominance.

I made eye contact with David and questioned his behavior. He knew we needed to stay focused. We couldn't afford to let our personal feelings get in the way of completing our mission. It was clear that David saw Mason as a threat, both to our mission and his sense of pride. As Mason backed away, David continued fellatio.

I inhaled in surprise as my cock pulsated, wanting to ejaculate prematurely. David didn't stop and continued to suck and stroke my hardness. The head swelled from my building orgasm. "I'm going to cum," I shouted, trying to hold back, but my body wouldn't stop trembling. "Oh, Jesus!" I moaned and backed up. The first stream shot on his face.

"Shoot it in my mouth!" David moaned.

The next three jets hit the appointed target. David sighed loudly, savoring the taste of my milky fluid. I leaned forward and kissed him as my body stopped spasming. My tongue pressed open his lips, and I tasted the gathered jizz at the base of his throat.

He pushed it inside my mouth.

As I leaned back, the flavor overwhelmed my taste buds. I closed my eyes and savored every bit of it. It was so delicious that I wanted to swallow it, but I knew that wasn't possible. So instead, I let the taste linger a little longer, relishing the experience before finally spitting it out.

"I'm multi-orgasmic," I said, turning toward Antonio and Mason. Their cock's stood at attention. "Who wants to get fucked first?

"I'll go!" Antonio said, stepping forward.

I remembered his ass. I smiled, wanting to devour him once again. Unfortunately, I had to restrain myself and not hurt him.

Antonio leaned forward and parted his buttocks. His anus tightened in anticipation of my presence. The fool remained oblivious, unaware of my identity as a vampire or my transformed state.

Excited, I rammed inside him.

He gasped and stood away from the pain.

"I'm sorry," I said, realizing my mistake. I bent him over again and slowly reentered him. This time, his moist hole engulfed my rock-hard shaft. It felt so good that my orgasm started building immediately again.

Antonio

I TURNED, taken aback, seeing the leather man had already reached orgasm. When our eyes met, I could sense the embarrassment he felt due to his premature ejaculation. Despite the situation's awkwardness, I tried to show empathy and understanding toward him.

He pulled out and quickly directed Mason to eat the jizz that seeped from my ass. Mason was all too willing. I bent over, and he started swallowing cum. At first, he moaned in ecstasy while tasting the warm fluid, but then his moans became shrieks. Shocked to see Mason's body collapsing, he shook uncontrollably before going still. Concerned, I knelt beside him, calling out his name repeatedly. His distant and unfocused eyes sent a chill down my spine. Panic began to grip me as I realized something was terribly wrong. I touched him gently, hoping for any sign of life or response. But there was nothing. Mason's body lay still, his once vibrant presence now reduced to a lifeless shell.

Then suddenly, he gasped, "Vampire," before taking his last breath and dying before me.

I was frozen with fear and confusion, completely unable to comprehend what was happening. My attention was captivated by a graceful movement unfolding mere inches away from me. I spun around and witnessed the transformation of these two men into themselves, revealing that they were Robert and David.

Without a second thought, I turned and ran into the catacombs in a blind panic. Enveloped in the abyss, I sought refuge, yet an elusive sanctuary evaded me. The darkness consumed, offering no solace. I could hear Robert and David's footsteps behind me. My mind raced with fear.

"Stop running!" David called out.

"Fuck you!" I screamed as I ran faster than I ever had before. I knew there had to be an emergency exit somewhere along these twisting hallways, a way out of this nightmare. As I rounded the next corner, my eyes scanned frantically for any sign of an outside door. My lungs burned with exertion, and sweat poured down my forehead, but I refused to give up hope.

I felt a hand on my shoulder. It was Robert — he had caught up with me! I tried to break free from his grasp, but it was too strong. I fell to the floor, gasping for breath as Robert loomed over me.

"You're dead!" he murmured, raising a switchblade.

The blade snapping open echoed through the air, sending a chill down my spine. I turned quickly to see Robert's knife descending toward me with deadly precision. Panic set in as I realized he would sever my head from my body if I didn't act fast.

I kicked Robert's chest with lightning-fast reflexes, sending him flying backward into the wall. He hit the ground and groaned in pain. I jumped up and ran as fast as possible, adrenaline pumping through my veins, but David was close behind me.

I shied away from his grasp, stumbling forward and nearly losing my balance. My ankle throbbed with pain — I had sprained it when Robert pulled me down. I gritted my teeth and pushed through the discomfort.

Despite my efforts, David was too quick and powerful. He tackled me to the floor. The impact knocked the wind out of my lungs, leaving me gasping for air as he held me down.

No matter how hard I struggled, David's grip remained unbreakable. It was like trying to move a boulder. With no chance of escape, I cried out and begged for my life. But he only sneered, his eyes cold and unfeeling. "I loved you!" I spat out, my voice shaking with emotion. "How can you hate me so much?"

In a last-ditch effort to change his mind, I leaned forward and kissed him with all the passion I could muster. I hoped that it would ignite something inside of him. But instead, the grimace that spread across his face told me everything. He hated me more than ever — and nothing would stop him from carrying out his plan.

"I have someone new in my life," David said, trying to make me jealous.

"Who?" I spat, not believing him.

"Me!" Robert shouted above us.

Turning my head, I saw Robert standing with his hand on David's shoulder. Everything suddenly clicked into place. It all made sense now. I spat at David, unable to hold back my disgust any longer. "You make me sick!"

David wiped the spittle from his face and snatched the

switchblade from his father's hand. Despite my desperate cries of "no," he remained indifferent. With a cold and calculating look in his eyes, he raised the blade and plunged it into my neck, causing blood to gush out of the wound.

Leaving the switchblade deep inside me, David stood with a twisted smile. He seemed to relish my suffering.

"G-Gabriel . . . help me . . ." I managed to choke out.

As my vision began to fade, I felt a sense of despair wash over me. I knew I was dying from blood loss and could do nothing to stop it. But just as the darkness was about to consume me, a bright, heavenly light appeared above us.

David looked up in surprise, his eyes wide with confusion. He seemed unsure of what was happening, but I knew deep down that this was no ordinary occurrence.

As the light grew brighter and brighter, the ceiling suddenly opened, and a figure descended from Heaven. It was Gabriel — the Archangel of God.

The sight of him descending gracefully with his wings spread wide was breathtaking. He landed completely naked on the ground, radiating peace and serenity.

Gabriel's presence was overwhelming, and I felt humbled by his grace. He touched my forehead without hesitation, sending waves of healing power through my body. I felt a transformative shift within, as if every ounce of negativity was dissolving into a radiant glow of pure light.

After Gabriel removed his hand from my forehead, he pointed toward my attacker. In response, David flew through the air and hit the opposite wall. The impact was so loud that it seemed to shake the entire room, causing dust and debris to rain down from the ceiling.

Robert stepped back in shock, knowing better than to interfere with what was happening. He watched in horror as his son slumped to the floor, his body broken from the impact.

The cold metal of the knife pressed against my skin reminded me of my danger. Every breath I took felt like it could be my last. "I don't want to die," I cried.

Gabriel touched the hilt of the knife.

"Don't worry," he said softly. "I'm here to save you."

And with those words, he gently removed the knife from my neck — taking care not to cause any further damage. Then, he placed his hand over my wound, and it began to heal with otherworldly energy that seemed to radiate from within him.

"These men will not harm you now," he said.

"Thank you."

"The exit is around the corner," Gabriel muttered, looking into my eyes with love and kindness.

"What about them?" I asked, pointing toward Robert, kneeling above David's unconscious body.

"I'll take care of them."

I stood with gratitude in my eyes.

"Go, now . . ."

After surviving another attempt on my life, I felt renewed with hope.

Robert

I GLANCED UP from my unconscious son, my heart racing with fear at seeing the angelic being standing before me. I knew better than to make any sudden moves in the presence of such a powerful celestial force. As I looked into his eyes, I felt a sense of awe and reverence.

The angel spoke in a voice that was both commanding and soothing at the same time.

"The chosen one is Antonio," the archangel's words echoed through the room. "He drank from the chalice and saved the Prince of Peace, returning him home."

My mind reeled as I tried to process what I was hearing. I lowered my head in disbelief, struggling to accept this new reality.

Gabriel's hand made contact with my head, and I felt an overwhelming surge of power emanating from him. My emotions got the better of me as tears streamed down my face while he addressed my forbidden incestuous relationship. The archangel's words echoed in my mind, filling me with dread and despair. I had committed a serious sin that carried the punishment of eternal damnation. I couldn't fathom any way to make amends, and then the angelic being delivered the final blow.

"You are forever banished from your son."

Looking up, tears continued to flow as I realized this would be my eternal fate. Gabriel motioned toward the exit, indicating that I should abandon my son. The mere thought of being separated from David ignited an intense and uncontrollable anger within me. Instead of accepting my punishment, I fought back and formulated a plan.

"Leave now."

As Gabriel stood before me, undressed, I firmly grasped his genitals. He remained motionless, seemingly shocked by my actions. Without hesitation, I proceeded to pleasure him orally, catching him off guard before he could comprehend the situation fully.

Antonio

I QUICKLY DESCENDED the metal staircase as the emergency door swung open. I ran toward the bathhouse on Bourbon Street, aware that the first light of dawn was starting to appear in the sky. I was in turmoil as I tried to process what had just happened. Mason's passing hit me hard, and it was difficult to comprehend that he was no longer with me. The weight of his absence felt heavy on my heart.

As I turned my gaze toward the alleyway beside the bathhouse, my eyes fell upon a semi-truck with the unmistakable signage of a casket supply company emblazoned on its side. The truck's back door was open, and to my surprise, it was empty. I realized Peter and Jackson must have completed their mission and found the caskets they sought.

Entering the bathhouse, I noticed a man standing behind a plexiglass barrier. His name tag read George, and as our eyes met, he was clearly frightened of me. Despite my attempts to appear non-threatening, something about my presence put him on edge.

"Antonio?"

I nodded.

The man behind the plexiglass let out a sigh of relief. He lifted a walkie-talkie and spoke into it, alerting someone that I had arrived. His voice filled with a mixture of excitement and apprehension. Seconds later, the speaker's voice erupted, saying he'd be right down. I took a deep breath, hearing Angelo's voice.

Suddenly, a loud, obnoxious buzzing sound erupted in the background, and the man motioned toward the door.

I pushed the rail, and the door opened. As I entered the bathhouse, George came out of the office.

"Welcome. I'm George."

I took a deep breath, catching my breath. "Thank you."

"You made it!" Angelo exclaimed behind us.

I turned and caught sight of Angelo walking toward me. My heart skipped a beat at the sight of his handsome face. He raised his hands toward me as if to say, "Come here." Without hesitation, I collapsed into his arms, feeling an overwhelming sense of safety and comfort. As we embraced, I looked into his eyes and saw his deep love for me.

As he drew closer, I felt my heart race with anticipation. And then, without warning, his lips met mine in a deep and passionate kiss. His tongue explored every crevice of my mouth, sending shivers down my spine. I couldn't help but let out a soft moan as I surrendered to him. At that moment, it was as if nothing else existed except for the two of us — lost in a world of pure romance and desire.

As I watched Angelo's eyes flicker open, I felt a rush of emotion wash over me. Even in my exhausted state, the mere touch of his dick under the towel ignited a fire. However, as much as I yearned to caress his hardness, my body was too spent.

Angelo's gaze met mine, and he seemed to understand everything — the pain, the struggle, and the sacrifices I made to get here. Without hesitation, Angelo lifted me into his arms.

"I've missed you . . ." I murmured, cradling my head on his muscular chest.

With a reassuring tone, Angelo whispered, "You're safe now," and gently kissed my head. He then carried me toward the staircase that led to the third floor of the building.

Robert

AS GABRIEL stepped back in shock and ascended quickly to heaven, I sat there stunned. Only then did I realize my mistake — I had done something terribly wrong. But thunder caught my attention before I could even begin to process what had happened. It started as a low rumble, barely audible at first, before escalating into a fiery storm that shook the very foundation of the building.

I could feel the floor trembling beneath me. The air crackled with electricity, and I knew this was no ordinary storm — it was a manifestation of something greater beyond my comprehension. It was God's fury.

At that moment, my focus shifted to my unconscious son beside me. I woke him up without hesitation and held him tightly in my arms, shaking him awake as the thunder roared on.

I raced to the emergency door and kicked it open.

Bracing myself against the howling wind and driving rain — I felt small and insignificant in the face of such raw power. Suddenly, a bolt of lightning crashed down on the staircase below us. At that moment, I started to shake uncontrollably, overcome with a sense of dread and terror I had never experienced before. My whole body trembled as every clap of thunder and lightning reminded me of the wrongs I had done and the monsters I had created. The storm seemed to intensify with each passing moment, as if it were closing in on me from all sides. My heart raced in my chest, and I could feel the sweat pouring down my face as I struggled to keep myself together.

Despite the fear that gripped me, I pressed on toward the bathhouse — determined not to let the storm defeat me. With each passing moment, I steeled myself against the wind and rain — moving ever closer to my goal.

Suddenly, another lightning bolt touched down beside us with a loud crackle. I felt the electricity flowing through my body as my hair stood on end. The smell of burning flesh filled my nostrils. I raised my voice and shouted profanities toward God — angry at him for this unjust punishment.

Yet in that moment of rage and despair, something shifted within me. As the lightning continued to strike around me, I knew it was time to ask for forgiveness. So, with tears streaming down my face, I cried out, begging for mercy. It was a desperate plea born out of fear and pain, but somehow it felt like the right thing to do.

And then silence.

The storm dissipated almost as suddenly as it had begun, leaving only a sense of emptiness. For a moment, everything was still — until finally, I heard my son's faint voice whispering in fear.

"The sun . . ." David moaned, covering his eyes.

The dark clouds that had filled the sky moments ago

were now rushing out as fast as they had come in. And with them, the intense heat of the morning sun began to beat down upon our skin. I could feel my body blister and burn under the sudden change in temperature, and I knew that I had to make a run for the bathhouse before it was too late. The pain grew more unbearable with every step, but I pushed onward. I knew time was running out, and if we didn't get inside soon, there was a real risk that we would combust into flames.

But despite the odds stacked against us, we made it. I set David on his feet and told him to morph into another man. I followed suit and opened the door, escaping the morning light.

Entering the bathhouse, the strong scent of chlorine hit me immediately. The sharp and pungent smell made my eyes water and my nose itch. But despite its harshness, there was also a sense of cleanliness and freshness to It — as if every surface had been scrubbed and sanitized to perfection.

As I looked around, I saw a man behind plexiglass looking in our direction. He seemed on high alert, scanning the room for any signs of trouble. So, I played it cool, running my fingers through my hair, pretending to be drunk from a night out at the bars.

Although I was nervous, my persuasiveness seemed to have worked, as the attendant accepted my payment and placed two clean towels, keys, and four condoms before us. It was a subtle nod of approval, signifying our warm welcome.

Peter

JACKSON AND I beamed with pride as we surveyed the room. Thirty coffins lined up in perfect rows were a sight to behold, and the newly added seating area with a television gave the place an almost homey feel. Under the direction of Angelo, we accomplished the task at hand. We also brought new immortality to Parker and Bennet, transforming them into vampires, and I couldn't help but admire their courage. As I looked at Jackson standing beside me, our eyes met, and I knew this wasn't just my mission anymore — it was ours. A silent understanding passed between us, full of admiration and gratitude for our shared journey. We were no longer enemies.

The night was filled with anticipation as we descended the stairs, Parker and Bennet at our side. With each step, the newly made vampires became more excited, knowing they would soon indulge in their first meal.

As we reached the bottom of the stairs and entered a selected room, we saw two men lying motionless. An aura of respect and solemnity floated through our group as we all realized the gravity of what was about to transpire. Parker and Bennet stared hungrily at their first victims.

We knew we had done something remarkable that would open a whole new world to them and us. Together, Jackson and I watched as our creations drank for the first time. It was one of the most beautiful moments I'd ever experienced, both exhilarating and terrifying at the same time.

We celebrated our accomplishments in the only way we knew how — with passion and unrestrained joy. Our naked bodies intertwined in beautiful harmony. We embraced and caressed each other, enveloped in pure bliss, cherishing the connection we had discovered as the air resonated with echoes of delight. Parker and Bennet joined us in intense connection and intimacy, reveling in their newfound powers.

Philippe

I OPENED MY eyes, feeling my skin burning as if it were on fire. The brightness of the morning light blinded me, making it difficult to see anything. I looked down at my body and saw steam lifting from my charred flesh. Despite being under a large tree, the sun's rays constantly attacked me.

Panic set in as I jumped and ran as fast as possible toward the nearest building — a block away. As I sprinted past a mother and child, she screamed in horror at the sight of my naked body and the flames sprouting from my back like demonic wings.

The pain was unbearable — an intense agony that terrified me. With each step, it felt like invisible claws ripped my skin apart. And yet, somehow, I stumbled forward, driven by sheer desperation and the need for help.

Suddenly, the pain became intolerable, and I stumbled to the ground. Consumed by fire, I could only crawl forward at this point. Across the street, cars screeched to a halt as drivers stepped out in disbelief at the scene before them.

As the pain in my body grew unbearable, I found myself slipping into a state of unconsciousness. My breathing became shallow and labored as my strength began to wane.

I lay on the ground, unable to move or even cry for help. The world around me faded away as I drifted toward the abyss of death.

As time slipped by, my consciousness gradually faded. The darkness fell upon me like a shroud, enveloping me in its cold embrace. And then, there was nothing — no sound, no sensation — only an endless void stretching out before me.

Antonio

ADMIRING the sight before me as we ascended to the third floor, I was struck with wonder at the rows upon rows of coffins filling the room. Clearly, Angelo had poured his heart and soul into the space, dedicating himself tirelessly to the task at hand. The meticulous attention to detail and skill on display left me breathless, and I couldn't help but inhale sharply as I took it all in. Alongside the impressive coffins, Angelo had also built a comfortable seating area featuring plush couches, perfect for vampires to relax and converse with one another. Completing the space was a giant television screen adorning one of the walls, allowing vampires to enjoy the experience of a sunrise or warm summer afternoon through the surveillance cameras outside the building.

All the newly made vampires had gathered as per Angelo's orders, including Jackson, Peter, Doug, Bennet, Parker, and Lucien. However, my father and Harry were nowhere to be seen. Their absence weighed heavily on my heart as sadness crept in, fearing they were dead.

Introducing myself as the new leader, I made it clear that Angelo was my right-hand man. Although I wasn't sure if military terms were necessary at this point, I knew we could implement them later if needed.

Once all the introductions were complete, Angelo stepped forward, commanding the attention of everyone present. With utmost clarity and poise, he proceeded to articulate the rights and responsibilities entrusted to each vampire within the sacred confines of the bathhouse. He also laid down a few laws, such as no fighting, no stealing, and a strict curfew at sunrise. And thus, the Vampire Bathhouse was born! I could feel the electricity in the air, knowing these vampires were now under my control and protection — it felt surreal yet invigorating.

The night ended with me ensuring everyone had a coffin to call their own before heading to bed. For the first time since becoming a vampire, I had found my purpose — this would be my new mission, and together with Angelo, we would make sure our makeshift family flourished and prospered. I bid goodnight to everyone, and Angelo led me to my bedroom. I couldn't wait to close the door and embrace him once again.

Angelo

EXCITEMENT COURSED through me as I let the towel slip from my waist, embracing Antonio in my arms. Our lips delicately met in a soft kiss as we gradually moved toward the bed, allowing desire to guide our every step. Gently laying him down, my eyes couldn't help but drink at his naked form, intensifying the fire of my passion.

Looking into his eyes, I sensed a deep concern, a worry stemming from his father's absence. It was evident that he carried a sadness, and at that moment, I made a conscious choice not to rush our intimate connection. Instead, I opted for a gradual and tender approach, aiming to make love to him in a way that conveyed comfort and love. And afterward, once our bodies had found solace in each other's embrace, I would hold him close, offering warmth and reassurance until his burden felt lighter and his heart found solace.

As I laid Antonio on his side, I gently caressed his back, feeling my hardness pulsate against his ass. Planting a soft kiss on his head, I asked if he was ready for me. His nod of consent was all I needed as I spread his cheeks and slid into him.

He inhaled as he felt my hardness. I took it slow and held him close. This moment needed to be sensual, not fast and furious. As we moved together in a passionate embrace, I showed him the love he deserved. I continued kissing Antonio's back slowly and sensually. The heat between us grew more robust with each movement, filled with love and tenderness. Our breathing became heavier as our passion intensified, but I took my time, savoring every moment of our intimate connection.

As we reached the pinnacle of our lovemaking, I held him tightly, never wanting to let go. Afterward, as we lay entwined in each other's arms, still joined together, we fell asleep without worrying about my seed poisoning him.

David

IT FELT GOOD to be inside the bathhouse again. I had frequented this place many times when the need arose. When I didn't feel like going to the bars, I would hide away and fulfill every kink I desired. Sex empowered me, and I knew I was good at it — pleasing men gave me a sense of satisfaction and confidence.

We entered the locker room and undressed. Once again, my father stood naked with an erection, drawing the attention of all the guys in the room. This made me jealous. We were here to kill Antonio, but I knew my father would use this time to experience gay sex. How would I deal with this? I could not react and tell him not to do it because he would see the jealousy in my actions.

We wrapped the white towels around our waists and headed into the maze of hallways. As we passed the showers, I turned to see a guy bent over getting screwed while sucking cock. My dad looked interested, and I could tell he wanted to participate.

"Come on, this way," I said, motioning him forward. I

didn't know how long I could keep him from participating in the activity around us. However, I understood his desire — I remember coming here for the first time and feeling like a kid in a candy store.

I stopped immediately, hearing Salvatore's voice inside my head. He said that he was leaving New Orleans and that I was not to harm his son. It seemed they had not made up but had agreed with the situation.

"Fuck that bullshit!" I murmured, disobeying his orders. He was no longer in charge. The vampire compound lay in ruins, its existence decimated.

A smile appeared on my face as I proceeded to walk, contemplating the idea of ending Antonio's life. I tightened my hold on the switchblade concealed within my hand. If I planned to succeed and Antonio was to meet his demise, the only acceptable method would be decapitation. Recognizing that I would need to catch him off guard to execute this, or otherwise, he'd call for assistance again.

"What are you doing?"

I looked up, breaking my train of thought, and turned around to see Robert standing at our room door with his hands raised in question. I had walked right past the door while lost in deep thought. "Oh . . ." I said, pretending not to see the room number. I unlocked the door and pushed him inside. I removed his towel and forced him to the bed, kissing him deeply. He tried to turn his head, but I held it firmly.

I kissed him passionately, our bodies trembling with anticipation. His lips were so sweet and warm against mine.

"This is sinful," he whispered, but his words contrasted with the physical desire emanating from his body.

I was determined to persuade him and convey the profound sense of destiny that bound us together. At that very instant, nothing eclipsed the significance of our love.

Desire coursed through my veins as I felt his hardness against me. The sensation only intensified my longing for what was to come next.

"I'm going to make love to you," I murmured, lifting

his legs. I knew Robert had never been fucked before. I would be gentle, and he'd enjoy it so much that he would never question our relationship again.

"This is forbidden . . ."

"Shush . . ." I murmured.

I raised his leg higher, and my tongue delved inside his tight hole. I continued to lick, insert, and suck until it relaxed, ready for my prick. I was glad I had changed into someone with a smaller dick because I knew he'd never be able to take my normal size. "Take a deep breath."

I heard him inhale deeply.

"Once you relax, the pain transforms into pleasure. I'll proceed at a slower pace." I kissed his mouth once more, and his tongue swiftly met mine this time. As we continued, we engaged in a passionate French kiss while I penetrated him.

"Oh my goodness!" he uttered in ecstasy.

He skillfully accommodated me, embodying the expertise of a seasoned receiver.

"Yes . . . it feels incredibly pleasurable. Make love to me!" he moaned.

I satisfied him thoroughly. His well-toned behind endured every thrust I administered. Robert transitioned from being a top to becoming my submissive bitch.

Robert

I GOT UP from the bed and saw my son lying on his back with his hands behind his head. "Son . . ." I began, but he interrupted me.

"From now on, you'll call me David," he murmured.

I nodded, realizing that he was asserting control over me and that I had lost my power over him. "I'm going to clean up," I said, placing the towel around my waist. David spoke again, asserting his dominance.

"No one is to touch you."

I nodded in understanding.

Turning away, I left the room. We both had room keys. As I walked, I contemplated showering and then fleeing the bathhouse. I knew that our sinful ways would result in punishment again. When I explained God's fury, David laughed in my face. His disregard for divine consequences frightened me endlessly. Should I run away? The thought crossed my mind again as a potential solution to the problem. But that wouldn't work. I loved my son too much.

Feeling overwhelmed by the urge to use the bathroom, I knew I needed to sit on the toilet. David's lovemaking had awakened my bowels, and I could no longer ignore the need.

Entering the shower room, I headed toward the commodes, and I could not help but notice the glory holes on each side of the walls. The lack of privacy surprised me, and I muttered in disbelief.

As I closed the stall door, I saw movement and realized someone was standing on the other side. Suddenly, a massive cock appeared through the opening, impressively veined. Despite my temptation to indulge, I pushed it away and muttered that I needed to use the bathroom. The man groaned and left the cubicle, leaving me alone to meet my needs.

As I sat on the toilet, I planned our revenge. I had already read the minds of a few vampires, and they were all located on the third floor of the building. Antonio's room was up there too. My mind wandered to Salvatore. He wimped out, I thought, knowing he was fleeing to Europe. I couldn't believe he had given up so quickly. What had changed his mind?

I yawned, getting tired.

I knew all the vampires were settling into their caskets on the third floor. I would go back to the room, crawl into bed with David, and we'd rest up to complete our mission.

The man reentered the cubicle next to me. He didn't waste any time and slid his erection through the hole. I became aroused, wondering what it would feel like to get impregnated with cum. Without thought, I stood and bent over, guiding him inside me. He was about nine inches, and it engulfed my rectum easily. My eyes rolled back as he started to thrust back and forth. I had never felt any sensation like this before. I loved every inch of his hardness. My cock spasmed, shooting fluid on the concrete floor. His moans increased, and suddenly, he creamed inside me.

The man pulled out.

"Thanks," he said and left the stall.

I didn't know whether to push the jizz out or leave it inside me. Not wanting to leave the room later, I sat back down and pushed it out. The amount of ejaculation surprised me — the man was a big cummer.

David came into my mind, asking where I was. I told him I was in the bathroom and would come to the room after showering. He never questioned if I was fooling around, so I kept it my secret. What harm could come from exploring?

William

AS HARRY led me to bed, I felt a sense of comfort as he spooned me and softly kissed my shoulder. The tenderness of his touch was so soothing that I rolled onto my back, allowing him to rest his head on my chest. His hand automatically found its way to my abdomen, providing security.

As Harry twirled my pubic hair absentmindedly, it reminded me of someone special from the past. However, I couldn't remember who it was for my life. Suddenly, Harry spoke up and mentioned my son's name was Antonio. My heart skipped a beat as I caught my breath upon hearing his name. It sounded familiar yet distant at the same time.

Desperately trying to piece together my memory of him, I asked Harry if we looked alike. Unfortunately, he said not so much. But he described Antonio as handsome with green eyes and a smile that could light up a room.

Harry shared the story of my son turning him into a vampire. It was heartwarming to know Antonio followed in my footsteps. His act of kindness was inspirational.

Minutes passed, and Harry's hand found mine as we lay there in silence until he finally spoke up again.

"You'll remember him soon enough. But for now, let's enjoy this moment with each other."

I nodded and closed my eyes, grateful for the peace I felt next to him. With Harry by my side, I was confident I could remember all the important things about me soon enough. Until then, I had him to help me piece together my past and rebuild a new future.

***

After waking up, we discussed the unique New Orleans cuisine and their strong chicory coffee. Harry suggested we feast on delicious food before heading to a coffee shop for dessert. I was thrilled at the prospect of experiencing New Orleans through his eyes. I felt so safe and comfortable with Harry that my arousal began to show underneath the white sheet. Harry noticed and smiled at me but waited for my permission before moving. "You have my permission," I said.

Harry sat up and removed the sheet from my body. My hardness stood at attention. Even though it was only six inches, it was impressive. The large vein that ran down my shaft was awe-inspiring, and my foreskin gave my dick a European look.

Lying on my back, I let Harry service me. He ran his tongue up and down the side of my shaft and licked my hairy ball sack. He even licked the area between my anus and scrotum. It was evident he knew how to please a man. In no time, my juice sprang forward, shooting into his mouth. I sat up, remembering my cum was poisonous. I watched as he savored the taste as long as he could and then let it flow from his mouth.

"It tastes heavenly," he said, wiping his jawline.

Salvatore

I WOKE UP in my New Orleans hotel room and made a reservation for a spot on a large cruise ship. It was one of those cruising companies that had thousands of people onboard. The ship had an impressive size and offered many amenities, including twelve restaurants, each offering unique dining experiences. There were also seven bars to cater to every guest's taste.

I paid the double occupancy rate to bask in the lap of luxury in the 'Sanctuary' suite. Despite the steep price of $4,000 per night, every penny spent was worth it. The suite spanned over 6,694 square feet and boasted three bedrooms, three full baths, walls of windows, and a breathtaking outdoor terrace with a hot tub and steam room. As an added indulgence, there was a butler at my disposal. However, what truly stood out was that the primary bedroom had no windows — offering complete privacy and tranquility. It was ideal for sleeping without any fear of sunlight disturbing my slumber.

The cruise was for seven days. Despite my initial fears, having the 'Sanctuary' suite guaranteed me privacy during my trip. I requested the best butler and instructed that I never be disturbed during the day and only be catered to at night.

I set the phone on the hotel desk and opened the blackout curtains, revealing beautiful New Orleans at dusk. My appetite was now my main concern, so I walked toward the bathroom to freshen up. As I stepped into the shower and felt the water flowing over my body, I couldn't help but think about my son's warning to leave New Orleans. Although I wished I could stay with him, it wasn't possible.

Without the vampire infantry to control, I found myself alone and depressed. The idea of returning to Italy was enticing. I could wander through the countryside and search for any remaining family members.

After finishing my shower, I rinsed before stepping out. I decided to indulge in the finest meal New Orleans had to offer. Before leaving this beautiful city, I wanted to treat myself. Dressed in my finest clothes, I left the room and stepped onto the street.

Opting for a celebrated restaurant with an exquisite outdoor seating arrangement, I quickly caught a waiter's attention and ordered a glass of Cabernet Sauvignon. Glancing at my watch as he left, I realized I had three hours before boarding the cruise ship. With all my belongings packed and ready to go, I decided to make the most of my time in the city before setting sail.

Sitting back in my chair, I sighed and finally released my tension. A jazz band in the corner played, filling the room with smooth and lively music. Taking in my surroundings, I embraced the atmosphere and reveled in every detail, determined to commit everything to memory for future nostalgic moments.

Robert

I OPENED MY EYES and sat up — my mind immediately overwhelmed with thoughts of the plan for our massacre. David was still peacefully asleep and snoring lightly beside me. I swung my legs around and placed them on the room floor, lowering my head as I thought of how best to ambush Antonio and catch him off guard.

Realizing that he had Angelo with him, I began strategizing ways to deal with two vampires simultaneously. I glanced at the switchblade on the bedside table. I knew this weapon would work if we could subdue him long enough to decapitate his head from his body. I snapped back to reality as I felt the gentle caress of David's hand on my back. He was awake now, and I could feel his gaze filled with concern as he looked at me. We had a mission to accomplish — but at that moment, I only wanted to keep basking in the warmth of his touch.

I turned and saw his erection. It pulsated in the darkness. It was massive and beautiful at the same time. I knew we didn't have time for this, but he brought my head to his cock.

"Suck me!"

Laying on my stomach, I started servicing him. When he was getting close, he pushed my head back and forth to signal that he was coming. David's orgasm shot into my mouth. I held it for as long as possible and spat it on the concrete floor.

"Thanks," he said, stretching his arms above his head.

He didn't ask if I wanted to come, but it didn't matter. We had a job to do and needed to get going before everyone woke up.

***

I gave David the switchblade as we hurried up the stairs paying little attention to the attendant in the front office. Upon reaching the top floor, we were surprised to discover the door unlocked, which caught me off guard and led me to wonder about the effectiveness of the security measures. Although someone had been careless, I was glad there were no further barriers to our progress. As we entered the room, we readied ourselves for whatever obstacles lay ahead.

My heart thumped as I stepped closer and closer to the coffins, and I was filled with awe as I gazed upon them. How did they accomplish this in one evening? The sleeping vampires were unaware that we were intruding in their den. We continued walking silently, taking care not to disturb the creatures.

We spotted the apartment door, and I motioned for David to approach it. He understood what he had to do — jump on Angelo while I attacked Antonio. We proceeded cautiously toward the door, and I felt dread when I encountered resistance — the door was locked! At that moment, my heart sank — this mission had become much more complicated than we had anticipated.

Lucien

I OPENED MY EYES while lying in the coffin, feeling more refreshed than I had in days. Despite the silence, my body pulsed with arousal — my penis stirring to life, begging for attention. All around me were still coffins, the vampires sleeping soundly within. Everything seemed too still and quiet — starkly contrasting what I felt inside. I reached down and grasped my hardness. It felt good in my hand. As I started stroking, my eyes closed, thinking of Angelo's eight inches. It was such a turn-on that I shot all over my hand.

As I lay catching my breath in the tight space, I could smell the fumes of my poisonous sperm, threatening to suffocate me. I had to move before it was too late. With a few deep breaths, I mustered up all my strength and opened the coffin lid. My eyes widened when they adjusted to the light, and I saw two men standing right outside Antonio's apartment door, attempting to get in. I called out to them, not sure of their intentions. Both men whipped around in surprise at my voice, their eyes zeroing in on me. The younger one stepped closer. His mouth quirked into a nervous smile. I didn't recognize him and wasn't sure who he was.

He discarded his towel and began to stroke his dick. It stood at attention. Did he want me to suck on it? I stepped out of my coffin, flicking my burning semen onto the hardwood floor.

"Kneel!"

I began tending to him on my knees, completely unaware of his actions. Little did I know, he raised a switch-blade and forcefully brought it down on my upper back. The impact caused my head to abruptly jerk backward. The relentless strikes from the blade caused me to collapse onto the floor. During the final moments, I sensed the blade piercing my throat. Within a matter of seconds, my head detached from my body. Then, without warning, all-consuming darkness overwhelmed me, and everything went black.

Robert

DAVID DEFTLY picked the lock using the switchblade, his movements precise and practiced.

As we transformed into our true selves, he passed the switchblade to me with a silent nod, its cold metal handle pressing into my palm. We moved stealthily, creeping into Antonio's bedroom like shadows.

I positioned myself over his sleeping figure. His companion, Angelo, was lying on his side, facing away from us. Without hesitation, I raised the blade above Antonio and thrust it into his chest. His eyes flew open, filled with terror at the sight of me standing above him. I repeatedly plunged the knife into him.

As I raised the switchblade and prepared to land the fatal blow, Antonio managed to reach out and protect himself. His voice came out weak but determined as he uttered Angelo's name. In mere moments, Angelo sprung from the bed, fangs bared and eyes blazing with rage.

Angelo leaped toward me, sending us both tumbling to the floor. The knife clattered out of my grasp and fell underneath the bed.

With a triumphant yell, David tackled Angelo, and our numbers became two against one. Despite his strength, it only took moments for us to overpower him. I grabbed the knife under the bed, wasting no time, and plunged it into Angelo's neck — his struggles ceased at once. The silence that followed was a clear indication of his death.

Salvatore

EATING MY dinner, I heard a familiar voice calling out telepathically. It was my son, Antonio, and he sounded scared. My heart pounded with fear as I stopped eating and listened intently to his message. I was horrified to hear that Robert and David had broken into the bathhouse and was trying to kill him. Without a second thought, I dropped my fork and ran as fast as possible from the restaurant. The bathhouse was only a block away, but it felt like miles as panic set in.

When I reached the bathhouse, the attendant behind the plexiglass seemed surprised to see me and quickly yelled for me to leave. Without hesitation, I kicked the door down and stormed into the lounge. My fury rising within me, I ran up the stairs two at a time.

Entering a large, dark room, I felt a wave of panic wash over me as coffins started to open. Vampire figures began to emerge from their slumber, their eyes filled with anger and surprise. I ran through the maze of bloodsuckers, hearing a commotion from the far wall. Without hesitation, I burst into the bedroom to find a horrific sight — Robert had Angelo on the floor and was severing his head from his body.

Seeing such unspeakable horror, I felt an uncontrollable rage surge through me. At that moment, my only focus was saving my son. I rushed toward him, lying on the bed, bleeding profusely, fighting for every breath he took. At that moment, David spun around and lunged at me. Despite his determined attempts to overpower me, I mustered all my strength and hurled him against the wall, knocking him out cold. With David temporarily incapacitated, Robert rose, poised for battle. With eyes burning with intense loathe, Robert leaped toward me. In a split second, I stumbled backward, my body crashing against the unforgiving floor.

"You're a coward for leaving the infantry behind!" Robert yelled.

His strength was overwhelming, and he pinned me, his hands closing around my throat as he tried to choke me. Gasping for air and struggling against his grip, I kicked him away with all my might — sending him tumbling backward.

But Robert was not one to give up easily. He jumped back onto his feet and charged me once again. Our eyes locked as we collided mid-air, rolling across the floor like two wild animals fighting for dominance. Our strength was perfectly balanced — neither of us could gain an advantage. We traded blows back and forth, each strike landing with a sickening thud as we battled.

I raised my fist and struck Robert's face with all my might. He winced in pain as blood flowed from his nose. I repeatedly clenched my fist, striking him relentlessly, until his eyes swelled shut and his incisors dislodged from his mouth. Finally, he lay silent on the ground — not dead but exhausted from our brutal fight.

Turning toward my son, I saw him looking at me with tender and forgiving eyes. Then, the weight of my mistakes came crashing down, and tears began streaming down my face. I cried out in anguish, realizing I had missed all the special moments in his life because of my selfishness and stupidity. How could I have failed so miserably as a father? How could I not have taken the time to truly get to know and understand this precious soul before me?

"I'm so sorry! Please forgive me."

Desperate to save him, I reached for his chest — trying desperately to stop the bleeding before it was too late. "Oh God," I cried, my words exiting my mouth without thought. "Please help me."

And then, as if in answer to my prayer, a heavenly light flooded into the room — filling every corner with its warm embrace.

Looking up, my eyes widened in awe and wonder.

Before me, I saw the figure of Jesus — a heavenly being whose radiance was beyond description. A warm glow surrounded him as he descended from above, his presence filling the room with a sense of peace and tranquility. All around me, the vampires who had been watching fell to their knees in respect — their eyes fixed on this naked figure before them.

"Jesus!" Antonio muttered, his voice barely above a whisper.

I watched as he touched down before us, his eyes scanning the room with a sense of authority that left no doubt about his power and majesty. For a moment, I felt small and insignificant compared to this heavenly figure who towered above us. As his gaze shifted toward me, a profound sense of comfort and understanding enveloped me, effortlessly dispelling all my fears and doubts.

As Jesus turned to Antonio, I watched in amazement as he rested his healing hand on my son's chest — his touch was gentle yet powerful.

Within mere seconds, a miraculous phenomenon unfolded — the bleeding ceased, and Antonio's body returned to its former state of health. Tears filled my eyes as I watched Jesus kiss the top of Antonio's head in benediction. I was overwhelmed with gratitude for the divine intervention that saved his life.

Jesus turned toward Robert.

Robert's fear was unmistakable as he backed away from his outstretched finger. Sorrowfully, Jesus said, "You are to live the remainder of eternity alone."

Robert bawled and ran to his son's side, unable to control himself. Holding David tightly, he whispered, "I love you," one last time. David stirred from his unconscious state and looked up in confusion.

"Your incestuous relationship with your son is sinful, and the men you have murdered are unforgivable. Leave now, and never see your son again."

With great reluctance, Robert accepted his fate and stepped away from the only thing that mattered to him

— his son. He looked toward Jesus with an expression of utter despair before he bowed his head and left the room. Before exiting, he stopped and turned around, hoping for forgiveness.

"Go now," Jesus spoke.

Robert let out a wail of sorrow, leaving the room.

Seeing Angelo's lifeless form, Antonio stepped from the bed and held him in his arms. "No . . ." he screamed, seeing his partially decapitated head. "Bring him back . . . please . . ."

Jesus shook his head, unable to help him.

Realizing there was nothing else he could do, Antonio cradled Angelo's body and kissed him repeatedly, struggling to accept the reality of his death.

With his eyes fixed on Jesus, David stood up slowly and started backing out of the room. Once at the door, he turned to race away, not wanting to face the consequences of his actions.

Jesus's voice resonated with an authority that was both divine and terrifying, "You are cast into the depth of hell for all of eternity." The words hung in the air, a chilling decree that promised eternal damnation.

David's response was a screech of pure horror, a raw and primal sound that echoed throughout the room. His terror filled the space, seeping into every corner, transforming the room into a tangible manifestation of his fear and desperation. It was as if the very walls trembled in his despair.

In a display of his survival instinct, David swiftly turned and sprinted away with all his might, hoping to outrun the impending doom. However, his efforts were in vain, and the divine punishment he had incurred caught up to him despite his attempts to escape. As he vociferously cried out, his distressing screams served as a chilling accompaniment to his fruitless escape. Suddenly, the ceiling parted, and a lightning bolt struck David, causing the air to crackle with electricity and momentarily turn night into day. The energy from the bolt was so intense that once the smoke and dust cleared, David was nowhere to be found. He had vanished without a trace, claimed by the pit of hell, a place of ceaseless agony and suffering. The charred remains of where he once stood was now a grim reminder of the divine judgment he had faced.

As calm filled the room, I looked up at Jesus. The air around him seemed to shimmer with a beautiful light that radiated from his body. It was as if a halo of pure energy and love surrounded him.

My heart swelled with joy as I stepped over to my son and embraced him. I could feel his hands clutching my shirt, seeking comfort and reassurance.

With tears streaming down my face, I held him tightly and told him everything would be alright. And then, I looked back at Jesus. He smiled warmly, lifting his hands in a healing way toward us before slowly ascending into heaven. The light surrounding him grew brighter and more intense as he floated higher and higher above us.

I watched in awe as the portal closed behind him, leaving nothing but the vampires gathered around us. Holding Antonio close, I repeatedly rocked him while murmuring, "Please forgive me," under my breath.

William

HARRY AND I embarked on a journey down Bourbon Street, searching for a renowned Cajun eatery. Eventually, we found one, and upon securing our seats, we requested drinks. Nestled comfortably, we relished our meals while engaging in light-hearted banter. I opted for the shrimp etouffee, while Harry decided on the red beans and rice. He divulged all he knew about my son — he had only encountered him once when they were both confined at the vampire compound. When the waiter approached to collect our empty plates, we passed on dessert and decided to enjoy beignets at a nearby café. As Harry finalized the payment, a cluster of men casually passed us. Harry raised his head in astonishment. His gaze fixated on the youngest member of the group.

"That's your son!" I heard Harry say suddenly. I turned quickly and saw a young man with white hair walking away from us — his face was indistinguishable.

"He has different hair, but I swear it's him," Harry muttered.

Reacting immediately, I leaped up from my seat, instinctively waiting for him to join me. Patiently finishing his last bite, Harry wiped his mouth with a napkin before rising and following my lead out of the restaurant. My son's unique white hair stood out like a beacon in the crowd on the bustling street. However, despite being able to spot him easily, the distance between us was too vast to close quickly.

"They're heading to the docks," Harry murmured.

I spotted my son and an older man lugging suitcases among the group. What struck me as peculiar was the uncanny resemblance between them. Desperate, I yelled my son's name, "Antonio!" But my voice was swallowed by the cacophony of noises from the nearby bars and clubs, rendering my call unheard.

Harry

THE JOY I felt for William was overpowering, though tinged with an undercurrent of fear — a terror that he might slip away from me. Despite the short span of our friendship, a profound connection had blossomed between us. His countenance, marked by determination, vividly reflected his longing to reunite with his son. His desperation became apparent as he firmly held my hand and led me in his persistent quest.

Acknowledging his steadfast resolve, I clung to his hand with similar tenacity. But as luck would have it, a misstep caused William to trip on the rugged path, resulting in a twisted ankle.

Despite his obvious discomfort, I reassured him, "We'll catch them." Lifting William to his feet, we moved forward, our determination ignited by a heightened sense of urgency. I voiced our mission with an indomitable spirit. "They won't elude us."

His suffering was tangible. Each wince was a harsh reminder of his physical distress. Yet, even amidst his torment, William urged us to hasten our steps. I supported him under his arm to alleviate his hardship, sharing his weight as we maintained our unwavering chase.

Antonio

I EXCHANGED HANDSHAKES with Peter, Jackson, Doug, Bennet, and Parker — my comrades who had gathered to say their goodbyes. Their reassuring words resonated in my thoughts as I turned to Salvatore and offered a smile. Dressed not in his customary military garb but in casual tourist clothes, he reciprocated my friendly grin just as the ship's horn announced our impending departure.

"We should board."

I nodded gratefully, thankful for this special moment together. Thinking back, Salvatore noticed my grief at my father's passing and asked me to come along on this journey. I eagerly agreed, hoping it would replace the emptiness inside of me.

The ship I was about to board loomed large, an impressive sight with its sleek white exterior and multiple decks. I marveled at the size of the vessel. It was like a floating city with restaurants, bars, shops, and even a casino.

Once on board, I took a moment to explore the ship. The interior was just as impressive as the exterior — everything was clean and modern, with elegant decor. No detail was overlooked, from the plush carpeting to the polished wood accents.

I felt excited for what lay ahead when I went through the various public spaces on board — from the grand atrium to the pool deck. This trip would allow me to connect with my biological father.

Standing on the pool deck, I waved to everyone who came to send us off. Salvatore and I stood together, feeling a closeness we hadn't felt before.

As the enormous ship gradually distanced itself from the worn-out dock, a sudden burst of noise and chaos caught my attention. Two figures were darting toward the departing vessel with an urgency that was impossible to ignore. My breath hitched in my throat as recognition dawned on me. The taller figure was Harry, my steadfast friend, and trailing slightly behind him was a figure that made my heart pound with a mixture of shock and joy — it was my father, William.

They had arrived just a fraction too late, the ship drifting away, creating a chasm between us. A desperate cry escaped my lips, echoing over the water, "Dad! Dad! I'm up here!" My voice seemed to bounce off the ship's steel hull, reaching out to him across the increasing distance.

My dad craned his neck upward, scanning the ship until his gaze met mine. The etched lines on his face, a testament to years of hardship and worry, seemed to soften as he recognized me. A wave of his hand signaled his acknowledgment.

A surge of relief washed over me, so potent that my knees almost buckled beneath me. The words tumbled out of my mouth, a shout that echoed across the water, filling the space between us with a tangible sense of hope, "You're alive!"

William

JUST ONE LOOK was all it took for my memory to return. Tears of joy cascaded down my face as I heard my beloved son express his love and tell me he'd return home. Harry grabbed my hand, his eyes conveying excitement for both of us. We embraced in celebration.

Surrounded by a circle of friendly faces, I couldn't help but feel a sense of trust and belonging. These men, who had revealed themselves to be part of the brotherhood, invited me into their inner sanctum, their headquarters nestled within the confines of the bathhouse. It was an offer that held both intrigue and promise. Among them, Peter, a gentle soul with a warm smile, approached me. His eyes held a glimmer of kindness as he spoke, his voice laced with sincerity.

"We have something that might aid your healing process," he offered, a hint of excitement in his tone. "Abundant blood."

Harry accepted the offer with great gratitude, understanding that my ankle wasn't healing correctly due to insufficient nutrition. As we journeyed toward the bathhouse, an immense peace filled me. We eventually reached our destination, and the men carried me upstairs to Antonio's bedroom, where Harry joined me.

Antonio

AS SOON as Salvatore and I stepped onto the terrace of our luxurious suite, my senses were immediately overwhelmed by the breathtaking panorama that stretched before me. The cityscape of New Orleans shimmered like a diamond-studded tapestry under the starlit sky.

The butler approached us, skillfully balancing a silver tray bearing two crystal glasses of effervescent champagne. He was an imposing figure, with a handsome visage enhanced by his dark features. His well-groomed hair and sleek physique suggested a disciplined lifestyle, while his olive skin and expressive eyes hinted at his Italian heritage. His manner was refined, a testament to his professional training. The crease of his immaculate black suit was as sharp as his attention to detail. A white pocket square peeked from his breast pocket, adding a touch of elegance to his attire. His rich burgundy tie was neatly knotted and aligned perfectly with the buttons of his crisp, white shirt.

We welcomed the offered champagne with grateful nods, our thanks reflected in our faces. As he acknowledged our appreciation with a nod, there was a sense of familiarity, a shared understanding between us. As he receded gracefully into the background, I turned my attention to Salvatore. His eyes sparkled with excitement.

"Here's to our journey," Salvatore initiated, his voice resonating with evident excitement.

The clink of our glasses echoed with the adventurous spirit that brought us to this point. "I don't know what to call you," I conceded, my voice laden with uncertainty and a hint of vulnerability. Taken aback by my question, Salvatore lowered his head, his forehead wrinkling in deep contemplation. Moments later, he raised his eyes, his lips adorned with a soft, comforting smile.

"I would never want to replace William, the man who

raised you," he began, his voice filled with sincerity. "If it's alright with you, I'm fine with being called Salvatore."

His thoughtful response made my heart expand with love and acceptance. "Thank you," I whispered, my voice laced with gratitude. As I gazed into his face, something clicked within me. I couldn't help but notice the striking resemblance we shared — the same eyes that held a glimmer of warmth, the same chin that exuded determination, and even the same smile that seemed to carry a world of untold stories.

"If only I could take back all the mistakes I've made," Salvatore's voice broke the silence, filled with regret and genuine remorse.

His words penetrated the protective walls around my heart, bathing me in a wave of peace and healing. In that instant, I was confident of the genuineness of his apology. I forgave him, casting aside the lingering resentments that previously overshadowed us. In this act of forgiveness, a profound sense of freedom and positivity took root. With renewed hope and resolve illuminating my eyes, Salvatore clasped my hand, leading me into the suite.

Once we crossed the threshold, Salvatore pulled me into his arms, enveloping me in a comforting hug that sent a ripple of exhilaration through me. I tilted my head upwards, soaking in his warmth.

"I have a surprise for you," he said, his voice brimming with anticipation and his eyes gleaming excitedly.

His statement caught me off guard, leaving me curious. What could he possibly have in store for me? I wondered, my heart pounding with uncertainty.

"You can come out now," Salvatore called out, grabbing the champagne flute from my hand.

My eyes followed his, confusion clouding my thoughts. And then, in the span of two heartbeats, recognition dawned. Stepping out of the bathroom was Angelo, my beloved. His mere presence ignited a surge of relief and overwhelming emotion within me. I ran to him without a second thought, his arms open wide to welcome me into his embrace. Angelo leaned forward with eyes burning with intensity. Our lips met in a kiss that spoke volumes. In that shared moment of intimacy, it felt like our souls were merging, knitting together the fragments of our fractured hearts.

Salvatore's voice broke through the haze of emotion, a smile gracing his lips as he looked upon us. "Enjoy, you two. I'll be outside," he said, his voice warm and accepting.

Turning my attention to my biological father as he stepped onto the terrace, I smiled lovingly at him. As he waved goodbye, I turned back to Angelo with questions flooding my mind.

"He brought me back by placing his seed on my ashes," he said, his gaze fixed on me, his love shining in his eyes.

The realization hit me like a thunderbolt, leaving me breathless and unable to comprehend the depths of Salvatore's sacrifice.

"He did that for me?" I mumbled, barely able to form the words.

Angelo nodded and scooped me into his arms, carrying me toward the bed. He gently laid me down, and our bodies intertwined in a ballet of desire. Slowly, our clothes disappeared, cast aside without a second thought, as we reveled in reunited bliss. In that sacred space created by the union of our bodies, we found solace and unadulterated pleasure.

As Angelo's length entered me, I gasped as exquisite pleasure surged through every fiber of my being. I surrendered to the sensations that engulfed me, giving myself entirely to Angelo and the love that enveloped us.

Later, bathed in the soft, warm glow that lingered after our passionate encounter, we lay entwined in each other's arms, our spirits melding together. A profound sense of peace washed over me in that beautiful, tranquil moment. It was a powerful affirmation that love had emerged victorious, and a promising future was brimming with limitless possibilities, waiting for us to explore.

THE END

Acknowledgments

I want to express my sincere gratitude and appreciation to the amazing individuals who have contributed to the creation of this novel. First and foremost, I owe an enormous debt of thanks to Aurora Delvaux, whose unwavering guidance, profound expertise, and infinite patience served as the cornerstone of this book. Her insight and dedication were pivotal in bringing the dormant story within me to life. I am forever grateful for her tireless efforts and unwavering support.

Eduardo Santiago, the skilled developmental editor, played a vital role in shaping this narrative. His expertise and discerning eye for detail helped refine the story's structure and flow, enhancing its overall impact.

Words cannot express my gratitude to Abby Hale, a true wordsmith whose keen eye and unfaltering dedication helped polish and refine my words to a shine. Her unwavering commitment to excellence and profound love for the written word has propelled the novel to unprecedented heights, surpassing even my wildest dreams.

To my cherished circle of friends, who have endured multiple revisions and provided invaluable feedback, constructive criticism, and encouragement at every turn — I cannot overstate the importance of your contributions. Your unwavering support and perspectives have enriched the text and helped shape this book in countless ways.

Additionally, I extend a special acknowledgment to my book designer and publisher, Mark Anderson. His unshakeable faith in this project and commitment to overseeing the book's journey from manuscript to reality was truly inspiring.

Finally, to my husband, your love and support are my everything. The life we share brings me immense joy. Thank you.

Printed in the USA
CPSIA information can be obtained
at www.ICGtesting.com
LVHW041107131123
763661LV00080BA/3385